"An absolute gem of a debut! With her breathtaking prose and captivating setting, Amanda Dykes weaves a tale of utter charm along the rugged coast of Maine. *Whose Waves These Are* transcends to the highest level of fiction. The author has paused to see humanity at its most real and precious, leaving the reader to tuck this one among the classics. It's a novel that wraps around the heart, breathing of hope and light in every scene. Equal parts relevant and nostalgic, this is a novel for the ages."

—Joanne Bischof, Christy and Carol Award–winning author of *Sons of Blackbird Mountain*

"This is the book everyone will talk about all year—lyrical, lovely, full of heart and heartache, secrets kept and revealed. These characters, this town, and their stories will seep into your soul and leave you wanting more. A novel of hope and reconciliation you won't forget for a long time, probably not forever."

—Sarah Sundin, bestselling and award-winning author of *The Sea Before Us* and *The Sky Above Us*

"A lovingly woven tale. Climb into these pages and be buoyed by this story's journey, alternately rocked and lulled by its waves. Full of heart and poetry, Amanda Dykes proves why she is such a beloved voice in lyrical fiction."

—Jocelyn Green, award-winning author of *Between Two Shores*

"With a gorgeously inimitable voice, Dykes sets herself apart with a debut novel as timeless as its themes of redemption and everlasting love. I dare you not to be swept into a yarn of age-old tales and seaside secrets deftly penned by a lyrical pen that pliantly shifts between contemporary and historical frames. Romantic, spellbinding, and wonderfully unique, Dykes's sense of setting and emotional resonance is nearly unparalleled. A book world to be savored and returned to again and again."

—Rachel McMillan, author of *Murder in the City of Liberty*

"When an author can capture me in the early words of a story, hold my attention on every page, and make me care this deeply about the characters and their struggles, the author has proven her skill as a storyteller. Amanda Dykes does all that, but with lyrical language that textures the experience and illustrates the power of well-placed words and their effect on the soul. I'll not forget *Whose Waves These Are*. Beautifully done."

—Cynthia Ruchti, award-winning author of more
than two dozen hemmed-in-Hope books

"Amanda Dykes's voice is as powerful as the waves and as deep as the ocean in *Whose Waves These Are*. Readers will love the thoughtful imagery and poetic language without losing sight of a well-crafted plot that will offer courage and hope in the face of the storms of life."

—Elizabeth Byler Younts, author of *The Solace of Water*

whose
waves
these
are

whose
waves
these
are

AMANDA
DYKES

BETHANYHOUSE
a division of Baker Publishing Group
Minneapolis, Minnesota

© 2019 by Amanda Joy Dykes

Published by Bethany House Publishers
11400 Hampshire Avenue South
Bloomington, Minnesota 55438
www.bethanyhouse.com

Bethany House Publishers is a division of
Baker Publishing Group, Grand Rapids, Michigan

Printed in the United States of America

Library of Congress Cataloging-in-Publication Data
Names: Dykes, Amanda, author.
Title: Whose waves these are / Amanda Dykes.
Description: Bloomington, Minnesota : Bethany House Publishers, [2019]
Identifiers: LCCN 2018048925 | ISBN 9780764232664 (trade paper) | ISBN
    9780764234132 (cloth) | ISBN 9781493418787 (e-book)
Classification: LCC PS3604.Y495 W48 2019 | DDC 813/.6—dc23
LC record available at https://lccn.loc.gov/2018048925

Scripture quotations are from the 1977 edition of the New American Standard Bible®, copyright © 1960, 1962, 1963, 1968, 1971, 1972, 1973, 1975, 1977 by The Lockman Foundation. Used by permission. (www.Lockman.org)

This is a work of fiction. Names, characters, incidents, and dialogues are products of the author's imagination and are not to be construed as real. Any resemblance to actual events or persons, living or dead, is entirely coincidental.

Cover design by Kathleen Lynch/Black Kat Design
Cover photography by Ashraful Arefin/Arcangel

Author is represented by Books & Such Literary Agency

Map illustration by Najla Kay

19   20   21   22   23   24   25   7   6   5   4   3   2   1

To Dad and Mom,

who have always shone light
in the darkness.

Ansel by the Sea

Joe's Landing

Ed's House

Jenny's House

The Gables

Sailor's Rest

Everlea Estate

Weg Von Blitz

Read from some humbler poet,
Whose songs gushed from his heart,
As showers from the clouds of summer,
Or tears from the eyelids start;

Who, through long days of labor,
And nights devoid of ease,
Still heard in his soul the music
Of wonderful melodies.

—Henry Wadsworth Longfellow,
from "The Day Is Done"

"He who . . . changes deep darkness into morning . . .
who calls for the waters of the sea
and pours them out on the surface of the earth,
The Lord is His name."

Amos 9:6

prologue

"Every wave in that big old blue sea is a story."

Bob told me this a long time ago, his voice brined with wind and water.

I laughed and focused on the cresting peaks from his old dock. They disappeared faster than a ten-year-old could count.

"Too many waves," I said. "It can't be."

His smile pushed wrinkles around blue eyes as he squeezed my hand tight.

"So many waves, Annie. You remember that."

It would be decades before I'd learn the truth of that. So many stories. In this pocket of a harbor where broken lives, like waves upon the shore, are gathered up and held close. I never imagined then that it would be my breaking place, too.

Nor how beautiful the breaking could be.

one

One minute a guy is splitting wood in the northeastern corner of the country, stomach rumbling and heart afire with ambition in the wake of his eighteenth birthday, and the next minute he's pumping water from the old kitchen sink to clean the work off his hands and pick up a letter from the president of the United States of America himself. It lies there on the red, paint-chipped kitchen table, like an old friend who has let himself in and put his feet up, the most natural thing in the world.

But it's anything but natural.

Somewhere in transit on the postman's boat ride across the bay, the letter has taken on some drops of water. The mail usually does in Ansel-by-the-Sea, and the postman doubles as a sleuth, delivering letters with partial addresses with infallible accuracy. This time the name is blurred, only *Bliss* and the house name legible. Usually just a name suffices, or if one was being very formal, the house's name. Sailor's Rest.

Robert Bliss rips it open, grips it too hard.

ORDER TO REPORT FOR INDUCTION

His pulse pounds in his ears. This is it. Almost exactly four years now, he's waited for this day. Ever since he'd gathered along with the rest of the town to watch President Roosevelt announce the first number of the draft. They'd watched on the town's only television, over at the Bait, Tackle, and Books shop, craning to see the capsules filling a towering glass bowl on the screen. Tiny white papers, each inscribed with a number and rolled up tight. A man had lifted a wooden spoon—hewn from the very marrow of the room where the Declaration of Independence was signed long ago—and stirred. Slow and sacred, moving the numbers until they were as mixed up as the war-torn world outside their country. Even through the television's grainy image, Robert could feel the thick gravity of the moment in that room of Washington men, electric with awareness that these numbers . . . they were people. Families. Lives about to be turned upside down by this thing called the draft.

Four years later the electricity pulses through Robert still, assurance that this is what he was made for. *For such a time as this.*

He holds the letter a moment longer, feeling a thousand nights of prayers gathered up in it. Answered here. That finally, at eighteen, he could go. Finally—though they'd closed enlistment "to protect the home-front workforce" and he couldn't just sign up— the draft is calling him to rise and fight. Protect. The only thing he has ever been good at.

He runs a thumb over the crookedly stamped return address in the upper-left corner—the local draft board.

The President of the United States,

Not yet ready to read the salutation, Robert skims down to the bold word GREETING in all capitals.

Having submitted yourself to a local board composed of your neighbors for the purpose of determining your availability for training and service in the land or naval forces of the United States, you are hereby notified that you have now been selected for training and service therein.

Selected. Training. Service. Robert's breath comes quick at those words.

> *You will, therefore, report to the local board named above at*

The next words are hand-typed in.

> *Machias Railroad Station at 7:15* A.M., *on the 17th day of October, 1944.*

He scans the rest and then closes his eyes. Swallows. There's one line yet to read, and a part of him doesn't want to read it. It'll be his name. It has to be. Still, a knot twists in his stomach at the knowledge that there is one other soul in this family whose name might appear there instead.

The clock ticks into the silence as Germany rains fire over Britain across the ocean. And he returns to the top of the letter.

> *To—*

The screen door slams, jolting Robert. Instinct closes the letter, tucks it behind his back. It's his brother, Roy, giving him a mouth-shut grin as he chews, a half-gone apple in his hand. He is Robert's twin in every way but two: Roy came two minutes earlier into the world, and Roy now wears a simple band on his left ring finger. One that, try as Robert might to stop it, still sears something awful into him every time he sees it.

"Come on," Roy says. "We're going for a clam dig."

Robert folds the letter slowly, hoping not to draw attention to it. "We?"

"You. Me. Jenny. And . . ." Roy takes a breath, his shoulders wide. There's something of the little kid in him, some untold excitement. "Someone else, too. You'll see when we get there. Let's go."

Robert nods, slides the letter into his back pocket. He's been avoiding these outings with the newlyweds, but the letter drives him, wanting to get Roy as far from it as he can. But Roy's grin freezes. He's spotted the empty envelope on the table.

Two lanky strides and he's spun the envelope still on the table to read its nameless text. Sees, no doubt, that it's from the War Department.

Heaviness rolls through the room like a tide. They both know there are only two people it could be for, and they're standing face-to-face.

Robert's jaw locks.

Roy gestures to Robert's pocket. "Is that the letter?"

It's like lifting lead, but Robert pulls it out.

Roy snatches it, unfolds it, reads it from the beginning—and his face goes white.

Robert's heart lands in his stomach. He can't see the letter, but he can read his brother's face. And it's not the answer Robert hoped for.

The screen door creaks open but doesn't slam this time. That would be Jenny, the gentle closing of the door so like her. A month and a half a wife and, as their mom liked to say, she had the glow of a bride.

"Poor as church mice and rich as kings," Jenny had said when Roy showed her the wedding bands. He'd carved them from the wood of an old-growth tree Dad and Mom had found on the mountain many years ago.

Robert's gaze settles on Jenny as she approaches behind her husband, wood-and-wire clam hod in hand. Cheeks touched with the chilly wind, she looks brighter than ever—with a quiet beauty that can take a man's breath right out of him. Robert looks at the floor.

"Did you tell him?" She slips her hand into Roy's. Robert forces himself to look. This is how he needs to see her. Together with Roy. He must look, so his heart will see, so his soul will follow. She's Roy's now, Roy's forever.

"I . . ." Roy looks at her as if there's a whole ocean between

16

them. She squeezes his hand and chatters on, her melodic voice at an excited tempo, weaving through the silent currents the letter has brought.

"Well," she says, "your mother was thrilled. You should have seen her, Roy." She laughs, and it's music. "She jumped right in the Ford and took off for Machias to see Mrs. Laughlin about some yarn. She says she has to get started knitting a blanket . . ." She talks on, her hand falling to her stomach. The leaden weight inside Robert grows. He looks from Jenny, to Roy, to the letter. And back at Roy. *A baby.* And Roy standing there with a letter that may as well be from the grim reaper.

His brother locks his stare with Robert's. Everything fades away, and they're ten years old again, looking out over the ocean as a storm bigger than their whole universe approaches and Dad motors off to town to fetch Mom home before it hits. *"Stick together, boys,"* he hollers, and disappears around their island. *"Keep inside away from the storm, and don't let each other out of your sight."* Robert had failed then. He could not fail now.

Jenny has stopped talking, the flush on her face fading as her smile does, too. "What is it?" she asks, watching this unspoken knowing go on between the brothers.

Roy shakes his head. "Nothing. I'll tell you later." He grasps for—and finds—a smile, pulls Jenny close until her head is leaning on his shoulder.

And just as they've done a thousand times since their youth, the three of them walk down to the clam flats by Milton Farm and dig up a bounty. Jenny swinging the basket, Roy hauling a clam rake and grinning at her as if she's gold itself, and Robert's chest yawning into a cavern over this injustice.

"What's got you all tongue-tied?" Jenny's sprinkling of freckles over her petite nose drives the stake deeper in him. But for her . . . even now, he tries to muster some semblance of a smile. It feels so mangled and forced on his face, he probably looks like a bloated puffer fish. She laughs, all silvery, and some of the edge falls away inside him.

He knows, despite everything—looking at her and looking at his brother, who wouldn't hurt a fly—he would do anything for them.

"You two meeting up tonight?" Jenny looks between them, entwining her fingers with Roy's. "For your birthday tradition. I didn't hear you mention it, so I wasn't sure . . ."

Roy looks at Jenny, drinking her in, knowing what she doesn't know yet. That any time spent away from her now is time that cannot be reclaimed in this ticking clock of a draft. Any time spent on the island of their boyhood, resurrecting their juvenile midnight-birthday traditions, is priceless time away from his bride.

"I was thinking we'd maybe skip it this year," Roy says. He looks at Robert, and the message is clear: *Please understand*.

He understands more in this moment than he ever has and prays Roy won't hate him for this. For there is only one thing that can make this right.

"No," Robert says. He flinches at how abrupt it sounds, sticking his foot in his mouth like always, fumbling with words. "I mean—let's meet up." He pastes that puffer-fish grin back on his face. "Please? For old times' sake. Just one last time."

Those words hit Roy harder than Robert intended. Too much silence passes, and Jenny looks quizzically between them. "Go ahead," she says, laying an arm gently over her slim stomach once more. "Who knows how many more times you'll be able to do this?"

The question, meant in kindness, socks Robert hard. If all goes well tonight, Roy's days with Jenny will never end.

two

Robert plunges his oars into the night-black Atlantic. He drags them back as his skiff skims closer to the craggy shore behind him. A small island, looming in castled silhouette—pine trees for parapets and ridges for ramparts. There is urgency in his motions, determination in the pull of his practiced muscles.

He scans the island's edge over his shoulder and spots a lantern hanging from a low branch, illuminating an empty rowboat. So his brother has beaten him again. One step ahead since the day they were born. He was probably already at the top of the hill, starting the bonfire for this midnight tradition. By rights they should have done it a week ago on their actual birthday, but time changes for a married man, and this is the first chance they've had.

Pebbles scrape under the weather-beaten boat as Robert jumps ashore and knots his rope to the spindly trunk of a young cedar, then strides into a night spiced with pine.

This had been their wild place, their first taste of independence. Where since the age of nine they'd come on their own to etch their names in rocks, swap spit-handshakes over secret pacts, and camp under a sky as big as their dreams. An old wooden box tucked beneath a rock shelter—the closest thing they could get to Tom Sawyer's cave—held their treasures, pacts, and maps scrawled on an old notepad within.

19

But they'd traded away boyhood when a war across the ocean came crashing into their worlds. Their games had turned into strategies, maps drawn in dirt. Their island stopped being the stage of their adventures and became home to their grief the day the war became personal—the day it had taken their father's life. Alastair Campbell MacGregor Bliss, who had wanted nothing more in this life than to leave a legacy of courage and faith for his family, had done just that to his dying breath.

Tonight, Robert would honor that. He is there for the fire and the dares, yes, but it will be different this time. Robert's pulse pounds harder thinking of it—he won't leave the island tonight without their two futures certain.

Cresting the high ridge, Robert breaks into Rogue's Clearing, plants his boots in the hard dirt, and studies his brother. Roy sits on a rock across the fire, bent over his knees as flame-cast shadows chisel over his creased forehead. He rubs his hand across his eyebrows, just like Dad used to do when some great worry had descended. It's no wonder, after all the hours he'd spent with Dad in the boat shop, that Roy was the mirror image of the man.

"Hey," Robert says. Shaking off the old envy that used to eat at him whenever he thought about those two, he steps into the orange light.

Roy sits bolt-upright, smile too quick on his face. "'Bout time!" A crack of sparks flies from the fire.

A scratch of static registers, followed by strains of a big-band orchestra and Frank Sinatra singing "Stardust." A sound so out of place out here in the September air, Robert jerks his head to find its source—a hand-crank Victrola, balanced on a rock with its cone tilting like a curious dog.

"What in the world?"

"Oh." Roy looks sheepish. "Jenny was here with me yesterday. She brought it." Roy strides over, pulling a hand from denim pants marked by stray bits of sawdust. He moves to halt the spinning record.

"Leave it," Robert says.

As Roy cranks the Victrola, Robert thinks of the girl who brought it. It's just like her. The island has always belonged as much to Jenny as to them, though it is Bliss land by rights. She'd tromped across these rocks with them over the years, lighting up their rustic misadventures with her magic. So natural a part of this place that for most of Robert's life, he'd thought of her about as much as he thought of breathing. But one day, he'd taken her hand to help her up from the clamming beach—a gesture as ordinary as the day was long—and something broke wide open inside him. Her freckles sported a smudge of dirt, blue eyes alight as dark hair fell over her face and brushed the bottom of her jaw. She pushed her lips to the side and puffed, blowing her bangs back in that funny way of hers. She smiled, and his chest hurt. She looked straight into him and just settled right in his soul. He'd known in that instant he'd do anything for Jenny Thomas, give anything if she could be Jenny Bliss one day.

Trouble was, they'd been thirteen back then. Little more than kids. By the time the years ticked by enough that he could say something to her, he wanted just the right words. And while he'd formed the words and switched and pulled them around in his mind, searching for just the right shape, Roy woke up to what Robert already knew—the girl next door was more than just the girl who once played pirates with them—and Roy beat him to telling her so. Roy and Jenny had been goners ever since. And Robert had found a sudden need to be at sea every chance he could.

Jenny liked to say Roy looked just like a young Gregory Peck. She'd never once said that to Robert. Didn't matter that they were identical. Maybe because Roy was the one with "those dimples," as she liked to say. But probably, more likely, because at day's end Roy smelled like clean-carved pine and Robert smelled like lobster bait and sea water. Girls didn't say things like that to guys like him.

"So . . ." Roy pushes his open flannel coat back to stuff his hands in his pants pockets. Natural and easy, as if the incident of the letter had not happened just hours before. "We going to do this, or what?" Roy socks Robert on the shoulder with a half grin and starts to gather rocks over by the precipice, where the island drops away into the sea. They'll need nine apiece: one for each of their eighteen years.

The idea of tossing rocks into an ocean and inventing dares to go along with each one—ridiculous tasks they'll each have to complete before the year is up—suddenly doesn't seem right. Not tonight.

Robert studies his brother. He's never seen him quite like this— like the eternal optimist everyone knows him to be is wrestling hard with some swift current carrying him away.

Roy pastes on a grin. "Come on," he says, palming the rock into Robert's hand. "You go first."

Robert turns the gray stone, still warm from Roy's grip. "Can we talk?"

Roy's jaw twitches. "Later."

What is going on with him? It's like this tradition—this fragment of their boyhood—is some sort of lifeline.

When Robert still doesn't throw his rock into the waves rushing far below, Roy pulls his own arm back. "Fine. I'll go first."

Maybe it's the tradition of it, a sense of duty. These are the things Roy is made of. It's his way, his half of their namesake: Rob Roy, the folk hero rogue of their forefathers back in Scotland. Roy got all the *hero*, and Robert got all the *rogue*.

Roy's arm freezes mid-swing. He clears his throat, drops his voice dramatically. "'Far and near, through hill and vale—'"

Robert throws him a look. "Really?" The old Walter Scott poem grates.

Roy swings his arm wide in challenge. "Come on. They're just words."

"Yeah, but they rhyme."

"So what?" Roy whacks him in the chest with the back of his hand. "Rhymes won't kill you." His eyes grow somber. And it

22

doesn't take much to figure out what he's not saying. This might be the last chance they have to declare the words Dad carved into their imaginations with many a tale of Rob Roy's daring.

"Fine." Robert pulls in a breath and joins in with all the enthusiasm of a periodic-table recitation. "'Far and near, through hill and vale . . .'"

Roy jumps in, and his voice sounds so much like Dad's, each word ignites as they speak into the dark.

"'Are faces that attest the same, and kindle like a fire new stirr'd, at the sound of Rob Roy's name.'"

Silence sifts through them.

Roy hurls the first rock into the dark, into Cauldron Cove below, where the waves are stirred by rocks into a constant roil. The rock splits the air, landing in a far-off splash. His reach is getting stronger.

"Normal people throw confetti at their birthday parties." Robert looks warily at the rock in his hand.

"Ayuh," Roy agrees, the Mainer word for *yes* as much a part of home as the salt air. "No confetti for the likes of us. Throw your rock." He lets the implication hang and steps back to gesture Robert's turn.

"So what's the dare?"

Roy hooks his thumbs in his belt loops. "Dare you to actually put something in the offering plate at church this week. *Something*, meaning money, not snails."

Robert smirks. "I'm not seven anymore."

"Coulda fooled me."

"Oh yeah?" Robert hurls his rock out. "Then I dare you to tip Mrs. Jenson's cow." *Splash*. They both know he'll never do it.

"Dare you to fix the side of the barn you ran into." *Splash*. Roy grins.

Then, a pause. As if the whole evening—maybe their whole lives—has been building up to this.

Robert summons every ounce of strength and sends his rock sailing far. A very distant *splash*. "I dare you not to go to war."

And suddenly any illusion of that faraway boyhood burns off like sea smoke.

"What?" Roy turns, fixes a steely stare on Robert.

"You heard me."

Roy shakes his head. "What are you even saying? You want me to . . ." He looks over his shoulder, drops his voice. "What? Dodge the draft?" A shadow crosses his face, as if Robert's plunged a knife straight into him. "You think I'm a coward?"

"*No.*" The word comes out quick. "I'm saying . . . don't go." He pulls in sharp air. "I'll be you. I'll go. They do that sometimes—let a guy go in his brother's place. Or if they won't . . ." He tries, and fails, to make his voice light. "We're twins. We could always just . . . switch names. It worked in grade school."

Roy gawks at Robert. "Do you even hear yourself? You know I couldn't do that. Not after Dad—"

"Please." Robert's voice is low now with contained ferocity. "You have a wife." The word *wife* comes out hard. The ache in him groans wider, but this is right and true.

To love Jenny means to give her a life with the man she's chosen: Roy.

Roy's jaw works. Robert pulls out the second punch. "You have a kid."

Roy lifts his chin, points his gaze across the bay, a toss down from the home they grew up in, where a light at the end of Jenny's dock glistens. Robert tenses—something's off. Any mention of Jenny usually makes the man glow like a lighthouse. But tonight it's the opposite. Something shuts down in his brother.

And when Roy speaks, there's a husk to his voice, like a boat dragged over gravel. "You think other soldiers don't have wives? Families? You think those loved ones aren't the very people they're willing to go to war to protect?"

Robert knows it too well. It was the reason Dad had enlisted, back when they still allowed men to enlist. And it was the very reason Robert had to try one more time. "*Take care of them, son.*"

Dad had looked fifteen-year-old Robert in the eye, as if he were a full-grown man, and left him with those words. He wasn't the oldest, but they both knew he was the one who had the fury of a nor'easter inside him, a fury he could use to fight.

Rocks clatter to the ground as Roy releases his grip on them. Shaking his head, he pushes past Robert, refusing to look at him as he shovels dirt onto the fire. A spiral of dust and smoke replaces the pillar of light.

Robert's lungs burn as he buckets a pile of dirt on the last wayward sparks, ready to continue his argument. But Roy strides down the darkened path, down the island bluff, a man caught between logic and duty.

"Wait!" Robert pounds the ground after him. "Just listen. What am I going to do, just keep pulling lousy shellfish from the ocean? But you—" Roy won't stop, just stomps around the dark bends of the path, making it nearly to the bottom of the hill.

Here, where the lapping of the waves is loud and steady above his own erratic heartbeat, Robert grabs his brother by the shoulder and spins him around. "You're the one who can *do* things. Build boats. Help Mom." His arguments are not adding up to enough, and he can see it on Roy's face. He shoves a pointed finger at Jenny's house. "You have a family."

At this word, Roy hangs his head.

Robert's chest heaves. Catching his breath, he whispers, "I'm going for you."

Cold moonlight glances across Roy, and a gust kicks up from the water. There's a strength in his stance, as if his feet are putting roots down into the very granite. Immovable. Somewhere in the distance a buoy bell tolls, and tolls again.

Robert locks his mouth closed around the string of arguments pounding their way out. Whatever torment is at work in his brother is doing its work. Roy's breathing is stiff and fast.

"They need you here," Robert says. He spits in his hand and thrusts it out to a brother who stares, swallows. He's torn, Robert can see it. Maybe they've outgrown the old spit-handshake, but it means one thing still: an unbreakable promise. Though never before has it meant life or death.

Roy clenches his fist, raises it, and for a split second Robert breathes easier. *He's going to do it.*

But then he sees Roy stand taller. Robert knows that look. That's the Eagle Scout right there. The one who vowed on his honor to do his best unto God and his country.

And instead of opening up into a handshake, that fist pounds right into Roy's other hand, and he shakes his head. "Remember the storm?"

Robert turns his head, looking away from his brother. They'd battened down for a thousand storms in their lifetime here, but he knows instantly which one Roy is talking about. When Dad had gone to town to fetch Mom home . . . and told the boys to stick together.

They had. But they hadn't gone straight home. Robert had spotted the new rowboat Dad had just finished for Mr. Simmons, cut loose and drifting up shore near Gretel Point, where the bay opened up to the ocean. That boat represented four months of work, and to a ten-year-old, there was only one thing to do.

"That stupid boat," Robert says. "I should have gotten us home, gotten you inside."

Roy shakes his head. "That's just it. All our lives, you've been the one to go out ahead, like you were born with a guardian badge or something, and you and Dad were always talking about looking out for me."

"Well, I didn't do a very good job of it that day," Robert says. He can almost still feel the rain pelting their faces, the wind blowing so fierce it pummeled their jackets out behind them like capes. He can still remember how he heard the gull, felt sorry for it crying out from somewhere far off, farther off with every step—and finally looking back and seeing no gull, but young Roy calling out "Help! Help!" with the moaning fall of a gull's cry.

He'll never forget the slickness of those stones as he flew over them, unheeding of the ankle twists and scratches until he got to

Roy, who was hanging over a precipice, sea foaming below him like a ravenous beast. He'd slipped, and Robert hadn't even noticed.

"You were strong," he says to Roy. "Hanging on like that. How you managed to find a grip in that storm . . ."

Roy's jaw twitches, and his gaze is far away. "I managed it because I knew you were coming," he said. "You always came. You still do."

Yes, he'd made it, but if he'd been doing his job, he'd never have let Roy out of his sight to begin with. As it was, they ended up with a shattered boat, a dislocated elbow for Robert, which ached to this day whenever a storm was brewing, and a nearly lost life.

If Robert hadn't lain himself down on that cliff and pulled Roy up while his brother's feet scrambled on the cliff side, they'd never have made it home to confess to Dad about the shattered boat. Nor would they have seen the desperate relief on Dad's face, nor felt the strength of his embrace around them both.

Roy looks tortured by the memory, though everything had turned out. "I've always thought the view must be better from up there."

"Up there?" Robert couldn't imagine what he was thinking.

"Yeah. Looking down at someone like you did that day, knowing you're saving them. Not looking up, knowing you're the one causing trouble."

"Shoot, Roy, you know that's not how it was."

"But it was. It is." He pulls in a deep breath and claps Robert on the back. "My turn now, brother. You're a good man," he says. "Let me try to be one, too."

And then he leaves.

Under a high moon, so high it must be well past midnight, he shoves his boat off into those waves. Unspoken dares forgotten in a pile of rocks at the top of the hill, unseen futures before him as he crosses some threshold in the dark.

Robert's feet crunch in determination across the small beach, as if his body hasn't yet heard what his ears and heart have. His hands work mechanically to untie his boat, and he gets in. But there, facing the deserted island of their youth, he launches a prayer from the mess inside him, to the God who—if there was any justice about Him—would let Robert go to war and keep the good brother home.

three

Numbers swim in front of Ann Bliss, blurring on her computer
screen to the cadence of her stomach rumbling. *Lunch hour*. After
jotting a few quick notes on the latest buying trends of consumers in their twenties and thirties, Ann closes her notebook and
navigates her way through the maze of elevators, lofty atrium,
white-marbled corridor, and pillared entry of Chicago's Calloway
Building. Once outside, she slips into the big-chain coffee shop
next door on the bottom story of a building that stretches up to
approximately, by Ann's estimation, twelve thousand stories.

Placing a hand on the glass door, she hesitates a moment, closes
her eyes, and imagines herself bursting through the door of The
Galley as a girl. An old ship's bell would clang over her head,
sunshine spilling happily on the dozens of mismatched chairs surrounding scattered tables, and red geranium sprigs would nod
hello from a tin can on the corner table where she always met Bob.
Little more than a transformed bait shop with whitewashed walls
inside and out and a kitchen tacked on as an afterthought, The
Galley was Ansel-by-the-Sea's only year-round eatery. It served
up three things well and without fail: views of the idyllic Maine
harbor, piping hot stacks of pancakes baptized in local maple
syrup, and stories as salty as the pier it sat on.

She is certain that, even after so many years, Bess would greet her with her customary "Glad you're here," her words arriving in the Down East Maine way, sounding as if they'd traveled through fresh air, touched with something of an old Hollywood accent, edges removed: *Glad yoa heeah*. Bess would wave Annie in with her spatula and flip a sizzling flapjack—Gretel cakes, she called them, named for the famed Gretel Point out at the tip of the harbor.

But Ann is not there, hasn't been for two decades. She pushes through the café door and tells herself this is home now.

The mingled scents of plastic and pastries surround a sea of people in dark suits. They are braced in neat postures against hard chairs, scanning virtual copies of the *Chicago Tribune*, the *Wall Street Journal*, or *TIME* magazine on their laptops. Their faces glow with the ghostly radiance of kilowatts.

Ann, in her navy pin-striped suit, places her order. The girl behind the counter slides a pseudo-fresh pastry into a corrugated sleeve and plunks a teabag into a paper cup. She calls Ann's name with the enthusiasm of one calling roll at a tax seminar.

Ann thanks her, plucks up her fare, and navigates the maze of turns to the table no one else wants. From here there is no view of the buildings—buildings that wall her world in, though they are the key to her someday ticket to an actual field project, if she can work up the courage to try for such a thing again. Two college degrees, a heap of student debt dwindling at the speed of decomposing granite, and three years of unused vacation and sick days were all steps toward that elusive *someday*.

But for now, the view for Ann is right here, facing the people. They are the keepers of stories, after all. And on their preoccupied faces she sees questions. Even in the robotic roll-call voice of the girl behind the counter, she senses a reason for the flatness.

She is careful not to watch too long, just glancing every so often from her "Intel-blue" eyes, as Judy and Jim at her office have dubbed them. They, the resident tech whizzes at their renowned design firm, like to speak computer. For now, she is just the unlikely anthropologist, her current abstract dig site the corporate jungle of Chicago's Loop. Instead of civilizations, she studies consumers. Buying habits instead of beliefs and traditions.

It won't always be this way, she tells herself. And it's a welcome position—a safe one—after her last job, which shackled her with a reputation she's still trying to shake.

She reaches into her canvas shoulder bag and removes a laptop case. But following the computer's tidy *zip-zip-zap* entry into the café buzz, a decidedly archaic rustle.

Newsprint.

Pressing each vertebra up and into the rigid lines of the bleached wood chair, she tucks a strand of auburn hair out of her face, lifts her cup, and sips her brew, warming herself.

As if her reading material, which flies to her apartment mailbox once a week, has brought the sea spray with it from away off in Maine, she closes her eyes, sees a little girl holding the hand of a weathered sailor.

She turns a page, and the sound draws a few eyes. Quickly, but with practiced grace, she flips the cover around back to hide the title: *Rusty Joe's Swap and Sell*.

She bypasses the Community Bulletin Board section, the Miscellaneous section, the Animals, Automobiles, and Real Estate. Makes a pit stop at the Livestock section, and the corners of her mouth turn up as she reads: *Wanted: Goats. Will trade lobster traps or surplus saltwater boots.* Her smile is a mix of pride and delight, with a tinge of loneliness. *Oh, Maine.*

Flipping on, she finally lands at her destination section. Boats. But before she reads the four ads set in their rectangular boxes, she riffles through her bag and pulls out a paper rippled with glued-on news clippings, like a first grader's art project. She reads a few of them and even laughs out loud once.

From four weeks back, Bob's ad, with all the familiarity and humor of a grandfather:

Lost: Marbles. Somewhere in the boathouse. Help an old man find 'em?–B

From the week after that, hers:

Found: Old man's marbles. Misplaced in a lobster trap. Will send certified mail.

And she'd sent him a bag of marbles, wrapped in a map she'd sketched for him of Ansel Harbor. She told herself that, technically, she was keeping her promise not to send him letters. She still didn't understand the standoff between her father and Bob. But long ago, catching the grieved look on her father's face whenever she slid a letter to Bob into the mailbox, she'd promised herself she'd find a different way to connect with her great-uncle. One that wouldn't hurt people so much. Her ten-year-old self had taken on the weekly mowing of her neighbor's lawn to earn the money to place the ads. She'd saved her seven dollars and fifty cents every two weeks and scrawled her first ad on a green index card, addressing it to Rusty Joe himself.

If there was any way to reach her great-uncle, she'd figured this was it. Next to his worn-out Bible, *Rusty Joe's* was Bob's most frequent reading material, despite his walls of books at home. And so it had continued, ads vaulting across time like Ping-Pong balls, right through that loophole.

His, from two weeks ago:

Wanted: Flatlander to get over here and dig up some clams. Enough of those citified scams.–B

And from last week, her own words:

Wanted: Sailor poet to stop rhyming ads. Poetry sows trouble in scads. (Egads.)–A

The messages went back and back, enough to fill two binders stuffed with pages back at her studio apartment. All from a relative she'd spent only a summer with, but who knew her better than anyone.

She inhales and casts her eyes back to the latest edition of *Rusty Joe's*. There are two ads with boats for sale, and stuck right between them, this:

Come home, Annie. Bess.

And suddenly Ann's face is the one telling a story. A look tied to the breaking that can freeze the entire world in time.

No one had called her Annie in twenty years. And there was only one reason Bess would write to her this way. The only reason Bob would not write.

Something has happened that made it so he couldn't.

The room mutes around her. She hears only her pulse and the paper rustling, distant, in a scramble of movements. Her hands somehow pack up her bag. Halfway out the door she turns back and puts her plate on the counter, hands trembling and feet not doing such a good job carrying her.

She fights the door's vacuum to push out into the wind. There, between skyscrapers and asphalt, Ann Bliss numbly puts one foot in front of the other until she is on a plane, bound for Ansel-by-the-Sea, Maine.

four

Ann stares down the aisle of the behemoth bus as it pulls up to her stop. Perhaps this was what Jonah had felt like in the belly of the whale. Aching for release, dreading what awaited. Jonah's exit certainly hadn't been lined with lumberjacks all the way up the aisle. Some were bearded; most wore one shade or another from Maine's color wheel of plaid flannel. All were bound for the great north woods after this final stop along the coast before the state's boundaries tuck up into Canada.

Ann tugs at her pin-striped suit, wishing for the hundredth time that she'd stopped long enough yesterday to change before her flight. She'd tossed clothes and books and a smattering of toiletries into a suitcase but hadn't had the presence of mind to trade in this shell of a uniform. So here she is, pin-striped suit and shattered heart, trying not to roll over the lumberjacks' heavy boots with her suitcase as she exits.

At last she steps onto Route 191. The bus departs with a diesel groan, a spray of dust.

She watches it disappear, then closes her eyes and hears it—the distant wash of the ocean in the harbor below. She breathes deeply before turning slowly, opening her eyes.

And there it is. Down the green hill, the harbor curves in a smile.

White houses dot the coast, where all is quiet, save the steady lap of waves. Offshore, a scattering of islands trail into the sea, right up to where the two peninsulas come together in a near-embrace around the protected cove. This is what makes this place a haven. Sailors seek it out as a "hurricane hole," a place to anchor until fierce storms pass, protected as it is.

Making her way down the road and into the village, she feels her pulse skitter. She pushes past her nerves and looks at the islands, the way they point from sea toward the village. She could almost hear Bob's friend Arthur telling of Old Joe's famous voyage here. *Lift your head, Josef Krause.* The famous line that caused the founder of this town to lift his eyes in a storm, see the lightning pointing the way to what would become his home.

"Lift your head, Ann Bliss," she whispers. She begins the walk down the winding road. Being here, even after all these years, feels more natural than returning to her loft in the city—and at the same time it feels like the most foreign thing in the world.

Once down to Main Street, she hesitates. She should go right and follow the trail around the harbor to Sailor's Rest—Bob's home. But she cannot. Not yet, not without knowing for certain. She'd had a cab, plane, and bus ride to think through every possibility, but it all comes down to this: Bess would never have written on Bob's behalf if he could have done it himself. No good news awaits her. She knows it in her deepest heart. Still, this tiny shred of hope lures her in. . . .

So she banks left and winds down the German-esque main avenue, the road pitted with potholes from a harsh winter. It's an honest-to-goodness cobbled street, tossing her rolling suitcase this way and that to prove it. Its tradition and charm match that of the tall row of buildings facing a central green and sloping down to the sea. Like something out of a fairy tale, its white walls are framed in half-timber details, the wavy lines of a thatched roof capping it and black window boxes freshly planted with flowers in every hue.

Market Row, they call it, and it looks as if it should house haberdasheries, patisseries, and purveyors of whimsy itself. But the hanging tiles over the doors ground the place with a dash of salt-of-the-earth:

Joe's Lobster Shack. The sign in the window says *Hibernating. Back in June.*

Pinch-a-Penny Thrift. The sign in the window says *Shut.*

The Bait, Tackle, and Books. *Gone Fishing. The BTB will BRB*, their sign says. Looks like Ansel-by-the-Sea, though far from the center of technology, has managed to pick up on modern acronyms nonetheless.

Starboard Home Realty, a one-stop shop for anyone looking to purchase barns, blueberry barrens, seaside shanties, or historic captains' homes is dark, telling her no one's home.

Ann bumps along the cobbles, a sense of eerie emptiness chasing her as she passes each shop. It's not just the lifeless shops. It's too quiet everywhere. Not a person out walking a dog, fixing a truck, painting a boat to ready it for the high season—for both tourists and lobsters.

Feeling the need to establish some sort of connection, she pulls out her mobile phone. Not even a glimmer of reception. So much for keeping a link to the outside world.

Looking out onto the harbor again, she is relieved to see a string of boats passing through the natural gates, weaving through the bay's buoys.

She checks her watch. Just after five thirty. It seems a little early for the lobstermen to be coming home from the day's haul, especially on a clear day like this. And certainly not one after another like that.

At the water's edge, long piers are piled with rectangular wire lobster traps. There should be two or three people on each pier, mending the traps. But other than the men piloting the approaching boats, not a soul appears.

White gulls circle in a bright blue sky, their calls chasing a bit of her concern away. A breeze picks up, delivering the smell of

Gretel cakes and maple syrup, like medicine for her soul. Maybe that's where everyone is.

With a *thunk-thunk-thunk*, she wearily rolls her suitcase down the last and longest pier reaching into the harbor and lands, finally, at The Galley door. With a deep breath, she pushes it open to the ring of the ship's bell.

But no row of old sailors occupies the counter. No tourists are packed in. She turns toward the corner table, half expecting to see Bob there, raising his hand quick in a static wave and slapping it back down on the table to usher her in with those smile lines around his eyes. Always, the smile lines.

But it, too, is empty. Her eyes sting. It hurts to breathe.

She steps toward her and Bob's table, tilting her head when she spots the envelope in the center next to the tin can of geraniums. The white paper is scuffed, like it's been stepped on, and a few drops of dried coffee dot the corner. Just as she reaches out to flip it over, a voice sounds from the back.

"Come in," it says without its source appearing. "Glad you're here." The voice does not sound glad. "Anywhere but the corner table."

Ann snatches her hand back, scanning the ceiling for surveillance cameras and finding only a few old buoys in chipped blue, green, yellow, and red hanging for decoration. How had the voice known which table she stood at?

She takes a seat at the next table over, back to the harbor. A woman appears, and the sight of her brings Ann the first true smile since she read the ad. Bess Stevens.

"How many orders can I get you," Bess asks of her one-item menu. She looks older, of course. Her wild black curls peppered with silver strands are held back just like always by a bandana kerchief. Bess always had a rugged beauty. Strength tempered with a jagged sort of kindness. Like Ansel itself.

From the moment Ann had stepped in here as a shy girl in a new place, Bess had chased her loneliness away with steaming plates of comfort and pointed words of wisdom. *"Pay no mind to the old coots, girl,"* she'd say about the fishermen at the counter. And then she'd lean in and whisper and wink. *"Well, maybe listen every once in a while. They do know a thing or two. Don't tell 'em I said so, though."*

She'd given Ann a place to belong when she had none in the world. And her first job. Flipping Gretel cakes had been Ann's very own miracle that summer.

Bess is waiting with pen poised over notepad and finally looks at Ann. "One order of cakes?"

Ann shakes herself loose from the memory. "Yes," she says, casting a quick glance out the window to the end of the peninsula the flapjacks take their name from—Gretel Point, just beyond Sailor's Rest. "Thank you. And . . ." She falters. What should she say? *I'm here about the ad in the Swap and Sell?*

"Yes?" Bess is scrutinizing her now, eyes narrow. No flicker of recognition crosses her face. Ann's heart sinks. But why should she recognize her? Their friendship was a lifetime ago. A world away, when she was a gangly girl in cutoffs.

"A cup of coffee, please?" She refrains from ordering a miracle on the side—the only thing, she's convinced, that will make Bob appear.

Bess nods and retreats to the kitchen. Ann turns her sights back out to the harbor, where the boats are now anchored and bobbing their farewell to the lobstermen headed toward the piers in their skiffs. With Ansel's tides that rose and fell a dozen feet twice a day, no lobsterman would bring his boat any closer to shore. With the speed they were moving, they must be using outboard motors. Bob had always rowed, and eventually taught her to, as well. She remembers the odd comfort and mingled terror it gave her, being in control of where she was going for the first time in her life.

One of the skiffs nears, disappearing from view over the edge of this very pier. Another joins it, then a third. It seems the whole pack is intent on doing the same. Stopping in to gab after the day's haul over coffee, no doubt, as was their way. Ann gulps back a wave of nerves. The sudden urge to flee overtakes her. She can't do this, can't bear the thought of meeting a pack of people who may or may not recognize her, still not knowing what's happened to Bob.

The back door beckons. She digs in her purse, leaving enough cash on the table to cover her order. A head appears at the end of the pier, right where the ladder down to the water is. A man climbs up and stands, offering a firm grip to another, pulling him up. And that man turns and does the same for the man behind him. As the gathering grows, so does her panic.

She crosses the room to the back door quickly. Grips the doorknob, turns it.

A shriek halts her, along with the sound of metal clattering.

Stashing her suitcase against the wall outside the kitchen, Ann dashes around the corner. "Are you all right?"

Bess whirls—her eyes, blazing blue amid the redness of pooled tears, narrow. "I'm fine. I'll have your coffee out soon." She removes her hand from the sink's streaming water and grabs for a clean white coffee mug, only to wince and release it with a second clatter.

"Don't worry about the coffee." Ann shakes her head. "Is it a burn?" She dips her head toward Bess's hand, taking a step toward her and ignoring Bess's warning look, as she'd learned to do long ago.

"I'm fine," Bess repeats.

A distinct scorched smell overtakes the tiny space, smoke wafting from crisping puddles of batter on the griddle. Bess lunges for a spatula on the floor, but Ann beats her to it.

"Here," she says. "Let me help." And before Bess has time to protest, Ann has removed the burnt cakes to a plate and pointed Bess back to the still-running faucet.

Bess is speechless, but that won't last.

Swiftly Ann moves to the corner cabinet next to the black rotary phone on the wall. If she's remembering right . . .

Eureka. She pulls out the metal first-aid kit and finds a bandage roll, bundles some ice from the dented steel freezer chest below the counter into a bag.

"How'd you know where to find that?" Bess's brows furrow, keen eyes sparking. Ann doesn't know if she's ready to be found out.

She purses her lips, letting the question linger as she reaches for Bess's hand. The woman extends it warily, wincing again as she unfurls her fingers. The skin is red, the burn clearly painful but not critical. Ann gently places the ice against it and begins winding the bandage to bind it.

The woman rubs her temple with her good hand. "Thank you," she says. "It was a stupid mistake. I haven't been burned in years. My mind isn't where it should be today."

Ann glances up into Bess's face. "Oh?"

"Worst timing, too. Got a heap of folks coming any minute now."

Right on cue, the bell rings.

Bess jerks her head up. "They'll be wanting their cakes. I promised . . . ." She picks up the coffeepot with her good hand—sets it down and goes for the batter bowl. "I can't let them down."

"Here." Ann reaches for the bowl. "Let me."

Bess pulls back on it. "Kind of you. But there's a trick to that old griddle."

"You have a burn to tend." Ann softens her voice. "Give me a try on it? I'll help you through your rush. They sound hungry."

It's true. The voices are low, but their intensity grows each time the bell rings. This is no ordinary dinner rush.

"Fine." Bess grabs the coffeepot and heads out.

Ann spots the stick of yellow butter and slides it back and forth across the black rectangular griddle, then ladles batter into sizzling circles. She arms herself with a fresh spatula.

Bess turns at the doorway. "Steer clear of the hot spots," she says, sloshing the pot toward the griddle. "Do five in the top row, three in the middle, five on bottom. Just like—"

"An hourglass," Ann says, joining Bess to finish the sentence.

The color goes from Bess's face. She opens her mouth to speak.

Bess's blue eyes study Ann's face, peeling back years. Ann can almost see the calculations, the rapid-fire adding and subtracting as Bess surveys the present, trying to reconcile this stranger in her kitchen with the Annie she'd once known. *Add freckles. Subtract two feet from height. Add waifish lost-girl looks. Subtract citified nonsense.*

"Where's Fletch?" a burly voice booms. "Bess, you seen Fletch?"

Bess shakes herself present. "Ayuh!" she hollers over her shoulder. "But not since right before he headed out to tow the sun up this morning." She peels her eyes away from Ann and sets to serving.

For the next hour solid, the kitchen is a time machine. Erasing years as Ann and Bess work around each other with practiced coordination. Lifting plates above each other's head in a smooth dance. Flapping jacks, brewing coffee, Ann reaching into the past to anticipate Bess's needs.

As she works, snatches of conversation blow in from the dining room.

The one that takes the wind right out of her—"Bob would've been proud of you boys today."

The one that pummels her with physical force—"He'd have done the same for us." Past tense.

She reaches for the counter to steady herself, bent over it as tears start and the truth sinks in: This is a wake.

A wake is the ripple left after a departure.

Bob has . . . departed?

Numbly, she goes back to flipping Gretel cakes, thankful somehow for the blessing of this mindless task. It keeps her breathing through water-blurred vision.

As she flips and passes plates, again and again, the same question pops around the dining room. "Where's Fletch? He should be here."

"Hard tellin' not knowin'" comes the reply. And "Maybe he wasn't up for it."

No one asks *"Where's Annie? She should be here."*

And when the dance is done—when the room quiets in the lull of content diners—Bess sidles up to Ann, takes the spatula from her hand, and places it gently on the counter.

"Time we talked, girl."

five

As Bess leads her outside and around to sit at a table on The Galley's patio, the growing dimness closes in around Ann. She knows this feeling—the cold hollow pit inside, the way it grows, trying to block out what's coming. Last time she'd felt it she'd been nine years old, almost ten, her father and mother taking her small hands to break hard news to her. To pull the anchor from her world, much as they wanted to spare her.

This time, it's Bess. And instead of her childhood living room down the coast in Casco Bay, it's Ansel as the backdrop, birds singing their evening song in the greening square behind them.

Ann spins her ring around her finger and wishes away the words she knows are coming. When she looks up, she can feel the pleading in her eyes. Begging whatever Bess is about to say to be untrue.

Bess, who always has a word ready for everyone, only purses her lips now. When she speaks at last, there are no pleasantries or catching up. No clean-cut words to tell Ann what's happened.

What comes out is a story. And that's a kindness. They could both feel it, Ann thinks. To say it straight out would be too much.

"Bob came in about a week ago," Bess says. "Sat in the corner, just like always, joked a bit with the fellas at the counter." She looks up, remembering. "He got his coffee and cakes like always . . . and when he got up to leave, he turned at the door and

43

said, 'Bess, would you keep an eye out for my Annie? Keep that table for her when the time comes, will ya?'"

Bess shakes her head with a sad smile. "The bell clanged when he left, and the gab went right out of Ed and Arthur. They just sat there with their heads turned, watching him go. He walked down to the landing"—Bess gestures down the harbor, where a line of piers juts out into the waves, joined by a rustic boardwalk—"and just sat there, mending lobster traps next to Fletch all day long."

There was that Fletch again. Ann blows into her cobwebbed memory, trying to find him there and failing. One of Bob's fishing friends, probably.

"Ed and Arthur each went and talked to him that day and said he seemed fine. Figured maybe he heard you were coming and that's why he'd spoken that way. But our spirits weren't easy about it, none of us. A trouble settled in this place, a fear that maybe Bob knew something we didn't. He went home that evening and . . ."

Ann bites her lip. Nods, as if to tell Bess it's okay to say what was coming, that she understands it must be said. Even so, a knot burns in her throat.

Bess's face falls and takes Ann's heart with it.

Ann tries to offer words. "He's . . . gone."

Bess jerks her head up, eyes sparking. "For pete's sake, is that what you think?"

Something twists inside. She tries to quell it, keep it from reaching the place marked *hope*. "He's okay?"

"Well, he's a far cry from okay, but he sure isn't gone yet. Gonna take more than something like that to put a cap on Bob's life. That's for sure. Subdural hematoma, indeed." She spits the diagnosis as if it's edged in fire.

Ann exhales, shoulders relaxing from their fierce place.

"It is serious," Bess says. "And he may yet . . . well. Fletch found him the next morning, did what he could and got him quick to the hospital. They had to do a surgery to relieve pressure on his brain.

The doctors say he's not out of the woods, not by a long shot. His injury was so bad, they put him in a coma. If Fletch hadn't found him when he did . . ."

Ann winces. "But . . . he's alive."

"Yes." Bess reaches across the table, squeezes Ann's arm. This from prickly Bess is like a warm and enveloping hug from anyone else. It's a gigantic gesture for her. "He's alive. Over in the hospital in Machias." Ann remembers it as a town a few harbors south. "Fletch can take you there tomorrow for visiting hours. They're over for today, or we'd get you there straightaway."

"So this"—Ann gestures to The Galley—"isn't a wake."

"*Pssshh.*" Bess waves off the suggestion. "You know this lot. Someone's down, they hop to action. They gave up the day to go lay Bob's traps for the season."

Relief and worry intertwine. "Bob's still lobstering?"

"That man is as wiry and strong as the day is long," Bess says. "Prides himself at being almost seventy-five and still out at sea. It's not the record-holding age for it, but he's aiming to beat that someday. Still takes the *Savvy Mae* out most days, along with some of the younger men. Says they gotta learn, and he can teach."

It's not unheard of. These rugged lobstermen know hard work, and they know it long into their lives—working the ropes and rigs with a fierce pride. The work fueling them as they fueled the work. Still, Ann had hoped some days of leisure might find Bob one day. Then again, leisure is akin to torment to some people, and Bob is one of them. He lives hard, and he loves hard—cost him what it may. This she knows more than anything.

"I'm sorry for the ad," Bess says. "I didn't know how else to reach you. Bob always showed us your notes, so I knew you'd be on the watch to hear from him. I got it in right before press time."

"Thank you, Bess." Ann places a hand on the woman's worn one. A glance toward Main Street tells her it's still as good as deserted. "I don't suppose I could find someone to take me to Sailor's Rest?" Daylight is fading fast.

"That shouldn't be any problem." Bess smiles warmly and says,

"Come inside, Annie." She says it as if *inside* might be a soft place to land.

But Ann isn't so sure. It means facing all those people. She may be one of Bob's closest relatives, but compared to these people—who know him so much better than she, who share his language and life and the very rhythm of this place—she feels like an absolute imposter.

As Ann contemplates, Bess stands. "Come in whenever you're ready, Annie. And take a look at your corner table. He left something there for you."

The sun is dropping behind Birchdown Mountain, which stands sentinel over Ansel. The chill ushers Ann back inside, where the din has steadied to a warm hum, one that she skirts as quietly as she can as she makes for Bob's corner.

With daylight slipping into evening, there's a glow from the lanterns at each table and the patio lights strung back and forth across the ceiling, and the familiarity of weather-beaten friendship. At last she stands before the corner table. The sight of Bob's empty chair pulls her heart down. She curls her fingers around the top of the chair across from it, seeing a flash of the freckle-faced girl in haphazard braids who was beginning to believe maybe she could be something in this world. All because of the old sailor with the kind eyes across from her.

"You can't sit there."

The abrupt voice from behind rips through the memory like a knife. That awkward-braided girl would have stood up, planted her hands on her hips, and said, "Wanna bet?"

But pin-stripe-suited Ann turns slowly and levels her voice. "Pardon me?"

A man stands there, arms crossed as if he's the lone guardian of this plot of planks. He's maybe thirty-five, but the look on his face is older, much older. Shadowed and resolute, with a wildness about him. Like someone has anchored the wind and trapped it, chains and all, inside of him.

"Sorry," he says. "You can't sit there." The words are polite,

AMANDA DYKES

his voice resolute. He has nothing of the Maine way of speaking and yet all of the Maine ways of being. Strong, wary.

Dark stubble lines his jaw. Like it's been a long day. Or a long few days. "That table isn't . . ." His eyes shift toward "that table." He tries again. "It isn't . . ." It's as if his words are tangled somewhere in there, caught. And suddenly Ann doesn't feel so indignant. His gray eyes land on hers at last, and what she sees there is sorrow. A depth of it that mirrors her own and makes her ache.

He hangs his head. And without a glance or another word, he strides to the door.

"It's okay," she says, raising her voice to be heard above the growing noise as the door slams behind him with a ring of the bell. "I won't sit there." Realizing she is talking to no one, she picks up the envelope.

The room has quieted, and suddenly her voice is too loud. People are staring. She feels the walls go up between them, the suspicious looks. She is the PFA—Person From Away, as they like to call outsiders. She feels the burn of questions, of intruding into this gathering that so honors her great-uncle.

"Hey!" A spry voice wound with age and spunk comes from the counter. "It's her!"

She searches out the face that belongs to the voice. A grinning man, weathered and rounded, stands from his stool and points. His fishing hat dangles with lures and joy. "It's Emma!" He points, finger bent.

At first she's embarrassed—for her, for him. She's not who he thinks she is. But then something tugs at her from the corners of a memory.

An image of Bob and his two friends, Ed Carpenter and Arthur Baxter, perched like barnacles on barstools.

Bob had brought her to The Galley to introduce her the summer she'd stayed with him. "Emmanuelle Bliss," he said. "William's girl." They'd felt like two mismatched puzzle pieces back then, not sure how to fit together while her parents were deployed.

47

"Emmanuelle." Arthur had turned her name over as if Bob had just spoon-fed him something bitter.

Annie felt the heat of defense, and with Bob's hand clutching hers safely, she had told the man that her mother picked her name, and she liked it. That it meant "God is with us," so that she would never forget that truth. She thought that would put his protests to rest.

"Emmanuelle?" Arthur's face scrunched up as he repeated it. "That name's too big on a girl like you. What say we call you Emma," he said, putting his hand out.

"Why not Elle?" This from the man her great-uncle had introduced as Ed, Arthur's counterpart in every way. Voice warm and deep. Words southern. Tall as the pines, skin rich black, and with a gravitas about him that balanced Arthur's jolly ways.

Bob studied her, stooped to look her in the eyes. "What do you say? You want a nickname?"

She'd bitten her lip, shy in this foreign place so far from home, ducked her head. "Annie," she murmured. "Mama calls me Annie."

How faraway her mother had seemed, with her an ocean away in a country she couldn't even disclose to her family. Military life. That had been the first time her parents' deployments had overlapped—for three months. And her mother insisted she go to Ansel, something her father seemed strange about. Not quite angry . . . and not quite sad.

At her admission of her mother's name for her, Bob squeezed her hand and turned to his friends. "This is Annie, and that's that," he'd said.

But that whole summer, any time she entered the diner, the string of greetings had sounded in a row like a familiar song.

"Emma!" Arthur would say.

"Annie." Bob would correct.

"Elle." Ed would lift his hand for a high five. He had a scar on his arm, knotty and otherworldly to her. At first Annie had high-fived him gingerly, worried she'd hurt him. "Don't you worry, Bob's Annie," he'd say. "Nothin' can hurt that any more than it already has. Good Lord heals, you know." And he'd thrust that hand out again for another high five—a real one, which she'd give with glee.

She blinks, bringing herself back. "Arthur?" Crossing the room to the hatted man, she holds out her hand. He takes it, searches her eyes, and she feels that in this instant she is standing trial. Whatever comes next will determine her fate among these people.

He drops her hand, eyes lined in troubled creases. Her stomach sinks. But a split second later, he extends an arm slowly, pulls her in, and wraps her in an embrace.

There's Ed, farther down the counter. He stands more slowly, and his eyes seem to focus through Ann, rather than on her. "Now, can that be Elle?" He reaches out, waiting . . . and she realizes he cannot see her.

"Ed," she says warmly, enfolding his hand in hers. "It's so good to see you both."

"Bob's Annie." Ed shakes his head as if witnessing a miracle. "He always said you'd come back home. Just a matter of time."

Home. The word hits her hard in the chest. She'd given up on feeling anything close to home a long time ago.

Arthur turns to face the rest of the room, a ragtag collection of onlookers. "Bob's her uncle!" he announces with glee.

"Bob's her uncle?" someone echoes.

He turns to Ann and winks. "Bob's your uncle."

"Well"—she tips her head to the side, confessing—"great-uncle."

"Sure as shootin', he is great," Arthur says. "Grab a seat." He pats the stool that sits conspicuously empty between him and Ed. Bob's stool.

She slides onto it tentatively, clutching the letter in her clasped hands.

Arthur's laugh goes low, then high, and he grips Ann's hand into a fist and thrusts it into the air as if she's just won a boxing match. "The girl is back!"

"Well," Ed says, "you'd best open that envelope, then." And he nods like he can see through his blindness to what she's holding.

She doesn't want to. She wants to squirrel it away, read whatever's inside when she's alone. But one look around the room tells her these people would give anything for a word from their friend. If there's something in here that can help them . . .

She slips a finger into the envelope and gingerly opens it.

six

At first she thinks it's empty. No missive containing Bob's wisdom.

Ann peers over the envelope at the people before her. Their hope is palpable.

She peers farther into the envelope. There, in the bottom corner, is a single slim object. Scratched metal, but bright enough to catch the light a bit. She pulls it out and holds it up.

A key.

Not the pretty, mysterious sort of skeleton key from the tales of old, but just as storied in its humble, clunky form. A padlock key with the word *Master* nearly rubbed off its worn surface.

She holds it up, a question on her face. But no one in that room has an answer for her.

"That's Bob for you." Arthur slaps his knee and spins back to face the counter. "Never one to waste words."

Ann has to ask. "Do you know what this unlocks?"

"Beats the tar out of me," Arthur says, then turns to Ed. "You know what an old padlock key unlocks?"

Ed takes his time answering, and Ann gets the sense he knows more than he's letting on. "I suppose," he begins in his southern way, "if Bob wanted to spell it out, that's what he'd have done. But it seems like an invitation to me."

"An invitation to what?" Ann asks.

Ed whistles low. "No tellin' with Bob. Adventure, maybe. Riches, if he's been holdin' out on us all."

Arthur howls with laughter, and Ed grins but sobers as he faces Ann, seems to see right through her. "Answers is where my guess is."

"Answers?" Ann turns the word over, and it breeds a thousand more questions.

Bess slips in through the front door, the bell sounding softly.

"Sorry, fellas," Bess says, bustling over to Ed and Arthur. "Gotta steal this girl away. Sure you'll see her again soon, though." She raises her eyebrows to Ann.

"Yes," she says with conviction. "That's right. I'll see you soon." And as Bess pulls her to the front door, she asks, "Where are we going?"

"Fletch is here," she says, as if that's all the explanation needed. As if she should know who that is. And maybe she should. She presses her eyes closed, trying again to remember. Two decades have passed, and she's finding the limits of a child's memory are no small obstacle.

Bess pulls her out into the chill air. Ann opens her eyes to the fresh flow of it and finds herself looking straight into a pair of eyes as stormy and changeful as the Maine sky. She looks away from their intensity. If this man, who only minutes ago ordered her away from Bob's table, wants her to be uneasy, he's certainly succeeding.

He's tall. Young, for these parts. And by the firm set of his jaw, clearly none too thrilled by her sudden appearance.

He's wearing a blue-and-white plaid flannel shirt, unbuttoned just enough to show a gray T-shirt underneath reading *Go Away.*

Such a welcome.

"Annie, you remember Fletch."

"Fletch?" She tries to keep surprise from her voice.

"Oh, I forget," Bess says. "You both seem so much a part of this place, feels like you should already know each other." She shakes her head. "Annie Bliss, this is Jeremiah Fletcher."

It's minuscule, his movement, but she sees it. The way he pulls back, narrows his eyes just a fraction.

"Annie." He says her name slowly, like she's a puzzle, and one he's wary of. "You came."

She straightens, trying to shake this feeling that she's in an interview, every action being assessed.

"Yes," she says. "As soon as I knew to come." As soon as the words are out she wishes to snatch them back. Shouldn't she have known right away? If she was a good relative? If she were as invested in Bob's well-being as he had been in hers? Guilt crawls up her spine.

"I'm sorry," she says. "I feel like I should know you." No one is explaining who Fletch is, why his name peppers every conversation connected with Bob. And he doesn't even look like a Fletch. The name suggests someone charismatic, vivacious. This man is . . . well, Jeremiah Fletcher has the air of someone who's been around since the beginning of time, and is as serious as that history, too.

She tucks these bits of him away in her mind, readying them to pull out when it's time to unlock this man. She imagines people as combination locks, each bit of information a tick on the dial as she works to build up their story in her mind, to unlock them.

"Yeah, you probably should," he says, and it's clear he believes there's a lot she should know, and doesn't—and much she should be doing, and isn't. He looks to her suitcase up against The Galley, where Bess has placed it. "Yours?"

"Yes," she says, and goes to retrieve it, hating the way her heels click unnaturally against the dock. What she'd give for her old pair of L.L.Bean boots, worn leather and blue rubber and comfort and warmth.

"I guess you'll be wanting to stay at Bob's," he says. His voice is distant.

"Of course she'll stay at Bob's." Bess waves off Jeremiah's question. "It's as good as home to her. Isn't that right, Annie?" She doesn't wait for an answer and turns back to Jeremiah. "Anyway, I thought you could take her up the Weg and across the bay, seeing as how—"

"I'll do it," Jeremiah agrees, his expression even more unreadable as the sky grows darker.

"And to the hospital in the morning? I'd drive her over myself, but . . ." She glances at the restaurant, her meaning clear. In a one-restaurant town, and a one-employee restaurant, she can't get away.

"Yeah," Jeremiah says. Ann notices the absence of the Mainer *ayuh* of agreement, thinks of how in communities like Ansel, the breaking down of their colloquial language is often the first sign of a town in danger of "irrelevancy." You lose the language, you lose the history. Sense of place. Tradition. Cultural Anthropology 101.

After saying good-bye to Bess, Jeremiah leads her down the wharf, to where a boat bobs in high tide. Bright Tardis-blue hull, white everything else. The words *Glad Tidings* are painted with precision over the blue.

Jeremiah's frown deepens as he motions toward a fold-down jump seat inside the cabin. It's a tiny space. Not the sort of confined quarters she wishes to share with a man who's clearly less than thrilled at her presence.

"I'll sit outside, if it's all right," she says, gesturing to a bench bolted to the deck just outside the cabin.

He shrugs, eyeing her thin layers. "Suit yourself." He tosses her a sweatshirt from the back of the helm seat. "It'll be cold once we're on the water."

"I'm used to the cold and wind," she says. "Chicago." When he fires up the engine, she feels the vessel tremble beneath her feet and gulps. Cold and wind are one thing. Being out on the waves is quite another. She sits quickly, wraps her fingers tightly around the weathered wood of the bench.

He steers the *Glad Tidings* out into the dark, and Ann presses her eyes closed. *No worse than an airplane,* she tells herself. And promptly disbelieves herself.

She looks around the vessel, fixing her attention on the details, hoping to anchor herself to the truth that this is someone's normal. They're just crossing the bay, for heaven's sake. Barely leaving shore.

Jeremiah mercifully takes it slow. He skirts the harbor a bit, guiding the boat past shingled buildings, white clapboard homes tucked up into the surrounding hillside, and docks capped with fishing shacks. Some homes are German-esque, like those in the town square. These, she knows, date back to when Josef Krause settled this place, his vision to fashion it after his hometown in the motherland.

Jeremiah eventually points the boat away from the harbor, weaving through anchored lobster boats all around. His boat is different, she realizes. It doesn't have the same stout look as the lobster-fishing vessels. His deck is longer, his cabin taking up nearly the entire front half of the boat. Around his deck, lidded plastic bins sit squat and straight, roped against the metal railing. The vessel is devoid of the ropes and trawl nets she remembers from Bob's boat. To her right, a mound of oddly sized clear plastic bags rattles in the breeze. She leans in for a closer look. There are boxes inside the bags, some small, some large, and a few in between. *What is this? Mail?* She fights hard not to look closer at the address labels. All her training—the drive to get to the bottom of the story—tells her to observe everything she can. But there's this other side, the side she likes to hope bears some resemblance to a normal human, that tells her to respect the man's privacy.

She turns, directing her gaze to the cabin. Inside, his light glows, and his eyes rove over the water. He grips the helm with ease and whistles a tune. Something slow in a minor key.

A stack of books sits on a case bolted to the wall, with railings at the bottom of each shelf to keep the books in on rough seas. She strains to see their titles. It's not the same as the mail. Books, people know will be seen. Spines outward, on display. They are the best sort of clues to figure something out about a person. And judging by his remarks, he already knows way more about her than she does him.

The titles are alphabetical, she realizes. *Advanced Emergency*

Care. Guitar for Dummies. Maritime Tradition and Lore. Microbes of the Sea. The Moonstone.

Well, his tastes were nothing if not eclectic. And perplexing. On the next shelf down, two books lay on their backs, faceup and dog-eared. Ann leans closer. These are the books he reads most, by the look of things.

A small Bible, its thin pages rippled and its spine long gone. Next to it, *Postal Laws and Regulations of the United States of America.*

She looks from the book, to the bins, to the bagged packages, and to the man at the helm, dark hair sticking out in slow curls from beneath a blue beanie.

"This is a mail boat?"

He gives her a sideways glance and fixes his stare back out on the water. "Mostly," he says. "Sometimes it's a ferry. Sometimes ambulance. Mostly a mail boat. Delivering packages and people to Ansel's inland and islands since 1934." He speaks as if he's the droll narrator on a documentary. "The boat, that is. Not me."

Ann swings her legs around to the edge of the bench to face him. "And when did you become a part of this delivery service?" She tries to reconcile Bess's account of how Fletch found Bob, helped him.

He scoffs. "That depends on who you ask."

"Well," she says. "Let's say I ask the town of Ansel."

"Three years ago."

"And let's say I ask you."

"Then . . . never." His face pulls into a half grin. "I came up here for an EMT job. Turns out a town like this only needs a very part-time EMT, and since the fire station shares a building with the post office, I inherited the postal deliveries as part of my responsibilities."

"You're kidding."

"Only in Ansel." He shrugs one shoulder. "It's not so bad. Keeps me out of trouble."

She studies his scruff, the way he speaks little but sees much. He doesn't seem the type to go about making trouble. Even so, there's something going on below the surface in this man.

"That's an interesting shirt." She points at the bold black *Go Away* lettering.

He glances at it, then at her. He lifts his eyebrows, tipping his head toward her. His message clear, and only half-joking.

"Your wardrobe should learn some manners," she mutters.

She's about to turn away, let this guy sink into his own world, as he clearly wants to, when he makes a quick movement. He grabs a Sharpie from the bookshelf, uncaps it with his teeth, and holds the shirt out with one hand. With his other, he scrawls atop it, lettering carefully from his upside-down perspective.

PLEASE, he's written at the top of the shirt.

Oh, this guy is rich. She does not respond to the look of smug victory he gives.

They're pulling into the dark side of the harbor now, the night so black she can barely make out the silhouetted horizon of pines and mountains beyond. They pass a long, narrow island and enter the Weg. A stretch of sea that's bordered by a string of islands on one side and the remote arm of the mainland on the other. Other harbors in Maine would call this a reach. Moosabec Reach, Eggemoggin Reach . . . and Ansel's Weg.

The pronunciation was all wrong, she'd learned since leaving Ansel—the locals all said it with a true *W*—but it had a tale that brings a thrill to her soul still. "Old Joe," as they called Josef Krause, was a humble fisherman who lived with his wife, three kids, and new baby in a tiny fishing shanty up near Saint John in New Brunswick. He had gotten swept down the seaboard after a heavy mist disoriented him and turned into a fierce night storm. With just him and the herring aboard, he had little hope of surviving. Seeing no sight of land, and having lost all hope, he fell to his knees and begged God to deliver him, that he might get the herring back to his little one's bellies and live to see them another day.

His only answer was a deeper churning of the waves, which splayed him onto his belly, facedown, repeating his prayer. And then, as the story went, he'd heard a voice, stronger than audible, as if it were speaking straight into his soul: *Lift your head, Josef Krause.*

It was not a promise for deliverance nor an opening of the sea as for Moses . . . but Josef did it. He lifted his head, and in that very moment the sky lit with a blinding streak of lightning. Enough to see an island in the distance.

Scrambling to his feet, he took the helm and navigated as best he could to where that fleeting glimpse of an island had been. When he got nearer, the pounding in his chest echoed that heavenly voice again. *Lift your head, Josef Krause.*

He looked to the sky, another dash of lightning revealing the island looming large to his left, and another island ahead, and another beyond. The next bolt of lightning stretched long enough to show a whole string of small isles, dropped like bread crumbs to lead him to shore. One by one, flash by flash, he'd followed their path.

Come morning, he awoke where he'd sheltered himself once reaching the mainland: beneath a stalwart pine tree, looking out at a harbor blue and promising, its waves gentled. The storm had brought him here, the islands leading him like the bread crumbs from the fairy tale of his childhood. Here, he knew, he would live.

In the weeks that followed, he moved his young family down into Maine and named the one-family town Hansel. Hansel-by-the-Sea, which grew to be a place of safe landing for many a weary traveler, just as it had for Josef. He erected a hand-carved sign to spell out its name. In the decades that followed, the wind mischievously wore the *H* clean off that sign, and by the time anyone noticed, the newcomers had already started calling the place Ansel.

Ann smiles over the story as they turn to exit the Weg and cross to the far side of the bay. "The Weg." She laughs.

"What's that?"

Oh. She'd forgotten about Mr. Fletch.

"The Weg. I was just thinking of the old story. You know it used to be called the *Weg von Blitz*?" She pronounces it as Germans would, the *W* as a *V*. "The Way of Lightning."

"I wondered," Jeremiah says. "Weg seemed strange, even for up here."

"They stopped saying it the German way during the war," she says.

He nods, and she can't tell if he's bored or just focused. He's steering the boat toward a dock in the dark shadows, and it's a few seconds before she recognizes it.

"Oh my," Ann breathes. "This place . . ." The old dock is the one she dangled her feet from a thousand times, laid back to watch the stars, scampered out on to bombard Bob with questions and ideas, finding a home for them in his listening heart.

Part of her aches to return. And part of her can't stand the idea of finding Sailor's Rest standing cold and silent and empty.

"Something else, huh?" Jeremiah slows the boat, and a gentle bump against the wharf says they've arrived.

Her suitcase rolls behind her, click-clacking across boards until she hits land. Soft earth, the path leading up to the Sailor's Rest.

She freezes.

Tucked up in the trees, steps turn and climb to the old Victorian captain's house. And it's anything but cold . . . or silent . . . or empty.

The lights are on inside.

seven

The doorknob is ice in her hand. And yet a light from the window—there, to her left, where she used to sit on the window seat and watch for Bob's boat every evening—washes her with warmth. A perfect collision of past and present. Pulling in a deep breath, Ann pushes through the entryway, nearly two hundred years creaking in protest with the old hinges.

A step inside feels like she's trespassing, the house assessing her every step as if to say *Who . . . are you . . . ?* Full of inquisitive accusation. She is Alice, the house is the caterpillar, and every creaking step she takes is a step through a ring of smoke. The house does not know her. She is an imposter—gone too far, too long.

A hand is on her shoulder then. She jumps nearly out of her skin, whirling to find Jeremiah, three logs of firewood under his other arm. He pulls his hand back as if he's been burned, and for the first time, she sees something softer than hard steel on his face.

"Sorry," he says. "Didn't mean to scare you."

"You didn't." The words come out like a defensive swing. "I just . . ." She has no way to finish that sentence. "W-why are the lights on? Is someone here?"

Jeremiah's face goes grim again. He points through an open door on the left, to her favorite room. "The couch is through there." He steps through to lead the way.

AMANDA DYKES

This is all sorts of wrong. She's Bob's only remaining relative. Well, the only one speaking to him, anyway. But this man she's never laid eyes on before is the one walking around this place making introductions.

And who's to blame for that? The voice of reason shames her.

Jeremiah stacks the logs next to the cold brick fireplace. This was a sitting room, once upon a time, but Bob . . . well, he was never much for sitting. He lined the shelves of this room with books upon books, a rainbow of muted colors from bygone ages. A globe sits on its stand in the corner, right where she used to spin it, close her eyes, and open them at Bob's bidding, to see where she might live someday. He'd taught her how to dream, how to think of the world beyond her. There's a piano on the wall by the door, and sandwiched between bookshelves, her window seat. It had been her ship, taking her to a thousand shores those hours she lost herself in books when she was too afraid to step on a real boat. But Bob had coaxed her even from that fear, eventually. Mostly.

The memories are sparking like fireflies all around her, leaving her breaths shallow and quick. She runs her hand over the sofa, the softness of flannel draped over it. It's only then she realizes that blanket is moving, sliding right out from under her fingers.

Jeremiah is standing opposite her, pulling a sheet toward himself. He freezes, scratches his beanie uncomfortably. He finishes wadding the flannel under his arm. "Blankets are there." He points to a cupboard back out in the hall. He grabs the pillow—a bed pillow, she realizes—from the couch and snatches a replacement for it from a crate in the corner, giving it a whack to release dust.

"There." He tosses it onto the couch. "All yours."

She eyes the mangled bundle under his arm. "You were sleeping here?"

For a second he looks like a kid caught red-handed, boyishly sheepish at six feet tall.

He shrugs. "It didn't feel right," he says. "This house empty." That's the only explanation he gives before striding across the room. He pauses in the doorway, then faces her. "There's some

61

food in the kitchen. Not a lot, but some. And . . . well, I guess you know your way around."

"It'll come back to me."

He pauses, as if deliberating about whether to tell her the next bit. "Bob . . . he lets me dock my boat out there."

Ann nods, trying to follow. There seems to be something else he's trying to communicate. It's endearing, a little, the way he stumbles around his words. A man after Bob's own heart, wherever on earth he came from.

"It's a houseboat."

He waits, watching for understanding to click.

Ah. He . . . lives here. Just a stone's throw from the front porch.

"I won't bother you." He rushes forward. "Meet me at seven tomorrow morning out at the dock. Visiting hours start at eight."

"Okay," she says. "Thanks . . ." She tries to call him Fletch, but it feels too familiar, something about it not quite fitting him.

"Jeremiah," he says, lifting his eyes to meet hers and hold them. Study her. He is direct. Maybe too direct. "Jeremiah Fletcher."

She gives a quick smile, a vestige of social niceties. "Jeremiah," she says, taking his true name as a peace offering. Offering hers in return. "I'm Annie . . . Ann . . . Bliss." Neither feels quite right. Besides, he already knows her name.

"I know," he says, and with a duck of his head, he's gone. Out the front door, a click behind him. His footsteps recede into the night, and from where she stands at the front window she sees him, hands in jeans pockets, bent forward against a night wind until he vanishes onto the *Glad Tidings*.

The day hits her hard then, exhaustion overtaking her limbs, her body, her soul. But the house is calling, memories tucked around every bend. She answers the call, surprised to find her feet remember which spots in the floor creak.

Just inside the front door stands an old phone table, the sort with a bench attached to it. Bob even has an old black phone—the kind with a cone to hold to the ear and a mouthpiece mounted on a pole to speak into. The cord is cut, frayed where he'd severed it with a pocketknife years ago. *"Who needs a phone,"* he'd said. *"If a body's got something to say to someone, they should just go find 'em and say it."* She smiles at how vivid his gruff voice is— and how that gruffness always wrapped up the value of people.

On the side table of the bench stands what looks to be a home-made receipt stake—the sort chefs use to spear their paper orders— but this one is just a long nail, hammered through a square of splintered two-by-four, pointed end protruding up. Staked upon the nail are not restaurant orders but envelopes. Each one bearing one name in Bob's handwriting: *Mr. Spencer T. Ripley.*

Down the hall and to her right is the kitchen, where they used to take meals at the little wooden table. She runs her fingers over its chipped red paint. Summoned by the sound of sizzling bacon mingled with the warm scent of fresh-baked biscuits, they ate here morning, noon, and night, never once setting foot in the formal dining room at the front of the house. A scan around the room shows it just as she last saw it, down to Great-Grandma Savannah's copper pie plate that Ann had learned to bake the family's famous hazelnut pie in, and the picture of Bob and his beloved bride, framed in silver, without a hint of tarnish. Except—there is one thing new. A framed document, beside the door to the back deck.

Flipping on the light, she crosses the room to read it . . . and her stomach sinks.

DARTMOUTH GRAD BRINGS PLAN FOR NEW LIFE TO ALPINE VILLAGE ON VERGE OF IRRELEVANCY.

She remembers the article. They'd wanted to print ON VERGE OF EXTINCTION, but she'd felt the word *extinction* would dis-hearten the residents too much if they ever got wind of it.

It still turns her stomach, eight years later. How she'd presumed to know how to save a Swiss village older than her own country. All its residents retired but the mayor, and houses sitting empty all up the mountainside. But she'd had that anthropology degree and a vision untempered by humility—a combination that caused her to promise them the impossible.

Maybe Bob never knew that part of it. Maybe he'd only learned of this part—the hope-filled part. *Please, God.* Words she'd sent heavenward countless times, that somehow the hurt she'd caused in Alpenzell might be undone. *Please.*

Pulling in a deep breath, she did what she'd had to do to survive the guilt—let the past stay boarded up in the past.

Upstairs, she rounds the railing and peeks into her old room, which had been her father's old room, and Bob and her grandfather Roy's old room before that. She smiles, recalling how she'd holed herself up in the closet when the wind was up. To turn the closet light on, she'd had to pull a chain, and she'd loved the way it made her feel secure, clicking on audibly to her pull and nestling her close in that warm closet. Her own little sanctuary.

She pulls the closet door open. But when she reaches up to pull that old chain—it isn't there. In fact, the whole closet is stacked floor-to-ceiling and front-to-back with cardboard boxes of every shape and size. Each one with a number scrawled across it in thick black ink.

"What on earth?"

She reaches up, feeling above the top layer until she finds the cord coiled up. When she gives it a tug, the whole thing takes on an eerie silhouette, backlit like another world is behind it.

She itches to look closer, to open a few of them up—but something turns her back. Human decency, maybe? This isn't hers. She has no right to search through any of it.

Quickly, before she can change her mind, she reaches to shut off the light and retreat. But her watch snags on a box on the way down, causing it—and two others—to tumble down. Pain shoots from her toes, where one of them has landed. She winces and bends to pick up the offending box. As she retrieves it, the contents tumble out on the ground.

Is that . . . ? But that makes no sense.

Kneeling, she confirms that it is, indeed . . . a rock. Gray and unassuming, angular on one side and round everywhere else, it's just a lump of hard earth, released from its cardboard prison.

She eyes the closet once more. There must be at least fifty other boxes in there. Are they all . . . rocks?

With care, she replaces the opened box and the two other boxes as well, noting the slow and heavy roll inside one of them.

It sure feels like a rock.

"What are you up to, GrandBob?" she whispers into the emptiness, but the rocks tell her no secrets.

eight

Sleep doesn't care for places outside normal. Cloaked in the scarlet afghan her great-grandmother Savannah had knit, Ann curls up in Bob's library, thoughts playing chase with slumber. Counting moonlit books filling shelves floor-to-ceiling around the empty brick fireplace, she pictures Bob reading them, aching that he's not reading them now. She can't stop thinking about the closet of rocks, troubled at their presence and wondering what they might mean. But finally her bleary mind registers the waves—breaker after breaker upon the shore—as the familiar Chicago wind and carries her off to sleep.

And then a deep-throated rumble grabs her awake. Rushing to the window, she spots a light bobbing in the dark at the end of the dock. Her thoughts are heavy, sluggish as they try to catch up to where she is, who that is, what's going on—and the fact that something is not right.

That is Jeremiah Fletcher's boat . . . and she is late.

Clutching the blanket around her, she's off into the predawn.

"Wait!" she shouts, but he's pulling away from the dock already. Had she overslept? Not heard the alarm? "I'm coming!" Bare feet fly over frost-cloaked grass, crunching and jolting her further into awareness. "I'm here!" But he's too far out to hear, his back to her as he plows the *Glad Tidings* into the dark.

Her feet collide with the dock, and she slides like a puck on ice, arms flailing as she scrambles for balance and grabs it none too soon. Breath coming in quick white puffs in front of her, she shivers. "Great. Thanks for nothing, Fletch." The name the locals say with such fondness comes out bitter. And that's when the sound of the alarm jangles from back in the house. *Five o'clock.*

Oh. She flushes warm, her mistake clear as the coming dawn. And where twenty seconds ago she was loathing him for not hearing her, she is suddenly thankful. She takes herself back inside and spends the next two hours keeping busy in the too-quiet house, where creaking floorboards, the ticking grandfather clock, and poets of the ages are her only companions.

Seven o'clock on the dot finds her dangling her feet over the dock into the morning sea smoke, watching as the *Glad Tidings* curves around the islands and back to the dock.

"All aboard who are coming aboard," Jeremiah says, and she stands. The moment of truth. It had taken her almost a whole summer to feel comfortable crossing the deck of Bob's boat . . . and she doubted it was like riding a bike. She couldn't just get right back on the boat as if twenty years hadn't passed and her dream wasn't just as vivid as back then. She grips the rail as Jeremiah waits. He checks his watch.

"Hey," she says. "I'm not the one who's late here."

"Nope," the man says, arms crossing in front of his gray-and-white baseball T-shirt. "I'd say you were about two hours too early."

Indignation rises in her, and she clambers up until she's standing right in front of him, arms folded to match his. "You heard me?"

He shrugs.

"You could've said something."

"Didn't think you'd hear me above all that hollering you were doing with that shawl thing around you." His mouth pulls up on one side into a dimpled half smile. He's not so scruffy today, his face clean-shaven.

"Shawl?" The man, with his Mariners baseball hat shadowing his eyes, doesn't look like the type to volley words like *shawl*. She feels it—the click of the first wheel of the Jeremiah lock turning. "You mean the blanket."

"Same difference." He motions her in, and she steps forward. She's dressed practically, ankle jeans and a T-shirt, her favorite hunter green cable-knit sweater draping around her to help keep the bite in the air at bay. But even so, she freezes just before boarding the boat.

"Ah," Jeremiah says. "It's got you."

"What's 'got me'?"

"You're sea-scared," he says. "Don't worry. It's pretty common. Navigating the bay is doable for most people, but something about the open sea feels different." He puts on a voice he probably intends to be soothing, but it sounds condescendingly slow to Ann. Her blood begins to boil accordingly as he continues. "I'll tell you what I tell the kids from the school when I ferry them over to their islands. Just take a deep breath, close your eyes, and—"

Her feet want to root down deep, remnants of an old nightmare resurrecting, but she blows past Jeremiah, lifting those leaden feet and planting them firmly on the *Glad Tidings*. Satisfaction surges through her, and she spins in triumph to face the man who's staring, brow furrowed.

"Ready," she says with a smile, trying to shove the shakiness from the cheerful proclamation.

Jeremiah moves slowly toward the cabin, leaving wary eyes on her. "As you wish," he says, like he's Farm Boy from *The Princess Bride*. "Just . . . try not to break my boat?" He nods at her fists, which grip the railing for dear life, despite the smile she's plastered on.

She removes her hands quickly and clasps them in front of her, feeling her face go hot. As the boat pulls into the bay, those hands fly right back to the railing. She thinks she hears a low laugh coming from that man, but when she looks, Jeremiah Fletcher has his eyes fixed on the ocean out in front of them.

Once out of the bay and into the open water, she inches closer to where he stands checking the screen of his plotter.

"So," she says, "are you from around here?"

He looks at her, and she feels as if they have come to a moment of reckoning. Not the same measuring-up that the other people of Ansel seem to be doing, but some kind of looking-in.

She takes a step back.

"I'd say I'm as much from around here as you are," he says at last.

What kind of answer is that? She's about to follow up, but he beats her to it.

"You've been here before," he says. It's a statement, but it feels like an invitation. Warning bells go off. She doesn't know him. He couldn't have that part of her, not yet. So she gives an answer about as good as his was.

"Ayuh," she says, using the local word for impact. "It was a long time ago."

". . . with Bob," he says, filling in at least one of the blanks.

She nods.

"Listen, Annie . . ." He uses the name everyone around Ansel knows her by. But it's different with him. He's new, not from that world. Yet there's something in hearing him speak it that feels . . . right. He's looking at the water again, and the pause is so long she wonders if he's forgotten to finish his thought. He blows his cheeks out, releases a breath. "When you see him . . ."

She swallows, curls her fingers around the door frame. There is true pain on his face, so much so that his heaviness fills the cabin and overflows, wrapping around her, too.

Jeremiah seems stumped, unsure of how to go on. His jaw works, and he looks her straight in the eye.

"A man who can take on the world, like Bob . . . to then see him unconscious to that world . . . I don't want it to shock you. He's changed." There's a gentling in Jeremiah's eyes. "But he's still the same inside. You'll see."

The boat blows on, and the waves part into a wake behind them. At last she speaks. "It's kind of you to visit him like this."

Jeremiah shakes his head. "It's the least I can do. He's done more for me than I can ever repay."

Ann wants to ask what he means, feels another round of clicks go by as she works to unlock what drives this person before her. He bristles, perhaps sensing her studying him.

"He just . . . got me through some stuff when I first came here," he says.

He stiffens, his vague words a wall going up between her and whatever "some stuff" is.

"Stuff he'd been through before," Jeremiah says. He's still standing at the helm, but he's a thousand miles away.

He remains so as they dock in Machiasport, taxi all the way to the Northwest Regional Hospital, and ride the elevator. The orange light lands on floor three, dinging as Ann reads the corresponding words. *Intensive Care Unit.* Jeremiah's long strides take him across the waiting room quickly, to where he speaks in hushed tones with a receptionist perched behind a light oak desk. The woman flashes Ann a glance, and her face softens. She nods to Jeremiah and reaches beneath the desk. A loud click sounds behind her, the unlocking of the double doors, and she motions them through.

The corridor is dim, lights low like the voices from the nurses' station. Jeremiah glances back at her, pulling one side of his mouth into a sad smile. There's a tenderness there that she doesn't want, for it can only mean that what's coming will be hard.

"You can do hard things, Annie." She hears the encouragement in Bob's voice from decades past, sees his blue eyes crinkled at the corners.

Jeremiah slows near the end of the hall and places his hand on the doorknob. Room 308. He pulls the door open and holds it for her. She takes a deep breath. Everything around her seems to slow—except her heartbeat, which is racing. She steps through, but something stops her. Jeremiah's hand. Just a quick clasp around her hand. It is warm. Reassuring.

Inside, the morning sun slips through open blinds. The smell is sterile. Clinical and empty. Every possible opposite of Bob.

And then she sees him there on the bed, attached to machines and lying still but for the slow rise and fall of his broad chest. Her hand flies to her mouth, stilling the cry threatening to escape.

At his side, she studies his face etched in kindness, and she knows those etchings did not come easily. She does not fully know the stories but has heard rumblings enough to know this man has lived through loss deeper than she can imagine. And yet it's his laughter that echoes in her mind.

Early in her summer visit, she, a scrawny girl of ten squinting past the freckles she wasn't yet old enough to despise, plopped down next to him on the end of his dock. He sat in an old Adirondack chair and raised an eyebrow at her. He didn't know what to do with a gangly girl any more than she knew how to live with a relative she did not understand her relation to.

"Mister," she said, "what do I call you?"

"Well, you better stop calling me mister—that's for sure."

"What, then? Are you . . . my granddad?"

He let out a slow exhale, as if she'd asked the meaning of life. "Now there's a question." He paused, never in a hurry. "Let me ask you this. What's a granddad do?" He said it as if he were wrangling a wet sheet through a laundry crank.

She screwed her mouth to the side. "I don't know. Cook grilled cheese grinders. Play cards. He looks a little wrinkly, maybe."

That made him hoot. "Well, that sounds about right. Tell you what. I'm your great-uncle Bob. And my brother, Roy, was your dad's father, your granddad. He'd have busted his buttons for the chance to know you, and I'm honored to have the chance. How 'bout you call me . . . grandguy?"

Annie laughed. "Nah, how about Grandpa?"

"Gramps?"

"That makes you sound grumpy."

"Well, aren't I?"

"Only when the wind's up."

"Okay, then. You pick a name."

She'd pondered a bit. "I like GrandBob."

He'd turned to her. She turned right back at him.

"GrandBob," he said, spreading his hand across the sky as if seeing the name in lights on Broadway. "That'll do." And suddenly Ansel had felt a little more like home.

Here in the hospital room, Jeremiah approaches, bringing her out of the memory. "They say you can talk to him, that it's good for him," he says.

Annie nods, unsure of what to say to the man who knows her best, here in the presence of a near-stranger. Everything about it feels wrong. But the silence ticks on, and at last she speaks.

"Hey, GrandBob." Her voice feels too big in the stillness of the room. She darts a glance and sees Jeremiah has moved to the corner, pulling a book from a stack on the table. *Backyard Boat Building.* A further look around shows a plant on Bob's bedstand, his jacket hanging in an open closet as if he's just come in from one of his "blusters down the beach." And in the corner to her left, the dull gold gleam of the knob of a cane shines from a barely open storage closet. She reaches for it, smiling.

Even twenty years ago Bob had spoken with longing of having a turn with this cane, ebony with its hand-engraved gold knob from over a century ago, inscribed for the town's oldest citizen. It has been in the town's possession since *The Boston Post* gifted them to New England towns lucky enough to receive them back in 1909. Ansel's, she knows, is one of the few canes still present and accounted for, holding up the tradition of supporting the lives that for so long had supported the town. But something doesn't quite add up. Bob is only seventy-four . . . not the oldest citizen by a long shot, if she isn't mistaken.

She runs her hand over the engraving, thinking of the hands that had leaned upon it.

Presented by *The Boston Post*
to the
Oldest Citizen
of
Ansel-by-the-Sea,
Maine

And in parentheses along the lower curve of the knob, the words *To Be Transmitted.*

Sharp, those words are. To be passed on, once the life of the holder is no more. A shallow intake of breath, and a vague prayer. *Please, not yet. Don't let him . . . transmit . . . yet.*

Where the outside world might look upon such a tradition as morbid, those in Ansel still hold it as a high honor, and a testimony to the natural handing down of life, love, and wisdom between generations. And no one deserves that honor more than Bob—though she still wonders at his possessing the cane.

She leans it back in its place and takes hold of Bob's hand. "We never were much for words, were we, GrandBob?"

There's no dry witty comment in response, and her heart aches. She squeezes his hand and pulls out her backpack. A quick zip and she pulls out her mandolin, lays it on her lap.

A nurse comes in, and her quick pace and efficiency is cheerful. "Hey, Bob," she says, as if he had greeted her wide awake. "Got some visitors, I see. Looks like your friend brought a girlfriend." She smiles and winks at Ann.

"Oh, um . . ." Ann stands. "No, that's not it." She blushes as Jeremiah looks up from his book.

His face is set, his jaw clenched as if that should tell the woman there couldn't be a more preposterous idea. The rigid lines dissipate as he turns toward the woman. "Hey, Shirley. How's Jim holding up?"

"He is about to go crazy, being kept home all day. He's itching to get back to work. But it'll be a while yet before he can get back on the boat."

Jeremiah shakes his head slowly. "It's enough to drive a guy mad, having to sit still." He looks to Ann. "Her husband was in a fishing accident."

"I'm so sorry," Ann says.

"Now, don't you worry," Shirley says, her warmth easy. "We all know it's part of the life, and we're lucky he escaped the rope before it dragged him into the water." She nods emphatically. "But,

Fletch, if you wouldn't mind droppin' in for a visit this week, I think it'd make his sanity stretch another day at least."

Jeremiah tips his baseball cap. "I'd be honored," he says, and Ann can tell he means it. He changes the subject. "This is Annie Bliss. She's Bob's niece."

"Great-niece," Ann says.

"I'll say." Shirley smiles. "The way Mr. Robert talks about you, we all think you're pretty great around here."

A flicker of hope dances around Ann. Bob had talked? "But I thought he couldn't—"

"Bless your heart, sweet girl, I'm sorry. He is unconscious, yes. I meant before. We all know Mr. Robert from way back."

"Mr. Robert?"

Shirley waves a hand. "Oh, you know. Your Bob. My mother always called him Mr. Robert. There was a sort of hallowedness about his name for a while, you know. 'Til he up and started going by Bob, as if he's just your average fella. But he'll always be Mr. Robert to lots of us around these parts. And rest assured, we're taking good care of him. Has anyone gone over things with you?"

She nods, recalling what Bess said at the diner. "A little. Do you think he'll wake up?" Ann distances herself from the words in order to speak them.

"Lord knows we're hoping and praying—and doing everything we can." She puts a hand on Ann's back and rubs her thumb in the gesture of a mother's care. "The doctors put him in an induced coma, to give him time to heal. When they think he's ready, they'll take him off the medication. Then after that . . . well, it is serious, but we're hopeful he'll wake up."

She checks some tubes and monitors, then turns to go. "Play that thing," she says, jabbing her finger toward the forgotten mandolin. "It'll do him good. Do us all some good, truth be told."

She nods and, as Shirley exits, begins to pick. Slow, bright notes. No song in particular—just a wandering melody. There's an intensity coming from the corner, and she opens her eyes to see

Jeremiah watching her. He looks quickly back at his book and she can't help smiling.

"Where'd you learn to play?" Jeremiah asks.

She keeps picking, remembering what it was like to hold this instrument in her hands for the first time.

She dips her head toward Bob. "Him," she says, and Jeremiah nods as if he already knew, as if that made all the sense in the world. "I came to stay with him for a summer when I was ten. My father was already deployed, and my mother was sent out before he returned. There was a three-month overlap, and he took me in. I was as lost a thing as you could find." The notes ease the air and coax more words out. "Not a clue who I was, where I was going, or even where I came from. I didn't feel like a whole person. Just a handful of pieces, not sure how they all fit together."

She laughs dryly. Some of that is still true. "One day Bob brought me into his sitting room. The dust was dancing all around in the sun shafts, and this was sitting on the sofa. I remember . . . just touching it, afraid to pick it up. He told me I wasn't going to break anything by picking it up, and when I held it, it felt as if I were holding a whole unopened universe in my hands—one I didn't have the keys to. And he said . . ." She squints, remembering.

"Let me guess," Jeremiah says. "Something like . . . if everything around you is broken, it's time to unbreak something."

"Yes," Ann says, studying. How did he know? "He said it was time to be a part of the unbreaking, of the making of something. He told me there was a Carpenter who was going to build me right up, too."

And that had been what it felt like in those early days of stumbling around notes on the mandolin. Stringing together notes that by themselves did a markedly clumsy nothing, but woven together they were magic.

Jeremiah nods. "Yep. Sounds about right." His is the look of someone who knows.

She stops playing and offers the instrument to him. "Do you play?"

"Not so much." He shoves his hands in his pockets and wanders to the window. "Hey, I'm going to go get some coffee. What'll it be?"

And just like that, he's halfway to the door, withdrawing from whatever it was they had just shared. "Tea? Coffee?" He snaps, pointing. "Smoothie."

"Water?" She reaches to grab her purse, give him some money. But he waves her off.

"I got it."

When he's gone, she stands and wanders the room. Someone has made it feel as much a home as possible. A worn book of Robert Frost poetry, and beneath that, an even more worn Bible. Same one he'd had all those years ago. She pulls out the drawer, and inside there's a paper folder, the kind with pockets and three bronze-colored fasteners. She runs her fingers down notebook paper inside, filled with clippings from *Rusty Joe's*, just like hers. All her thirty-word messages to him, going back and back for years.

Several pages in, there's a torn piece of paper stuck in like a bookmark.

"What are you up to, GrandBob?" She looks at the man and can almost see a smile hiding just a millisecond away on his face.

Something starts to beep, and she steps back. Has she broken something? Is Bob okay? She makes for the door, for help, only to be met by Shirley walking in.

"Don't you worry, honey. I just need to change his IV bag."

Ann breathes her thanks, relieved. She leans against the stack of books near Bob, feeling she should be doing something to help. "It looks like someone's brought some of Bob's things," she said. "Has Bess been here?"

Shirley looks at her, amused. "Yes, indeed. But if you want to know who made it like this, think again. There's only one person who's come every single day. Hates being here as much as Bob would if he were awake, but he comes, and never empty-handed."

"He?"

Shirley looks at her as if she's dull of brain. "Jeremiah Fletcher," she says.

If Jeremiah Fletcher brought the folder, had he read her clippings? She doesn't know whether to feel glad for Bob . . . or utterly mortified for herself.

"He sits and reads Bob's two favorite books." Waving a finger between the Bible and the folder of clippings, Shirley continues. "That man. You'd have to pull all his teeth twice over to get him to stand up and make a speech in front of a crowd. But give him a solitary soul, and he'll sit for hours with them."

She clicks a button on a CD player on the other bedstand. The sound of ocean waves rushes in around them. "He brought that contraption, too, but I gotta say, what he brought today takes the cake." She winks and leaves.

Ann follows her out into the hallway and catches up. "What did he bring today?" She hadn't seen Jeremiah bring anything in.

"Why, everything, honey." She smiles. "He brought you."

Jeremiah is shuffling down the hall from the other direction, water bottle in hand. She watches him pause outside the hall window, face somber as he studies Bob. And it occurs to her he's giving her his own time with the man.

"Shirley?"

"Mm-hmm?" The woman is busy at the computer, noting numbers on a chart.

"Is there a business center here? Somewhere I could check in with my work?"

"Now, what kind of people do you work for that won't let you alone to visit a loved one in the hospital?" She plants her hands on her hips as if she's offering to take them on.

"I just need to send a quick email," she says. And to clear out to let Jeremiah have some time with Bob. "They're waiting on a report I was supposed to have in two days ago, but they gave me an extension."

Something goes cold in her. It's a report about consumers.

People, turned into numbers, taking her away from the one person who set her heart to beating for others in the first place.

"Sure, honey. Go on down a floor. There's a place near the coffee kiosk."

The "place" turns out to be a table in the corner with a yellowed plastic-framed monitor and a dial-up Internet connection that beeps into a static stream. But the slower pace of things matches this corner of the world, where people are out working land and sea instead of tapping fingers and staring into computer screens all day long.

Accessing her email, she sends the report she'd saved in her drafts and, finding she has cell-phone reception in the hospital, makes a couple of calls. She takes her time walking back to the room, stopping to look at the large historical photographs lining the corridor. Lumberjacks. Men walking on islands of logs rolling down rivers, breaking ice and tangles of great tree trunks upon water. Courage.

When she rounds the hall to Bob's room, a new voice drifts from within. ". . . hopeful," it says, deep but subdued. "But too soon to tell."

She peers through the open blinds and sees a doctor, white-coated. He faces Jeremiah, who stands tall with his arms crossed, nodding. Shirley stands near the window, taking notes. Jeremiah asks a question she can't hear, and the doctor answers. "Weeks," he says, "if not months. Coming back from a coma at an advanced age . . ." He goes on, talking of residential physical therapy, out-patient physical therapy.

And all she can see is Bob's strong hand wrapped around hers, pulling her up when she tripped, as if she weighed no more than a feather. Those same hands, cradling hers to pull out a splinter with a gentleness to rival his strength.

"Will you be available to assist him in his recovery?"

They're asking this guy. A stranger. Some scruffy man who's nothing to Bob? She lets the burn of it scorch right over the fact that there's a reason they don't know to ask her. She's in the room now, and just as Jeremiah opens his mouth to say something, she speaks.

"I will." Her words are firm, much bolder than she feels.

Three pairs of eyes are on her, the machine's quiet beeping ticking off seconds.

"I'm sorry." The white-haired doctor adjusts his glasses. "You are . . ." He flips through the clipboard in his hands, as if that will tell him.

"Next of kin," she says. "Almost. I'm his great-niece. Ann Bliss." She draws up her shoulders, offers her hand. He takes it.

"You understand, Ms. Bliss, that his rehabilitation, if he awakes, will be extensive."

As had been hers. And he'd never given up on her. "*When* he wakes up"—she knows the odds are stacked against him, but she refuses to use that cutting word, *if*—"I'll learn whatever I need to, get him wherever he needs to go."

Jeremiah's looking at her as if she's just jumped off a cliff . . . and maybe doesn't know how to swim.

Shirley, on the other hand, is beaming. Ann stands a little taller and hushes the nagging voices clamoring for her to remember reports, limited vacation days, to-do lists.

But then she looks at Bob lying there, face mapped in wrinkles carved from compassion.

There's a way. There has to be.

nine

"So," Jeremiah begins as they make their way back to the wharf, "that was . . ." The corners of his mouth turn down as if he's pondering, searching for just the right words.

Ann raises her eyebrows, waits.

"You're going to care for Bob," he says.

"Of course." She could do without his skepticism, but she does like the way he leaves off that dreaded *if* clause at the end. "Well, maybe not if he has anything to say about it. If Bob knew we were talking about him convalescing, how to help him along, he'd bark at us to quit our nonsense and tell us he'd do just fine on his own."

Jeremiah chuckles. "True."

At the boat, she hesitates before getting on. *This is ridiculous.* Pressing her eyes closed, she swallows back nerves and steps aboard.

"You okay?"

"Yeah." For some reason wanting him to understand, she reaches for a story. "It's stupid. When I was a kid visiting Bob, he figured out I was pretty scared of the ocean. I shouldn't have been. I was raised on it. My parents had a boat and started taking me out when I was a baby. My mom would tie up a scrap of old sail like a miniature hammock between two posts on the deck, and the ocean would rock me to sleep."

The past uncoils like a fiddlehead fern, a tender ache with it. "So what happened?"

Ann shrugs. She's not ready to go there, not with a stranger. "Things change," she says, and moves on. "Anyway, when I got here, Bob tried to take me out on his boat every day for a week. I couldn't do it. I could hardly get up courage to talk, let alone face a whole ocean. So on the seventh day, he brought me down to the dock and started whistling an old hymn. He had something rolled up under his arm, and I watched him unroll it. It was a rectangle of canvas. He'd drenched it in glue and covered it in sand, then let it dry." She could still feel the way fear dropped away to make room for curiosity.

"He said, 'Sand's nothing but little rocks, Annie. And rocks are nothing but little earth. Solid ground, no matter what waves are thrashing around you.' He pointed at the sand and said, 'Get on your rock and let's get on with living. We're going to sea, girl.'"

It wasn't until much later that she realized he'd been talking about a whole lot more than literal rocks and water.

"Sounds like Bob," Jeremiah says, the edge gone from his voice. He motors the boat out of the Machiasport harbor, and she can't help but notice he seems to be going slower, turning more gently. They ride in silence, green islands rising like low hills from the sea, all pine clad and granite skirted.

On the left, sheer bluffs rise as towers—Gretel Point, as she recalls, the signal that they're nearing Ansel Harbor. But where they should have turned, hugged the point to head on home, Jeremiah continues straight.

"I have to make a stop." He tips his head toward the bins of mail.

Ann checks her watch—12:37—and can almost hear his eyes rolling. She doesn't blame him. He's been up since before dark, going who knew where, and is probably tired, hungry, and behind on his own work. Sure, she needs to find some sort of Internet, catch up on more emails. But he'd given up half of his workday to bring her to see Bob.

"Of course," she says. "Let me know what I can do to help."

"You could steer this boat, for starters." He leaves the wheel and tromps toward the bins. "That'd free me up to get the mail ready—"

"What?" She springs to her feet, panicked. No one's at the helm. Helm? They called it that still, right? No one's there. "I don't know the first thing about steering a boat."

"Sure you do," he says. "Just hold us straight."

She gulps, grips the wheel, and holds it, eyes glued to the dizzying waves. They pass Bob's island on the left, and she sees something in the daylight that escaped her when they passed it last night. There's a fence around it now. Chain link and sad, like a worn and saggy garment. It captures her attention, and she realizes with a start that she's let her hands follow, veering the boat closer to it. Quickly she corrects, feeling the boat respond, and stiffens as it registers that she's really steering this thing. And knowing her, she'll go horribly wrong somehow.

She doesn't realize how tense she is until Jeremiah returns and steps behind her. He's careful in the small space, but his hand brushes hers as he slides it onto the rung beside the outer rim. There's a steadiness to his touch.

"See? Nothing to it." She notices again how he doesn't drop his ending Gs, like the Down Easters do.

She inches away, pulling back to the doorway to let him have space.

He docks on an island near the head of the harbor. She remembers this spot—Everlea Estate. Her family had some history here, though the details are foggy. Something about her great-grandmother Savannah. It wasn't in the family now, but she'd seen pictures of a Victorian house with pointed roof, gazebo, pond—all of it.

"Be back soon," he says, and picking up a beige messenger bag, he disappears up a trail and into the trees.

The boat bobs gently, sun warming her shoulders.

This is what some people give their life's savings for, she tells herself. To come here and soak in silence and bob away on the waves. This is nothing to be afraid of.

Still, she can't stop herself from planning her quickest exit and pinpointing the location of the life jackets as she waits.

And waits. Time stretches out, and finally so does she, stretching her legs as she ventures back into the wheelhouse. Just as it looked yesterday, but in the full daylight the details are clearer. In the corner, a backpacker guitar—she'd know that shape anywhere, too small to be a full-sized guitar—in a soft case, with straps to live up to its name. She'd guess Bob was behind that, too.

From the bookshelf she pulls out the old copy of *The Moonstone*, thinking to fill her time with the old mystery. But as she settles back on the bench outside and opens the cover, something flutters from the crisp yellowed pages.

She retrieves it and, as she's returning it, takes in the first lines. *Hey, Fletch* . . .

A letter.

She looks away.

The handwriting, snapshotted and filed away in her mind, is loopy and smooth, slanted like a breeze blew through it. A bit of a tremor in spots.

She hadn't meant to see the next words, but there they were, branded in her mind before she could look away: *I know you're not going to want to read this for a while* . . .

Her college textbooks come back to haunt her near-photographic memory, taunting her to read more. *The study of written communication is crucial*, one book had said, *for gaining insight into the structure and function of human interactions. Society itself, modern or otherwise, cannot be fully understood without such examination*. . . .

She shuts the book hard on the letter. "Stop it," she says, scolding the phantom textbook. Maybe what it asserted was correct, but if she'd learned one thing in her disastrous and short-lived career as a field anthropologist, it was that knowledge means nothing without trust.

And trust has to be earned.

A crash sounds from somewhere in the trees, like a tower of dishes clattering to the ground, and Ann flies from the boat. Pounding up the trail Jeremiah had taken, she breaks into a clearing where the house from all the old photographs stands as big as life—pale yellow and trimmed in flaking white paint. On the porch, Jeremiah is on his hands and knees, a concerned look on his face.

EMT. He's an EMT. The crash, the look on his face, him on his knees—he must be helping someone. She rushes to join him, pulling out her phone to call for help. *Useless.*

"Oh, that won't work here, darling." A woman with a long white braid and a floppy straw hat takes Ann's phone, holding it as if it's a three-day-old fish she's about to toss back into the water. "Do you need to make a call? You're welcome to use the radio if you need shore."

"I . . . it was reflex. . . ." Ann takes in the scene—Jeremiah gathering bits of a broken china plate, the woman's face smudged with soil. Her denim pants, tucked into tall black galoshes, marked with dirt at the knees. "I heard a crash. Is everyone all right?"

"Everyone but that plate," the woman says. "And the scones. Not that they were much to write home about." She thumbs over her shoulder toward the house. "There are three cases of shined-up silverware in there from this place's heyday. Just gathering dust while I eat over the campfire. Seems a waste, don'tcha think? They say you can't teach an old dog new tricks, but I'm determined to figure out how to make civilized food. Starting with the infernal scone. That silverware *will* be used again for something other than dust-gatherin'."

"Those scones . . . if you were aiming for *infernal*," Jeremiah says, "you got it just right."

The woman narrows her eyes at him, and Ann's just about to rise up on her behalf when she tosses her white braid over her shoulders and laughs at the sky.

"That's a good one, Fletch." She points at him, and Jeremiah gives a stiff, shallow bow.

84

Ann can tell this woman has never met a stranger. And she likes that. Envies it, really.

Jeremiah stands, plate pieces stacked, and the woman points him to a galvanized bucket. "Stick 'em in the ash bucket, where they belong."

Ann glances over her shoulder to the bucket and sees, sitting on a heap of ashes like Job himself, a pile of blackened triangular would-be pastries.

"I've gone and skipped the hiya's again, haven't I? Sylvia Phelps." She sticks out a garden glove–clad hand, and Ann shakes it, thinking how the grit of the soil that clings to her afterward matches Sylvia.

"They called me Sully on the mountain," she says. "But you call me whatever you like. Call me Sully. Call me Sylvia. Call me Mary Poppins, for all I care. Names don't make a person. What's yours?"

Ann's mind races to catch up with this whirlwind. "My name? I'm Annie." The name slips out in a fluster . . . and sounds strange in her own voice. She's been plain Ann for so long, but being here, back in this place . . . "Annie Bliss," she says. It sends a small thrill through her.

"Annie." Sully curves the name, like it doesn't make sense. "Bob's Annie?"

She'll never tire of how that phrase drapes her in belonging. "Yes," she says. "I'm here for Bob."

"I thought you were off in San Francisco or Miami or Beirut or somewhere."

"Close." She tips her head. "I'm up from Chicago."

"Huh." Sylvia put her hands on her hips and looks Annie up and down.

Jeremiah's been watching all of this with amusement, but then he grabs a shovel and starts digging a hole beyond the deck, out where the makings of a garden are. "Right here, Sully?"

"You got it, Fletch. Thanks!" She turns back to Annie, gesturing to the white wicker chairs, where they sit. "I'm puttin' in a fence. Infernal deer around here make a habit of eatin' my dinner."

Sylvia takes out a pocketknife, starts to whittle a stick. "For the fish," she says, pricking her finger with the knife point to test it. "Nothin' beats catching 'em the old-fashioned way."

Annie considers Sylvia, the rugged woman all mud-streaked and fierce, sitting on the prim porch of an old Victorian. She and the house are as unmatched as can be—and yet there's a rightness to her out here on this island, the wild sea all around. There's a story here—Annie can sense it.

"What are you growing?" Annie plies the tools of her trade, hoping that the questions will lead to connections. It was what brought her into anthropology in the first place. When she was a painfully shy teenager, she discovered the magic of questions. If she asked the right questions, the other person would talk, and talk, and talk. And she could listen. She fell in love with listening, marveled at the magic of the things she found out, just by asking a few questions. Treasures buried in every conversation.

"Growing!" Sylvia spits the word with disdain. "Mud—that's what. It's mud season, don'tcha know? Summer, fall, winter, mud. Spring's a myth here, and summer sprouts up sometime after the mud."

Annie had forgotten about the season of mud. After the long winter these hearty people endured, the cold melted everything in sight into . . . well, mud. This part of Maine was a place like no other spot in the universe, and being back was like finding an old patch of sunlight in a long-lost home, and settling in.

"Was the mud bad up on the mountain?"

"Mountain?"

"You mentioned a mountain. Is that where you came from?"

"You don't come from the mountain. The mountain *makes* you. I was a guide fifty years up there until I finally turned in my compass." She points at Annie accusingly. "Not that I needed a compass. Knew Katahdin like the back of my hand." Annie recognizes the name of Maine's tallest peak.

"You must have so many stories from your time there," Annie says.

Sylvia hoots. "Stories!" She glances at Jeremiah, who's leaning on his shovel, posthole all dug, listening. "Tell you what. You two come on back later this week and I'll serve you up an earful of stories. I'll start with the one about the rabid chipmunk and the troop of corporate know-it-alls from the city. And I'll give you lunch, if you're lucky." She glances at the ash bucket. "Or unlucky."

And just like that, it seems their visit is over.

Sylvia walks them back to the *Glad Tidings* and waves her floppy hat as they pull away from the dock.

The whole way back, Jeremiah shoots Annie furtive glances. His expression is stolid, and it's maddening. She should be able to tell something about what he's thinking, but he's got a poker face like no other.

"You do that often?" she asks at last.

"Do what?"

Annie waves back at Sully's island. "That. Dig postholes while you're delivering mail."

"Can't say I've ever done that before." Jeremiah's smile is wry.

"But that sort of thing. That's part of the job?"

"That's just part of living here. You don't remember that?"

That silences her. She's used to city life, rich in its own way, with an energy and bustle from the lives there, but where eye contact is a safety issue and a good neighbor is your insurance company's tagline. The perfect place to skate by on the surface of society . . . which she told herself was a blessing. Safer that way.

But the growing hollow place inside says differently.

They ride in silence until they arrive at Sailor's Rest. Jeremiah offers his hand to steady her as she steps onto the dock, holds her hand for just a few seconds longer than needed—as if she might bolt. "Where'd you learn how to do that?" he asks. He's searching her eyes, and it takes everything in her to not look away, hide from this intensity.

"Learn how to do what?"

He releases her hand. "Sylvia. I've brought her mail every week for the last three years, and never once have I heard her open up about the mountain."

Annie smiles. "It's the magic."

"Oh, great." He rolls his eyes. "Next you'll be telling me it's phases of the moon and—"

"No," Annie says, feeling her defenses rise. "Just the magic of questions. People. You ask, you learn."

He studies her. "Not always."

"What's that supposed to mean?"

Shooting her a maddening glance, he heads up the path, as if she's proving his point and he's just won the battle.

She jogs to catch up.

"What did you mean?" she demands.

"Not everyone will answer your questions. Especially around here."

"What—like you?"

"For starters."

"Why not?"

"Bob told me about you."

She stops fast in the path.

"What did Bob tell you about me?"

"You and your . . . people-detecting."

This guy is nuts.

"You're a people detective. It's what you do, right? Study them, figure things out about them."

His summation is so simple, it cuts away the fog of the last four years of people boiled down into numbers and trends.

"I'm a consumer insights analyst," she says dully. "I just crunch numbers." She walks around him to make a beeline for the sanctuary of the house as he rounds the corner of it, heading out back for who-knows-what reason.

But there, planted on the steps between her and safety, is a man in a gray suit. Annie registers little else, her mind going into overdrive. He must be from the hospital, or maybe Washington County, here to deliver a notification she doesn't want.

It must be. He looks grave, his wire-rimmed glasses framing somber eyes.

"Good day," he says, voice polished. "I'm here regarding Robert Bliss."

"Oh," Annie murmurs, eyes growing wide. "He isn't . . . he hasn't . . ."

"I've a standing appointment with him and have been waiting over an hour."

Shackles of apprehension click open, and she can nearly hear them fall away. "I see," she says.

The man seems to notice her for the first time, and a polished smile emerges. "Spencer T. Ripley," he says. "I don't believe I've had the pleasure."

She introduces herself, folding her arms and backing up a step. "You have an appointment with Bob?"

"No, he doesn't." She turns to see Jeremiah, face as stone and a package of shingles under his arm. He strides toward them, slows as he passes Spencer T. Ripley, never taking his eyes from him. Two more steps and he's in the house.

"Hey!" Annie goes after him, only to find him pulling an envelope off the stack of speared notes next to the door. *Spencer T. Ripley*, it says. That's why the name sounded familiar.

Jeremiah strides back out and presses it to the man's chest. Spencer scrambles to gather it up, rip it open. Jeremiah stands back, arms folded, waiting.

Spencer scans the paper as if he's the hunter and it's the prey. He stops. Scans it again, the spark dying in his eyes.

"Very funny," he says. "Please tell Mr. Bliss that the Committee for Excellence in Maritime Poetry will continue to await his earnest next installment, for display at the upcoming summit." The man talks like a form letter.

"Good luck with that," Jeremiah says.

Spencer T. Ripley turns from him, directing dark eyes to Annie. "Ms. Bliss, was it?"

Annie nods, pulling a water bottle from her bag and taking a sip.

"I'd be much obliged, Ms. Bliss, if you'd convey my message to the venerated Mr. Bliss."

She nearly spews her water—not because Bob's not worthy of being venerated, but because she can picture his face twisted up if he ever heard himself called so.

The man removes a business card from his suit pocket and hands it to her. It's crisp white with bold black type. "If you learn of Bob's promised installment, do look me up." He turns to leave but stops and looks over his shoulder, as if he's Spencer Tracy instead of Spencer T. Ripley. "Or if you'd just like to enjoy a coffee together sometime, I'm staying above the Realtor's office in town," he adds with a wink. Ignoring her shocked expression, he continues. "I've rented the flat there for the next two weeks, in preparation for the festival."

Jeremiah drops the package of shingles, its *slap* piercing the air and sending Spencer jogging down the harbor trail in his Oxfords.

The paper he'd pulled from the envelope falls behind him and dances a circle inside a whirl of breeze. Snatching it up, Annie reads Bob's words.

> A life well-lived
> is a life well-given.
> And a poem well-wrote
> is a poem goodly-smote.

She looks from the paper to the retreating man and back. Jeremiah's watching, his expression as serious as ever but his eyes laughing.

Annie scratches her head. "What just happened?"

Jeremiah stoops to gather the shingles, which have escaped from their brown paper wrapping. "You just stepped into Bob's worst nightmare."

Annie kneels to help him, and he goes on to explain how Spencer T. Ripley is a thorn in Bob's side. How his department at the New England Oceanic College is putting together a festival—the

Summit for the Celebration of Maritime Literature. How they'd descended upon Ansel's town meeting three months ago with no warning and announced that they'd chosen Ansel-by-the-Sea to host the prestigious inaugural celebration. How the town board had informed them that they might have trouble securing a venue and lodging, seeing as they'd chosen the same weekend as the annual Ansel Lobsterfest, which pulled in no small crowd. And how Spencer T. Ripley and his Committee for Excellence in Maritime Poetry were undaunted and planned to descend on the town that weekend anyway, choosing local poet-hero Robert Bliss to be their keynote speaker and headliner.

To which they'd been met with a room of blank faces and not a few chuckles. Mr. Ripley had never met Bob—nor had he seen the way his on-a-good-day gruff manners grew coarser by a thousand whenever someone mentioned his single poem, penned some fifty years ago.

"How did Bob react?"

"As you might imagine," Jeremiah says. "Bob wasn't at the meeting, but Spencer showed up here to give Bob the 'good news,' and Bob shut the door in his face. He flat out refuses to take part in their literature fest, which the rest of the town has started calling Bobsterfest. Bob's dead set on going to Lobsterfest and won't set foot near Bobsterfest. He's written a pile of"—he looks at the paper Annie is holding and holds his fingers up in air quotes— "'poetry' to feed the guy whenever he comes around. Made up words, cheesy rhymes, the gamut."

Annie smiles and aches all the more to hug that gruff old man.

"Since then," Jeremiah says, "that guy has plagued every town meeting, bringing updates that no one cares about. He gets to town a day before the meetings and shows up on Bob's doorstep, begging for more poetry, convinced he's going to be the one to summon the great poet who united a nation back into writing."

Annie had heard the whispers around town, of Bob's famous poem written back in the forties. She didn't know the details, and though she'd gone hunting for a copy of it when she lived with

Bob that summer, she'd turned up nary a clue. Still, she knew it had gained him some renown, and he'd loathed it, refusing to call it poetry. *"They're just words,"* he'd grumbled.

"All they had to do was open up *Rusty Joe's* classifieds, if that's what they wanted," Annie says.

And Jeremiah—for the first time—laughs. Deep and alive, it's the sort of laugh that frames his mouth in kind lines and reaches right inside everyone around. She joins him, and he glances up, their eyes meeting and holding.

He's the first to break the hold, fixing his eyes back over his shoulder. "I've got to get these to the boathouse," he says, but he lingers, as if torn.

"Yes," Annie says. "I won't keep you."

He pauses. She's learning that this guy is never in a hurry. Whatever he's thinking, he gives it time to be thought. She tries not to squirm under his gaze. "Come with me," he says. "You haven't seen inside the boathouse yet. This visit, I mean."

"Actually . . . I never have."

"Never?"

She shakes her head. "It was always locked. The padlock looked like it had been there for decades. I used to imagine what was inside."

"Like what?" Jeremiah starts walking, and she beside him.

"Well, you have to remember, I was ten."

"Okay. So what did ten-year-old Annie conjure up to live in the boathouse?"

She feels heat creeping up her neck. "A dragon."

"Huh."

"What? What would you have thought, with the place always locked, and a whole corner of the roof missing, and a light glowing inside some nights?"

"I guess in some ways you weren't too far off," he says.

"Oh?"

"There is something larger than life in there that I've never been able to make sense of."

"What is it?"

"Here." Jeremiah pulls a key from his pocket and hands it to her. For a moment, her pulse hammers. It looks like the one from the envelope at the diner. Same tarnished metal, though this one looks significantly more scratched up. Were they duplicates? Had Bob been granting her access to the boathouse when he left her an unexplained key? She digs into her pocket and pulls her version out, handing Jeremiah's back to him.

"I think this might work," she says, holding her key up, a thrill coming over her.

"Where did you get that?"

She remembers Jeremiah wasn't in the diner when she opened her envelope.

"This was in the envelope Bob left for me on our table—nothing else, no explanation."

She can see Jeremiah's mind sorting through the possibilities, but he just nods and says, "See if it fits."

The boathouse appears as they round the corner, its brown shingled sides and flaked-white trim lending it an air of timelessness, its tracks to the sea underused and overgrown.

One corner is in ruins at the roof, just as it had been when she was a kid. But someone's been working on it—a ladder is propped against the shingled side, and a blue tarp flaps over the opening in the roof.

"Are you fixing this?"

He tips his head to the side. "In a way. Bob was doing it. I tried to talk him out of it, but . . ." He narrows his eyes at the building, regret on his face. "This is where I found him after he fell."

Oh. Annie's stomach sinks, thinking of it.

"I aim to get it fixed before he wakes up. Like I should have done before."

"Jeremiah, I'm sure it wasn't—"

"It was my fault," he says. And the set of his jaw says the conversation is over. He strides toward the door, and Annie follows. She knows the weight of this regret and has thought more than once the very same—that this is her fault. If she'd been here . . .

Jeremiah gestures toward the door. There, hanging on the metal latch, is the same rusted padlock, greeting her like a long-lost partner in adventure.

She slips the key in.

Nothing.

A second try is met with a hard wall of failure, lock not budging.

Jeremiah holds his key up again, and she takes it, hope blistering as she sticks her own back in her pocket. Its mystery will need to wait a little longer.

Jeremiah's key slips right in. She holds her breath, the vivid picture of that childhood dragon breathing into her memory. The metal clicks . . . and releases.

ten

Thousand-ton metal shrieks, slowing the train as it pulls into Boston's South Station. Robert's gaze wanders from the old copy of *The Count of Monte Cristo* in his lap, past Jenny, and on through the window. Outside, soldiers in navy blue uniforms and white caps mill about with those in army green. Lieutenants and privates, corporals and captains, paths intersecting in this tangle before they head off to their next assignments, furloughs, trainings, missions.

Robert sits a little straighter, watching them. So this is Boston. Two flags wave high above the station's massive columns, carvings, and clock tower. Red, white, and blue moving in the wind, the flags remind him why they've come.

Jenny is fidgeting in the seat next to him. She rummages in her handbag and pulls out the telegram—the one she's read at least ten times since they left Ansel. Robert has nearly committed it to memory, too.

JENNY. ON LEAVE TWO DAYS STARTING NEXT MONDAY. BOSTON. SHIP OUT AFTER THAT. MEET

95

ME FOR USO DANCE IF YOU CAN. WILL SEND DE-
TAILS SOON. 21 FATHOMS—ROY.

She smiles at that last part. It was their code, those fathoms.
Each time a letter passed between them, they added one more to
the number. Another letter passed, another bit of life experienced
together. For a boat builder like Roy, whose thoughts were fixed
on nautical miles—fathoms—beneath a boat, this was a story of
the growing depths of life and love beneath their vessel. It grew
and grew, fathom by fathom, letter by letter.

In the six weeks he'd been away, the distance hadn't hindered
their fathoms in the least. By now all of Ansel knew of it, and
they'd ask her in the street, *"How many fathoms now, Jenny?"* It
did them all good to see her lovestruck face beam back the answer,
even in her heartache at missing her husband.

"Two days," she murmurs now. "Two days until he's away."

Roy had hoped to come home from his training before he left.
But with such short leave surprising them all, it made more sense
for them to come to Boston, else he spend the whole of it on the
train.

Her hand rests on her stomach, a reminder that there is another
present in this row.

"I won't be like all the other girls at the dance," she murmurs. Her voice is lined with sobriety and wonder all at once.
The life within her is changing her in more ways than just the
small bump that's barely beginning to show. Changing who she
is, how she grapples with this world. She's both stronger and
softer, somehow.

Passengers around them start bustling, preparing to exit the
train. "I hate to break it to you, Jenny," he says, "but you never
had a chance of being like all the other girls."

Her head jerks up, dark hair curled into the style of the day
around her face. "Why, Robert Bliss!"

"Ask Roy," he says. "He'll tell you you're fathoms more than
the others."

She laughs. "That's kind. But don't put those other girls down too quickly. Roy and I have schemes of setting you up at the dance, you know."

Robert cringes. Not if he can help it. He wants as little to do with dances, people, and this city as possible. The last thing he wants is to spend the evening spinning girls he'll never see again, as if somehow that'll help the war.

He'll make sure Jenny gets safely to her aunt Millicent's house and home. And that will be that.

But once they meet up with Roy outside the station, Robert learns his brother has other plans, starting with dinner at Jenny's aunt's house—a beef roast and biscuits, exorbitant in times like these and attained only by the whole neighborhood's donated meat rations when they heard a soldier was being sent off to war. Jenny and Roy are awful companions for table conversation, staring starry-eyed at each other the whole time, but afterward, they insist on dragging him along to the dance. He resists at every step, but Roy's "I dare you, little brother" tips the scales.

It's dark when they exit the subway at Symphony Station and make their way toward the Roseland-State Ballroom. Big band music jigs out into the air, ushering them into the lobby. The USO has reserved the whole hall for the night. Smiling faces beam from pretty girls all in a row, hands clasped behind backs or taking the offered arms of soldiers, stepping through the inner doors and into the dance. Light reflects from a mirrored spinning globe above them, sprinkling them with beams as they move in and out of the light, the dark, the light.

"Come on." Roy steps up to the front table, where a lady sits with clipboard in hand. Roy, looking smart and proud in his uniform, pulls a paper from his jacket pocket, slides it her way.

The Boston USO formally invites
Seaman Roy A. Bliss
to
An Evening Beneath the Stars

The woman flips through her papers, and as she does, Robert's attention drifts past the junior hostesses lined up and beaming in their party frocks, over to where a woman in a dark red dress hesitates in the doorway to the ballroom, watching the couples inside.

His gaze lingers there—not the way other men in the room do, though she is certainly beautiful, but because there's a story written on her face, a sadness etched deep there as she watches something or someone on the dance floor. And as the music crescendos, she stands taller. Her blond-crowned head gives a small shake, and her jaw sets. He recognizes that look—that of a battle raging inside a human soul. She turns and, with head held high and not a glance toward anyone in the room, strides out the front doors and into the night.

"Ah, but can't you make an exception?" Roy is leaning on the table, flashing his biggest grin at the clipboard lady. "He's my brother. And he's doing as much for this country as anyone in uniform—"

"I'm sorry, Seaman Bliss." Her voice is like molasses, thick and too sweet, melodic as she says, "Rules are rules. And the USO is, after all, for our soldiers."

"But look at that mug!" Roy straightens, cups Robert's chin, and squishes his cheeks crookedly. The kid wasn't doing his argument any favors.

"Yes, very handsome indeed, but—" She stops, looks between them as puzzlement, then delight, plays across her face. "Why, you're identical!"

"That's right." Roy bounces his eyebrows up and down, as if they have an inside secret. "Wouldn't you like your dance to have twins? We're quite an act."

Speak for yourself, Robert wants to say, but he bites his tongue.

The line behind them is growing, the fellas in it growing impatient.

"No," Robert says. He feels the appraising once-over of the

lady as she takes in his brown slacks and white shirt, his worn wool coat devoid of military insignia, and the humble newsie cap he holds between his hands, a relic from Dad's youth. He takes a step back. "It's all right. I'll meet up with you later."

Jenny steps forward, bedecked in finery that's a patchwork of loans from the ladies of Ansel—Mrs. Crockett's blue gloves, a silver silk dress of his mother's that she shortened for the occasion, and what Jenny called "slippers" from Liza Montgomery. The whole town had gone into a tizzy, readying Jenny for this dance when Roy's telegram came. The town square had looked like an explosion of someone's attic, with dresses and shoes and all the women draping Jenny in what they were sure would still be the finest wear. Jenny had just laughed—her first genuine smile since Roy had gone. When she'd turned those blue eyes on Robert and asked, *"Would you take me there?"* there had been only one possible answer.

She leans toward the matron and whispers something, eyes dancing. She slips her hand into Roy's and points in a conspiratorial way between Robert and the lined-up girls.

Would that the floor might open up and swallow him whole.

The lady turns her head to the side, looking the three of them over as a smile tickles at the corners of her stained-red mouth. But just as Robert is afraid she's about to assent and throw him to the lions, she releases her pent-up breath from behind pursed lips and says in defeat, "I'm sorry. Rules are rules."

Robert's nerves release and propel him forward until he's picked up the woman's hand, pen and all, and kisses it. "Thank you," he says.

"Young man," she says, pulling her hand back, "I said no, you may not enter. I'm sorry, but—"

"I know," Robert says, sticking his cap back on his head and making for the door. "Thanks!" He turns to the astounded Roy and Jenny and points. "I'll meet up with you tomorrow." And the blast of cold air as he exits, parting a crowd of soldiers filtering in, is freedom itself.

Outside, it's lightly snowing. Robert walks toward the corner of Huntington Avenue, where his room at the YMCA awaits him. Just a few minutes more, and he'll be safe from all this socializing, alone in his room for the night.

But his feet carry him the opposite way. He knows this feeling. The pull of the ocean, the only familiar thing in this bustling city— and the only thing wide enough to break free of this closed-in cell the buildings create.

He wanders several blocks, through the Boston Common and Public Garden, where a lit tree and a cluster of carolers remind him that tomorrow is Christmas. The falling snow melts on contact and forms rivulets on brick sidewalks, and like the water, all he knows to do is follow the slope. Down and down until the ocean will appear.

Gas lamps hiss, strains of music from the dance are only a memory now. Another sound rings. His footsteps fall in sync with metal on metal, pounding, so much more music to his ears than the strains of Glenn Miller back at the dance. These are surely the sounds of the harbor. Someone at work. Doing something. This is a dance he can understand.

The clink of metal grows louder. Whatever it is, he can help. Someone building a shed, maybe. He looks around at the reaching white-stone mansions and laughs. Okay, this isn't Maine. So maybe it won't be a metal shed. But still . . . he'd give just about anything to set his hand to something, help a guy out, get the patronizing look of that USO lady out of his head.

He turns the corner . . . and a crowbar nearly slices into his face. His elbow flies up to protect it as he ducks away. The figure in front of him—shadow shrouded, with back to him—brings the crowbar down upon its mark: the bumper of a Buick Roadmaster gleaming in the gaslight. Its grille—surely not more than a year old—is dented, misshapen from this assault.

"I don't think that's such a good idea," Robert says, straightening and turning to face the figure full on for the first time.

And he takes a step back. The "guy" isn't a guy at all. He . . .

she—for she steps from the shadows, and there's no mistaking her distinctly feminine figure—is in a dress of deep crimson and a coat of richest fur. Her dark eyes flash, hair like very tangled gold falling into her face. The same face he'd just watched leave the USO, envious of her escape.

eleven

"It most certainly is a good idea." The woman plants her fists on her hips, crowbar leaving a smudge across her skirt.

"You might not want to—"

She jabs the crowbar in his general direction, and he steps back. "I'll tell you something, mister. It's the first good idea I've had in a good long time. Tell *that* to the Misses Hampstead and their *ladies* college." Another crowbar jab, for emphasis. If this keeps up, someone's liable to happen along, figure he's cornered her, toss him into jail.

He should leave.

But he looks at her, standing there like Zorro with sword extended, and he can't leave. Some magnetism keeps his eyes glued to her.

"I don't know the Misses Hampstead."

"Oh? Well, you're lucky. They'd have you speaking the 'four languages of the Romantics'—their words, not mine, thank you very much—in no time." She ticks her fingers off on the crowbar. "French. Latin. German. Italian. Ha! One of those is dead, and two will get you labeled a traitor these days. They've crossed German and Italian off their list now, like proper wartime citizens, but—"

"Seems they'd be more useful now than ever," Robert ventured. "In a war job somewhere."

She was becoming more conversational, less tyrannical. He imagined she might be the sort of creature Shakespeare invented when he wrote of a shrew to be tamed.

"Tell that to my father," her rant continues. "'Go to the dance,' he said. 'Do your part to help our soldiers,' he said. 'Be a hostess.' As if spinning around all night will end the war."

Maybe she wasn't as crazy as she'd seemed at first.

"But will he let me *actually* help? Take a war job? Become a nurse? Anything at all? No!" She turns to the car again, hits the bumper hard. "He"—*clank*—"will"—*clank*—"not!"

She slowly lets out a deep breath and turns to face him. "Do you know what the widow in the Good Book did when she had only two mites to give?"

"She . . . gave it." He's caught her eyes for the first time, and he keeps them, hopes maybe holding this stare will help steady her.

"That's right. And do you know what I have to my name?"

"I don't even know your name."

"Names." She waves an arm. "Quite the most unnecessary contrivances that ever were. But for argument's sake—do you know what I have to my name?"

He doesn't like to judge, but by the fine dress and coat, the satin gloves and gleaming shoes, it might be a good bit.

"This car—that's what. It's the only thing of value I've ever had to call my own. And only because it was a gift from my grandmother. She was never one to stand by and let life roll over her, so I figure I've got her blessing."

He eyes the car. "Her . . . blessing to pound holes into your car?"

She rolled her eyes. "To give my fender to the war effort."

It's the bumper she's attacking, but he doesn't correct her as she continues. "Let them melt it down and make ships out of it or whatever it is they do with all the donated metal. Maybe it'll help save some soldier's life someday. Even if I can't." She looks away at that last part, voice quieter.

Ah. Now, this is a spirit he understands. He steps forward, thinking to help.

"You can't stop me." She brushes her hair out of her face, leaving a streak of grime behind. It becomes her.

"Wouldn't dare." He kneels next to the bumper, slides his hand behind it, searching for the bolt. He finds it, then stills under her gaze. "If you're not opposed to a fella sticking his nose in . . ."

She crosses her arms. "I . . ." She clears her throat. "That would be fine." She catches his eye, and her posture eases. "Thank you."

"So long as you keep that crowbar still for the duration," he says, "and you have some tools in your trunk."

With a glimmer of a smile, she sets the crowbar gently on the brick sidewalk and opens the trunk.

Finding a wrench, he loosens the first bolt and moves on to the next. She bends to watch, sending him furtive glances every now and then. He matches them, glance-for-glance, and the steady loosening of the bolts weaves a calm into the atmosphere that had not been there when the crowbar was about.

"I . . . um . . ." The woman—phoenix, force, conflagration, whatever she was—seems to be replaying the whole scene that's just passed in her mind. She winces and brushes the dusting of snow from the shoulders of her fur coat. "I don't suppose you're from around here." Her voice has taken on the air of polite conversation, as if they've just met in a restaurant somewhere and not in a tangle between a crowbar and a bumper.

He laughs. Even in his best attempt at would-be dance attire, he didn't fit in, not even out here on the streets. "I guess a fisherman from Maine doesn't know how to camouflage himself for Boston," he says. "Was it the clothes? They didn't want me at the dance, either."

"Good heavens, no." She looks at her own dress. "I'm not one to talk about clothes. Mother brought this back from New York so as to 'dazzle those soldiers.'" She smooths out the skirt where the crowbar left its black mark and laughs. "So much for that notion."

"Don't give up too fast. I'd say you just gave a dazzling performance with that crowbar," Robert says. "I'll give you that."

104

She laughs, and it's musical. Straight from some place of light inside her.

"It wasn't your clothes," she says at last. "You're just not entirely . . . Boston. You've got a sort of"—she waves her hand in a circle in the air—"wilderness about you. But steady, too. A wild peace."

"That doesn't make sense."

"Certainly it does. There's no wilderness quite like peace." She studies his face. "You do remind me of someone, though."

Something in him sinks a little, and he doesn't want to think about why. It feels too familiar. "You might have seen my brother around town." He turns his attention back to the bumper and pulls the final bolt off. "We're twins. Mostly."

She pushes her lips to the side, thinking. "No, sir, it's not your mostly twin." She snaps her fingers. "It's that man from the movies. The one with that sort of . . . knowing look." She pauses, the gaslight behind them hissing. "Gregory Peck! Gregory Peck."

"Gregory Peck with a knowing wild peace," Robert says.

"That's right. Gregory Peck if the wind got into his hair a little, and his soul, too. That's you, mister."

He holds her gaze, thinking how if he's knowing, she's seeing. The way she looks at him, studies him openly, as if he's the most fascinating mystery she's ever encountered. She'll be disappointed once she finds out he's just a plain man of the sea, no mysteries to be found.

"Robert," he says at last. "Robert Bliss."

"Robert Bliss." She turns the name in her mouth and nods. "Yes, that's a good name for you."

"Can't take any credit for it." He wriggles the bumper until it slides off.

"Well, Mr. Bliss . . ." The phoenix stands and offers her hand. He shakes it, and the shake slows until he's just holding her hand, wrapped in night. "It's nice to meet you."

"Likewise, Miss . . ."

The smile on her face disappears.

"That's right," Robert says. "What was it you said? Names don't matter?"

"Unnecessary contrivances," she says. "Unless it's one like yours. But if you must know, my name is Eva. Eva . . . Rothford."

She drops the last name as if it's a shadow, a heavy one.

"Well, Miss Roth—"

"Eva."

"Well, Miss Eva." Her hand relaxes in his. "I gather maybe that name means something around here, but—I'm sorry to disappoint—I don't know just what that might be. I do know, though, if you point me in the direction of the nearest scrap pile, I'd be glad to take this bumper there."

"Oh, but I wanted to—"

"With you." The words push out too fast, as if he's flinging a lobster cage out into the deep. Good gravy. Words were never his strong suit.

His face heats. He should not hurl clumsy ideas at this woman, who's looking rather too amused just now. "That is, uh . . . if you'll have me."

And now it sounds like he's proposing marriage. She seems to find no end to the amusement in all this, but thanks be to God, Eva Rothford brushes her grease-streaked hands against her skirt as if it were a dish towel, leaving black smudges across the crimson sheen, and holds out her hand, awaiting his escort.

"All right, mariner," she says as she takes off her fur coat, tosses it in the trunk, and slams it shut, "let's scrap some metal."

He takes one end, she the other, and they turn down a cobbled road—Acorn Street, the white metal sign upon a brick house says. The road is narrow, with black-shuttered brick homes all in a row, wreaths and red ribbons upon their dark doors, and garlands wrapping the gas lampposts. They make a sight, he knows—she in her fine dress, he in his civvies, and a shiny, dented bumper between them. All is quiet, and though this city still gives him the urge to loosen his collar and run until he reaches wide open sea, this . . . this is nice.

At the end of the street, a mountain of tangled metal grows up from the sidewalk. Bed frames, wrought-iron fence panels, pots and pans, and every other form of metal imaginable. Someone's chalked SCRAP METAL FOR VICTORY onto the brick wall the mountain leans against.

"Feel better?" Robert asks as they slide the bumper into the mound.

"Much." Eva brushes her hands together, satisfied. "But I wonder if the whole car would fit in the pile. . . ."

"Now, listen," Robert says. "We make a good team, but I don't think even the likes of us could carry your car."

There's something about her laughter, the way it slips right into his chest like it belongs there.

Something tumbles from the pile, pinging to the ground with its tinny clash. He stoops, retrieves it. It's a metal deer, a child's toy. Cherished, for the way its details are worn nearly smooth.

She comes close. He opens his palm, offering it to her, and she takes it—her touch light. She holds it as if a treasure, and there's a sheen across her eyes.

"Well," she says, sniffing and pulling herself up straight. "If that doesn't just smite me." She places it atop the bumper, toy on a throne. "Come on, Robert the Fisherman. If you don't mind a walk, I'll show you a sight a touch closer to your home. Wherever that might be."

Concerned she might be getting cold—her dress's long sleeves don't seem warm enough to ward off the increasing chill—Robert starts to take off his coat, but she shakes her head. "Thank you, but I'm fine. Walking will warm me."

She leads him through her city, talking all the way. It's as if she's been storing up words for a lifetime and has decided he'll be the one to hear them all. Not that he minds. The opposite, actually. Her warmth and ease spin a spell that makes him feel not so far from home. She talks about the jobs she's tried for and how her parents have not allowed her to take one, no matter what. How her father, with his connections in the city, has thwarted her attempts at welding, ship work, even selling war bonds. "The only thing I can contribute to the war is to 'engage myself to a worthy young officer.'" She deepens her voice for this impersonation and though she smiles, it's a sad one.

"I . . . take it this officer has a name?"

"My parents like to think so. But we already know how I feel about names." She's quiet for a moment. "What about you? You have a girl holding that heart of yours?"

He takes his gaze from her, directs it to the body of water ahead. She'd told him it is the Charles River, reflecting Boston's lights and Cambridge's across the way. "No," he says, but his pause muddles the straightforward answer.

"Ah," she says. "That's the look of a man in love." She tilts her head, waits. It's an invitation, and that spell she's woven reaches into him, beckons an answer.

No. The word lingers, its roots digging around for explanation. "Maybe once. But not now."

"What happened?" Her brow is pressed into compassion, concern. And a spark of that driving fire.

The short answer is best, he decides. "Sometimes love is a choice."

"And you choose not to love?"

"Sometimes the best way to love is to choose to let go."

She's studying him. He feels the warmth of it, hears it in how everything is silent but the black river currents and strains of music—a slow accordion, so unlike the brassy pomp of the dance.

Ahead he sees cafés that have come alive for the evening. Their warm, tantalizing smells swirl—garlic and cheese and herbs—and he hopes his stomach doesn't betray him in this moment. He doesn't want to shatter whatever is going on in this stitched-together connection of theirs.

"You don't seem like the type to let go," she says at last.

His jaw shifts. She's right. He is not, and it's taken more than he ever imagined to do it, dug out his very nature. He has never spoken a word of this to anyone. He'd entrusted the heaviest burden to the safest of vaults. She slips her hand into his as if it's a key, unlocking this truth.

"Maybe not," he says. "But it's a different story when the feeling"—he can't call it love, because he's worked long to carve it into something different—"is not returned." He should just let the rest of the story lie still, but he speaks it. "And when your brother loves the same girl. And marries her."

She tilts her head, contemplating. Narrows her eyes, stays this way for a moment too long, and the silence begins to stretch until it burns.

"Now, look here . . ." She's going to give him a speech. Tell him he should have fought. Make him regret ever speaking a word of this.

"I'm going to dance with you," she says.

He opens his mouth. Dumbfounded, trying to find words to protest, but she holds out a hand to stop him. "The way I see it, you and I were both bound for a dance tonight, and though neither of us looked too keenly on the notion, you're a fool if you think you can lug a girl's fender—"

"Bumper."

"—through the city and not have it do something to her heart. You're downright chivalrous, Mr. Robert Bliss, whatever you may think, and I'm going to dance with you."

And there on the banks of the Charles—with the soldiers and girls all jitterbugging in a dance hall across the city—the fisherman slowly, perhaps not so smoothly, but deliberately, pulls the woman close in his sea-hewn arms. When she, in her grease-streaked dress, places a hand on his un-uniformed shoulder, it feels for all the world as if she's given him some medal of honor.

And they dance. Snow-dusted sidewalk for a dance floor, stolen strains of music coming in snatches on the December wind.

He feels how she is like him. They are the same—lonely souls beating against the walls of war, asking in, being denied. But tonight they find a home together.

The chill in the sky thickens the falling snow, and together they look up. They still. There's something about this moment completely outside Robert—a sense they are standing in the calm before a coming storm.

She shivers, and he releases her long enough to place his humble jacket over her New York dress—and this time she doesn't resist. It should be something better, he thinks, than the worn wool that's seen too many winters. But she slips her hand back in his and tugs him over to the railing.

They're at the mouth of the river now. She points out Charlestown Naval Yard across the harbor. Always an ocean between him and the navy.

Eva gestures toward the docks. "There," she said. "I thought you might like to see that."

He scans, trying to pick out what she's brought him here for. There are ships, docks, buildings. . . . But one ship sticks out from the others, its tall wooden masts strung from history itself, lines running to deck in perfect symphony.

This is not a gunmetal-gray warship, all bulk and might.

It is a frigate from another era, one when ships began as saplings in a forest and grew their strength from the earth. Steady and great, like the men who hauled those logs from the deep, snow-laden forest. The men who labored them into vessels mighty enough to traverse unkind seas.

"Is that the—"

"USS *Constitution*," Eva says with pride. "Named by George Washington himself."

Unseen sinews unfurl in the dark, reaching over the black shimmer of water and gripping him.

"Why . . ." He clears his throat. "Why did you show me this?" he asks, trying to sort out this feeling of being stitched to that ship with iron thread.

Eva studies him, then gives a light shrug contrary to the depth in her eyes. "It reminds me of you."

There's a stirring deep in his chest as he watches the wooden hull rock over the harbor waves effortlessly.

"That boat," she says, "was carved by time. It's not like the rest of these." She sweeps her arm out over the harbor, encompassing the fleet of warships. "They were churned out in a hurry, all for utility and speed and power. Sure, we need them right now. But that?" She lifts her delicate chin toward the *Constitution*. "That one tells a story that's taken time. And it's one that'll be around long after this war is over. No less needed, either. Just as important and courageous as the others."

Why is she saying all this? They've only just met, yet somehow she knows him better than he understands himself.

"Think of this harbor without that boat. Think of what those seamen see as they embark. When they look back at that frigate, they see inspiration—the reason they're going. It gives them hope, strength . . . and if someone hadn't been willing to put the time in to build it . . . well, this would be one sorry harbor."

She closes her eyes and lifts her face to the falling snow, leaning back and letting her hands catch the rail to hold her. "I get that feeling about you, fisherman Robert. You're meant for something great."

He's about to protest, to tell her the truth—that he's just a humble man of the sea, better with waves than people. But he's interrupted when a black Bentley pulls up to the curb next to them.

"Fiddlesticks," Eva says. She brushes her dress straight, and the way she tries to look dignified with her face streaked in axle grease drives her further into Robert's heart. "Don't mind whatever he says. He has eyes all over the city and likes to remind me of that."

He? A backseat window rolls down, and a man speaks from the shadows. "There you are, Evelyn." He gives a cursory glance over Robert, then apparently decides he's not worth acknowledging.

"Hello, Father. Are you having a nice evening?" She speaks with polish, presumably imparted by the famed Misses Hampstead, and acts as if it's nothing out of the ordinary for her to be found here, blocks away from the dance, in such a state. Unchaperoned with a strange man.

"I was, yes. Passing a very pleasant night at the club, until the proprietor of Giovanni's telephoned that you seemed to be lost way out here."

Eva gives Robert a quick glance as if to say, *See?*

"How kind of him," she says, "to care so for a damsel who has no idea of her whereabouts in this foreign city."

Robert has a feeling these two match each other wit for wit just as strongly as they collide.

"Yes," Mr. Rothford says. "Well, do come home now. Your mother has wedding details she'd like to sort out, and you're clearly free of other obligations tonight. . . ."

He lets the insinuation settle.

"Oh, I'm *very* occupied this evening, Father." She looks at Robert, and back at the car. A flicker of concern. She seems to want to spare him something. "But it's nothing that can't be continued— *soon*—another time."

She turns her back on Robert and starts to lift his jacket from her shoulders. Placing a hand on her shoulder, he leans forward ever so slightly.

"Keep it," he says. He has no need of it, not when she's given him something that brought far more warmth tonight.

"I will," she says. "For a time. I'll find you, Robert Bliss."

He watches, torn, as she slips into the Bentley. His sense of honor tells him that she clearly is—at least in the eyes of some— committed to a different future. A different man. And he knows now he is capable of schooling his heart away from love.

But something deeper pleads with the heavens that she might be free. That someday he might be the one to find Eva Rothford.

twelve

The boathouse door creaks open. Annie holds her breath, the darkness within conjuring up images of her imagined dragon from the past. She'd always thought Bob kept this place locked to keep her safe from whatever was inside.

Jeremiah slides in and disappears into the dark abyss. After a moment, the light of a kerosene lamp hisses to life. She peers in, not seeing Jeremiah, and nearly jumps out of her skin when he reappears suddenly, thrusting the lantern at her.

"After you," he says, holding an arm out to gesture her in.

She takes a tentative step inside. Crossing the threshold is like stepping into another world—one where the dark air hangs heavy with the spice of sawdust, the mellowed fragrance of old wood, and a tinge of campfire smoke.

A quick shine around of the lantern flings ghoulish shadows of a workbench and stool. An old canoe hangs from the rafters, creaking back and forth in the breeze. The paint on its hull looks freshly sanded, revealing bare wood beneath.

"Roy's boat." Jeremiah looks at her warily, as if unsure whether to say more. "Bob's letting me try to restore it. I hope that's . . . okay."

It's a moment before she realizes he's waiting on her reply. "Oh! With me?"

"Well, you are his granddaughter. By rights, this is yours."

It's strange, looking at this vessel created by a man she never met . . . a man whose very blood runs through her veins.

"Yes, of course. It looks like it should be at sea," she says.

"So do you." Jeremiah's eyes crinkle into a smile at the corners.

"Ha. I beg to differ."

Jeremiah shrugs and steps aside as she explores the space.

In a far corner of the boathouse—the one marked by fire—the walls are cloaked in black, artifacts of hungry flames. A ladder stands there, stacks of wood shingles bundled in neat rows next to an orange power drill.

Jeremiah gestures to the corner. "I'm hoping to have it all repaired by the time Bob gets home." A flicker of doubt crosses his face, but Annie is tempted to hug him for the way he speaks of Bob's homecoming as if it's a certainty.

"And here"—Jeremiah strides to the center of the barn-like space—"is your dragon."

It's a large block of something, as wide as ten of her and reaching nearly to the rafters, draped in paint-splotched drop cloths. Its shape is oddly lopsided, like it's trying to be a perfect cube, but chunks of whatever is beneath are missing.

Annie approaches and with a tentative look at Jeremiah, lifts a corner flap.

Her pulse revs up, breath catching.

She runs her hands along the edge of the drop cloth until she has a wide grip on it, then flings it up into the air. Dust rains down, around, and upon them in sunlit shafts. Annie coughs, waving away the cloud, and the cloth pools into a pile on the ground.

Layer upon layer of containers are lined up in near-perfect precision. Some humble brown cardboard. Others, pristine—if dusty—hatboxes that look as if they've come straight from Bloomingdale's. A dented oblong tin, lid secured in twine. Some are just oddly sized lumps, wrapped in packing paper or newsprint, scrawled with an address. The packages speak of every walk of life. They look to have hailed from shanty towns and mansions and everywhere in between. Each one, like those in the closet inside the house, marked with a number.

"Rocks," Annie breathes. Jeremiah flashes his gaze to her.

"You knew what they are?"

She shakes her head. "No, not these. But there's a closet inside packed full of boxes just like this."

"They've been here since you were a kid?"

Again she shakes her head. "Those in the closet weren't there when I was here. But these . . ." She picks up one from the corner. A neatly opened flap of the brown packing paper is postmarked 1964 and reveals a Knox Gelatine box inside, its lid open to reveal a Sedona-red rock inside. "It looks like these have been here awhile." She narrows her eyes. "How did *you* know what was in them?"

He looks sheepish, shrugs. "I'm the postman."

"That means nothing." Annie shoots him a look that says she can see right through his nonexplanation. "These are from decades ago. And they're addressed to . . ."

She squints in the low light to read the address. *Postmaster, Ansel-by-the-Sea, Maine.* "Oh."

"Maybe I shouldn't have looked. But when you find something like this"—he sweeps an arm over the scene before them—"in a place like this"—she follows his gesture at the shadow-dancing walls—"sometimes you just have to snoop." He stuffs his hands in his jeans pockets. "And it *is* addressed to Postmaster."

"A job you did not come here to take," she reminds him, replacing the box.

"And yet, here I am." He pulls that dimpled half grin.

"But what does this have to do with Bob?" she asks, serious again.

"No clue," Jeremiah says. "But there's one thing I do know."

Annie waits, listening.

"Town meeting tomorrow. If you want the best chance of finding out, that's the place."

———

The next evening finds Annie walking Market Road, white buildings adorned with flower boxes spilling over with red geraniums and blue lobelia. Its European feel ushers her back to evenings spent walking the streets of Alpenzell.

She shifts the still-warm pie over to one hand, shielding her eyes against late sunlight to scan the buildings around the square. Jeremiah had warned her that to "get in" with this crowd, she'd need two things: to be born and raised in Ansel, and to bring food. Since she had no chance at the first, she'd spent extra time on the second, pulling out an old family recipe that was famed around these parts. She checks her watch—6:50. A respectable ten minutes early.

She crosses the green and enters the library. At least . . . she thinks it's the library. Last time she was here, it had just been an old railcar, pulled from the abandoned track behind Birchdown Mountain and outfitted with floor-to-ceiling shelves along its walls. Now the old red railcar appears to be the foyer for a new building rising up behind it.

She steps inside and crosses the narrow space to the double glass doors, through which she sees a small clutch of people have already gathered. A woman presides at a table in front of three rows of chairs framing an aisle. They appear to be in session. Had she gotten the time wrong?

Pulling the door open as quietly as she can, she winces at the sound of its creak. Immediately, all eyes are on her.

"Can we help you?" The woman at the front looks at Annie over wire-rimmed glasses.

"I'm so sorry," Annie says. "I thought I was early for the town meeting, but—"

"You are, dear," the woman says, her voice softening a bit. The brass nameplate in front of her says *Margie Lillian*. "This is a meeting of the Ansel Keeping Society. We adjourn in five minutes, at which time the town meeting shall commence."

Annie is caught off guard by Margie's formal speech.

"You can wait outside in the foyer."

Annie withdraws, thankful for the shadows of the railcar, its humble comfort. She takes a seat on a long wooden bench next to the glass doors, and drinks in the magic of this small space. She imagines the journeys the railcar must have been on, the people it must have carried in its heyday. The children flooding it for story time when it was the little library on the green.

It's fitting, she thinks, for the keeping society to meet here. They are the keepers of history in towns too small to warrant full-on historical society meetings, and it appears they've turned the railcar into their own display room of artifacts. A worn calico day dress with sprigged yellow bouquets presides at the head of the room from behind a glass. It looks more like something a southern farm girl would wear than a lady from the wilds of Maine. The front door is flanked by oil portraits depicting the beloved town mascots from the sixties: Homer the Maine coon cat and Johannes the dolphin. Bob used to tell her tales of the unlikely friends who skirted the harbor together. One picture shows Homer crouched over the seawall, resting a paw on Johannes's bottlenose. In the other, Johannes buoys himself enough to rest the underside of his dolphin beak on the cat's head, as if dubbing him knight. For a time, the pair drew in crowds from nearby towns, who came just to eat popcorn on the harbor benches and watch their antics.

Annie makes a mental note to return to further study the displays when she can spend some real time in this treasure trove. It's things like this that send her heart skittering, wanting to preserve the character of this place, to plumb its history and preserve its future.

No. A sharp pang at the memory of what she does to places like this when she tries to help stops that train of thought cold. Redirecting her thoughts, she again practices in her mind what she'll say to these people who know her so little and yet know more of her own family's story than she does.

The door creaks open, and Arthur steps out. He flips the

Keeping Society sign over from its suction cup hook on the glass, so that it now reads *Ansel-by-the-Sea Town Meeting*.

"Come on in, Emma." He winks. "Just kidding. I mean Annie."

She follows him inside, where small groups are talking throughout the sun-bathed room. Sully, white braid swinging down her back, is making the rounds with a silver platter.

"Scone?" she says to a man who is holding up his cell phone as if it's a beacon. He pushes a button, and the colored screen freeze-frames on an image of Sully with a hopeful open-mouthed smile.

"Remarkable," he says, turning the phone in his hand.

"Did that contraption just take a picture of me?"

"Sure did. Pre-market technology. Everyone will have one within a year from now, if you want my guess."

Sully waves him off. "Who needs a phone that takes pictures? That's what cameras are for. Passing fad, if you ask me." She raises her platter until it's nearly in his face. "Care for a scone?"

"Why, sure, Miss Sylvia. Thank you kindly."

Sully scurries off, radiant to have found a taker, and Annie watches as the man takes a bite—or tries to. He crunches down hard on it, and the triangular pastry crumbles to smithereens. He fumbles, trying to catch the downpour of crumbs, and drops his phone in the process.

Annie grabs it and hands it back as he brushes crumbs from his button-down white shirt. He looks out of place here, more Wall Street than Ansel. Mid-fifties, hair salt-and-pepper and combed with care.

"Thank you." He offers a handshake. "Richard Wilkins. People call me Rich."

"Annie Bliss." She shakes his hand, and points at his cell phone. "Do you have service here?"

He laughs as if she's just told the joke of the century. "No, ma'am. No one in Ansel does. That's the draw of the place, you know."

He grins and gestures to an open seat near his when the lady up front hammers her gavel like she's a judge. Margie Lillian stands, turns to face a flag hanging from the railing of the loft above and behind her, and begins to lead them in the Pledge of Allegiance.

Arthur twists in his seat in front of them to face Rich. "Looks like we might get by without seeing that rascal." He raises his eyebrows in glee, but just then, the door creaks open behind them and in strides Spencer T. Ripley.

"Spoke too soon," Rich grumbles back to Arthur.

"Pardon me." Spencer gives a quick bow to the lady up front. "Are we open for public comment?"

"Does it look like we're open for public comment?" Ed chimes in from across the aisle.

"If you'll have a seat, please," Margie says coolly.

Margie takes attendance for the three selectmen present—herself included—and gives the agenda. One man stands to give a state-of-the-roads address, citing multiple potholes and one oversized sinkhole from the winter. Another man gives an update on the upcoming Lobsterfest.

"We've got vendors coming from all over the state," he says, and the room buzzes with excitement. "Of course, we're hoping to bring in the usual revenue, but more than that, we hope to attract new folks to these parts for good. So Starboard Home Realty has generously offered to be our main sponsor and will be hosting open houses all that weekend."

Rich leans in to Annie and whispers, "This town's dying."

Annie's pulse picks up. "What do you mean?" She whispers, too, not wanting to incur Margie's wrath.

"Can't keep the young people here. No jobs. Tourists only come in summer, and not so much anymore." He shrugs.

"Is there something you'd care to share with the group, Mr. Wilkins?"

Rich stands. "Yes, ma'am, if you're amenable to it."

Margie Lillian checks her watch, and the agenda paper in her hand. "If it's relevant to the issue at hand, proceed."

Rich scoots past Annie, up to the microphone at the end of the center aisle. He leans in and clears his throat, as if he's about to give an address to a coliseum.

"I propose to offer the services of my Skyblaster 3000."

The audience exchanges befuddled glances.

Margie slips into monotone questioning mode. "And can you tell us what a . . ."

"Skyblaster 3000," Rich says, feet shifting as if he's a kid in line for a roller coaster.

"Yes. Do tell us what that is, please."

He pulls his hands from his khakis and waves them overhead. "Picture it." His voice sounds as if he's attempting the drama of a movie trailer, but he doesn't quite have the timbre to pull it off. "Lobsterfest. Epic summer festivities. People drawn from miles around. Why?"

Ed cups his mouth and pipes up. "For the lobster!"

Rich points at him. "Yes. For the lobster. And because of the light, streaking across the sky, summoning people from far and near. Sixty thousand lumens, pulling them in."

Arthur hangs an elbow over the back of his metal folding chair and shifts to face the man in the aisle. "Why'd you up and buy a searchlight, Rich?" Then he twists to face Annie and whispers loudly, "That guy is always buying some new gadget. Came to us from New York and seems like he wants to bring that whole city here, one gadget at a time."

Ed chimes in again. "Why's he do anything? He's rich!"

A wave of laughter curls over the small crowd, appreciating the pun.

Rich draws back a little. "I . . . bought it for hunting."

A dark-bearded man stares at him. "You don't hunt."

Rich raises a finger. "But I might!"

"And you bought a *searchlight*? What are you hunting? Godzilla?"

Another voice pipes up. "They make hunting lights, you know. The kind that aren't so powerful they'll chop down the whole north woods."

"Go big or go home." Rich shrugs.

A woman across the aisle pauses her knitting and shakes her head. "City folk. You can take them out of the city, but you can't take the nonsense out of them."

"Listen," Rich says, his smile good-natured in spite of their jesting. "The fact is, we've got a powerful searchlight that we can use to make a big impact during Lobsterfest. Take it or leave it." He steps away from the mic, then leans back in. "But I hope you'll take it."

He returns to his seat, whispering "Skyblaster!" as he fists his fingers in triumph and winks at Annie.

The lady knitting stands. "Public comment?" she asks. Margie Lillian gestures her toward the microphone. Spencer T. Ripley looks irked. He hops to his feet and lines up behind knitting lady.

She begins to speak, standing at least two feet from the microphone.

"Lean in, Mrs. Blanchard," Rich urges. "This is being televised."

"For who, young man?" She plants a hand on her hip. "Most of the town is here!"

"It's your moment." Rich winks. "Lean in."

She obliges. "I don't think we need a searchlight, Rich." Her voice is so kind, like molasses, that her words come out sounding like a favor rather than a censure. "Look at everything we have already. The tides—biggest in the country! The lobster—best there is. The stars—which we wouldn't want to drown out. Part of the reason people come to Ansel is *because* there's no light pollution here. Not even streetlights." After a pause she continues. "And the growin's. People always like to see the growin's."

Annie has never heard of the growin's. It sounds strange, even for Ansel. She makes a mental note to ask about it later.

With a smile Mrs. Blanchard sits down, and Spencer T. Ripley steps up to the microphone.

"Good evening," he says with a polish that clashes with his youthful face. "As you know, the Committee for Excellence in

Maritime Poetry is in the final stages of planning the First Annual Summit for Excellence in Maritime Poetry. As a courtesy, I come bearing the latest developments. . . ."

He drones on, and the more intense he becomes about the details of his summit, the more detached the audience seems. Annie almost feels sorry for him. After speaking of agendas and breakout sessions for both iambic pentameter *and* free verse—"If you can believe that!"—he finally closes his black portfolio. Just as he's about to duck away from the microphone, something he says makes Annie sit straight up. "Our plans remain unchanged for the presentation of the lifetime achievement award to your very own Robert Bliss. The committee sends their well-wishes for his swift recovery and looks forward to his acceptance of this prestigious award."

He directs that last bit at Annie, whose face warms red. She'd been to the hospital again today, praying the very same for his swift recovery. She can tell the whole room has put up a wall between themselves and Spencer. She's teetering on the edge of it—wanting to earn their trust but desperate to learn whatever history Spencer knows about Bob.

"If there are no other public comments at this time—"

Sully hops up, platter in hand, and steps to the microphone. Margie gives a reminder that public comment should be limited to three minutes, and Sully dives in fast.

"There's a *light* coming into my windows at night," she says with disgust. "Now, you all have been most welcoming to me since I came off the mountain, but try as I might, I can't get to sleep because of that light." She goes on for several minutes about her conundrum, and when she's given the thirty-second warning, she starts moving around the room, distributing her scones and ignoring Rich's whispered hisses to get back to the mic.

Annie leans forward, asking Arthur, "What's she doing?"

"Smart," he says. "She's extending her time by distracting them."

"But the scones are . . ." Annie stops herself. She doesn't want to be unkind.

122

"Worse than eating dirt? Doesn't matter. Food's important to these folks."

She thrusts one at Annie, who takes a tentative nibble of the artifact as Sully returns to her microphone and points at Ed.

"The light is coming from *his* island. I can't help it if my house faces it, but he can help where he puts his light."

The room stirs awkwardly. No one wants to take the blind man to task for having a light on the end of his island. Ed stands, dignified. "Did you ever think I might have put it right there for a reason?" And without further explanation, he walks out, a cane of driftwood guiding him.

"Ed, where's your real cane?" Arthur whispers, but it's too late. Ed's gone.

"That's time," Margie says to Sully. "And we'll adjourn for the night if—"

"Wait!" Annie has been so caught up in the meeting that she's nearly missed her chance. She springs to her feet, and for the second time that night, all eyes are on her. "Three-minute limit, right?" She smiles, rushing to the microphone.

But once she's up there, all the words fly straight out of her head. What does she say to this apparently dying town that needs so much more than her nosy questions? She who is the grim reaper to dying villages, as proven at Alpenzell, but who might be able to help, if she could find the courage?

"Time's going, Miss . . ." Margie narrows her eyes.

"Bliss. Annie Bliss."

"Bob's her uncle!" Arthur hollers, and the air turns compassionate.

"Great-uncle, yes. Which is why I've come to ask . . ." How does she put this? How does she ask about a literal box of rocks—boxes, actually—without sounding nosy and presuming? *Is* she just being nosy and presuming?

"Two minutes left, Miss Bliss," Margie prods.

"Well, you see, I'm hoping the kind people of Ansel might be able to help me figure out something. For Bob." Yes, that's it.

And the moment she speaks it, she knows it's true. She wants, more than anything, to have something to offer him if—*when*—he wakes. If she can help with whatever these rocks are, surprise him by finishing whatever project they belong to . . . "I wonder if anyone knows anything about a number of boxes being delivered to Bob. It seems he has acquired quite a collection over the years, and I'd like to . . ."

Something shifts. Not a person in the room is looking at her. They're looking at their shoes, or the wall, or the clock. Someone clears their throat.

"Thirty seconds," Margie says.

What she'd give for Sully's platter of scones right now, to extend her time. Too late, she remembers the pie, which she's left out in the railcar.

"If anyone could help shed light on the rocks—"

A soft laugh comes from the knitting lady's corner. "Your word choice, dear. It's too ironic."

"And that's time." Margie looks apologetic. "Meeting adjourned."

Annie retreats in defeat, face burning as she slips into the dark railcar foyer and gathers up her pie. She can't escape fast enough. But out on the green, she hears footsteps behind her.

"Is that the famous Bliss hazelnut pie?" Bess, capped in her red kerchief as always, her dark, tight curls trying furiously to escape, closes the distance between them.

"Bess." Annie's smile saturates her voice. "I didn't know you were in there."

"Only at the end," she says. "I had to close up The Galley and snuck in the side door." She chuckles. "Sometimes I'm in time to watch that Spencer kid dig himself deeper into his hole."

"Yeah, well, he wasn't the only one doing that tonight."

"So I saw." Crickets sing from the shrubs around the green. "A little tip?"

"I'll take all the tips I can get."

Bess stuffs her hands in her pockets, looks up at the stars. "All right, here's two." She holds up one finger. "One, next time bring that pie in. Savannah's hazelnut pie will get you into any locked door. Two . . . if you really want to know about those rocks"—she looks conflicted—"talk to Ed."

That's right. Ed had left before she'd had a chance to sputter her request.

"I'll do that. Thank you, Bess."

"You bet. How's Bob today?"

Annie tells of her visit this morning, how not much has changed but that the doctor had seemed reservedly hopeful.

"Good." Bess nods. "I'm planning to get over there myself tomorrow." She lifts her chin at something over Annie's shoulder. "Looks like your ride's here."

Jeremiah is approaching, moonlight making him seem taller somehow. Like he's a natural part of night, like it's his homeland. Bess gives him a wave and walks toward her apartment over the shops.

"Hey," Annie says. "How come you weren't there?"

His eyes crinkle into a smile, though the rest of his face stays stoic. "The Keeping Society and I . . . we don't quite see eye to eye."

"I sense a story there," Annie says.

"Yep. A story for another day."

Mrs. Blanchard shuffles up to them, her knitting needles stowed in a quilted handbag. "Oh, Jeremiah, would it trouble you terribly to relight my pilot light tomorrow on your rounds? I hate to ask again, but—"

"Consider it done," he says.

"Use Bob's torch!" Rich approaches with his confident, khaki-clad walk.

Annie furrows her brow. "His torch?"

"Yeah. From the Sharper Image. I brought it for him last year. It's for crème brûlée."

Annie shuts her mouth around laughter. The mention of Bob in the same sentence as Sharper Image is two shades beyond ridiculous. She can just picture the way he would have screwed his face up at the gadget, like it was an alien spaceship in his callused hands.

Rich laughs, shaking his head. "He just pulled an old book of matches from his pocket and looked from that to the stainless-steel torch and back, like he couldn't figure out why anyone would try and stuff fire inside a can when matches worked just fine. He uses the torch to cauterize ropes on his boat, though." Rich turns to leave, still talking as he goes. "You should grab it. For the pilot light."

Jeremiah leads the way to the *Glad Tidings*, docked at Joe's Landing down the harbor road. Boats around them are chugging to life, carrying townspeople home from the meeting. Others are walking trails and roads to their harbor homes.

Jeremiah sets to work on the rope, untying as he whistles. He glances her way when she hesitates near the gangplank.

His stare just makes things worse, and she forces herself forward with feigned courage.

"Be right back," he says. He disappears around the back of the small building on the wharf, returning with a bucket. Three long strides up the plank and he's on board, headed her way, bucket in hand. She tries to step out of the way, but he follows her. She sidesteps again, and he does, too.

"What are you doing?"

"Would you stay still?" He moves to dump the bucket, and she jumps back, expecting water.

But it's not water. It's a stream of gravel and sand.

"What . . . ?"

He turns and, with no explanation, strides off the boat, resuming his work on the rope. Once the knot is loosened, he pulls the rope on board, hands her the end, and gestures for her to wind. She does, recalling how Bob taught her to loop it gently around forearm and shoulder.

He whistles on, as if he hasn't just up and dumped a pail of earth at her feet.

"So . . . what's this all about?"

"Dirt." He shrugs, as if it should be self-explanatory. "Like Bob's."

"Bob's?"

"For you." He reaches behind his neck and scratches, trying to play it off like it's nothing, but awkwardness is slipping through. She's finding it rather . . . endearing. He finally stops and looks her straight on. "Like the dirt mat he made you to stand on." He gestures an open palm at the pile.

And she cannot keep from breaking into a smile.

"Mr. Jeremiah Fletcher," she says, "if that isn't the most thoughtful thing—"

"What is it you do again, exactly?"

She clamps her mouth shut. That puts a damper on the moment. How to admit she's a washed-up anthropologist who makes spreadsheets about buying habits all day? How to explain that she had an internship in the field straight out of college—one that her classmates would've done anything for—and that she'd ruined it?

"I'm a consumer insights analyst," she says. Same answer as yesterday.

He moves into the cabin, starts checking devices on the bridge. "Ah," he says. "CIA."

"Pardon me?"

"You're CIA."

"Shhh!" Annie stifles a smile, eyes darting between the other boats. "I'm trying to earn people's trust here. You aren't helping."

"Well, neither are you, looking over your shoulder every two seconds."

Annie looks him straight in the eye. "Actually, my company is in the middle of a reorganization. My boss recently told me I will soon be a network consumer insights specialist."

"Oh, yes." Jeremiah turns his key, firing the boat to life. He narrows his eyes, as if pondering something weighty. "You're right. NCIS. That's much better."

A second passes, and she doesn't know whether to be furious or whether to laugh. His stone stare challenges her until she can't keep in the rogue laugh that escapes.

The boat rocks, and Annie's stomach drops. H_2O, she reminds herself. *These waves are just molecules. Do not fear the molecules.*

She digs her feet farther into the sand, and Jeremiah watches. Is that . . . a smile she sees cracking through?

"Speaking of insights." She clears her throat. "What do you know about Ed?" *And the rocks? And the growin's? And this key?* The questions are piling up, and she can't shake the feeling that they're like a line of dominoes. If she can knock over one, the rest will follow.

Jeremiah looks sideways at her. "Not much. He's hard to read. Surely you've figured that out by now."

He turns his attention fully to weaving through the boats around them, and Annie assumes he's hit his conversation limit for the night, but as they head to open water, he clears his throat. "How about you join me on my walking rounds tomorrow. You might find what you're looking for."

thirteen

That man is gone before the sun again, but this time he doesn't return for her. He'd said he meant to start his rounds at eight, but when seven forty-five rolls around and there's still no sign of him, Annie sets out on the harbor road to track him down. Maybe he'd meant for her to meet him at the post office.

The morning is dewy, lupines blooming as she passes the white steepled church and the footbridge over the creek. Smoke curls from a few chimneys to chase off the morning chill, and Annie pulls her cable-knit sweater sleeves down over her hands to do the same.

In town, she passes the landing, the green, The Galley—all with no sign of Jeremiah. The post office is empty, a sign scrawled in straight letters reading *Mail's coming. Just wait.*

It isn't until she curves around to where the harbor's other peninsula arm begins to reach out into the sea that, through the light fog, she spots Jeremiah in jeans, a Carhartt jacket, and a baseball cap. Messenger bag slung crossways over his shoulder, he's kicking pebbles as he walks toward the schoolhouse north of the harbor.

"Jeremiah!" Annie shouts. He doesn't turn. Even at the sound of her mud-slogging footsteps along the shore.

Nearly caught up, she extends her arm like she's coming in for the passing of the baton in a relay, touches his cold shoulder. He whips around, jaw tight. It isn't anger she sees in those eyes but puzzlement.

"Annie?" He tugs headphones from his ears, looks behind her, then back at her. "What's wrong?"

She's winded but trying not to be. She tucks wild vagrants of hair behind her ears, as if that will do anything to tame the mist-born mess. "I thought we were meeting."

He nods. "So did I, at the post office."

"Sorry about that. I misunderstood. Is it still okay if I tag along?" She hopes so. She's packed her canvas tote with a notebook, three sharpened pencils, a granola bar, and an apple. Oh, and three slices of last night's pie, with hopes of coaxing Ed to share what he knows. "And do you mind if I ask a question?"

Without a word, he keeps walking.

She stops trying to match his lengthy stride, stops altogether. A few paces later, so does he. He turns and says, "No, and no."

"Oh . . . okay." He seems a different man this morning. "I'll leave you in peace, then." Her words sound as cold as she feels, and she can't help leaving with a dig. "I'll just ask at the keeping society instead."

"No, I don't mind if you tag along. And no, I don't mind if you ask a question."

She can feel her ears reddening. How could she misread one man so much?

"You think too much," he says, lopsided grin dimpling. "Nice touch with the keeping society, though. You're catching on."

She matches his smile, making a mental note not to take this man as seriously as his somber façade would have her do.

They're rounding the curve to where the opposite side of the harbor from Sailor's Rest meanders out past the Weg von Blitz. Annie hasn't been to this part of Ansel before and finds herself a bit disoriented when Jeremiah veers off to the right, out onto what appears to be a narrow strip of land connecting to an otherwise sea-locked island.

Jeremiah checks his watch and carries on.

"Making good time?" Annie tries for small talk. Which, as she'd learned, could sometimes lead to large talk. Which made the small talk bearable.

"You could say that," he says.

They walk in silence, the path of damp earth before them dotted in slick rocks and barnacles. The wind is whipping the mist away and whipping more great clouds of it in around them, until they set foot on the land mass.

"Welcome to Long Island," Jeremiah says.

Annie looks at the expanse before them—trees, boulders, granite, and more trees. Not quite the image conjured by a famous name like Long Island.

Jeremiah is drinking in the place like a man parched, and she gets the feeling he's waiting for her to notice something.

"Long Island," she echoes, and shields her eyes to search the horizon. "Yes, I see it now. There." She points to a clump of pines hovering above them on an outcropping to their right. "Jay Gatsby's house, right? Oh, and there." She points to the rise ahead of them, where, in truth, she cannot see what lies beyond. "The Hamptons."

Jeremiah lets out a low whistle. "Good one."

"It's not a good one if you have to say it's a good one and you don't laugh."

This, he laughs at. "Come on," he says. "Ansel's Long Island can beat out that other one any day."

They follow the sandy path up to where it curves into a forest dense and dark. A keeper of secrets, this place is. Her smile fades as they enter, and she feels as if they've just stepped into Narnia or Middle Earth or Sherwood Forest. This is a storied place—she can feel it straight through her. And when they round the next bend, she sees the proof.

A shanty of sorts, tucked into a clearing. Path lined with carefully placed rocks, moss hugging the cracks between. All this leading up to a structure that is as otherworldly as Narnia or any of the other legendary places of literature. Walls of horizontal driftwood, planked with their curves in a closeness that makes it appear someone has piped each one with an icing bag, one layer on top of the next, curving with and around each other tightly. The jagged edges of the interlocking sloped roof give the appearance of turrets topping this humble castle. A window has even been woven into the structure. Not cut square, like a proper cabin or fish camp, but formed from the poetry of the wood to create a lopsided porthole.

Who would build such a place? Could someone really live here? Surely not when winter blew in like ice.

Jeremiah is watching her, amusement on his face. "Go ahead." He gestures toward the abode. "Take a look."

"Do you have a delivery here?"

"Not exactly," he says. "Don't worry. No one's home."

Curiosity piqued, she ducks through the low arched doorway, where inside, gray shafts of light filter in. A rough-hewn stool with three legs sits next to the porthole window. The room is as close to a perfect rectangle as it can be, a stone hearth tucked into one of the corners. In another corner, an old straw broom leans into a tangle of sparse cobwebs. Its presence is a puzzle, since the floor is just hard-packed dirt.

There's a scuffing sound on that dirt behind her, and she turns to see Jeremiah leaning in the door frame. He's stepped inside, and his tall form looks even taller beside the dwarfed entrance.

"Who lived here?" Annie breathes the question in wonder. She runs a hand over the stone mantel, her touch reverent.

"You're the people detective," he says. "What would you say?"

She plants her hands on her hips as gentle thunder sounds in the distance. She takes in the way the driftwood planks, in their multitudinous lengths and breadths, are stacked like layers of shale, perfectly level but for a few little wobbles and warps.

"Someone meticulous," she says. "Probably someone who values order, detail. Values home, and all the things that seem right. Justice. Hard work. Art." She gestures to the stones, and they beckon her back, tugging at the mystery she's after. Could the

132

stones in Bob's closet and boathouse have something to do with this?

They seem to capture a ballad, but in a different key and cadence than the other rocks. These stones match each other well—gray with layers of white, every one. Not like the multicolored stones of the boxes.

Still, there's something here. A mantel so permanent, here in the home built from sticks. She thinks of the three little pigs, how the house of sticks collapsed with a huff and a puff from one hungry enemy. But this . . . these sea-worn sticks rest against the hearth with permanency, even as the chill wind blows through the seams.

"Anyway. That's all just speculation. I'm probably not even close," she says.

The corners of Jeremiah's mouth turn down as his eyebrows arc up and he shrugs. "Come find out," he says, and departs.

He's ten steps up the path before she catches up. "Wait . . . the builder is here?" She looks around the island, no sign of life. "But they can't still live there. There's nothing there. No way someone could exist . . ."

"I think you'll enjoy this person," Jeremiah answers. "And I think he'll have a thing or two to say about your idea of 'nothing.' Where you see nothing in that shanty—where probably all of the rest of us see nothing—he sees . . ." Jeremiah shakes his head slowly. "Well, you'll see."

And that's all the maddening man says as they hike on another ten minutes, the sea coming in and out of view with the rise and dip of the terrain. The island is narrow, probably less than half a mile wide, but the thick pine groves make it seem bigger. Just as she's about to ask if he is leading her on a wild-goose chase, they enter one such grove, where smoke curls from a log cabin's chimney.

fourteen

Jeremiah lifts his hand to knock, but the door swings open and a dark, weathered hand reaches out to clap him on the shoulder.

"Fletch," a rich voice says. "Your coffee's on. Come on in."

Annie steps to the left to see who it is, and surprise overtakes her.

"Thanks, Ed," Jeremiah says. "Is it okay if—"

"Yeah, bring Miss Elle on in." Leaning on a gnarled but smooth length of driftwood, he holds his door open for them. "Thought you'd be comin', Bob's Annie. Didn't think it'd take you so long, though."

Annie's fishing for words and not finding them. How did a man who could not see know they'd arrived before they even knocked? How could he tell she was with Jeremiah? How was he even out here, living alone on this island, so isolated from everything? But all she manages to get out is a clumsy, "How . . . ?"

Ed waves off her unfinished questions. "Old Ed just knows things," he says. "And you know what they say about the blind. . . ."

"That . . . all of the other senses are amplified?" Annie offers tentatively. "Did you hear us coming?"

"A deaf elephant would've heard the two of you coming." That chuckle again. "No. They say the only thing worse than being blind is having sight but no vision. Deaf, blind, and mute girl said that some time ago. Seems she understood quite a lot."

His words sober as quickly as his expression. "Word is you need some vision, Bob's Annie."

His directness catches her off guard. She clears her throat. "I admit, I am looking for some answers."

"Have a seat. Jeremiah's got a thing or two to say to me, I think, and then I'll tell you what I know."

Barefoot, he shuffles over to the far wall, which constitutes his entire kitchen. He leans the length of driftwood against the counter, pulls an old kettle from the top of his woodstove, and pours coffee into two metal cups, blue with white specks and straight out of a lumber camp somewhere. He shuffles back—not the frail shuffle of an invalid, but the maneuvering of an archaeologist, digging for sure footing. His bare feet are his eyes, Annie realizes, noting the bright white of his pristine Keds, placed with care against the wall near the front door.

"Where's your Citizen Kane, Ed?"

"Citizen Kane?" Annie asks. "The movie?" This place doesn't look like it has electricity, let alone a movie library.

A low chuckle rolls out from Ed as he leads them to a cozy gathering of chairs. "No, ma'am. It's the old cane from *The Boston Post*—the citizen cane. The one with that fancy brass knob on it that they like to give out to remind you you're about as old as Methuselah."

"So, where'd it run off to?" Jeremiah asks.

Annie can visualize it tucked away in Bob's hospital room closet.

"Oh, I just . . . found someone who'll have more need of it than me," he says.

She wants to burst forth with the truth, to thank him for such a gesture toward Bob, whose bucket list is simple but includes walking with that cane. It had special meaning to him that, for some reason, he'd never explained to her.

But Ed's downplaying the gesture, and she decides the best way to thank him is by honoring that. And by pulling out Savannah's pie, which she does right away. Forget using it as story-bait.

He inhales appreciatively. "Now, that is a smell I'd recognize anywhere. May I?" There's so much of the southern gentleman in his ways.

"Of course." Annie pushes it across the coffee table—a suitcase perched on four log legs.

"Driftwood suits me better than that cane anyway," Ed says after his first bite.

"Why is that?"

"That, Bob's Annie, is a long story. We'll see if we get that far today." Ed eases back into his rocking chair and creaks back and forth, rocking as he directs the next question to Jeremiah. "What's the news from Mississippi?" At the mention of the place, his words move deeper into the accent of his southern roots.

Jeremiah hands him a letter. "Open it, Fletch." There's teasing in Ed's voice.

"You know I can't, Mr. Ed." Jeremiah's smiling, parentheses creased around his grin.

"Postal regulations," they say in unison, and Ed's laugh rolls in easy and slow.

He slides a finger beneath the flap, pulls out the letter, and hands it back to Jeremiah. This is a ritual they've repeated often, Annie senses, and she presses herself farther against the deep blue sofa, trying to make herself as unobtrusive as possible.

Jeremiah clears his throat and begins reading. A letter from Hosea. A nephew, apparently. It opens *Dear Uncle Ed* and carries on with news from Mississippi. The homeplace. Word of Hosea's grandson Jimmy's high school graduation coming up, a mishap involving a crock of gravy and a poorly sealed shaker of pepper, and reports of the cicadas waking for summer.

Warmth floods Annie at the easy cadence of the letter, the world it comes from. It takes a blustering wind blowing through Ed's cabin to ground her back in Maine.

Finished, Jeremiah tucks the letter inside a lidded tin box on the coffee table. The box is full of countless others. By the lingering smile on Ed's face, this is his treasure trove.

"Your nephew," Annie says. "He writes often?" She likes the

thought, thinks of her own banter in the classifieds with Bob. She pulls in a sip of her coffee, its bitter notes rounded with smooth cream.

"Hosea writes every week like clockwork." Ed's grin tugs into lament. "But he's not my nephew."

Regret floods her, and if not for the coffee in her mouth, she'd be backpedaling. She should know better. *Never assume*—one of the basic tenets of anthropology.

But the coffee doesn't go down quickly enough, and Ed presses on.

"I have your GrandBob to thank for these letters," he says.

"Bob?" Annie turns the mug in her hands, and Jeremiah leans forward. The story is new to him, too, then.

"Yes, ma'am, and your daddy, William, too."

Annie sets the coffee down. Never has she heard her father's name mentioned in tandem with Bob's. People skirted around the subject as if the Berlin Wall itself stood between the men, and no one would tell her why. *"Water under the bridge,"* they'd say. But there was no bridge. Only a dam, barely holding back the crackling tension.

"Do they know Hosea?"

A clock on the mantel chimes, and Ed listens intently, counting. "Figure we got time for some of the story before the tide comes back in and traps us here all day long. I've got to get to America." He laughs at the islanders' name for the mainland. "I'll walk back over the sand bar with you before the tide's too far up, if you don't mind an old codger slowing you down."

"As if we could keep up with you," Jeremiah says, and the old man smiles. But it's true, Annie has noticed. Ed is careful but swift, reading the earth with those feet.

"Well, let's see, then. The story goes back further than we've got time for, but we can go back to the war and start there."

There it was again. The war. Everything was beginning to go back to it. It had always been this dark knot of history, ever since Annie watched the documentaries as a wide-eyed eighth grader in history class, feeling for the first time the weight of a darkness that should not be real. And now . . . it seems everywhere she turns, mystery calls her from its shadows.

"There was a time the world dropped a curtain around me. I lost my way. Hitchhiked and walked 'til I reached the edge of the world and couldn't go farther."

"This was after the war?" Annie asks.

"That's so, yes. Some time after. And after another war, too," Ed says, gravity pulling the room tight.

"Were you with my grandfather during the war?" Annie knows so little of Roy, she's hopeful Ed might hold some insight.

Ed's laugh is a sad one. "No, ma'am. Troops were segregated back then."

Annie's face burns. "I'm so sorry." She should have known this.

"It was a different time," Ed continues. "And most of us . . . we understood better than most what the people over there were going through, what it meant to be rounded up, shoved into certain neighborhoods, denied the rights of being a human. Threatened and killed for our heritage. So when we went off to war over there, it meant a whole lot. And when we came back . . ."

Ed shakes his head. "We'd fought, gave life and limb, as people say. But even though the government tried to help us out with that G.I. bill, some things back home hadn't changed. We were G.I.s, sure. We could apply for those home loans, sure. But most of the banks wouldn't loan to people like me, or would only give loans for homes in white neighborhoods. And if a black man up and moved into a white neighborhood . . . well, the neighbors didn't care much how you got the loan. They just wanted you gone. Same with the colleges, and that G.I. school money. White universities wouldn't take us. Black universities were flooded to past full and near to breaking with everyone trying to use their G.I. benefits and only so many schools willing to take us. Not enough teachin' to go around."

His wizened face holds these memories, pinching deeper into chasms as he pushes his eyebrows together. "We figured out how to win the war, figured out how to set all those captives free across the seas, but we couldn't figure out how to liberate Jim Crow back home on our own soil.

"I was one of the lucky ones. After a few months back home in Mississippi, I found a job up at the university in Alexandria. Cleaning blackboards at night, keeping watch. Every morning come the sun, I'd go home, and every night come dark, to work I went. For nigh unto ten years after that war ended I worked in the building my own great-granddaddy laid the foundation for way back when."

He falls silent awhile, but Annie feels the undercurrents of something coming.

"I got a fool notion in my head one day. By then the law was sayin' they should let us into any state school, but not everyone agreed. I couldn't forget the men we'd left behind back in Italy, in those mountains where we made horseshoes for donkeys out of melted-down barbed wire just so we could keep going one more day, where men pushed in and pushed Germany back, where they laid down their lives because they knew this was about somethin' bigger than them. They never got to come home. I figured I owed it to them, to keep marching. So I did.

"I marched right into that university and registered. At first no one took note, they were used to seeing plain old Ed around with his broom. But when they caught wind that I was aimin' to be a student . . . well, I didn't mean for it to, but it struck up a new war. Riots and protests and armed guards walking me to class. It wasn't right, but I think I could've taken it. It was what happened next that changed it all."

Annie is right there with him in that beautiful, shadowed university. In her mind's eye, she's standing amongst those columned buildings, watching something about to crumble. And all this somehow ties to Bob and her father?

"One day the crowd showed up to march, and someone brought a gun." Ed's breath rakes over rubble. He rubs an arm, that scar etched there.

"You were shot," Annie murmurs, wishing her words were a salve on that wound.

Ed nods, pursing his lips. "But not so bad," he says. "There was another man, though—Michael. He was younger than me, with a baby at home. He built houses for a living. That wife of his worked hard just like he did, the both of them just wanting to give what good they could to their son. I s'pose that's why Michael came out that day to march on behalf of a man he'd never met." Ed swallows. "The same bullet that grazed me, pierced right through him."

Annie winces.

"We thought he was gone. But somehow instead of carrying him on home to glory, that glory must've wrapped itself right around him. A week later he was home, holding that boy of his. Just . . . he came home without one of his arms. That man made it all the way through the war over the ocean in one piece—and then this happened."

Annie blinks, tears splashing her folded hands. Jeremiah leaves and comes back, slipping a soft cloth napkin her way. Shoving his hands into his pocket, he lingers by her chair a moment before lowering back into his.

Ed shakes his head. "Michael lost his livelihood that day. He never once complained. Said he figured it just meant God had somethin' new in mind, and when the Lord did a new thing, it was good."

"What was Michael's new trade?" Annie makes sure to speak the man's name with the same respect Ed does.

Ed chuckles. "As it happens, there was an openin' just then for someone to clean blackboards at night. And that man washed those slate walls like it was a science. He helped me study. We'd walk the corridors and rooms cleaning boards and windows, him drilling me on human anatomy 'til my ears bled. He's what kept me going, all those years. Right there in the building my great-grandpa helped build. Same building Michael's own son would grow up to teach in one day. Hosea Jones, Professor of History."

"Hosea?" Jeremiah unfolds his arms, taps the letter box twice. "This Hosea?"

"The very same," Ed says, beaming. And then his smile fades, melts into sorrow itself. "Shame Michael didn't live to see that." The man closes his eyes and is silent so long, Annie wonders if they shouldn't step out, give him space.

But something draws her forward instead, fingers tentatively sliding beneath his.

"That bullet ended up killing him in the end. Seven years later, sepsis got to him from that old wound. I was graduating, finally, and when they gave me that piece of paper, something snapped. A man was dead—a child, fatherless—all for a piece of paper. And what did it matter? Not a lick. I was planning to go on for more training, but no one wanted a doctor who looked like me, not down there."

The clock in the corner ticks on. Closer and closer to when the ocean will cover up their road home. They should be going, she knows, but Annie is yearning for just a little more of his story. Of how he'd come from Mississippi to Maine, and how on earth Bob had a hand in all this.

"What happened?" she asks tenderly, hoping to show she's holding his words with care.

Ed shakes his head slow, sorry. "Nothing to my credit," he says. "I'm ashamed to say I let the bitterness take me for too long. Even took to the bottle. Drank more than a man should one night, sitting there by Michael's grave, and got it into my head that the man who did this should lose somethin', too. I took a rock from near Michael's grave and stumbled my way across town, across the tracks, to that man's house, fixing to punch a hole right through it with that rock. But . . ."

Annie is on the edge of her seat now. "But . . . what?"

"I took one look through the window and saw him. Sitting at his kitchen table, gas lamp lighting a face that told me life hadn't been good to him. He was bent over some paper, rubbing his head. A baby started crying, and he got up, left the room, and came back with that child in his arms."

Ed's chin trembles. "That rock felt heavier than iron in my hand. Something weighed it down, tellin' me this wouldn't be what Michael wanted. Truth be told, Bob's Annie, I could nearly hear the good Lord tellin' me somethin' that night."

"What was it?" Annie's heart is beating harder. To think of hearing something straight from God himself. Something Josef Krause had heard, something Ed had heard . . . and something she doubted she'd ever hear. God was distant, in her experience. Real enough on the pages of the Bible, but not one to speak directly to the likes of her.

"Wait."

"Wait?"

Ed nods. "Yes, ma'am. That's what he said to my heart. Just . . . *Wait*. Loud and clear."

"So . . . what did you do?"

"I waited. I wrapped my hand around that rock, stuck it in my knapsack, sobered up, and took to the road. Outrunnin' the fact that Michael could never run again. Sometimes I walked, sometimes I hitched a ride. Didn't care where I was going, just as far from that place as I could get. The place I'd fought a war for—two wars—and the place that denied me a home, nearly an education, and that took the life of my friend. Must've been weeks I was on the road."

"That's how you got here?"

"No, ma'am. I was headed the other way. Somewhere long about New Orleans, I scraped my last coins together and bought a po' boy sandwich on a street corner. It was wrapped in newsprint dated three months before. The same day Michael passed on. And you know what was in it?"

Annie shakes her head.

"A sandwich." Ed winks, and she gets the feeling he knows she's sitting on the edge of her seat, and he's enjoying tormenting her.

"Aw, now. I'll tell you, Bob's Annie. It was his words."

His words . . . ? Then what he is telling her begins to fall into place. She'd heard rumblings of Bob's "words," but they'd mostly

142

been grumblings from the man himself, about how the words he'd penned had run away farther than they were ever meant to. All the way to New Orleans, apparently.

She feels silly admitting she's never read them and holds her tongue.

"They were an invitation to come here," Ed says. "As close an invitation as I needed, anyway. So I switched directions and headed north. Worked when I needed to, walked whenever I could. I must've looked like Moses himself, with a beard long as the Nile and covered with the grime of the road, when Bob found me. I'd reached the end of the country, the end of my rope, the end of having hope to ever help someone, after all that with Michael. I had only a soiled newspaper clipping and a simple rock from a grave site to my name. And there Bob came, whistlin' down the road, pocket bulging."

Ed closes his unseeing eyes around the memory. "Bet you can just see it. Bob comin' upon a person new in town from away. Far, far away. So far he don't rightly know where he's come from or where he's going or why he should even keep on or whether he will. Gangly fella without a cent to his name, looking like ten thousand yesterdays piled in a heap, sittin' on a rock at the jetty."

Ed pauses, and Annie realizes this is her cue. This is a dance, as it should be. He offers a story, she receives it, shows she's going to care for it. "Yes," Annie says. "That sounds like Bob."

"I bet this does, too. He pulled a wad of cash from his pocket. He was on his way home from hauling in the day's bugs." He uses the Mainer word for *lobsters*. "Melvin down at the dock had paid him thirty dollars even. Come to find out later, that was all the money he'd got all week, but Bob looked at me and said, 'Here's thirty dollars. It's yours if you'll help a guy out.'"

"And . . . did you go with him?" Annie loves picturing this. A younger Bob, seeing right into somebody the way he always has.

"Yep. Didn't care so much about the money as the other thing he said."

Annie's eyes flick side to side as she recalls. "Help a guy out?"

"It probably didn't seem like much to him. But to me . . . they were the words of life. A chance to do something good for someone, though I knew deep down it was him doin' something good for me.

"It was then I took to this island, nowhere else to stay." He inhales deeply, soaking this place in. "When the world gets to feeling too awful big and dark, it's time to get on an island."

Annie nods. "I can see that. An island would offer some . . . refuge, after all you'd faced."

Ed's smile is slow and knowing. "That's what I thought, too. I needed away from it all. But I tell you what, a few decades on a piece of land surrounded by sea tell a different story."

His voice holds a spark of invitation, just waiting for her to ask. She obliges. "Oh?"

"It's not the isolation that's medicine for the soul. No, ma'am. See, an island is a world unto itself. And if God can keep the tides comin' and goin', if He can use the sky itself"—he leans forward, elbows to knees, truncating the last three syllables into exclamation marks—"to pull back an entire ocean, just roll it clean away twice a day, easy as pie . . ." He whistles down like a waterfall. "Why, then He can walk us through this life. Did it at the Red Sea. Does it for us now. One step at a time. There's little here to get in the way of seein' that, and boy, did I need to see it."

This unsettles Annie. These words might crack right into her thinly ordered universe. She had grown comfortable with the idea of God only being a creator, someone who maybe watched things from afar off. But this God that Ed speaks of . . . He seems close. Powerful.

She clears her throat and tries to encourage him on in telling his background. "It made a good home, then?"

He takes the subject change in stride.

"Yes. I couldn't afford a house, so I pulled planks from the sea. Maybe the country denied me a home, but the waves went so far as to do the sanding down for me and deliver my materials right to my doorstep." He gives a wry laugh. "Maybe it wasn't much to

144

speak of for most, but it felt like a mansion to me. With meaningful work to do and the sea singin' me to sleep . . . I think I became a small bit human again.

"When Bob found out I was livin' out here on the island in a driftwood shack, he and some of the others came over and built this cabin. Brought the logs over from his family land up the mountain. Just towed 'em behind his boat, and before I knew it, this here house was mine. The house that Bob built."

Annie can almost feel the walls smiling, keepers of another of Bob's secrets.

Ed blows his cheeks out and stands, moving toward the door. "Best be gettin' on," he says. "Else the water will swallow us all right up." It's jarring, to be summoned out of his tale so abruptly, like waking from a vivid dream in a world before her time.

The man is up and out the door, hat on head, shoes in one hand, clam hod in the other, ready to be filled with the day's bounty. Wind whips around him, and he stands tall nonetheless.

Annie has to work to keep up with him as she and Jeremiah follow. They stop first on the south end of the island, where he plucks a solar lantern from a tree branch. "Tell me somethin'." He places his hand over its light sensor. "This shining?"

The lantern blinks on, bright as can be.

"Yes," Annie says, and looks across to the next island. Sure enough, Everlea Estate stands there like a grand Victorian lady. "Can I ask why you put the lamp here?"

He tucks it behind the tree, on the ground, where Sully won't see it. "Just thought she'd like a sign of life, alone out there on her island. Sometimes a body likes to be reminded there's a heart beatin' close by." He slides his foot over to it, pushing loose dust up against it, and chuckles. "Guess old Ed doesn't know as much as he thought."

He leads the way back across the island, and as they arrive at the sandbar, which is quickly narrowing in the rising tide, she thanks the man. The haze of his story world has cleared in the bluster out here, and there's a question pressing in.

"Mr. Ed," she says, "how was GrandBob involved with you and Hosea?"

Ed stops, back to her. Drinking in the air, drinking in the past.

"Hosea's father deserved to be honored," he says at last. "Your Uncle Bob helped me find a way to do that."

She waits, hoping he'll explain. *What way?* She pleads the question silently, something telling her his answer is just the tip of the iceberg.

"Best be gettin' back to the cabin." He points at her. "You left your knapsack."

Annie grabs her side where her bag should be hanging. He's right.

Warily watching the rising water, Jeremiah says, "I'll go. You start back. I'll catch up."

Annie's torn—Ed tromping over the thin line of sand, Jeremiah jogging back to the cabin.

"Go on," Ed hollers back at her. "Time's a-wasting." He chuckles, and takes the rest of his story on with him.

She starts to run after Jeremiah.

"Annie." Ed's voice is solemn again.

She turns to see him, back to her, head hung in thought. He then lifts it to the sky, letting the beginnings of soft rain baptize his deeply mapped face with fresh life. He waits, as if trying to choose his good-bye. "How does a blind man, with no boat, who can't swim, cross an ocean?"

Is this a riddle? "I don't know. How?"

The way he turns and faces her, eyes alight with a sight sprung from his darkness, makes her hold her breath to hear his words and hear them good.

"One step at a time." He winks, tips his worn-down fedora toward her like the gentleman he is, as if he's spreading all the warmth and welcome of the south right at her feet. "Answers are right in front of us, most times. 'Specially when something seems impossible. You've just got to open your eyes.

"And," he adds, in the tone of an afterthought, "don't wait too long to go there."

"Go where?" Annie takes a step toward him.

"The growin's. Bob's island. I think you'll find some answers there." He sinks his callused feet into the wet sand, and a slow grin starts as he shakes his head in appreciation. "Mm-mmm."

He sets off. In a chain of movements that should have been stilted and harrowing, his leaning in to the driftwood cane, stepping out and digging his toes into his Maker's earth, Annie's breath catches. The more so as a song starts—"Be Thou My Vision"—rolling in deep and slow in his rich voice. She watches his complete abandon, haunted by the fullness of the song of this man with two letters to his name and a million to his story.

The blind man walks on, leaving her in an unleashing sky.

fifteen

Annie pounds up the small rise, into the wooded part of the island. The rain is bucketing now. She passes the driftwood shanty, finally curves into the cabin clearing, and blinks away water—only to collide straight into something solid and warm.

Hands wrap around her shoulders, steadying her.

"In a hurry?"

Jeremiah's eyes swim with mirth. She stares, momentarily caught by the way the rain falls on his face, clean and rugged. He tips his head toward the overhang over the porch. It's shallow but gives them some protection from the rain.

"Thank you," Annie says, catching her breath, "for coming back for my bag."

"Don't thank me yet." He nods toward the house. "Ed's taken it captive in there." He mutters something about Ed being up to his old tricks.

"What's that?" Annie asks.

"Nothing." He lifts his baseball cap, then sets it back in place. "The man just sees more than he lets on."

Annie can agree with that. His words would not soon leave her. Still, if they find a way in, maybe they would still have time to make it to "America." She jiggles the doorknob to no avail. "The sole resident of an entire island, with an ocean for his personal moat, and he locks his door?"

"Some habits die hard," Jeremiah says. "The man was in charge of securing an entire college building for a decade."

The wind punctuates that thought with a gust, shoving rain sideways at them.

"How long does the sandbar stay open?"

Jeremiah snaps his fingers. "I forgot to check the sandbar hours when we came. Was the neon Open sign flashing when you last checked?"

Annie rolls her eyes. "You know what I mean."

"I do, and I think we missed our chance," Jeremiah replies more seriously.

Annie shivers. "When does it . . ." She searches for the right term. *Open back up* was about to come out, but she didn't want more of Jeremiah's clever remarks. "When's the next low tide?"

Jeremiah checks his watch. Annie looks on—it's ten thirty. They'd passed nearly two hours with Ed, and it had seemed only a few moments.

And now they were stuck.

"Around eight tonight. We will be able to get across a while before that."

Annie, hands planted on her hips, spins around, surveying the lay of the land. Trees, trees, boulders, rain . . . and a locked cabin.

Jeremiah shifts his bag, and a thought strikes Annie. A hand flies to her mouth. "Your mail," she murmurs. "I'm so sorry. I'll help you deliver it, I'll make up for this—"

"Relax," he says, and starts to walk back up the path. "How's it go? Neither snow nor rain nor heat nor—"

"Nor gloom of night," Annie fills in for him.

"Right. None of that will stay us couriers from our rounds. Doesn't say a thing about tides. Or forgetful people-detectives who leave their belongings in locked cabins."

"This could turn into a pretty bad storm though, yeah?" She tries to keep her voice casual, all the while recalling Bob's tales of fierce nor'easters that swept down the coast with a vengeance. Or thunder squalls, pouncing out of nowhere and churning those waves into giants to be reckoned with.

"This?" Jeremiah waves the notion off. "It's nothing." He veers to the right, toward the driftwood shanty. "This'll keep us."

Once inside, he pulls up a stump and sits in front of the hearth, motioning for her to take the stool.

But Annie is doing the math, looking around the place warily as the wind howls its warning moan. *Eight hours,* it laments. *Eight hours before I release you back to the world. . . .*

She gulps. "Be right back." And ducks out, returning with an armload of mostly dry wood.

Jeremiah gives an approving nod. "Good thinking," he says. "Where'd you find that? I'll go for more."

"Underbrush," Annie says as she sets to laying the fire. One log horizontal, two logs leaning on it to form a lopsided tent of sorts. Just the way Bob taught her. "In the trees. If you dig a little, it's not so damp down there."

Jeremiah lingers a moment, his gaze on her.

"Could you get some tinder while you're at it?" she asks, stacking the rest of the wood near the hearth to dry out and laying some twigs inside the log-tent for kindling. She stands up and looks around. "What are the chances we'll find some matches here."

Jeremiah gives a quick light whistle to grab her attention, and when she looks he tosses her something small and metal, pulled from his messenger bag.

"A lighter?"

"Mrs. Blanchard's pilot light. The way the wind takes to her house, I learned fast to carry that with me always."

When he returns, he's got a huge armload of wood, and Annie's got the fire going.

"The chimney smoked a little at first," she says, "but I think it's all clear now."

They settle into their makeshift seats, and Annie rubs her arms through her sweater, warming goose bumps away.

"So, you forage a lot for firewood in Chicago?" Jeremiah leans back and crosses his arms.

Annie laughs. "Yeah, in the concrete jungle, for my fifth-story walk-up with no fireplace."

Jeremiah's grin adds more warmth to the room. "So how's a city girl know how to whip up a fire like that? Wait, let me guess. Bob."

Annie smiles. "Yes, and no. Bob taught me the basics when I was a kid, but a year in the Alps living in a drafty stone hut drove me to the woods for kindling."

She rarely—no, never—talks about her time in Alpenzell. The shame had a way of flooding in whenever she thought about it. But Jeremiah waits, head tilted, asking for more of the story.

"I spent some time there working for a village, right after college," she says, thinking that's about all he's going to get. But he just waits there, listening. Maddeningly.

And maddeningly, part of her wants to tell him. To confide it all and leave it once and for all. If that's even possible.

She sighs, remembering the beauty of that place. Not unlike Ansel, actually, with its tall pines, wind whispering through bending boughs, snow running in veins down the mountains. Cobbled homes and humble, hardworking people. One crack in the dam of memories, and they're flooding the place as she tells Jeremiah.

"They were in trouble," she says. "They had one employed person in the whole village, and that was the mayor. The rest were retired artisans, all the young people lured away by jobs in cities. It was a town 'on the verge of extinction.' I thought . . . I don't know. I'd gotten good grades, studied how people thought and worked and how societies built and thrived." She lifts a shoulder, drops it. "I thought I could help."

Jeremiah leans forward. "And . . . did you?"

"I hoped so . . . at first. We put on an artisan festival that summer. People came from all over to buy the yarn, watch it being spun, taste the cheeses. . . . And they kept saying, 'I wish I lived here.'" She smiles. "You'd understand if you saw the place. Enough people said it, that this idea I had . . . it was drastic, but it didn't seem completely preposterous."

"What was it?" Jeremiah looks truly intrigued.

"I thought we could use the village funds and all the empty cottages as incentives."

"For . . . ?"

"To draw people in. Promise them a free home, and a small moving stipend, if they'd relocate."

Jeremiah leans back, crosses his arms, thinking. "It sounds . . ."

"Stupid? Naïve? Shortsighted? I know."

"I was going to say *creative*."

Remorse drags her tone down. "I drained the town's funds in advertising and stipends. And do you know what happened?"

Jeremiah shakes his head.

"People came. Stayed a month, two, maybe three. And then . . . they left. Just up and left for their real homes, back in the cities that had stolen the village's life to begin with."

Jeremiah blows out his cheeks, exhaling and shaking his head. "People are jerks sometimes."

"Yeah. I was the jerk. I should have realized. . . . It would have been so *simple* to put in some protective clauses—minimum commitments, sole residencies, that sort of thing. I mean, I study people. I should have seen what would happen. How not everyone loved that place like I did. How they just wanted easy summer homes, and they left the place poorer than when they came."

The wind is slowing, rain taking on a steadier rhythm above them and finding its way through the narrow cracks, giving the room the feel of a cave.

Jeremiah's face is thoughtful. "What happened to the town?"

"Alpenzell? They're better off without me, for one thing. I took a job in Chicago, where I couldn't hurt anyone." Couldn't help anyone, either, but she tried not to think about that. Whenever that little ball of fire inside ignited, driving her to do something big, she knew just how to tamp it down and turn her attention back to the computer, to skate across the surface of society and never plunge in again. She wouldn't do that to a place again—especially not a place as dear as Ansel, tempted as she was to give in to the ideas spinning in her mind for this place.

"I saved up. Paid back their funds. And vowed never to do that again."

"Do what?"

She hangs her head, shame washing fresh over her. "Put people on the line like that for a poorly considered idea."

Jeremiah's eyebrows lift as he considers. "I think it was a pretty good idea, honestly."

"Tell that to those empty cottages." She stands, hoping to steer this talk away from painful things. "Speaking of empty houses, it's crazy that Ed built this place."

"Yes, he's something else."

Annie thinks back on his account. Michael's and Hosea's lives, their tale and Ed's, linger like a shadowy cloak about her. "What did he mean when he said Bob gave him a way to honor Michael?"

Jeremiah shakes his head. "I'm not sure. I'd never heard that part of his story. But you saw the look on his face. There's a story there, and he's relishing making us wait."

Annie scrunches up her nose. "It's so strange. Bob didn't seem like one for secrets. But the last time I was here, I was so caught up in my own . . ." She searches for the right word. Trauma? Confusion? "My own world, maybe I just didn't notice. Or maybe he shielded me. But there are things I should have cared about enough to ask."

"Like what?"

"I don't know. Like my own grandfather. I know he was buried at sea, but shouldn't there be some sort of memorial for him? A plaque or something? Maybe a bench or a marker in the graveyard? I never saw anything like that here."

Jeremiah rises then, crosses the room and stoops to look out the porthole window. "You know Bob," he says at last, stuffing his hands in his pockets. "He never does things the way you'd expect. Some memorials . . . they're living and breathing ones.

People, walking around, carrying that other person with them until the day they die."

He looks far away then, and Annie doesn't speak, doesn't want to break into whatever world he's in.

Jeremiah sucks in a breath, as if to ground himself here, in this rainy reality. "You know what I mean. Bob and Roy," he says. "People who knew them both talk about them as if they're the same person. Never apart. Someone can be so much a part of you that . . ." His eyebrows pinch together. "You know what I mean."

She doesn't. She can imagine such a strong connection between people, but she'd never felt such a closeness, not to anyone. Had he? He'd looked so bereft when he spoke of it, and yet there was a light in his eyes, too. Something in her aches.

"Yes," she says at last. "I think I do."

And if any one soul could keep a fire burning within him as memorial for the one lost, it is Bob.

Even so, there are things that don't add up. A key. A closet and a boathouse full of rocks. They have to mean something . . . and she intends to find out what that is.

The stress of the last days is catching up to her here beside the fire, with the world all gray outside. Eyelids heavy, head resting against Ed's driftwood wall, and settled into a communal quiet with the enigmatic postman beside the crackle of the fire, sleep sneaks in.

She awakes to low embers and an empty room. She should be cold . . . but something warm and secure is draped around her. It is Jeremiah's jacket, smelling of pine. And the man, she sees when she rises and pulls that jacket tight against a shiver, stands outside, silhouetted against a setting sun. He leans against a tree, staring out over the waves.

She moves to go to him, but something stops her.

Wait.

The very word from Ed's story that kept him from shattering something. Is she about to shatter something, too? She watches as

Jeremiah lowers himself to the rock the tree grows against, until he's sitting. He pulls something out of his back pocket—a paper.

Annie's breath catches. It is the letter from his boat, the one he'd stowed away so carefully inside a book.

He opens it. Studies it. Holds it long . . . and then, folding it back up, bows his head. Brings his hands, folded together, up to his forehead. A posture she has seen her mother take when bringing her very heart before her God. It is the stance of unanswered questions, of troubles too heavy to carry alone.

No sound emerges, yet she knows with an anchoring within her that this moment is sacred.

She waits until he rejoins her, and the two of them at last cross over the sandbar, to freedom.

And yet she has the sense that somehow she's leaving it behind in the dark.

sixteen

The air crackles at night. Tensions tangling like invisible warriors in the atmosphere above them all. Radio waves bringing news to their homes: of the April death of President Franklin D. Roosevelt, the man who had led them in this war, of the masses of ships headed for Japan. Will they invade that country? How high will the casualties be? Numbers, higher than high, are tossed about as if they aren't faces or lives. The war on the European front ended months ago, but this turmoil with Japan shows no end in sight, and the world war rages on.

That mid-August evening, Robert leaves the radio and heads for the dock.

The dew on the wood is real, something he can see, touch, feel. It is not full of questions too lofty for the human soul. It's just here, reminding him the way forward is to keep on with the work at hand, reminding him there's a God out there who can create dew, water from air, and if He can do that, then He can see them through this war.

He wonders if Roy's sitting in dew on his ship, wherever he is. He prays for the thousandth time—*Bring him home*.

A light shriek from the house—his mother. The screen door

156

slams. Her footsteps hurry down the path toward him. He's up on his feet, heart pounding, running toward her.

They meet at the shoreline, and he searches her face, hand to her shoulder. "What is it?" With relief, he sees joy there.

"The war. It's—"

A whoop sounds from across the bay.

"It's done," she says. Astonishment boils into laughter from deep inside her. Tears spring to her eyes. "It's done."

Her words skid off Robert, trying to sink in.

Lights begin to come on in homes whose windows usually go dark about now. Fishermen go to bed with the sun in order to wake with it again tomorrow, but their windows blaze tonight.

One boat engine fires up, then another.

Mom squeezes his shoulder. "They're gatherin'."

A laugh tumbles up from some locked-away place inside Robert. "I'll get the boat ready," he says, grinning. It's all he can do to keep from jumping in the boat right now and opening up the engine full-speed to search the Atlantic for his brother and bring him home. Last they heard he was on board a destroyer somewhere in the North Atlantic—somewhere right out there in the dark waves beyond.

His mother disappears into the house, returning minutes later with a lidded basket and thermos. What she has in there, he can only guess. Their cupboards are as sparse as any in the country just now. But that was one of Ansel's workings of magic, the way the women could pull up a feast out of anything, at a moment's notice, war rations and all. And no one worked the magic better than Savannah Bliss.

Dark settling around them, they stop long enough for Jenny, babe in arms, and even her stalwart Aunt Millicent. After William was born, Jenny's parents had returned briefly from Minnesota, where they had moved soon after Jenny married Roy. But when they left, Millicent had insisted she join Jenny while she learned to care for her son.

They make their way across the harbor, around Long Island,

and into the Weg. There, sure as Sunday, on one of the tiny islands is a telltale bonfire on the beach. Ansel's setting to celebrate in Picnic Cove. It is aptly named, for the boats can get close to the shore without danger of run-ins with hidden rocks.

The celebration is already in full swing, fire reaching heights twice that of Tall Reuben, who's roasting a hot dog on a branch over its flames. Ethel and Pearl provide music, one on the guitar while the other one sings, pulling a ring of children in a circle round and round. Picnic blankets slapped down on the earth stake a claim on this newly announced victory. Mrs. Crockett scurries around, heaping slabs of her blueberry cake onto everyone's plates.

People in cities are probably throwing confetti, tossing hats, but they haven't known celebration until they've tasted Mrs. Crockett's cake, cooked with plump berries that just hours before were soaking in the sun and breathing in the sea air.

Robert stands back, watching joy beat with a pulse. This, then, is liberty.

Before long, a square dance forms, and Robert is pulled into the flurry of movement. It's not his gig, this dancing, and he feels the awkwardness of his lanky form trying to fit into the measured maneuvers.

He thinks of another dance. A snowy December night, when a girl with fire in her soul slipped into his arms alongside the dark waters of the Charles River. Three letters he'd written her since then, with only months of silence as an answer. Perhaps tonight he'll try again—one last time.

The memory is cut short when Mrs. Bascomb, old enough to be his great-grandmother and crabby enough to land in a crab trap, grabs him by the elbow and hollers, "Do-si-do, yow'un!" He grins like a fool at being called a kid in her Down East way—and feels a little like one, too, as he spins her.

The party lasts until the moon is high above them and they've spent themselves in rejoicing. And the afterglow of it lasts and lasts, buoyed by the letter that comes from Roy a few days later:

He is coming home. Their ship will be docking in Boston within the next two weeks.

Yet with each day that passes, there's a growing feeling inside Robert that he cannot stamp out. Something is amiss in that letter. It was Roy's voice, but it lacked his usual vivacity.

The feeling festers like the storm clouds that roil into the week that follows. Robert does his best to carry on as usual, the best thing he can think to do.

As usual, he stops at Joe's Landing every morning for gasoline and bait. And as usual he pulls his traps in and stops there every afternoon to trade with Hal, accepting his folded payment from the cash the man keeps in an old pail.

Wednesday morning is the same. Robert's earlier than usual, as Ma woke early to prepare to leave for Bangor.

"We need supplies for your brother's homecoming," she'd said. "We'll make it a day to remember, when he and Arthur get back. Maybe the other boys will return the same day!" As they'd prepared to leave, she'd talked on about the whole plan. Millicent was to drive, and Jenny and the baby were going, too. It'd take them three hours to get there, and who knew what schemes the three of them would concoct in that time. Fireworks and confetti, maybe a full brass band, if they had their way.

Still dark outside, the lights had been aglow with hope when he'd passed Jenny's house. Docking now at Joe's Landing, Robert winds around other shadowy fishermen milling about on the dock, some jovial, some still enrobed in sleep—all purchasing bait, filling gas cans.

Robert does likewise and is just about to head out when he hears footsteps pounding. He narrows his eyes, straining to see down the Harbor Road in the morning sea smoke—and a figure emerges.

"Robert," the man pants. It's Jim, the postmaster. He heaves, not used to running. "I caught ya."

Robert closes the distance between them. Jim's blue shirt is buttoned wrong, half tucked in. His billed cap is askew. "What's doing, Jim? Anything wrong?" He can feel a knot forming inside.

The other men sense it, too—they've stilled, watching from the landing, like pawns staggered on a chessboard, frozen in time.

"This just come in." Jim hands a scrap of paper to Robert. "Over the wireless. Didn't have time to put it on the right paper." This explains the torn scrap of envelope the scribbled words are on. "But it seemed important. Wanted to get it to ya before you headed out."

It's a string of numbers—coordinates.

N 43° 4' 7.9
W 66° 0' 21.1

Robert had drawn enough lines on navigational charts, consulted enough compasses to know these numbers indicate a location somewhere just south of Nova Scotia. Not home, but not an ocean away, either.

"What is this?"

Jim taps the paper. "It's from Arthur."

"Arthur Baxter?"

"Ayuh. Didn't have time to write down the rest of the message. It said . . ." Jim presses his eyes closed, nodding as he recites. "Come now. See Roy. Arthur."

Vaguely, the sound of movement registers behind him. The men doing something. Maybe giving him space, sensing this is no ordinary message.

Arthur must have broken a thousand protocols to send this message. He would never divulge that their destroyer is stalled, vulnerable, but that had to be it. Otherwise why send coordinates?

A sinking sickness sets Robert's feet to running. He's rounding the fog-wrapped building to where Joe keeps the gas cans, and nearly collides with the man himself.

Joe's lugging two cans—one in each hand. "Grab that one, too." Joe tilts his head to a green paint-chipped can. This will take Robert's gas rations for the next week, at least. But he'll worry about that later.

They approach the *Savvy Mae,* and she's bobbing, as if she

knows, too. Lined up like soldiers beside her are Tall Reuben, Gus Packer, Melvin Buck, Tim Baxter, each with a gas can. Their rations. Everything they have to fuel their livelihood. The widow's mite, right there in rusty cans offered at odd angles.

Robert wants to refuse, but he knows he may need it all to get that far and back. He wraps his fingers around the metal handles and dips his capped head to the men in their yellow oilskins. The overalled uniform of the fishermen is as valiant in this moment as full navy uniforms and medaled chests.

Tim grips his shoulder. It's his boy, Arthur, who sent the message. But he doesn't send a message for him, just purses his lips, gives a solid nod. A man of few words, like his son. It's a benediction, that grip. One Robert would have given anything to have from his own father just now.

Robert nods back and steps through the opening they've left for him to board the boat. Sloshing cans tucked inside, he turns to thank the men for these cold vessels of hope. "Thank you," he says. "I'll pay it back."

Joe shakes his head. His Harry's still out there somewhere, too. "Get to your brother," he says. "Get him home."

"You be careful, young Robert!" Gus chimes in. And they disappear into the curtain of fog as he navigates toward the Weg.

"Get to your brother." There is something final and dark in those words. They drill into him, out through his heart and into his veins until he's turning hard starboard, over to home. Docking, running. *Let them still be here.* Ma should come. Jenny should come. He pounds up the weathered steps, shoves the heavy oak door open and feels the emptiness.

"Ma!"

Silence.

He runs out back in case she's digging in her garden, but all is still.

Jenny's house is next, and it's the same—all silent. Breakfast dishes neatly put away, and a hand to the kettle on the stove burns him with the knowledge that he's just missed them.

161

There's a twisting in him, a heavy sickness. They are gone to Bangor. And something is wrong with Roy.

He stops long enough to scribble a note for Mom, that he'll be gone a good piece of time and not to worry if he doesn't return for a day or two.

Out on the open sea, he lets the engine loose.

seventeen

Robert navigates toward the USS *Franktown*, weary after five hours at sea and another spent chasing down the ship's whereabouts, after it drifted from Arthur's coordinates. The *Savvy Mae* is like an ant in the shadow of a mountain. He cuts his engine, bobbing out there in the open blue with nothing in sight but this behemoth ship. There's a reason they call these ships destroyers. He is David and it is Goliath, fifty fold.

It's quiet. Eerily so. He hears the sound of the Naval Jack flapping in the breeze, the solid blue flag spangled with forty-eight stars in perfect rows.

His pulse hammers. Somewhere on board his brother's heart beats, too. *Please, God.* The heart that beat beside his own before they'd even drawn breath. This friend he'd shared a lifetime with. Only a wall of war-thick steel and military protection between them.

He'd had hours to come up with a plan. Considering every possible way to board a well-guarded military ship whose crew was almost certainly not in the practice of letting civilians aboard.

And every possibility—from sneaking aboard, to feigning distress, to masquerading as his brother—led him down a path of near-hope, only to be dashed with the final verdict: *This will never work.*

He can almost hear his father, picture him casting a sidelong glance, eyes creased the way they did when he smiled. *What're you gettin' so all-fired-up and tangled about, son? The answer's always the simplest. No matter how mixed up the problem is. Scale it back, son. Peel it back until you find the simplest truth. Then do that.*

The simplest truth in this moment that so much hinges upon comes down to two things—the sun coming out long enough from its storm-threatening sky, and a piece of glass no bigger than his palm.

He waits. In the distance through his binoculars, he sees men on deck. Some moving about, and some—two of them—watching him. A third joins them, and Robert sees from the black-billed white cap that he's an officer. Probably the officer of the deck. He can't see faces. Uniforms, yes. Navy and white upon the gunmetal gray of the ship. He's hoping, praying, that one of them is Arthur.

He doesn't blame them for their diligence. The war may be over, but times are still tense and no doubt will be for a long while. There are those who have not been pleased with this outcome. Saboteurs even on American soil that they'd all heard about. If it were him on board the destroyer, he would be watching and wary, too.

He glances at the sky, clouds still scudding en masse. "Come on," Robert mutters at them. "Move!"

They do, but still no sun.

When at last they break, he whips his mirror into action, tilting until it spells his message in Morse code. *PERMISSION TO BOARD.*

A pause. One of the three men disappears, and the other turns to face the officer.

Their signal light flashes back: *IDENTIFY YOURSELF.*

He does, feeling the humility of answering: *THE SAVVY MAE. ROBERT BLISS.*

The third man reappears, a fourth with him. That man takes charge. Flashes back: *ONE TO TWO.*

It's Arthur. Their old code, the one he used to flash across the bay to signal that one man, Arthur, was trying to get the attention of the twins. Relief undoes Robert's muscles, and he realizes how stiffly he's been standing.

Arthur says something to the officer. The man gives a nod, and Arthur flashes: *BOARD.*

The *Savvy Mae* advances, tying up to the destroyer. A rope ladder comes over to Robert. He grips it, swings his body toward it, and in his haste, does not check the integrity of the ropes. A wave has slapped the ladder, and it's slippery. He falls but grabs the ladder and climbs, soggy but thankful no one appears to have witnessed his fall.

On deck, only Arthur awaits him. His face is a mix of joy and dread. He hesitates, different in his uniform, but breaks right past its formality and grips Robert with both arms. It's the embrace of a brother. And the embrace of grief. His green eyes are haunted—whether from war or whatever he's about to say, Robert cannot tell. He is changed. It's been nearly a year since Arthur got on that train at Machias . . . but it's been a lifetime, too.

A figure comes around the corner, and Arthur is quick to salute in the man's presence.

Robert does the same. He shouldn't, being a civilian, but something comes alive in him. All the pages he's read from the Blue-jackets' Manual, all the knowledge he stored up for someday. He just never expected "someday" to come this way.

"As you were," the man says.

The gold of his insignia declares him chief petty officer. He gives them both an even assessment.

"Bliss?" He furrows his brow at Robert, looking him head to toe. Registering, no doubt, the drenched state of his entire being. But he chooses not to acknowledge that, instead asks, "Where'd you get civvies?"

Robert shoots Arthur a look. Navy men did not carry civilian clothes with them. "I . . ." He clears his throat.

The man raises a brow. Robert has not used the proper form of address. This is not going well.

He summons to mind those yellowed pages of the Bluejackets' Manual.

"Sir. Permission to explain, sir."

"What happened to your face, Bliss?"

Robert's mouth hangs open, searching for an answer. He knows he isn't generally considered as much of a "looker" as his brother, but . . .

The officer steps closer. "Remarkable. Not a trace of your injury." He shakes his head in wonder. "Glad to see it. Glad to see you above deck. Take your constitutional." He gestures toward the deck, indicating Robert should continue walking. "Take ten, if you like. From what they told me, I feared you might not see the light of day again." He pumps Robert's hand. "Here's to doctors being wrong, eh?"

Arthur hangs his head. And Robert understands.

The officer's voice suddenly sounds distant, as if he's in a tin can somewhere faraway. Talking about how the ship's boilers are being repaired and they'll be out of this forsaken stall by day after tomorrow, if they're lucky. Headed home. How that wave got them good, but they'd have victory yet. "You're proof of that, Bliss."

Robert presses his eyes shut, opens them to see the officer watching him.

"Sir," he says at last, "I need to see my brother."

It's not eloquent. It's not even an explanation. But the man hasn't gotten to his rank without sharp wit and quick thinking. Robert, trying to summon more coherent words from the fog that's filling him, sees the man look questioningly at Arthur, who nods, points overboard to Robert's boat, and finally says, "Sir, Bliss is still . . . below deck. This is his brother, sir."

The man narrows his eyes. "Is that right?"

Robert feels it—a thousand weights balancing on this thin

thread of a moment, ready to snap. A civilian shouldn't be on deck, shouldn't even have known where the ship was. He's so close. He can't be this close and not see his brother. He's about ready to burst past them all, charge below deck. But something tells him to *Scale it back, son.*

"Yes, sir," Arthur says. He's quiet, but he stands tall. Standing by what he's done.

Seconds crawl by. The ship's bell tolls in two pairs—it's six o'clock. *Eighteen hundred hours,* Robert corrects himself. And the officer finally breaks his iron stare, shifting into a feigned informality. "A wonder, that."

"Sir?"

"For Bliss's . . . twin"—he looks to Robert for confirmation, and Robert's mouth goes grim—"to find us way out here in the blue by chance." He's looking at Arthur again. "Well, I guess we've all seen a wonder or two in this war. Best get down to the infirmary, Second Bliss. We do take on sailors in distress from time to time. And you"—he looks at the puddle of sea water at Robert's feet—"are that. Baxter? Escort this man."

"Aye, aye, sir." Arthur and Robert speak in unison.

Arthur leads Robert through a maze of narrow passages. A crypt of walls groaning with the clink and hiss of machinery and ship movement. Shouts echo from some deck within.

"Try again!" a voice barks. The boiler problem apparently still unsolved.

"Aye, aye, sir!" The younger voice sounds weary, determined.

Arthur leads on. The ceilings are low, or maybe it's just the space going out of the world as Robert draws near to his brother for what, he now understands, will be the last time.

They pass a sailor coming up from a narrow stairwell, a dark abyss below. "Sleeping quarters," Arthur says, and Robert squints to see canvas cots stacked bunk-style, four high and what seems like a thousand deep.

At the end of the passage, they reach an arched door with a porthole window. Faint light glows inside.

"The sick bay," Arthur says. He removes his round white cap, and Robert does likewise with his news cap. Through the window, a man holds up a finger, telling them to wait. He disappears from view, moving the stethoscope to ears as he does.

Arthur looks over his shoulder, and seeing the passage is empty, he speaks on. "It's not good, Robert."

"Tell me."

Arthur takes a deep breath. "It seemed the ocean woke up the second the war died down. We got a distress signal—a Polish ship, bound for New York. They'd been taken in by the storm, started to list soon after. We were the closest to them, got there as fast as we could and started to search. Thought we had every survivor, when Roy spotted one more lifeboat. Two children inside, lying so still we didn't know if they'd lived. And their mother, hollering. We couldn't hear a thing—the storm was still raging—but her face . . ." Arthur's voice cracks. He cups his face, runs his hand down the length of it.

"Men went down on bowlines to get the children. But our ship was creating waves, tossing her boat. We threw the rope to her, but the moment she touched it, a swell came up under her, tossed her into the sea she'd been fighting all night.

"She didn't come up at first. It was dark, and when we finally got a light shining down from on deck, there was Roy—already down there. He'd rappelled down and was reaching for her where she was trying to grip the hull of the lifeboat. She couldn't catch hold—not of the boat and not of him—so he lowered himself 'til he was in the water, reaching. I was sure she was going to give up. But he shouted something to her, and somehow she mustered the strength to grip his arm."

Images flashed across his mind. A hand reaching in the cold. Desperate to save a life. Only instead of him looking down this time, it was Roy. He can hear his brother's voice in his memory—*"The view must be better from up there. . . ."*

Arthur continues. "He secured the rope around her, and we pulled them up. He wouldn't get on board until she was safe. We got her over and turned to pull Roy up, but . . ."

There is a sick, desperate weight in the silence.

"A rogue wave moved the whole ship, came over the top of it hard. Slammed him so hard we felt the impact."

Robert winces, the noise of flesh-on-steel penetrating the scene so alive in his mind.

"I don't know how . . . but he held on. We pulled him up and got him to the sick bay."

In the sea of pictures, Robert's mind reaches for something solid, some piece of logic to hang onto, to thread through all the horror. He clears his throat for the words to get past the ache. "When was this?"

"Three nights ago."

Three nights. Why was Roy still here, if things were so bad? Why hadn't they gotten him to a hospital ship, or a hospital?

Maybe sensing the question, Arthur explains, "The survivors spent the night in the engine room. Sailors offered to give up their beds for them, but the engine room was warmer. A passenger ship came for them the next day. Roy was coming to by then. Doing good. He had a concussion, Doc said, and some scrapes, a gash or two, but with us headed to port, we expected to have him there in plenty of time if he needed more attention."

"But . . . ?"

"But we took on more water than we realized during that rescue. The wave flooded the boilers. It keeps looking like they've got it fixed, and then keeps on failing. Roy . . . he started showing signs of infection. Took on quick, and it's gone deep. Doc says he's never seen it this bad."

Robert braces himself. He knows there is more.

His friend's green eyes, rimmed in red, look at him straight on. "He says . . . he won't see the night."

It's a gut blow.

The door creaks open, and a doctor ushers them in.

"You've told him?" The doc's voice is grave, directed toward Arthur. He must have been in on the plan to summon Robert.

"Yes, sir."

The older man releases a slow breath through his nose, shaking his head. "It won't be long now. I'm sorry, son." He puts a hand to Robert's shoulder. "I'll give you some time."

They weave past three open beds. In the back corner, there is a man, face swollen and discolored, nearly beyond recognition even to the man who sees its likeness in the mirror every day. His chest barely rises, barely falls.

Roy attempts a deep breath, eyes opening. They roam around the space above him, not seeing.

When Robert speaks, his voice is gruff. "I'll get him home," he says. "Or to Bangor, Machias. Or . . . or . . ." He reaches for a map in his mind—whatever place is closest. "Halifax. Or home." He hears himself talking in circles. "He'll do better there. I'll get him help. He'll see his son . . . and . . ."

"It won't be long," Arthur repeats the doctor's words, turning his hat in his hands. "I'm sorry."

Arthur leaves, and Robert kneels, looking at his brother's swollen face, the way his brows crease even in his sleep.

Robert doesn't know how to fix this. He grips his brother's limp hand, as if to give it strength. And he bows his head.

Oh, God . . .

They are the only words he has.

There's a makeshift bedstand, crates stacked up, and on it rests a Bible and a copy of *Rob Roy. Armed Services Edition. Condensed for Wartime Reading.* A picture of Jenny and William is pinned to the wall. She's beaming in that way she saves just for Roy.

"Knew they couldn't keep you out of the navy," Roy mutters. His lip is split, but he pulls it into as much of a grin as he can. "Leave it to my brother to get on board a ship with security tighter than a vault."

"It was nothin'," Robert says. "Piece of cake."

"Mmmm . . . cake." Roy winces. "I was really looking forward to that when I got home. Guess that's not going to happen."

There's a furious fight simmering in Robert. He restrains it, measures out his words. "You'll get all the cake you want. When you get home."

Roy's eyes are steady on him now. And there's this wisdom in them, like he knows things Robert doesn't, like he's closer to eternity than Robert is or ever has been, and it's gathering a peace around him stronger than the storm clouds gathering outside.

"It's okay, brother," Roy says.

It's not okay.

"This is why I came."

This is why Robert was supposed to come instead.

"Just . . . tell William . . . when it's time, tell him I love him. And it's gonna be okay. Life is big. And God is bigger."

Silence.

"And Jenny . . ." He closes his eyes. "Give her this." He pulls his far hand up, opens it to reveal a scrap of paper. The rope burn on his palm is an angry red, proclaiming courage. "She'll know."

Robert takes it. "I will," he says. "You're a good man, Roy."

They long remain this way, in silence, and Robert wonders if Roy's gone back to sleep. But then he whispers, "Bob."

Robert's chest burns. The only person in the wide universe who calls him that is speaking it with his last ounces of strength. Roy's voice is breathless, fading. "Don't get stuck in the dark, Bob."

It doesn't make sense. Maybe he doesn't know what he's saying. But right now Robert would promise his twin anything.

"I won't," he promises, shaking his head.

"There's a whole lotta light," Roy says. "Go there instead."

"I will."

Roy's slipping. His breaths are too far apart. Erratic. Robert quickly spins out words, willing his brother back from where he's going, pulling with his whole soul on this invisible rope tethered to his brother. "You gotta come back and show me," he says. He swipes the heat from his eyes. "Come home with me."

But his brother's hand becomes heavy and still inside of his own.

He has gone home.

And the world has gone dark.

Robert doesn't know how long he stays there. He's slipped into a world without time, vaguely aware of the doctor coming in, checking for pulse, uttering some final words. Time of death. Some of the men come in, hands crossed in front of them, heads bowed in respect, and Robert senses they have work to do. He steps back, and they begin to stitch canvas around his brother's body.

Grave words are uttered about bringing him home. He presses his eyes closed and sees his brother, ten years old and all sunburned, pirate patch over one eye. Jenny stands watch as he points out over the water from Rogue's Clearing with a stick he'd been wielding as a cutlass. *"Out there,"* he'd said, with all the conviction of someone seven times his age. *"That's where to bury me when I die. Lay me to rest with Granddad and the good soldiers out there."*

But Granddad had perished during months at sea in the Great War—when water burial was the only option. Roy . . . he could bring him home to Jenny. But he pictures her as a girl, nodding with gravity at Roy's boyhood burial wishes.

In the numbness he steps in to help. He can't stand by as strangers attend to him, family though they are to Roy. His words come out all jumbled, a request for water burial. They all look askance at him. This close to home, it makes little sense to them.

But they hadn't known that ten-year-old pirate. "It's what he wanted," Robert says. One by one, they nod, drawing themselves up to complete this task with all the honor they can offer this fallen hero.

At some point in the haze, when the work is done and voices drone low around him, he numbly pulls the pin from the wall, grabs the picture of Jenny. The book on the bedstand, where Roy's wedding band lay, too. The Bible, the paper Roy entrusted to him. He follows Arthur back out through catacomb passages and above deck where even the dying sunlight is too harsh.

Arthur pauses, placing a hand on Robert's shoulder. "I-I'm sorry, Bob."

It is only a few words, but Robert doesn't miss that Arthur has called him by Roy's name for him. It means the world, in just one word.

Sailors still from their work as they pass, pulling off their caps. The chief petty officer is there to lower Robert back to the *Savvy Mae*. It's a job far below his station, Robert knows, and he feels the reverent respect in it for his brother.

"Stay out there 'til sundown," the chief petty officer tells him in parting. "Your brother was a fine sailor. A good man. We'll see to it he has the burial he deserves."

And so, out there in the middle of nowhere, with Robert half a mile out from the ship, white-uniformed sailors line up against a sky, red-blazing into night.

Robert cannot hear, but he knows what's being said. A prayer. A benediction. Capped heads bowed, sailors' feet wide in strong stance, as words are spoken over his brother's body.

Robert speaks them, too.

"'The Lord bless thee and keep thee.'" He thinks of Roy's grin. Those blasted dimples. An untethering starts in him. A severing of soul he is not—could not ever be—prepared for.

"'The Lord make His face to shine upon thee.'" He remembers Roy's rasped words. *"There's a whole lotta light . . ."*

"'The Lord—'" His voice cracks, and an unearthly noise comes in its place. He presses his eyes closed and wetness courses down his face, tears gone off to an ocean too big.

"'The Lord give thee peace. Amen.'"

A solemn order echoes over the waters, and the men line up to salute volley one gunshot into the air. Then another . . . and a last. A wordless proclamation soaring over the sea.

Robert knows that if he could take flight, too, view the scene in aerial, he would see the sailors and officers lined up, row upon row. Saluting—a stance of fiercest heartache schooled into firmest respect.

He would see himself there on his humble lobster boat, facing them, an ocean between them, saluting too. Numb to the throbbing of his elbow. Trembling.

And in a split-second's time that will be burned in Robert's mind forever, his brother, wrapped with care, slips down into the deep.

The waves swallow up the boat maker . . . and all is still.

eighteen

How did I get here? Robert pauses outside the picket fence around Jenny's yellow house. The journey back to Maine was a blur, at best. And then he's spent most of the day wandering the headlands of the bold coast north of Ansel, trying to find what to say to Ma, to Jenny. He hadn't gone straight home to them. Maybe it was wrong, but he'd asked Arthur to hold back his telegram a day. He couldn't fathom the weight of the truth emblazoned onto paper, couldn't let rigid type on a cold white backdrop deliver this news. So he'd navigated back to a nation awash in joy, newly at peace, to bring the news himself.

He's come to Jenny's house first. There is still protocol to follow. The widow gets the notification. He half expects his mother will be here anyhow, doting on her grandson.

The house pales in the waning twilight. There's a peace here, with the red climbing roses on a white trellis. Shutters frame glowing windows, the sound of laughter and the radio coming from within. It's such a picture—everything bright and good, like Jenny. He's about to crash into this world, slice it clean through. This is a home awaiting a long-expected homecoming.

A lifetime ago, he'd dreamed of standing here at the gate with a bouquet at his back for her. He'd hoped back then to win her heart . . . and now he must break it. The only bouquet to fill his hands is the clutch of his brother's belongings.

God, help me.

The gate creaks open to his touch, and the laughter inside falls silent. A porch light comes on, and Jenny rushes out. "Roy?"

Her voice is so full of hope she could buoy the whole world. She grabs his hand. Freezes. Takes in his civilian clothes. Peers closer against the fading light. "Robert?"

She looks around him, down the lane both directions. It is empty.

"Sorry," she says, sheepish. "We heard you got a message and thought you went to get him, to surprise us." She gives his hand a quick apologetic squeeze. "I . . ."

She looks down into the hand, where she's felt Roy's hat. She sees the picture, the Bible.

And she reads his face, reaching with her eyes for hope he cannot give.

She pulls back, wrapped in a thousand shades of knowing. But she shakes her head, not wanting to know.

Her aunt Millicent has followed her out and arrives at her elbow just in time to loop her wiry arm through Jenny's, guide her toward the house. "Come," she says over her shoulder to Robert.

The war has done a number on words, he thinks numbly as he follows them. Most of the time they all need words, words, words. Whatever news they can get, never enough words. And then—times like this—those words just fall to the ground, no chance of being big enough to say what needs to be said, what they all so desperately need to be unsaid.

Millicent guides Jenny to the blue curved sofa in the sitting room. Robert pulls off his hat, goes onto a knee before her. "Jenny, I . . ." He pauses, then begins telling her of the wound. The infection. As gently as he can, but she stops him.

She looks at him in that straight-on way of hers. Blue eyes of their youth, desperate. She takes his hand. "Just . . . tell me he wasn't alone."

His throat swells, aches. "He wasn't."

Her eyes fill, chin trembling. She lifts that chin and nods. Keeps nodding, as if that will keep her breathing.

Robert pulls in a shaky breath. "We were together. He was safe . . . comfortable. And . . ." He reaches into his pocket for the box. He'd bought it in Halifax, stopping there before coming home. Wandered in a haze through the city, disregarding the wary looks the ladies at the jewelry store gave him when he said he just wanted an empty ring box. If he had to deliver its contents to Jenny, it should have the wrappings of the treasure it was.

"He had you, Jenny." He slips the deep red velvet box into her hand. She opens it, pursing her lips as she pulls out Roy's worn wooden ring . . . and the slip of paper Roy gave him in the sick bay.

Jenny's hand flies to her lips, where she presses them to gather herself long enough to whisper, "Thank you."

She wraps her fingers tightly around the ring. Thinking, no doubt, of the hands of her love. Hands that carved it, sanded it, crafted hers to match. "Poor as church mice and rich as kings," she murmurs. The paper flutters, unread, to the floor. And then she's up, gripping the ring and running from the room, into the kitchen, out the back door, onto the porch—where silence falls, soon broken by a wail the likes of which he's only heard in the winter wind, so haunting it rends the night.

He picks up the fallen paper and follows to the kitchen, but Millicent brushes past him, hand up to show him to stay put.

It is warm in the tidy room. A log snaps in the potbelly stove in the corner. His attention is drawn to a brass-framed picture sitting on the table next to a jar of lupine—a picture of Roy, proud in uniform.

Then a tiny hand springs up from a basket on the table, nudged up against the wall. Robert steps close, and William's fair face peers back at him, eyes wide. A miniature Roy, hair dark and with Jenny's sky-blue eyes.

Outside, Jenny's voice slips into a battle of ragged breath and restrained sobs. It is the sound of loss and life colliding, the one pulling the other right out into the night. Unearthly, growing. It is not any lullaby this child has ever heard.

William begins to whimper, and for a second, Robert steps back. These arms that battle the sea do not know how to cradle a baby. He feels in every stiffened muscle, the burn of not knowing what to do. And yet his legs bend him near, carry him where his arms won't go. Stiffly . . . and then not-so-stiffly, he reaches in, cups the tiny face as gently as he can in his callused hand.

Fingers so young wrap around Robert's hand, the hand that swaddled this child's father unto his grave. Robert's hand begins to shake. He wants to stay here, cocooned in this grip of innocence that doesn't know, doesn't see how these hands are stained with death. He pulls away ever so gently from the grip, from the lie. Shaking still, he turns his life-roughened hands backward, fingers curled around his calluses, and lets his knuckles brush that soft cheek.

William smiles and a dimple appears, just on the left. It is good and pure. Light flickers in those tiny, trusting eyes. Something deep in Robert begins to crack. Like granite from the shifting of earth miles below the surface.

Out in the night, Jenny's wail morphs into muted words, and the back door creaks open. Clipped steps come in an efficiency only Millicent could bring, but Robert cannot look at her. Setting down the scrap of paper, he slides his arms beneath the child and pulls him close.

This should have been Roy standing here, pulling his son against his chest, feeling the flutter of this tiny heartbeat strong through the blankets. So much *life*. He presses William close, mustering all the strength he's ever known and letting it gentle around this child. *This. Should. Have. Been. Roy.*

Millicent, for once, does not intrude. She goes to the stove, turns off its flame, and the bubble of the savory meal begins to quiet. She waits. In the corner, the cuckoo clock ticks on as if to remind him time is short.

The cracking inside is spreading. Tendrils webbing, chasm widening. He has to say these promised words somehow. He presses his lips to William's head. And yet in this gesture given to show comfort, it's he who feels the comfort in the downy softness of that dark hair, the smell of soap washing his soul clean enough to say, "He loves you." He can't bring himself to say *loved*. "And . . . it's going to be okay." There is more to Roy's message, and though Robert doesn't feel the truth of it just now, he says it. "Life is big. And God is bigger." He'll tell the boy these words all his life. He vows it.

The child has stilled, relaxed into his arms with more warmth and trust than the whole world outside knows.

Millicent shuffles her feet. "His mother . . ." She lifts a hand to rub a slow circle on the child's back.

Of course. Jenny needs William. William needs Jenny. This is right and good. And yet as Robert lowers him away from his chest and into Millicent's arms, the cracking down below rends deep. He trembles with the way it grows as Millicent disappears through the door.

A breeze tumbles the paper across the kitchen table, and Robert catches it. He means only to anchor it there for Jenny, for later. But as he turns it in his fingers, he sees the message his brother wrote with his last bit of strength, for his beloved:

77 fathoms. And more. Always.

Jenny's shuddering sniffles calm into the rhythmic creak of the rocking chair out back. A fragile calm descends, walling him away. He can't stay. The cracking grows, he can nearly hear it. It'll shatter everything he touches if he stays.

He secures the paper in a fold of the baby's basket, where Jenny will see it in good time. He slips out the front door, locks the knob behind him, and silently pulls it shut. The night swallows him up. He should go on to tell his mother. But her windows are dark through the pines, and he cannot wake her to this living nightmare. Not yet.

Breath comes thick in this sea of clean air. He walks, then runs, then pounds to the dock. Into the rowboat. Out into the waves that are wretchedly gentle. He spears them with his oars, willing them to fight. All the way to the island, a one-sided battle, the cracking driving him harder with each movement.

By the time he reaches the shore, he's in a thousand pieces, held together by he knows not what. He's at the top of the trail and can't even remember taking the steps to get there. Yet here he is, this place untouched in the months since he and Roy were here. Cold in the white moonlight. Black coals where their bonfire last lit the night. Their chest of boyhood loot tucked into its rock shelter. The Victrola perched crookedly, its coned speaker tilted like a curious dog, watching him.

"What are you looking at?"

It just stares, stupid and silent.

A few strides and he's cranking the thing. Picking up the needle. Placing it on the record, desperate for it to work. But the wood is warped from too many fog-drenched mornings, rain-soaked afternoons, freezing nights. Its song, gone.

The cracking inside him has webbed so far that it's stopped, and all that's left for him is to either crumble or explode. He presses his eyes shut and strains to hear reason. But all that comes is Roy's voice: *"You're a good man. Let me try to be one, too."*

The words kick him in the gut. He shoves the needle blindly across the record's ridges, feels it scratch and destroy. He steps away, and its silence mocks him.

Blind heat floods him. Shards of consciousness register him snapping a branch from an overhanging tree, wielding it like a bat. The splinter of the Victrola five times, ten. The wires inside the demolished box stringing its mangled parts together. Him gripping it, flinging it into the waves, the boil in Cauldron Cove matching his own. Him falling to his knees in the graveyard of stones he and Roy left behind the night they'd left their dares untossed. He grips one hard, sobs retching from him in silence.

A hand falls on his shoulder.

It is his mother, lantern in hand. She's dwarfed in his father's plaid flannel shirt over her nightgown. She looks at the scene before her, shrapnel. Kneels. Gathers up her one remaining son.

And together they weep.

nineteen

The days that follow are a haze. At any given time of any given day, there's a boat crossing the harbor from the village to Sailor's Rest or Jenny's cottage—bringing food, lugging tools, telling tales to bring a smile, offering handkerchiefs to dry tears. Some bring news from a newspaper in Bangor reporting of U-boats brought ashore just down the coast to Kittery. How this will change things, give the U.S. more victory, both now and in wars to come. Not that anyone can think of wars to come, when the one just ended is still so ravenous.

Robert stays close at hand, torn. He needs to get back to the sea if they're to have a harvest of lobster this year. But he's anchored here, for Jenny, for his ma, sensing hearts need more tending than lobster traps.

And one lobsterman or another begins to show up every few days with a stack of money. "From your traps," they say. Which makes no sense. His traps need mending, some unable to hold a catch. And these men have their own traps to mend and set and tend, need the money as much as anyone.

So he thanks them and tells them to keep it, but without fail, he later finds the dollars tucked under a rock, the welcome mat, hanging from a bait bag on a nail on the porch post.

Millicent, Jenny, Ma, Robert—not a one of them has lifted

a finger to cook a meal in days. Not for want of trying, but because every time any of them goes to open a cupboard, a knock sounds at the front door and they open it to find a basket-o'-this or a bushel-o'-that. Ma was going fair crazy with it, loving the hearts and gifts but itching to do something, too. She's taken to canning up blueberries, since everyone brought a pail of them "for a sweet treat."

They gather for meals each night at one house or the other, trying to swallow around the ache of the empty seat, finding strength in one another and the normalcy of the supper prayers.

They all struggle with how returning to anything resembling a normal duty seems like a betrayal. A taking part of life, moving on without Roy, of leaving him behind. And yet it has to be done.

I dare you to. Robert could picture Roy saying it. And so he takes to the sea one September morning. Stops off for bait at Melvin's boat, grateful Mel doesn't refuse payment. A man of few words, he must sense that this corner of normal—of paying for bait—is needed.

"Looks to be a good'n." Mel raises a nod to the horizon, where the sun is igniting a ceiling of clouds with fresh color.

Melvin's right. The sun is bright, the air is fresh. Bob knows his work will be cut out for him, his traps sitting untended for so long.

There's something blessedly hard about the work, pulling him out of his fog as he pulls the traps in. He passes islands where the summer people have departed when he wasn't looking, windows boarded and flags pulled in. Signs of life moving into a new season.

The chatter on the VHF radio does him good, too. He hasn't chimed in yet, to the talk of tides, and winds, and fog. He hears Arthur's voice crackle through with a warning about southward gusts.

It's good to hear his friend's voice. Arthur has stayed away, and Robert can only speculate as to why. Maybe he's giving them space, doesn't want to intrude. Or maybe it's something more. Something akin to the way Jenny won't look Robert in the eye anymore. He can't blame them, really. He's a walking reminder of the one who's not coming home, ever. He can barely look at his own reflection most days, for all it looks like Roy's.

He wonders, then, why it feels as if someone's punched the air straight out of him when he trolls his boat past Jenny's place on his way home that afternoon. There's a sharp pounding, hammer on nail, reverberating like gunfire. She's kneeling before a hand-painted sign. It's lovely, like everything Jenny touches—fresh white paint, clean black letters scrolling across it. Has she given the cottage a new name? He squints, finally close enough to read:

For Sale

He cuts his engine.

She pounds a final nail into the post at the end of her dock and stands. Turns to face him. Hair falling around her face from behind the white handkerchief holding it back, overalls spotted with paint. Eyes stained red when she looks at him, and for the first time in weeks, she doesn't look away.

They stand this way, eyes locked, waves lapping the boat closer to her. And before he knows it he's on the dock, boat tied up, eyes still locked with hers.

She swallows.

He looks at the sign again, and up close he sees how the letters' soft lines tremble. They are not from a steady hand. Lovely at a distance, but they have cost her dearly.

She hangs her head, clasps Roy's ring, which she wears on a simple string around her neck, next to her heart.

"I'm sorry, Robert," she says at last. It's the most she's said directly to him, just him, since the night he broke her world.

"You're . . . leaving."

She nods, looking over her shoulder. Her parents' old black Buick is up by the cottage, shining like the day her father brought it home ten years before. No one had ever had an automobile out that way before. Robert and Roy had spent that summer helping him chisel the harbor road wider up to their gate, cutting away bracken.

"My parents are taking us in," Jenny says. "Selling the place here. Things are good for them in Minnesota." She tries to muster a smile, pushes a note of optimism into her voice. "They've got a room for us."

Us.

Of course. William, too.

"Jenny . . ." His voice rasps. *Don't go.* His chest pounds with the two words. They're strings pulling from all directions. The quickening of his heart at the sight of her years ago, the letting go of her, the sight of Roy's child in her arms.

They pull and threaten to snap, and all he can say is . . . "Don't go." He feels the desperation in his eyes, sees her see it too, and miles of words are spoken between them in this silence.

She exhales slow through her lips. "Part of me will never leave here, Robert. Most of my heart, truth be told." She looks east to their island, shields her eyes with her hand. "But if we stay here to live," she says, "we won't live. We'll just . . . exist." She looks to the cottage, to her mother who's stepped outside with William on her hip, toting a suitcase to the car. "I owe Roy more than that. William, too."

Robert can feel a divide, some wall between them, as if she's drawing a line in the sand with her words—past and future—and they're standing right in between. He reaches for her through that wall, grasping for more time here on the line. And he does what he long dreamed of. Lifting a finger, he traces her jawline, cups her face. But it's different, so different than he ever imagined. In that touch, he knows right through him that his love for her is the love of a brother—the love he's strived for, schooled his heart for—and it is strong.

He ducks his head, uncertain what to do with that. "You've a place here always, Jenny."

She smiles, lines gentle around her mouth. It is foreign on her face, but it becomes her. "Maybe when we visit Aunt Millicent in Boston, you'll come see us." Something of the old Jenny flashes across her face. The mischief of days gone by. "You know how warm she is."

He laughs.

She stuffs her hands in her overall pocket and retrieves something, picks up his hand and places it in his palm, wraps his fingers around it.

"Roy's rock," she says. "He kept it. From the place he almost . . . from the place you saved him, in that storm when we were kids." She lets her hands remain there, hers wrapped around his wrapped around a piece of earth his brother pulled from darkness.

As she pulls her hands back, he turns the stone in his hand. Its russet surface is smoothed by the waves. "He went back for this?"

Jenny nods. "He told me he kept it . . . to remember what courage looked like."

That sounds like Roy. Even the kid version of him, an old soul.

"Courage," Robert says. "I wish he could tell me what that looks like." Robert could use a dose of that right about now.

Jenny tilts her head and takes in the sight of him. "You really don't know?"

"Know what?" The stone is warming in his hands.

"He said courage looked like you. Reaching out. Pulling him up. And he said that's what you'd always do, because it is just in you."

She puts a hand on his arm and gives a gentle squeeze. "I'm thankful you saved him that night, Robert. I always will be." The wind picks up, snatching her gaze away to the horizon. "You know Roy." She speaks of him in the present tense, and it feels good. "Do something remarkable with it, Robert Bliss." Those blue eyes pierce him, and he knows she's talking about the rock, but so much more, too.

He smiles. "Minnesota's got another thing comin' with you, Jenny Bliss."

She pulls her hands away, waves off his words. "We'll see."

When he leaves, promising to return later to see them off, he points the *Savvy Mae* home to Sailor's Rest. But the rock is heavy in his hand. Before he can think, he turns toward the island instead.

"Do something remarkable with it."

Ashore, he sheds his waders from on top of worn jeans, pulls on his saltwater boots, cinches up their leather laces, and hoofs to the top of the trail.

Something is stirring here. A rising up inside him.

He tosses the smooth stone in his hand. A step away is the graveyard of rocks he and Roy left. He picks one up, granite rough against his skin, catching light among its white flecks. He thinks of what it represents—life yet unlived, life Roy would have dared Robert to live if he'd been allowed to that night, before the war crashed into their island.

He picks another one up. And as though he's lifted a key, it's unlocking a memory. Looking into the USO dance, seeing the spotlights on the ceiling, the way they created beams and the couples danced through them. Light falling on soldier, sailor, captain, lieutenant. Each one lit, smiling as they pass through, dancing their way to the battle-streaked future they would soon face. Immeasurable courage beneath those smiles.

Three rocks now nestled in the crook of his arm, and he picks up another. It's as if he's picking up bread crumbs and they're leading him somewhere. He's stepped into some otherworld, and this thing leading him is no small force.

He sees a sea of sailor faces. This time standing erect in salute on the deck of the destroyer. He hears the measured, reverent gun volley, the lone trumpeter lifting his brass, last rays of sun gleaming in it as it lays his brother to rest with the somber notes of "Taps."

Shards from the Victrola dot the clearing, and he tries to think of the song it last played, but a different one floods his mind. His mother's singing the night she found Robert here, gathered him up, wept with him. He rowed her home that night, towing her boat behind them, slipping through those midnight waves with numb pain. And though they'd each gone to bed, he knew neither of them slept.

When first light began to ease the dark, he'd heard his mother's voice. She had a lovely voice, like silver—but that night it had been raked over grief. Yet the song she offered up was all the more beautiful in its wavering and brokenness. Courageous, an offering. The laying out of her broken heart before her God.

"'*On Christ the solid rock I stand, all other ground is sinking sand . . .*'"

Words reaching through her dark, gripping truths she could not see.

On the cliff top he continues until his arms are full of rocks. This gathering up makes no sense, and yet it makes all the sense in the world. It's an urging-on so strong and sure, he cannot dream of resisting. And so he continues, stone by stone, memory by memory. Each one a weaving of light, of rock, of sacrifice and strength, until he can carry no more.

He stands in the middle of the clearing. The ocean before him, the mountain wall of the island behind him.

"What now?"

He speaks the question and listens—and somewhere in between the cry of the gulls and the sound of the buoy bell in the distance, a single word is chiseled on his soul. Unmistakable.

Build.

He listens, strains to hear more. But that's all there is. He sets the stones down in a neat pile, steps back. Plants his fists at his sides and considers them, the lives, the light. *"There's a whole lotta light,"* Roy had said. *"Go there instead."*

He knows what to do.

He crosses the clearing to the overhang where he and Roy kept their chest of tools and boyhood loot. Its aged wood is stenciled with block letters—*INE TEA*. They'd always joked about the missing letter *f*—that *ine tea* must be a step down from *fine tea*. Sliding the lid off, he pulls out an old notebook. It's warped, the pages dimpled from fog and time, but it is here, and that's all that matters. He brings out a pencil, sharpens it with his pocketknife. Words begin to line up, pour right through, like someone turned on a faucet and he's just trying to catch them. They're not his, not really, he's just the one scratching them out.

Several lines in, he stops. Pushes his eyebrows together. *Living? Giving?* It rhymes. *Oh, brother.*

And on cue his brother's voice pipes up from the past. *"Rhymes won't kill you."*

Robert shakes his head, lets out a dry laugh, continues on. And when three short verses have spilled themselves, he rips the paper out and takes it straight back across the harbor. He marches into the square, over to the newspaper office of *The Pier Review.* It's locked. Before he can stop himself, he slips that paper through the mail slot and doesn't look back.

Late that night, sleep eludes him once again, and he begins to replay the whole string of events. It's as though he was in a trance, and he can't deny that something beyond himself was leading, guiding. He was nothing more than an instrument. And that single word—*build*—tells him he's going to have to keep on being an instrument. For a long while, maybe. With any luck, Gus will run his words—a call for rocks, a way to honor Ansel's fallen sons—in the town paper. And in a few weeks, maybe a few months, this will all be over. An anonymous poem, a small island lighthouse to build—a way for the lives given to continue to shine on, save others.

It's a simple plan.

And it will all be finished soon.

twenty

If townspeople were soldiers, Ansel's residents would be the innocently masquerading guard of the most classified secrets. Pulling the door shut behind her as she leaves the Bait, Tackle, and Books, Annie is convinced that, though this town may have quaint streets and endearing people—the makings of a modern-day Mayberry—that was only one side of it. In secret, she was sure, they'd linked arms in some indelible promise to guard Bob's story at all costs.

Everywhere she goes, she is met with smiles . . . until she brings up Bob's poem or the ruins on the island—which apparently are *growin's*. Though from her place on Jeremiah's boat when they pass each morning on the way to the hospital, they look for all the world like the ancient, crumbling ruins of a castle.

Pulling her hair back into a ponytail, she savors a breeze cooling the surprising heat of early June. There's hope in the air—perhaps sown by the doctor's encouraging words about Bob this morning. His vitals are good, returning to a steadiness, and the doctor spoke of weaning him from the medication to see if he wakes from his coma.

She's standing in the middle of a puzzle of her great-uncle's life, praying she can put some pieces together and have something warm to welcome him home with when the time comes. His rusting key burns a hole in her pocket, cinching urgency around her mission.

With no one willing to shed light on any of her questions, she's left with one hope—that the land will speak where the people will not.

That afternoon, she summons all her courage and every bit of boat know-how she can pull from the recesses of her mind. She fastens a life vest around herself—a hundred decibels of screaming orange—unties Bob's old rowboat from its place bobbing at the dock, climbs down the ladder, and hops in, telling herself every step of the way that she is not stepping into a great abyss. She is simply stepping into a lovely wooden vessel that will skim over waves and bring her the answers she needs. Molecules, she reminds herself. She dips her oars in, closes her eyes, and pulls with all her might.

Something's wrong. Her eyes fly open, to see the dock post fast approaching. Her pulse hammers and she quick reverses the direction of her oars.

"Rookie," she mutters, rowing hard until she's a safe distance away. From there, it's a tug-of-war between her and the sea, as she feels her way into some semblance of maneuvering this vessel. When she finally hits a rhythm, winded and muscles burning, she feels a surge of pride. She, Annie Bliss, the confirmed landlubber, is *at sea*. Just her and the waves, and she's sure she can manage at least five more minutes of this rowing. Surely that will be enough to get her to Bob's island.

A soft wind slows her, and she turns back to see how far she is from shore.

There, not fifteen feet away, is Sailor's Rest.

She lays the oars over her lap, hangs her head, and laughs at herself.

The rumble of an engine draws close. The *Glad Tidings*, coming in to dock.

Annie's face heats, and she digs her oars back in, rowing as hard as she can toward the island, trying to make it look like this is a breeze. But she knows the struggle must be painfully apparent.

The engine cuts as the *Glad Tidings* drifts closer to her.

"Need a ride?" Jeremiah looks like he's straight off the page of an L.L.Bean catalog, hair blowing and eyes narrowing against the sun. Meanwhile, her ponytail is slipping down the side of her head, and she prays the sweat accumulating on her forehead doesn't choose this moment to cascade down her face.

"I'm fine, thanks." She keeps rowing.

"Where are you headed?"

"Just . . . out." More words would take more breath, breath she does not have.

He looks from her to where her boat is pointed. He disappears, then re-appears with a bright orange bundle under his arm. "Take this, then." He tosses it down to her and she catches it, unrolling what appears to be some sort of deflated diver's suit.

"What is it?"

"Survival Suit. You go any farther in that thing"—he circles a finger around Bob's rowboat—"and you're going to need it."

Ugh. The word *survival* pummels her, and she rolls the suit back up. Everything in her wants to just keep on rowing, to prove she can do this. But if she can't reach the island . . . well, that thought wins out over her pride.

"You sure you wouldn't mind? You've been carting me all over for days now, and—"

"Get in."

Once the rowboat's been hauled back ashore and Annie's on board the *Glad Tidings*, she wishes she'd just asked him to begin with.

"Where to?"

Annie pulls the key out of her pocket, runs her thumb over its scratches—praying she's bringing it back to its home. "Bob's island."

The island is unlike most of the others in the harbor. Not flat or with easy rises, it is more akin to a mountain right there in the sea. A small one, but still. Sheer granite makes finding a place to anchor difficult. They circle it twice, and Jeremiah gets as close as he can without endangering his boat. He points to a bench with a hinged top over near the stern, and she follows his instructions for pulling out and inflating the life raft inside. Together, they paddle ashore and find themselves on a small, rocky beach leading to an overgrown trail . . . guarded by a chain-link fence. A splintered piece of plywood proclaims *No Trespassing*. The gate is locked with a simple padlock.

The fence, the sign, the lock . . . Annie reminds herself that Bob left her this key. If it fits, it's an invitation.

She hopes.

Annie lifts the padlock, letting the weight of its small form fill her palm and thrill her soul. This little mechanism is what stands between her and so many answers . . . or so many questions.

Jeremiah stays silent, perhaps sensing that this moment means much to her. Annie lifts her key, inserts it into the lock, closes her eyes . . . and turns.

Click.

Its inside mechanism releases, unseen. The lock itself takes some coaxing, having sat for who knew how long, but soon she is removing it entirely and tugging the gate open as it scrapes over the rocky earth.

Heart pounding, smile overtaking her face, she turns to Jeremiah. "Shall we?"

They step through the fence and, without a word, begin the climb up the path. Long grasses and weeds brush against Annie's knees, as if whispering *hush . . . hush . . .* in sacred anticipation.

They reach the crest and enter a clearing. A fire ring lies cold, old coals nestled black at the base of the grasses trying to take over. A wooden box is tucked with care under a small rock outcropping, and an old ladder leans against the granite wall that backs this place.

She treads with care, overwhelmed by the feeling that she's slipping into a slumbering story.

And then she sees it. Or rather, she steps into its shadow and feels it. The cool of its looming shade, the call of its mortared seams.

A tower, there between the clearing and the cliff. Stones in every hue, nestled together as if they have been carved with care to fit one another's crevices. Rising cylindrical, like a turret right before her.

"Oh . . . my."

Jeremiah draws near, his presence warm in the shadow. "Whoa."

They stand together, wrapped in the place where words have no use.

A doorway, arched and empty, yawns with shrouded invitation. She shivers. It's the same feeling she got when standing in the ruins of Rievaulx Abbey in England during her semester abroad. This sense that time stretches so far beyond her, the walls holding life and a thousand tales.

Only these aren't ruins. They are growing. She sees it now. In place of the telltale piles of crumbling rocks lying here and there amongst ruins, here there are small groupings upon the ground. Rocks placed like jigsaw pieces, laid out in preparation for their addition to the tower.

The growin's.

But . . . what are they? Whatever they are, the "growing" seems to have come to a standstill some time ago. She steps forward, and Jeremiah steps back. He's headed toward the alcove, and she can almost hear his mind clicking with questions and theories.

But for her, there is no room for the hypotheses hammering to get into her consciousness. Not amid this stirring beckoning her in.

With caution, she moves to the doorway and stands on the dividing line of darkness and light. Looking in, she gives her eyes a moment to adjust and, shadow by shadow, begins to make out more of this giant mosaic. Round walls, a staircase of the same patchwork stone winding round and round against the inner wall. At the top, the sky beams in as through a long telescope. No ceiling. A makeshift wooden platform, with a wishing-well-type wooden roof, but open otherwise.

A single leaf drifts in on a breeze, spiraling down through the shafts of light as Annie stands there in the center of it all.

"What is this place?" she asks, and her voice echoes against the damp walls.

"Annie?" Jeremiah calls, excitement in his voice.

She turns and nearly collides with him. He's carrying the wooden box she'd seen in the alcove.

"You need to see this," he says. His eyes spark as he sets the box on a nearby boulder and carefully lifts the lid.

At first it looks like any boy's treasure trove. A stub of a pencil sharpened roughly with a pocketknife. An old Dick Tracy comic book. A pad of paper . . . and a rolled up, larger piece of paper. Jeremiah takes it out and hands it to Annie.

It's yellowed, rigid. Unrolling it gingerly, she spreads it out on the flat top of the boulder. Jeremiah stoops and grabs four stones, placing them on the corners.

And together, they stare at what appear to be precise hand-drawn blueprints. For a tower, yes—but there, at the top, is the answer.

A lens. Like a glass crown topping the tower, transforming it into . . .

"A lighthouse." They both speak it, hushed.

Jeremiah pulls something more from the box. A scrap of newspaper, most of it scorched away, the edge blackened and still smelling of smoke. Gothic print reads *PIER* before it drops away into nothingness, and a few lines of print read:

> So send your rocks
> And raise your hearts
> And set to the work—

There it stops, the rest of it consumed by flame in a black jagged edge. Annie's breath swells within her, too big for her lungs. "Is this . . . Bob's poem?"

Jeremiah slips his hand behind hers, so they're both holding it. "There's one way to find out," he says.

twenty-one

The Pier Review building is locked, a hand-printed sign hanging on the window reading *Closed. No News Is Good News.* Jeremiah fishes in his pocket for a quarter and goes into the pay phone on the corner of the square. It is a relic. Three walls of paned glass, framed with chipped black paint. It's missing its door, and Jeremiah exits after only a few seconds. "The editor's not answering his phone."

Annie plants her hands on her hips, turning to survey the buildings about. All closed so late in the day. But there is one light on, there, above Starboard Home Realty.

"Spencer T. Ripley."

"What?" Jeremiah's shoulders square. "No. Not him."

She faces him. "I can't think of any other Robert Bliss poetry experts who just happen to be in the neighborhood. . . ."

Silence pounds a path to Jeremiah's next words. "You're right." And without meeting her eyes, he gestures for her to lead the way.

Spencer's "flat," as he calls it, is a tiny apartment with barely enough room for the three of them. Especially with his stacks of binders and books, which make it look as if he's bent on establishing a second library in town.

The look on his face when Annie asks about the poem is that of sun breaking through sky.

"Robert Bliss's poem?" His enthusiasm pushes out a laugh. "You mean the poem that changed the tide of the nation? The words that transformed grief into hope? The poem that's—"

"Pretty sure that's the one we mean," Jeremiah says.

"I'm sorry." Spencer waves his hand in disbelief. "It's just that when it comes to poetry—war poetry, especially—this is . . . it's a phenomenon. You know the photo of the sailor kissing the nurse in Times Square on V-J Day?"

Annie nods. They'd studied it in her cultural anthropology class freshman year.

"Bob's poem is that. I mean—printed just as many times, known just as well. For a time. But where that photo captured the jubilee of that day, his poem caught the broken hearts that followed the war and gave them a place to go. A purpose for their pain."

Annie swallows, already knowing the answer to her next question. "Do you . . . happen to have a copy of the full poem?"

He laughs again, pulling out two of his binders from the stack near the front door.

He lays them on the round table and taps them. "And that's just the start."

Just the start? What is it, an epic ballad?

Her hand shakes slightly as she opens the first binder.

A clipped column of newsprint is held with black corner fasteners to the middle of the page, and the heading of the paper itself fills the rest of the page. *The Pier Review*, out of Ansel-by-the-Sea, Maine. Three humble stanzas line up:

LIGHTHOUSE

By: Anonymous

So send your rocks
And raise your hearts

And set to the work of living.
For the joy and the loss,
the gold and the dross—
The lives who were lost, still giving.

Stone upon stone,
strength upon strength,
Their courage shall rise from the sea.
Where their lives, at the shore,
Are igniting once more
To light the way home fearlessly.

And in the light . . .
At last, at last . . .
In the light, at last, there is life.

To honor a fallen soldier and help build a lighthouse to bring others home, send a rock in their memory to: Postmaster, Ansel-by-the-Sea, Maine.

Annie looks at Jeremiah. Jeremiah looks at Annie. Between them, the vision of the tower they've just come from rises up, understanding beginning to spark.

Her pulse skitters around the implications.

She tries to find words . . . but can't.

Jeremiah turns the page. The same poem, printed in a Connecticut paper a week later. She flips to the next page—New Hampshire. *Flip.* New York. *Flip.* Boston. On and on, all the way west to California and south to Texas, Florida. Everywhere beyond and between. 1945. 1946, '47. 1951, along with a clipping about the Korean War. 1965—Vietnam. The clippings grow sparser as the decades grow more recent but continue on into the '80s. The '90s, with Desert Storm.

Annie's heart is in her throat, wet heat stinging her eyes as she traces a clipping from 1981.

"Hard to believe, isn't it?" Bent over the paper, Spencer pushes his glasses farther up on his nose. "That something could continue to be reprinted for so long. Viral, before that was even a-a thing." He grimaces at his slip into casual language. "A phenomenon."

Across the table, Jeremiah watches with a look beyond just the wonder of the poem.

He's not looking at the binder. He's looking at her.

"Annie?"

She sniffs, feeling all manner of tangled up. Frozen on this clipping from 1981—Beirut.

"It's nothing," she says, and forces the binder closed. It feels like it weighs a hundred pounds.

"Wait." Spencer's voice is excited, hushed. "Wait until you see. . . . Now, where did I put that other portfolio? One moment . . ."

He wanders from the room, leaving Annie and Jeremiah—and the countless lives they're beholding in this moment.

Jeremiah has not budged, still studying her. Only compassion on his features, stoic though they are. Haltingly, he slides his hand across the table until it's next to hers, where she still grips the corner of the binder.

He takes hold of the cover, letting his thumb slide next to hers.

"What is it?" His voice is low. Inviting trust.

She lifts her eyes to his, and despite her steely resolve not to crack . . . the wetness in her eyes brims over, drops. Right into his hand, which he lifts to dry her face.

His touch is strong. Gentle.

Let him in. Something inside nudges her. Only it's more than a nudge.

Pulling in a deep breath, she opens back to the clipping about Beirut, taps it twice, pulling the cuffs of her sweater up over her hands.

"This . . . this is when my dad was there, in Beirut. And I was here." When she'd stood on Bob's dock, slipping her hand into his weathered one, understanding only that the great blue sea before her had taken her parents far, far away. Not realizing that at that very moment, Bob's boathouse was filling with rocks. Rocks that represented lives lost. Lives that could so easily have been her parents'. *"Every wave in that big old blue sea is a story,"* he'd said.

How little she'd understood then. How she is only barely beginning to skim the surface now.

Spencer enters the room again, attention on a document in his hand. Jeremiah's attention is still on her. Slowly, he releases her hand as she tries to focus on what the scholar is saying.

"Here," Spencer says. "The one that changed it all." He hands her a few pages.

Annie's eyes skim the page of tiny print. *TIME* magazine, 1947. *BUILDING THE LEGACY OF A NATION*, the headline reads. In smaller print, a subtitle: *Fisherman-Poet Robert Bliss gives hope to a country from the rocky shores of Maine, building a lighthouse one stone at a time.*

Annie's breath catches. The opposite page is a full photo of a young man. Shadows and light caught in time to capture an image of the previously anonymous poet. He looks off over the sea, one hand at his side, wrapped around a single stone. A universe of stories in his eyes—stories that had lain silent now, for years.

Unspoken words that she holds the key to.

twenty-two

A week after the Words came to Robert, they run in *The Pier Review*. He can only call it "the Words," for he cannot bring himself to call it a poem. It's not his fault the Words went and stacked themselves up in syllables, fell into lines and stanzas like soldiers into ranks.

The day it runs in the paper, he feels the way it follows him like a shadow—the fellas giving him furtive glances at the landing, Mrs. Stevens studying him as she serves him his plateful of Gretel cakes, her young daughter, Bess, peeking at him from the kitchen. They know it's him. It isn't hard to figure in this town no bigger than a bushel basket. But no one gives him any rocks.

The second day, he stays away from town. Still no rocks.

And the third day, Sunday, he slaps courage back into himself and goes to church. Ansel is on a loop with other small towns up in this corner of the country, where preachers only visit twice a month. Services, then, are twice the occasion, to make up for occurring only half the time. His mother should not have to sit alone, on top of everything else she's lost. Savannah Bliss is a strong woman—of that there is no doubt—but there's a stiff sort of protection that now rises in him when it comes to her. He and

202

AMANDA DYKES

she, half of the family they once were, carrying on with these phantom pains, glancing down the pew where Dad and Roy should be.

So he goes to church, and he sits. The visiting preacher continues through the book of Luke, and he's talking of the young donkey brought for Jesus. The disciples sent on this errand that surely seemed nonsensical to them, except for one thing—their King instructed it.

The preacher speaks of the way Jesus rode the creature down the Mount of Olives. At the base of that mountain just days later, darkest betrayal would deliver Him unto death, but as Jesus rode into Jerusalem, the people rejoiced with everything in them. The preacher asked the congregation to imagine how His heart broke wide open at the sight of the city that would soon endure much pain.

The peoples' complete outpouring, loud and jubilant in their praise of the miracles they have seen, made no sense to the Pharisees—they told Him to stop them.

Robert's ears pound with the rush of blood, for he knows what is coming. And then the pastor speaks it. "'I tell you . . . if these should hold their peace'"—more pounding in Robert's head, in his heart—"'the stones would immediately cry out.'"

The rest of the sermon is a blur. Robert tries to fix his mind upon it, but it's as if there's a foundation being constructed beneath him. Strength to stand upon, and he wonders if this is what God did for Noah, whose task was of significance ten-thousand fold more than his. A task that seemed downright crazy on the surface.

After the sermon, he's the first one out into the sunlight. People trickle out, lingering as they always do. Swapping recipes, swapping condolences. He stands in the shadows of a pine cluster, waiting for whenever his mother is ready.

And then there's a tug at his jacket. He looks down to see little Lainey Foster, face smudged with adventure and dirt, just like her Sunday frock. Wide brown eyes peer up at him, and she lifts a hand toward his.

He pushes off from the tree he was leaning against, kneels down, and takes what she offers.

And the weight of it—the warmth it's absorbed from her hands—takes his breath.

"It's for my daddy," she says. "Mama says it's a 'memberin' rock."

"A *remembering rock*." He turns her words in his mouth, her rock in his hand. She's said in two words what his clumsy rhymes took an eternity to say.

At a distance, her mother looks on, dressed in a coat of crimson, one hand to her mouth, fingers curled, the other holding the hand of Lainey's younger brother.

"So, can you take care of it?" The girl bends to pick up a pinecone, and another, bunching her hands around them. Ready to carry her next load to the next place, wherever that might be.

"Yes," Robert says. "Your daddy was a brave man, Lainey. Just like you're a brave girl."

"Okay," she says, and turns to go, shouting over her shoulder as her curls bounce to her run, "Thanks, mister!"

He stands, and raises a hand solemnly to Mrs. Foster, thanking her. For the rock, and so much more.

She nods, tears in her eyes, then takes the pinecone Lainey is thrusting toward her.

———

The next day, it's Lainey's little face in his memory that urges him on to the post office. He worries he won't get any more rocks—or maybe there won't be enough. What had he been thinking? A lighthouse? It's going to take a lot of rocks. Why hadn't he stopped to calculate, before going and printing those words? And what did he know of finding a light source for such a thing? But Lainey, her untainted gift of the rock, drives him on. Maybe there will be a package or two today.

Jim pokes his head out from the back room of the post office. "'Bout time!"

"Got somethin' for me, Jim?"

"Ayuh. But you got me in a pickle, son."

"How so?"

"You wrote that article"—*poem* isn't in Jim's vocabulary, either, it seems—"and didn't sign your dumb name to it, and now these boxes are comin' here without a name, and I can't bring 'em your way."

"What makes you think it was me?"

"Where do you think you live, son?"

"I hoped no one would figure it out," Robert mutters.

"The whole town knows it was you. We might as well have had front row seats when you were writin' it. If you don't want me to use your name, what do you want me to call you? Ansel Number Four Hundred and Fifty-Four?"

"Fine by me."

"Follow me, *Robert*." He gestures him back.

Ansel number 454 follows Jim into the back room, where there are thirteen packages stacked up behind the back door. Each addressed simply to *Postmaster*. The return addresses are, as he expects, from nearby towns—Machiasport, Cutler, Jonesboro. People close enough to have *The Pier Review* passed on to them by daily gabfests around town.

Jonesboro seems a bit far for word-of-mouth, but Mainers always did surprise him with the lengths they sometimes took things. Maybe he'd get a few from as far as Bangor, perhaps even Beals Island and Bar Harbor in time.

Jim pulls out a pocketknife. "May as well open 'em. Regulations say the recipient has to open them. That's me, unfortunately. But then you'd better believe you'll be hauling these away, young sir."

One by one they open the packages, each one containing a stone. Some the size of a fist, some half as big, some twice so. But what socks the air out of Robert is what else they contain.

Pictures. Men, most right about his age, smiling proudly in their uniforms. Names, written on the back. Histories, tributes. With one, the story of a man who went back, and back, and back, at Omaha Beach, to deliver soldiers in a U-boat. The beginnings of D-Day, his courage a cornerstone of that fate-altering day. A turning point in the war, without which the next stone's story may never have been told.

It is from V-E Day. A young American soldier in Paris, writing in a letter to his wife, telling of the streets filled with dancing. How every streetlight was turned on, after so much darkness. *It seemed good to see all the light. . . .*

And a man from Germany who came to America as a child. Faced with the challenge to use the language of his youth as a shield for his brothers-in-arms. Wielding words to draw German troops from their bunkers, without a single shot fired. Had it not been for his words, many lives would have been lost that day.

These are the stitches in the stone fabric. Each one connected to the next. These are the faces that tie themselves inextricably to these stones, and in doing so, give them life. That day, and in the many to come, Robert retrieves them—boxes already opened by Jim's trusty pocketknife—from the back door to the storage room at the post office, to his boat.

Land over sea the earth moves, rock by rock in the boat. Onto the island, these bits of others' worlds, and into their place in a great jigsaw puzzle in the clearing. It is here that Robert at last draws up a rough set of plans and begins to piece these broken lives together, each one with a prayer. And each one, with Roy's voice urging him on with his dying refrain: *"There's a whole lotta light."*

Months pass this way. The boxes coming in spades, postmarks from farther and farther away. He places the pictures and stories inside the boathouse, not sure what to do with them, how to rightfully honor them. And with the rocks, he builds. Nights, mostly. When he's pulled in his lobster haul for the day, washed the sea away, he rows to the island and works again until his eyelids burn with fatigue and his muscles rail against the strain . . . his soul taking flight with it.

Nigh on a year later, some paper down in St. Louis runs the poem, and goes and sticks Bob's name on it. *By Robert Bliss.* A reporter there knew someone in Georgia who knew someone in Ansel who knew the guarded identity of "Anonymous." The infernal transcontinental gossip chain found him out.

Bob hates it. He did not want to be known. Did not even write the words, really. He was only the hands.

The Saint Louis article brings rocks in a flurry for a while, but months later he looks at his dwindling pile of rocks and a tied-up sort of empty settles deep in his stomach—he needs more, so many more, to make this light reach high and far. Yet he does not want more, for he knows what they signify.

So he waits.

And part of him, still cursing that old gossip chain, begins to bless it when a reporter from *TIME* magazine shows up on his island one summer afternoon in 1947, wanting to interview him, to run a feature on the lighthouse that gave hope to a nation.

"You're a real legend, you know." The man in his plaid sports coat and bowler hat says, his shiny oxfords scuffed over with island dust.

Bob keeps working, keeps spreading mortar, piecing rocks together. "They are the legends," he says, pointing at the tower.

"Many a-folk would be much obliged to know more about the man behind the tower." The reporter draws a notebook out of his coat pocket, pen poised. "Can you tell me about him?" This reporter's sharp. Walking around things, referring to Bob like he's someone else not present. Weaseling his way in, really.

Bob stands beside the scant rocks remaining to be placed. Any other time, he'd run this guy off, and the man would never look back. But . . . he needs the rocks.

"Nope," he says at last.

The reporter just waits, like that'll make Bob change his mind.

"But I'll tell you about them." He gestures toward the tower. "The men. Their families."

The reporter taps the pad with his pen. "Deal."

"One more thing," Bob says.

"Lay it on me."

Bob lifts his chin toward the camera hanging around the man's neck. "No pictures. Not of me."

They shake on it, and three hours later, with the sun going down and the reporter's hands crusted with the mortar he stooped to help apply as they talked, the man leaves. With a notepad full of tales . . . and the stolen click of a camera, last thing before he hoofs it down the mountain trail.

Bob would loathe that picture in the months to come. He'd stash away the copies the people from town brought him when it was printed, biting back all the choice words he had for that reporter. Ansel was happy. They felt honored, somehow. Maybe even . . . proud? But Bob ducked beneath all that, thankful at least for the new influx of deliveries that came, and came in abundance—and even came by hand one Saturday afternoon.

Heat scorches and sun blinds as he works on the island. Footsteps sound on the path.

"Well, Mr. Robert Bliss," a voice says, a voice like music. Feminine and strong, with a story to tell. "I'd say names are quite the most unnecessary contrivances that ever were, but I'll tell you something. If I'd have known a year ago that the nameless fisherman building a lighthouse was none other than *you* . . ."

He stands, staring into the harsh sun. Before him is the silhouette of a woman. It can't be.

"Eva . . ." He clears his throat, unable to take his eyes from her as she steps into clearer view. "Miss . . . Rothford."

She picks up a stone from the ground, and he is tempted to kiss her for the way she handles it. With care, tenderness.

"That's Eva, to you," she says. She's different than when they met in Boston. The same strength—that spark igniting her—but different. She's wearing denim pants and a plain white blouse, for one thing, and a sky-blue kerchief with some kind of small flower print over her head. It makes her eyes sing blue and her cheeks glow pink. There's a quiet resolve, steely yet free, settled in her.

"Oh, don't worry." She sees the way he's noticed her clothes. "I've got other clothes. Better ones."

What is she talking about? Her dress, from that night?

"This, for one." She pulls a jacket from where it's looped over her arm. Worn wool that he knows too well, so many winters did it rest on his own shoulders. "A mariner loaned it to me more than a year ago on a snowy night in Boston. I hope he won't mind if I—"

"He won't."

She pauses, her smile growing. "Good." She takes a step forward. "And I have coveralls now, you know. They're just the best things. Ever tried them? They gave them to us in the welding shop."

"The welding shop."

"Oh, yes. After the rendezvous with the bumper—"

"Fender." He turns the joke on her, can feel mischief lace between them.

"After the rendezvous with the *bumper* . . ." She stands her ground. "My mother feared for the fate of their Art Nouveau balustrades—iron, you know—and convinced my father to let me contribute to the war in less . . . creative ways."

"I wrote to you," he says. It's a statement, and a question. She'd never replied. Not to the first letter . . . or the second . . . or the third . . . or the fourth. A man had to take a hint at some point.

"You wrote to a lot of people, it seems." She takes something from her back pocket, unfolds it. The *TIME* article.

He steps closer. "You didn't write back."

"You met my father." Her eyes are wide, sincere, but laughing. "One does not always receive one's post in the House of Rothford." Her turn to step closer. She smells of sweet peas. The sun lands on a stray wisp of hair, and he wills his arm down to keep from reaching out and touching it right then.

"I . . . should have gone to find you, regardless."

She looks to the tower. To him. To the article. "It would seem you've been busy, Mr. Anonymous." She winks, but there's a sadness there, too. An understanding of all that has happened, all he's lost.

209

Waves crash, and the sun sinks lower, birds striking up their evening chatter.

"Well," she says, inhaling and planting her hands on her hips, looking to the horizon. "It looks like we're losing daylight, mariner. Put me to work."

"You mean to stay?"

"If you'll have me." She bites her lip. It's the first crack in this cloak of confidence she wears, and she stands before him in an offering of vulnerability.

Suddenly they have switched. Instead of him awaiting her permission to help haul her bumper to a war-bound pile of metal, she awaits his invitation to help him build these stones into a battle-born tower of hope.

If you'll marry me. He bites the words back. They're reckless, even for him. There is more learning, knowing, unfolding of hearts before such words are fitting.

But when he opens his hand to hers, and she slips hers in as if it was tailored for this very moment . . . he knows he will not be able to hold those words back for long.

twenty-three

The morning after she learned of the history behind GrandBob's poem and tower, Annie could think of little else besides picking up the building of his tower. As soon as it opened, she entered the general store at Joe's Landing and left minutes later with mortar and trowel. When Jeremiah spotted her from across the green, he'd shaken his head, pulled that half grin of his into a dimple, and disappeared, only to return ten minutes later with tools to match hers. Every night for the past week, they had climbed that island trail and set to work repairing stray stones, piecing together where Bob left off, the whole time, an idea brewing.

It had taken her three days to work up the courage to confide it to Jeremiah, and two more days of him convincing her to bring it to the next town meeting.

So here she stands. Facing down the microphone in the library, with Spencer T. Ripley poised to take notes and Margie Lillian sitting before her like a force to be reckoned with. It's been a bad start. Her three minutes nearly up, she leaves her post and distributes slices of hazelnut pie—complete with Great-Grandma Savannah's "true Southern crust." The room falls blessedly, horridly silent and she continues.

211

"So you see . . ." She holds her hands out, wishing she had a chart, a graph, or some other visual aid to direct their attention to. But all she has are her open hands. "If we run a ferry to the island during Lobsterfest, it may pique enough interest to start bringing in more steady visitors for the rest of the summer. We can share some of the pictures and stories, the article from *TIME*, and let people find which stones match to which stories."

Margie Lillian chews her pie, eyes narrowed. Scrutinizing every angle of her plan. "All due respect, Miss Bliss. Please help me understand how, exactly, you think we can market a pillar of rocks as a tourist destination. No offense, of course. It's just . . . the growin's have lain abandoned for years now. We have public safety to consider. And frankly, I am concerned the hoopla will detract from the rest of the weekend, keep people out to sea when they could be spending money on shore. They might come to see a lighthouse, but with no light . . ." She shakes her head, letting Annie draw her own conclusions.

Her stomach clenches. These worries, and so many others, had nearly kept her at home this evening, shackled by memories of Alpenzell. She had a long list of ways this could hurt the town, rather than help them. Not to mention . . . how would Bob feel? She'd kneaded these worries as she rolled pie dough earlier that afternoon, and if not for the warmth of that pie in her hands, she might well have stayed silent tonight.

Face flushed, she looks around. Rich is examining his pie, nodding in appreciation. Has he heard a word she'd said? She could really use a vocal, business-savvy ally right about now.

Ed and Sully are seated across the aisle from each other, each of them refusing to acknowledge the other.

Jeremiah is seated in back, hat in hands, elbows on his knees, watching intently. He gives her a nod, encouraging.

Margie speaks up. "Should we have Jeremiah Fletcher come speak on your behalf?"

Annie's face burns. A quick glance shows Jeremiah's tall form, as still as possible, eyes wide as he gives her a shrug. Is he actually considering joining her? But Shirley the nurse had said he hated public speaking.

He leans forward, hands on knees, as if readying himself to join her, his face afire. Would he really do this?

"No," Annie says quickly. She won't ask it of him. Not after all he's already given. "Thank you." She flashes him a smile, then presses on. "Those are all valid concerns. I've drawn up a plan that reduces risk—keeping tours short, running them only a few times during the weekend. This would be a way to test the waters, so to speak. I don't have answers for all of your insightful questions"— she purses her lips—"but one thing I do know." Her pulse pounds with this truth that feels too big for her own life. "Drastic change requires drastic change. If Ansel is struggling, I can't help feeling it's worth it to try."

Remembering what a refuge this town had been for her, her passion starts to climb, reaching the heights of her fear—threatening to overtake that fear. "People need Ansel. I've heard it termed a hurricane hole, and I think that element of refuge extends far beyond literal storms."

Margie gives a thoughtful nod. She, as harbormaster, knows more than anyone how ships seek out this little pocket harbor for safety.

Annie makes a last-ditch effort to convince her. "A whole world of examples is waiting on that island."

"Time's up, Miss Bliss. This is a rather sudden request to decide on, with the festival commencing in only a few days, but we'll take it under consideration." She glances at the clock and concludes the meeting, saying they'll all need to turn their attention to the Movies in the Harbor event tonight. Something akin to a drive-in theater, but for boats, with an oversized screen erected at Joe's Landing.

Annie looks for Jeremiah, but he's vanished.

Outside in the early evening, the smell of popcorn drifts from The Galley, where the dining room is dark but a light glows from the kitchen.

"Nice speech." Sully draws up next to Annie, walking with her toward The Galley.

There's no sarcasm in her direct voice, and with what little she knows about Sully, Annie has no doubt the woman would have no reservations telling her straight out if she disagreed with her.

"Thank you," she says. It's unexpected encouragement, a balm to her still-quivering heart.

"I didn't know about the lighthouse." Sully's voice is thoughtful.

Annie laughs. "That makes two of us. It's hard to keep something a secret in Ansel."

Sully hoots. "That's the truth!" They walk in companionable silence a few steps, and Annie thinks of the woman living alone on her island, about the light that so irked her.

"Would you like to join me for coffee, Sully?"

She looks hesitant.

"I'd love to hear more about your time on the mountain." Annie hopes the invitation will entice her and is pleased when Sully gives a silent nod.

The Galley is closed, but she wants to check in on Bess, see if she can help, and she bets Bess won't mind them using two of her mugs if Annie can drum up the coffee.

Turns out she's right. Bess is busy popping popcorn for the show and doesn't mind them using the stools for a chat. Piping hot mugs before them, Annie nudges the bowl of creamer Sully's way.

"How's your garden?" she asks, before pulling in a sip of cream-laden coffee.

"Not about to win any awards," Sully says. "But I think I've got some carrots coming up, and that's something at least."

Annie smiles, wondering if she has any right to intrude but hating the fact she holds knowledge that might bring some good to this courageous woman's life.

As if reading her thoughts, Sully gulps down her sip and opens up her heart. "Tell you the truth, it's a mite lonesome out there. You wouldn't think it, me living up on the mountain so long. But

I lived there with my husband the past two decades of it. Late bloomers, both of us. When he passed on, he left me this old estate, and I started to get some hints that an old woman like me was more a hindrance out there in the wilderness than a help." She shakes her head, letting Annie fill in the rest.

"You're hardly an old woman," Annie says. "You've got more spunk and grit in you than most twenty-somethings back in the city." She laughs. "Including me."

"Now that's not true." Sully halts the thought with an open hand. "They can do a thousand things I can't. And I saw the way you lit up when you talked about that light tower tonight. That's really something." She sighs. "Guess it's just the solitude that gets to me. I feel it more in that empty house on the water than I did on the mountain."

This is it. The window she's been watching for. "Sully . . . if I may . . ."

"Oh, spit it out, girl. Not much can offend this old bird."

She takes a deep breath. "That light. On Ed's island?"

"That infernal thing! At least he finally took it down. I—"

"Did you ever wonder why he might have it there?"

"Of course I did. Why does a blind man need a light? But I couldn't come right out and say that to him, could I?"

"Maybe he sees a whole lot more than he lets on." Annie repeats Jeremiah's words, hoping Sully might pick up on some of the bread crumbs she's dropping. "A light appearing right about when you did? A light facing the island of a newcomer who lives alone, out there where he knows just how isolating island life can be . . . ?"

Sully is growing antsy on her stool. She stirs her spoon in her coffee, agitating the black surface of it.

"It's a sign of life," Annie says. "For you."

"Well . . . as if I needed a light to tell me something like that." Her words are gruff, but the lines on her face have softened, forehead pinching thoughtfully. She fingers the silverware laid out on the napkin before her, gaze intent on them. Foot tapping.

Suddenly she's up, shrugging into her jacket. "Time I did some-thing," she says. "Thanks for the coffee, Annie. You keep going on that tower." And with that, she vanishes out the back door.

Annie hardly has space to process what just happened before Bess pops her head out of the kitchen. "Got a minute?"

"For you? Always." Annie joins her in the warm room.

"Would you mind taking these over to the landing?" She points at a box of stuffed-full red-and-white-striped popcorn bags. Annie can almost taste the hot butter and sea salt.

"Sure." She lifts the box. "Who am I taking them to?"

"Fletch." Bess tugs at her red kerchief. "He's running the con-cession boat tonight."

Annie's face goes grim. That man . . . he is a puzzle. Anytime she thinks she sees a flicker of connection looming, up goes the wall between them.

"What's his story, anyway?" Annie shifts the box to the stainless-steel counter beside her.

"His story?" Bess empties the pot of fluffy white kernels, then pours in a slow drizzle of oil to coat it again, adding new kernels, clamping down the lid. She blows out her cheeks, shakes her head. "It's not for me to say, Annie-girl."

Annie nods. She respects that. "I just wonder about him. There are times he seems like he could be . . ." She struggles to complete that thought. "A friend." Maybe even more. "A real, true friend. The kind you only come across once in a lifetime, you know?" The kind who dumps a bucket of sand on his boat deck just because of a girl's silly fear. "But then he just . . ."

Bess nods. "Shuts down."

"Yes."

"That's Fletch, all right. He's as honest and good as the day is long, but try and get close, and you see how stubborn that wall around him is."

"There has to be a reason for it," Annie says, more to herself than to Bess.

Bess shakes the pot to keep the kernels from scorching. Annie opens new striped bags and starts shoveling some of the cooled, buttered popcorn in.

"There is," Bess says.

"I don't mean to pry," Annie rushes in, recalling Bess's earlier words. "Just thinking out loud." She thinks of his letter, that first line she read, and feels the guilt roll in.

"You know about his wife," Bess says. Her eyebrow peaks in a question.

"His . . . *wife?*" Her mind reels to make sense of this. Jeremiah Fletcher has a wife?

Bess nods. "Late wife. That much, everyone around here knows. He lost her some time ago, back in Seattle. Showed up here, locking himself away from everyone. It was like he'd run as far as he could from what had happened, hit the ocean, and had to stop. But even so . . . he doesn't. You've seen him head out every morning."

"Yes." Without fail, every single day before the sun.

"No one knows where he goes. It's like that heart of his is still running, and it does it in the dark."

Annie's motions are slow, filling the popcorn bags blindly, trying to make sense of this information. A pain deep in her chest pulses for the man and what he's been through.

"One thing you should know about Fletch." Bess pulls the pot from the heat, switches off the burner. "He doesn't let people in quickly. Or at all, sometimes."

Annie nods, trying to resign herself to this, to the fact that she's shared more of herself with this man than anyone she can think of. And yet . . . he is a vault.

"But when he's in . . . he's all in. No turning back. He's a lot like Bob, in that way. It's no wonder those two are thick as thieves. He's also a lot like someone else I used to know."

"Oh?"

"Ayuh. Your father."

"You remember my father?"

"There's not a soul in Ansel who doesn't remember him," she

says. "He won all our hearts back then." Something heavy settles upon her then.

"What is it?"

"We miss him, is all. I pray still he'll come back."

The question winds up through Annie, the one knit to her very bones. "I knew he came here for a time after my grandmother died, but what made him leave, Bess?"

The woman gives out a low whistle. "That is a long tale," she says. "One better saved for the light of day. Come back tomorrow, and I'll tell you what I know, if you really want to know. For now, though"—Bess winks, picking up the box of ready-to-go popcorn bags and placing it in Annie's arms—"get this to Fletch, or he'll have a mob of angry yachters pounding at his rowboat."

twenty-four

Bess's words travel with Annie down to the landing. Twilight is turning to dark, and the whole landing is lined with patio lights strung aloft, like an Italian street café. A huge screen stands upon the length of the landing, and like magic, it has pulled boats she's never seen into this harbor. There, mingled among the hardworking lobster boats, are yachts and luxury houseboats, taking care around rowboats and kayaks and canoes.

Hugging the box to her, Annie breathes in the delight of the scene. The screen flickers with *Columbia Pictures* arched over the woman with the torch, triumphant music striking vintage-film enchantment into the air. The opening credits to *It Happened One Night* give way to another ocean scene.

"Hey!" The loud whisper snatches her attention—Jeremiah over at the sea wall. She shakes herself back to reality and hurries over.

"Trying out a new career?" He's keeping his voice low, as if they were in a real theater.

"I think it suits me," she says, grinning.

His eyes are smiling. "Agreed. Want to help out tonight?" He opens an arm toward an awfully cozy rowboat. "Your chariot awaits."

Her first instinct is to run. From the boat, and from more time

219

with him. But something about the way he waits, the flicker of hope that steals across his features . . . it beckons her in.

Once seated in the boat with the popcorn nestled safely in the hull between them, he reaches up and flips a switch. Above them, a metal sign mounted from the boat lights up with round bulbs in old-world marquee letters spelling *Fresh Popcorn.*

"Where did you get a sign like that?"

"From Rich. A gift to the town."

"Ah."

Jeremiah rows in between boats, pulling up to anyone who flags them over. Annie's job, apparently, is to balance in this thing while offering up bags full of popcorn without spilling them—or herself.

Up on the screen, Claudette Colbert stumbles back on a bus, losing her balance. Annie laughs at the look on her face, and a swell comes up under the boat just high enough to tilt it, causing her to pull her own Claudette.

Jeremiah's hand catches her wrist, bracing her before she falls entirely. His touch is strong but gentle, sending a jolt through her.

"Thank you." Annie gives a halfhearted laugh. "Guess my sea legs are still finding me."

Jeremiah waves off her thanks, and the mirth on his face morphs into concern.

"You still haven't told me," he says.

"Told you what?"

"The sea." He dips his oars in, pulling them gently back into motion. "What happened, that it makes you . . ."

"A blubbering scaredy-cat?"

His laugh is kind. "Nervous, I was going to say."

That was a nice way to put it. She feels the pull to tell him, but at the same time, a roll of stubborn pride blocks her. Why should she give him more of herself, when he will not let her in? And a harder question—why does he care?

"I . . ." The words want past this tug-of-war inside her. *Just tell him.*

"I read your letter," she blurts. Her hand flies to her mouth.

That was not what she intended to say. "I mean . . . I didn't mean to, but that first day on the boat, a letter fell from a book and I read the first line." She hates the way guilt is fighting to be released into confession, seeking forgiveness, but it also is coming out fighting, pushing him away. As a weapon. Challenging him to tell her. Who was the letter from? Why did that person think he wouldn't want to read the letter for a while? Why was he so distant, always? For a brief second, something ugly overtakes her, wanting to challenge him. *See? I know something about you. Wall or not.*

He looks away. Plunges his oars in deeper, to where she can't see their tips in the black water beneath them.

Remorse sweeps over her, all feeling of retribution gone. "Oh, Jeremiah." What has she done? "I'm so sorry. I should have just put it back in the book without looking. It was just the first line, but—"

"So why are you sea-scared?" He looks at her then. Blazing right past what's just happened.

"What?"

"Listen, you don't have to tell me. People shouldn't be forced to explain before they're ready." He's talking about more than the letter. "But if you want to tell me . . ."

Annie sighs. "It's silly," she says. "It was a long time ago."

He waits. Paddles. Listens. Takes a piece of popcorn and eats it, as if he's settling in for a good story. The tension falls away.

"I was young. All I knew was that the sea . . . it was a friend. Something mighty but beautiful. Until one day, I was out swimming with my mom. I got too close to a jetty, and when she came to help me, a rip current got her." Annie's throat aches, and words rub it raw, trying to get out. She shakes her head. "I was a strong swimmer, but I thought that was it. Watching her disappear like that . . ." Hot tears prick her eyes, and she swipes at them. Jeremiah has stilled his oars, leaning forward in the gentle rock of the boat. Slowly, he takes her hand.

"She was lucky to get out. She was a diver in the navy. She'd trained for such things. Even so, that could have been it. She managed to break free, but the terror of that stayed with me."

Jeremiah nods. "Some things never leave you." These are words he owns, truths he knows deeply.

He waits. She feels too exposed and trivial to continue. Especially now, knowing what he has faced. But still, he waits.

"Over the years, the ocean did take her. And my father. Not forever, but far away. On deployments. Dad's dad, Roy . . . well, you know about him. And Mom's dad had been missing for years after that same war. They both vowed not to forget the way war marks a person—whether for good or for ill. They both joined the military themselves when it came time to honor that vow in the fullest way they knew how. They didn't take the cost lightly, but counted the sacrifice worth it, in order to protect the family they hoped to have one day, and their country."

Medals attested to their trailblazing courage over the years, though they never displayed them at home. *"It's my duty,"* Dad often said. *"Not something to brag about."* But Annie had. She'd bragged at school, whenever she had to explain why she lived with just one parent or the other, or when she needed to stay with a school friend for a couple of weeks at a time when her parents' deployments overlapped. She'd pulled out those bragging rights to justify why she'd been left . . . again.

They did it for her, she knew. But that wasn't always an easy thing for a young girl to wrap her heart around, when the heart was aching for them so badly. And over the years, that ache had turned into one of compassion for them. They each held so many stories she'd never know, held in the dark circles under their eyes after another sleepless night, or the way they'd let their gazes linger long over her, like they needed to be reminded why they did this as much as they needed air to breathe.

They were the first people she'd made a study of, on a heart level. The ones who first got her thinking of a career that could help others.

Annie brings herself back to Jeremiah's listening ear. "I counted the days until their retirements. My mom took up painting, and my dad took to reading. I'd send paints and books, anything to encourage that. I loved seeing their hands at rest. Touching things untainted by war."

She pulls in a deep breath. "But lately . . . it's gotten strange. They take these trips to Florida. Dad says it's consulting work, but he never gives any details."

When she'd asked, he had tried to explain, but the conversation left more questions than answers. *"It's . . . an important project. Something I have to do, Signal-Ann. Something I've got to make right."* He calls her by the childhood nickname, coined when she'd play signalman on his boat.

She continues. "That's where they are now. Otherwise, I'm sure they would have come to see Bob by now. Or at least . . . Mom would have. She tries to bridge the gap between those two. She's the one who sent me to live with Bob that summer. I don't think Dad would have done that. But Mom and Bob had talked some over the years, and when Bob lost his wife . . ." Annie shakes her head. She remembers how a sorrow had settled in their home. Dad away, she and Mom reading Eva Bliss's obituary in the paper. "I think she knew Bob and I needed each other that summer."

"Your mom sounds wise," Jeremiah says. "You talk to your parents often?"

"Yes. I called them as soon as I knew what happened to Bob. They should be home in the next few days, and Mom's hoping to convince Dad to come up here to visit Bob." She'd called with updates from the hospital whenever there was one, which wasn't often. "We're a hopeless bunch. I keep sending paints and books. They keep going to Florida to consult on whatever it is."

She shrugs, sheepish. "Anyway, that answered way more than your question. I guess I just learned early on that the sea takes people away. It got inside me, that fear, until it was as much a part of me as the blood in my veins."

"Things do that sometimes," Jeremiah says.

Annie waits, hoping—praying—he might go on. He looks as if he might. But whatever is trying to break loose in there comes up against the Great Wall of Jeremiah and tumbles back into the shadows.

That night, long after Claudette Colbert and Clark Gable have had their triumphant last moment on screen and the marquee lights have been turned off, they row home together. In the smaller vessel, they can glide closer to shore than usual and are skirting the edge of Everlea Island. Annie wants to sneak a peek just to see if she can catch any signs of Sully, concerned about how the woman is after her sudden exit from The Galley. But the house is dark, the island silent.

Across the narrow stretch of sea, Ed's island stands equally dark. But as they pass beneath a tree that hangs over the sea from Sully's place, a glimmer of silver light flashes. Moonlight, reflecting from something metal.

She points toward it, a questioning look toward Jeremiah. He rows closer, and as they pass beneath it, she sees a chandelier of individually strung silverware. Fine and Victorian—presumably the ones that Sully had been bent on finding a useful purpose for with her attempts at scone-baking. Delicate filigree twirls as a breeze picks up, swaying forks and spoons of every size, until they strike up into a silvery symphony. Carrying across the water in a westward drift . . . right to Ed's island.

A tall figure moves among the trees on his rocky beach. Annie holds her breath, not wanting to ruin whatever is at play here. He is bending, lifting something. Fiddling with it until . . . there.

His light shines once more. He adjusts it, pointing it right toward the sound of the homemade wind chimes. And there in the old Victorian house, Annie could swear she sees a curtain in one of the upstairs windows pull aside . . . and linger there.

Annie motions to Jeremiah. As quietly as they can, he rows. Gliding away from this waltz of light and wind and music, and whatever else is budding between the two islands.

twenty-five

The tides in Ansel are some of the greatest in the world. Surging twelve feet above its low-tide mark twice a day and rolling back again to reveal a hidden landscape. And like those tides, the rocks come in swells and pulls. A city across the country latches on to the Words, a new flood of boxes come. Jim transfers them to the shed behind the post office, and Robert and his plucky, beloved wife move them to their boat, lug them up the path on the island.

For years, it has gone like this. Months with not a package, then an influx, slowing to a trickle, and another lull. Bob and Eva layer them, life upon life, until they run out. And then they wait.

It is during one such lull, four years after the poem first ran, that Bob lays down the trowel, offers his arm, and escorts Ma and Eva into town for the Independence Day festival.

Ansel-by-the-Sea has always known how to work hard, rest hard, and celebrate with abandon. But since the war, this celebration in particular has taken on new extremes. Somberness and glee, both. The day begins and ends with a prayer, followed by a moment of silence as the fallen sons are remembered. And in between . . . oh, how they celebrate the freedom that was not promised, the freedom they'd wondered if they'd lose. It's as if

225

a long fuse on a firecracker is lit that day, burning in increasing fervor until the evening.

The town square is bedecked in bunting, swags of red, white, and blue. The high-school band—if seven kids with time-worn instruments could be called so—plays from the gazebo. Patriotic tunes put people in the spirit to loosen their purse strings for the pie auction. After a picnic, during which everyone partakes of everyone else's pies, Anselites sprawl on their picnic blankets in the sun, awaiting the highlight of the day—the crate races.

Everyone lines the shore from Joe's Landing to Mel's dock. Strung from the end of the piers, a line of wooden lobster crates skims the surface of the frigid ocean water, waiting for men to dash across them as if they are lily pads, challenging them to make it from one wharf to the other in record time.

The mayor opens the event, inviting "anyone brave enough among you lot" to take to the crates. A quiet hush settles over the crowd as they await the inevitable Melvin Buck.

The man steps forward, red baseball cap fronted in white, looking for all the world like a performer taking to the stage he was made for. "All right, all right. Twist my arm, why don'tcha? I'll go first." A chuckle rolls through the crowd. Melvin always goes first.

He takes to the wharf in shorts and his striped button-down shirt, lunges and holds his arms over his head like an Olympian stretching.

"Ready," Mayor Boone says. He holds his gold pocket watch high. "Steady . . . go!" And Melvin is off, wobbling to and fro as the crates do their best to toss him overboard. He makes it past the halfway point and two more crates beyond before the crate beneath him lists, throwing what little balance he had. And he's in the drink, bobbing up with a victorious shout.

"Whoooo!" No one can call Melvin a sore loser. "Two past last year's mark!"

Someone shouts that at this rate, he'd get to the end in twelve years' time.

"Twelve years, here I come!" Melvin shouts, as he clambers up the ladder at the end of the wharf.

Several more men go, most nearly reaching the end, and Tall Reuben doing so in record time.

"That's the time to beat, folks!" The mayor tries to hold Reuben's arm in the air, but his fully extended one only gets Reuben's to an awkward halfway point just over the mayor's head. Reuben glows red, shuffling his feet.

Eva turns to Robert, looking expectantly at him. "You going to give it a go, sailor?"

He raises an eyebrow at her. "Not on your life." Last time he'd competed was on a dare from Roy, and he'd learned then how the ocean is colder with an audience, more unforgiving with the whole town watching one's failure to stay upright.

"Maxwell Yost!" one of the young men calls from the crowd. He repeats it, and again, getting two or three of his boisterous young friends to join in the chant. "Maxwell Yost! Maxwell Yost! Maxwell Yost!"

They're calling for Mr. Max, the oldest man in town. Ninety-seven years old, Maxwell chimes in from his wheelchair. "Hear, hear! Let old Maxwell give it a try." He raises his stick—a gift from *The Boston Post* to be bestowed always upon the town's oldest citizen. One of a few hundred such sticks throughout New England, they'd had a hard time fitting the whole of *Ansel-by-the-Sea* in the scrolled script on its brass knob. But the crowded letters don't bother Mr. Max, and he lowers it back to his lap as the boys continue to call for him to give the crates a go.

Ire rises in Robert. He knows this jest that the oldest among them might try the hazards of the slippery crates is meant in good fun. But for pete's sake. Eighty-seven years ago almost to the day, Mr. Max was young Max, the eleven-year-old drummer boy who'd laid aside his instrument and taken up a cannon at Gettysburg when called upon. Doesn't he deserve more respect than this?

Robert lets go of Eva's hand, and she sends him a look that's both questioning and conspiratorial. "Go get 'em," she says.

A slow walk takes him to Mel's wharf and, on the way, past Mr. Max.

He leans in low to the man's ear, and says, "This one's for Gettysburg."

"Hear, hear!" Mr. Max shouts. "Make way for Young Bob!"

Robert grins at the use of his name. The whole town has taken to calling him by Roy's name for him. It feels nice. And kind of Mr. Max to call him young, too, for he does not feel so young anymore. Twenty-three, and it feels like he's lived ten lifetimes in the past five years.

On the mayor's cue, he leans his hands onto one extended knee. "This one's for Mr. Max!" he shouts, and the whole town erupts. The man is beaming, thrusting his cane into the air.

The crates drift about like a snake in the water, daring him to cross.

"On your mark," the mayor shouts. "Get set . . . go!"

With a leap and a splash, he's in. Pounding from crate to crate, sea swallowing his feet with every impact. Arthur rows along at a distance, ready to lend an oar if he should slip and fall, but there's an intricate dance of speed and muscle carrying him.

Breath coming hard and face splashed with ocean, he is six crates from the end. Five crates. Four—three—

His foot hits the second to last, victory surging through him. But just as quickly, a wash of cold reaches to snatch it back, crate tilting, set on casting him off. He's going fast and going hard. He thinks of Mr. Max and that doggone last crate, and in a thrust of gravity defiance, pulls his leg from the water, plants it firmly on that last crate, and falls headlong onto Joe's Landing. The finish line.

Jim claps him on the back, says something that's muffled among his own thrumming pulse in his ears and the cheering crowd on shore.

Jim grabs Robert's wrist and thrusts it into the air. "That's a record!"

The band pipes up, brassy in the distance, and the folks gather around to pump his hand, clap him on the shoulder. This, he could do without.

"It was Mr. Max," he says, face burning. He looks longingly toward the town square, which is blessedly empty. If he could just vanish away over there. "It's for Mr. Max," he says, dropping his gaze.

"Mi-ster Max! Mi-ster Max!" It's the same trio from before, the youngsters bent on stirring up a scene. They hoist Robert onto their shoulders to carry him through the crowd. "For Mister Max!"

And then they stop.

The crowd falls silent.

Robert strains to see what's happened, but the sun is in his eyes. He raises a hand to shield them and sees a woman in a simple black dress moving toward him—pointing at him.

He's never seen her in his life. And yet the very sight of her jolts some electric shock through him—the unshakable sense that he does know her.

The boys beneath him are slack-jawed, uncomfortable in the face of this sudden otherworldly figure.

"It is you," she says. She is singular—ice blue eyes, looking right at him, or right through him. Her face holds unknowable age. Circles beneath her eyes show she's lived more than he, worlds more, though she can't be much older than thirty. Dark hair drapes over her shoulder in a long braid.

He leaps from his unwanted perch, lands on the ground and senses a line. Like if he crosses it, he's crossing a divide there will be no coming back from.

She crosses the divide. Never breaking her gaze.

"You . . . you are good man." Her speech is measured. It's as if she's reaching far across to her homeland—somewhere in Europe, by her accent—and pulling those words here to speak, her conviction fierce with the strength they gather over the miles.

He should protest. She does not know. He is not a good man. But there is fierceness in her voice. Eva is beside him now. She's slipped her hand into his, and they both stand transfixed in a

229

sense that something momentous is happening—though nobody knows what.

Ansel, for once, is silent.

The woman lifts a hand to his face, and it trembles as she cups his jaw. "Good man," she says again. Her eyes seem to see universes where he only sees a moment, and they hold heartache beyond measure. With her other hand she does the same to Eva, her touch one of conviction. "Good people."

He drops his gaze. The only gift he can give such a one is the truth. "Ma'am, I'm sorry. I don't think I am who you think I am."

But she is not listening. Her face, marble-still until now, moves into a sad smile as she retracts her touch.

She is murmuring, words indecipherable. At first he thinks it is the way she runs her words together, the mournfulness of her voice. But then—word by word—he realizes she has slipped into another language. German, if he is not mistaken. A language few dare to speak in America, so wary are folks after the war, and after the escape of three German prisoners of war right here in Maine. None would soon forget the panic of that manhunt through the North Woods.

He catches a few words he knows: *Danke*—thank you. *Leben*—life. And two words that have the whole town holding their breath—*Auschwitz. Stutthoff.* They have heard the stories of these camps. Grieved the atrocities. But they never expected someone to arrive on the town's doorstep speaking of such things.

Eva tilts her head to the side as she leans in. She doesn't have much occasion to bring out her linguistic skills in Ansel, and she is alive with purpose.

"Ocean." she says. "She was in the—ocean—and—"

The woman discerns that Eva is translating, and her words speed up. "She had been in Auschwitz. Was freed but had no home. She was fleeing for America, a new life . . . but the boat . . . it was sinking. She was on a life raft—"

Robert's breath goes out of him. He knows this story. It was told to him in the gray belly of a warship. Could this be . . . ? He searches the crowd looking for Arthur but doesn't spot him. He does, however, see his mother standing in the surrounding crowd, her eyes wide.

Eva continues. "She was cold and nearly drowned and her . . . her children?" She flattens her hand and pushes it toward the ground, indicating the height of a child.

The woman nods. "*Ja! Ja! Drei!*" She holds up three fingers.

But that is wrong. There had been two children with the woman Roy saved, not three.

Still, the woman speaks on, her voice cracking with passion as she points at Robert. She pauses, pulls in a breath raked with tremors, shakes her head, purses her lips. Her eyes fill, and she nods at Robert. "*Gut.* Good man."

Robert looks her full in the face. "That . . . was my brother," he says. Eyes wide, willing her to understand as gently as he can. She does not know his brother's fate after her departure from the destroyer. And she has borne enough pain, he can see. "My twin." He circles his face. Pushes his hands down in an X across his front. "Not me."

"*Nein,*" she says.

"My brother," he says, and looks a question at Eva.

"*Bruder,*" she whispers.

"*Mein Bruder,*" Robert says. "He was a very good man."

To his left he sees his mother has moved close, a tear trickling down her cheek.

The woman stares long, to the point that heat creeps up Robert's neck.

Finally, she breaks her gaze and rummages in her purse, a tattered brown handbag with one wooden handle where once there were two. She pulls a paper out, unfolds it, and holds it out.

It's the piece from *TIME* magazine.

"You," she says, pointing first to him, then the picture. "*You* . . . are a good man." She shuts her eyes as if to recall something hard practiced. "Mister Robert Bliss."

His breath hitches. It's as if someone's unplugged an ocean around him and it's swirling, draining, leaving him exposed.

Not a soul stirs. A quick glance around shows the children who have clambered up beneath the docks onto the scaffolding timbers are just as transfixed as the adults—the ones floating in boats, the ones gathered about.

Eva breaks the silence with a soft strain of spoken words, making the German language melodic, building trust with this woman word by word.

"Come," Eva says at last, smiling and putting an arm around the woman's shoulder. "Robert, Savannah, this is Mrs. Liesl Rosen. We have some catching up to do."

twenty-six

Through the magic of Eva's warmth, the comfort of Mrs. Crockett's wild blueberry-rhubarb pie with its golden-brown crust, and the backdrop cheers and crack-of-the-bat coming from the town baseball game, Liesl Rosen picks up a cloak of hope and wraps it about herself at the foot of Josef Krause's statue.

Her English is better than it first seemed, and with only occasional help from Eva, she tells her story.

Of how she, at twenty-five, had found herself, her husband, and their two children in a concentration camp in Poland. How they lived on floors of mud, packed into barrack beds, all four of them in a bed built for one. How their stomachs grew empty, their limbs grew so cold they could not feel them, the roof leaked water so cold they sometimes awoke to ice beneath their feet—but hardly noticed, for the cold had been the only covers they'd had all the night long. But they'd stayed together, and they knew that was a miracle.

After a time, their captors had separated the men and women into different barracks. Liesl had felt an unraveling begin within her—a shivering that would not stop. A hollow sickness within her said her children would be next, for she had heard stories of other camps where children were exterminated because they served no use in the work camps.

"Served no use." Liesl repeats the words in a whisper. "As if they are not the keepers of life itself."

And soon her children were taken, but they appeared safe, at least for the time being, in a new children's block. She and Luka, her husband, hardly saw each other for long days—he in the quarry, pulling stones from earth, and she in the munitions factory, her soul rending at the work she was made to do, the lives these weapons would end.

They had one single corner of the universe where they could meet in the late afternoon. After the guards making their rounds would pass, there was enough time that she could brush her little finger against his thumb in passing. Or sometimes—once in a great, great while— they lingered a little longer together, hidden by a wall of sandbags.

The blessed winter rains, when they came, drove the guards away longer, sent the sandbags higher, and stretched their time deeper.

Some days she came bearing bruises and marks given her at the factory—and to explain them would only add to the pain inflicted by her overseers. So Luka would just run his fingers as gently as he could over her wounds, a silent lament, his gray eyes filling. And he would whisper to her, voice roughened by the injustice—*"Eines tages, Liesl."* Someday, Liesl.

She'd known he'd meant that someday . . . they would be gone from that life. To a better life. A place to breathe. Where the sun did not hide for years upon end, and where their hands could work the soil to grow things, not destroy things.

Eines tages. The man said more in those two words, and in the fierce hope living behind the torment in his dark eyes, than all the storytellers in all the world could have said together.

And so when it came to pass that she realized she had life growing within her—life there in that place of death—she'd taken her husband's hand fleetingly as they passed one afternoon and placed it on her sunken stomach, hiding such a secret in its dark. With cheeks flushing like a bride in her youth, and a magic she could feel come alive sparking the air between them, she whispered his battle cry back to him: *"Eines tages, Luka."*

Her smile said the rest, and his grin in return was as if someone had given him his youth back. And life right along with it. *"Ja,"* he'd said, and squeezed her hand. *"Ja, Liesl."* His voice so thick, so full even in its huskiness.

And then had come the march. Rumors of the Soviet forces encroaching brought hope and despair in a battle for life. The Soviets—they could free them! But the Germans—they might outwit the Soviets first. March them all off to their death before freedom had a chance. Which was exactly what they did.

"It was . . ." Liesl's voice here in the town square, telling the story in the shadow of Josef, her countryman, is haunted. Just like her eyes. She shakes her head. "I cannot bring the words to it," she says, her accent lacing the English she is able to piece together into tragic poetry. "They marched us through the winter, right up to the cliffs of the Baltic Sea. And then they forced us over a cliff . . . and the shooting began." She lifts her hand to cover her mouth, stifle a cry.

Eva reaches across the table and takes Liesl's free hand. "You need not tell us," she says softly.

Liesl is still as she composes herself, then draws a deep breath. "I will tell you what is needful," she says, "because there is a miracle yet."

She goes on to speak of how, though her children were with her, she could not find Luka among the travesty. But she could hear his voice in her heart, urging her on with those two words. *Eines tages. Eines tages. Someday.* She knew they were already as good as dead, and as that reality drove deep, something happened. Freedom.

"They could take nothing more from us than they already were doing," she said. "And so my shackles . . . they broke. No fear. Not a thing except this . . . this . . ." She presses a fist to her bosom, over her heart. *"Fire.* To try, one last time."

She broke away from the others before they were made to jump.

Holding fast to the hands of her two children, she pressed herself against the far side of a tree. Her children shook, one of them whimpering, and she pulled them close, praying for a way out. Praying, to the God who parted the sea once before, that He might do the impossible again and save them.

When she opened her eyes, she saw a break in the trees ahead. Footsteps came from behind them. "Quickly, my loves," she said, pulling her children toward the opening. It was a rough stairway, nearly unrecognizable as such for its rustic steps of rock and driftwood embedded in earth. At its base, a humble fisherman's shack. The steps neared. She whispered to her children to take shelter behind the shack and not to emerge, no matter what they heard. That if she did not come for them by morning, they were to be "quick and sneaky like foxes" and follow the cliffs west until they found a home.

With one eye on them, and one toward the tree line, she saw that she must advance toward the coming guard, lest he spot the children before they reached safety.

So she did. He caught her roughly by the wrists, would not look her in the eyes, though her stare dared him to. And when he did . . . what she saw there poured heartache and cold fear through her, twisting together like a noose around her lungs. The man—boy, really—had hardly tasted life, and all he knew of it was death. She saw it in his eyes. The coldness. The flicker of despair.

"Please," she'd said, voice low. Strong. Wrapped in a peace she could not account for. "You do not have to do this thing."

He'd looked away. Toward the sea. Then over his shoulder, to the massacre he'd left beyond the trees.

"It is all I can do." His voice broke. He released her grip, shoved her with the butt of his rifle. She hit the ground. Crawled backward, away from the approach of his black boots, crunch upon gravel.

She felt earth give way beneath her shin, a tiny tumble of rubble down the cliff. She would soon follow. There, on her knees, arms upon cold earth, she'd prayed for deliverance. A wordless prayer, spoken only in a wail, thinking of her children. *Spare them, Lord. May they not find me, not live with that picture in their minds. Keep them, Lord.* One hand struggled up to her stomach, to cradle her unborn child—desperate. And then she'd looked up.

The soldier looked at her. Mouth pursed grimly. And she'd seen it. He was going to kill her. Feed her to the sea, then shoot her to make sure. Just like the others.

He bent down, reached a palm toward her face as if to push her. A single tear trickled down her cheek, splashing a gray rock as big as her head, speckling it black.

The young man laid a hand on the back of her head. Let it linger there a moment—a benediction . . . or a death sentence. His struggle pulsed into the air. Was she a life worth saving? Or only a parasite, as he had been taught to believe? Hand to head, human to human, he was torn.

And then, in an explosion of force, he slammed her head against the rock—and all went black.

Transfixed, entangled in her story, right there on the cliffs of the Baltic with her, Robert cannot take his eyes from Liesl. Nor can Eva. His mother's head is bent in tearful despair.

"But you . . . you awoke?" Robert says at length. The woman is here, sitting before them, after all. "That was your miracle."

Eva shakes her head in wonder. "It is a miracle, Mrs. Rosen, to have survived that march, the fall . . . and to have—pardon me for assuming, but—to have also escaped with your children?"

Liesl's face lights, shadows chased away. "*Ja.* A miracle I thank God for every day. But that is not the miracle I came to tell you of."

"I did wake up. It was wet and cold, and I was covered in a thin layer of sand. It was first light the next day, and I awoke to two shadows blocking the sun. My children, murmuring their own prayers, holding tight to me. My whole self was numb, and as I began to move, every bit of me began to hurt. I had fallen a great distance—and I was scraped all over, new scratches crossing over my old scars like weaving. But—and I still cannot believe it—I was not shot. That boy." She shakes her head. "He breaks my heart still. I hope for him that the darkness does not win. Such a battle in him. Though he did toss me to the sea . . . he did not shoot. I choose to believe there was some shred of light left in him. A light I pray he fights for."

Eva squeezes Liesl's hand, and swipes quickly beneath her eyes with her free hand. "So much goodness in your heart."

"I wish that might be so," Liesl says. "But the truth is, I did not feel that way for a very long time after that. To have another person look you in the eye and decide that you are nothing—a pestilence to be squashed—it is very dark. I walked in darkness very long after that."

She gives her head a small shake, as if to realign her story, and continues. "My children and I made our way through the forests of Poland, surviving however we could. The land was alive with word of victory in Europe. Not the end of the war, but the end of it in our part of the world, at least. The beginning of hope for the rest of the world. We were met with kindness, enough to help us find passage to America. Luka had a sister here, and we had dreamed of someday joining her. If I was ever to find my husband again, if he by some chance survived, it would be here. I worked and saved and then had word from Luka's sister, with money for us to board a ship to take us across the Atlantic, several months after . . . after the cliff."

"Bound for New York," Robert says. There's a pricking in his memory, an echo of Arthur recounting the midnight rescue. He sits taller, leaning in.

Liesl nods. "When we went into the ocean that night, I had no hope. My children and I—all three of them, for my baby was still on the way—clung to that life raft and sang our song. They saved my children but could not return for me. But then, when all seemed lost, your brother appeared.

"When I saw his hand reaching down for me . . ." Her voice is choked by the memory, eyes red with tears. She pulls in a shuddering breath. "Suddenly I was upon that cliff again. A hand reaching toward me. But it was not the face of a killing soldier I saw, not a man who would toss me away like vermin. It was a face of kindness. A man who would come into the waves when he should not have. To risk his life for mine."

His mother's anguished face is laced with a haunting sense of pride that Robert, too, feels deep in his heart. He forgets to breathe. In his mind's eye, another dark night is replaying itself. His brother hanging on for dear life—the look of torment on his face when Robert pulls him to safety. Echoes of regret—and cast against this new image of him redeeming this woman's scars, with the one thing he had to offer: courage.

Liesl smooths her hand over the *TIME* article on the picnic table between them. "We came at last to my husband's sister, in New Hampshire. A tiny farm. Do you know what we grow?"

There is a childlike smile upon her face, as if she is about to reveal that they are the keepers of the sun, or that they sow gold and reap it in spades.

She leans in and speaks it with that much magic, too. "Corn." She shakes her head in wonder. "Corn! We grow something that brings *life*. My children—they are healthy. Not . . ." She churns her hand in the air, searching for the word. "Not *oysgedart*."

Robert looks to Eva, whose head is tilted in befuddlement.

Liesl laughs. "I am sorry," she says. "My English is still growing. *Oysgedart* is—in the Yiddish—not enough meat on the bones, I think you would say. My children are not like skeletons any longer. Thanks be to God.

"One day as I was cleaning the farmhouse, I found this. Luka's sister, she read it to me. It is not new, I know, but . . . I had to come when I saw your face.

"That night, all I could do was weep. To know that your brother did not come home from that night at sea . . . to know that for us to farm corn beneath the sun, he will never see that sun again. I went into the field under the moon, out in the corn. And I took this from the earth for him."

She reaches into the worn knapsack and pulls out a stone.

Large and gray, with streaks of blue. "It is for your lighthouse, if I am not too late." She cradles it in her hands and offers it this way, hands shaking. "For him, or for Luka, or perhaps for both of them."

Robert slides one hand beneath hers, and the other on top of the stone. "You're not too late."

His mother wipes her tears and lays a hand on Liesl's. Asks after her children, drinks in every detail as if they are her own family, her parched mother-heart storing up this healing treasure.

"I . . ." Liesl drops her gaze. "I am sorry. That he did not come home to you. Because of me."

Robert's jaw works, heat coming in waves inside. "There is something you should know, Mrs. Rosen." He tells her of the night of Roy's own rescue, how it changed his brother. How he longed to save another, as he himself had been saved.

And in his telling, a peace settles about Liesl like a shawl. A sad smile, and she says at last, looking out at the ocean, "Roy Bliss." She has not said his name until now. "He . . . how do you say . . . ? He changed"—she gestures toward the water—"the tide for us. Nothing can undo the evil that came before him, but he did more than undo it. He . . ."

She wrings her wrists. "*Unter wasser.*" She looks to Eva for help. She tilts her head. "Under water?"

"Yes, like that, but . . . more. All the way. S-s . . ."

"Submerged?"

"Yes! He *submerged* into the pain. And he gave himself into it. It is as my husband used to say, just what our *Yeshua* did for us, giving life through His death. And we wish to honor His life with ours."

"Your husband," Eva says gently. "Luka. He hasn't returned . . . yet?" Her wording is hopeful but gentle, and Robert wants to kiss her for it. He would have blundered that question a thousand ways.

Liesl's smile fades. "No," she says. "He has not. And we know he will not, unless there has been a miracle. But . . . I have had more than my share of miracles, wouldn't you say?"

240

"I don't think God keeps a count of those, Mrs. Rosen," Eva says.

The woman laughs. "This is true. Perhaps, Mr. Bliss, your light will help guide my husband home to us someday."

Late that night, when the echoes of the ballgame are long silent, and Mrs. Rosen has boarded the Machias train to her home in New Hampshire, Robert turns her rock in his hands, sitting at the kitchen table. Liesl's words play over him. And although it is far past midnight and the morning will soon call him out to sea, he heads through the night to Roy's boathouse. There, with chisel and mallet in hand, he begins to engrave the rock with two words:

Eines tages.

twenty-seven

JULY 1962

Years. Years, it has been, this scraping together of coins and wages, of occasional donations and a windfall or two. A war in Korea, come and gone. His mother departed to heaven, leaving him grieving the purest, farthest-reaching love he has ever known. She leaves him, too, with an inheritance of this place she loved—Sailor's Rest—and an old family tract of land up in the woods, and the most treasured inheritance of all: her hazelnut pie recipe, for Eva.

Now the war in Vietnam is making waves, everyone speculating on whether and when America will get involved. Every year, every war milestone and Memorial Day and Veteran's Day, the poem gets picked up again, the rumor spreading that the light tower is still being built, and fresh waves of rocks come. Enough to nearly finish the tower.

But though there is still plenty of building to do, the tower is not the problem now. It is the lens room, where the light will go. The light itself, when it comes down to it. Turns out the price of scallops doesn't hold a candle to the price of larger-than-life glass panels. Even after so many years, Bob has an ocean of distance between his bank account's contents and the price tag on the almighty Fresnel lens.

Freh-nell, he's learned. Corrected every time he opened his

242

mouth and pronounced it *Frez-null*. *Freh-nell*, the people at
Cornwell Company insist over the phone. They're awful high and
mighty about it, for a company that makes baking ware. And
lighthouse lenses, apparently.

It was usually the same woman—Titan Trish, Bob has dubbed
her in his mind since he'd first called them four years back. Her
voice became pitying when he explained his situation. How the
lighthouse needed a pretty big lens. Second-order, she called it.
That meant it'd be so big he could walk inside it, all six feet of
him. The light needed to reach as far as possible, but he knew the
first-order lens, the biggest of them all, was too far out of reach.

Imagining how it sounded to her ears, he didn't blame her for
the way her words took on a near-condescending tone, like she
was speaking with a child asking for the world.

"It's highly unusual," she'd told him back then. "For an individual to purchase a lens, especially these days. Not much call for
lenses now." She'd sounded morose, had gone on to bemoan the
modernization of lighthouses, the way they were being updated,
and lighthouse keepers—"those stalwart souls," as she called
them, who risk life and limb to the sea—are being thrown to the
wayside.

Today's phone call is no different. "Not many folks call up to
purchase lenses anymore," she reminds him, a tired edge to her
voice. "And never of that magnitude. Have you planned a char-
acteristic?"

"No," he answers, just like the last time she asked. He can't yet
think of the flashing light pattern she refers to, which will have
to be unique so as to be identifiable at sea. No, he can't think of
it yet—not when he doesn't even have the light. He says as much.

"Have you an organization to work with?" She continues her
barrage. "The coast guard, perhaps? We've dealt with them in the
past, and they have the means to—"

"Do I sound like a gull-blasted organization?" Bob huffs, only
slightly regretting the way his words stop her nasal chatter cold.

"No, sir, I don't suppose you do."

"I'm sorry." He rubs his temple. He's at the end of his rope, all these families counting on him to do what he promised. And he's taking it out on Titan Trish. "I'll call you back."

He hangs up the phone in the store at Joe's Landing, rattling the display of tape measure key chains on the counter, and shoves his hands in his pockets. Mrs. Crockett averts her clam-wide eyes quicker than a dart, busying herself with the paper-wrapped canned deviled ham as if it's the most urgent task in all the world.

Hal is hunched over *The Pier Review*, head in hand and elbow to desk, pretending nothing out of the ordinary has just happened. He turns the page, starting in on the article boldly heading the page: JOHANNES HAS SHOWDOWN WITH HOMER. There's a picture of the coon cat sitting on the end of a pier while the dolphin swims by in the distance. Slow news day, apparently.

"Didn't go so good?" Hal mutters, looking over rectangular glasses.

"No." Bob doesn't elaborate. Astronomical price tags to the tune of many, many thousands of dollars are busy pounding themselves into his brain.

"Too expensive?"

Bob rakes his hands through his hair. There seems only one option now. "I don't see it, Hal. How I'll ever get the money. At this rate, it'll take me . . ." He presses his eyes shut and does some numbers in his head. His savings are meager, and that was from living hand to mouth, shoveling every extra penny he could over to the lighthouse fund. Eva, God bless her, is just as determined as he to see the tower lit. She's plunged full-force into living off the land and sea like a true Anselite, clamming and fishing scallops with him and foraging fiddleheads, tapping maples . . . all of it.

She'd been cut off from any family money after she'd married him but hadn't blinked twice. Had rolled up her sleeves and blundered her way into learning how to cook, clean, harvest, build, all so they could be together, and all to save a penny for the light.

They'd started a dedicated account eight years ago, thinking

244

they'd have enough saved by the time the tower grew high enough to put a lens in. If he was to scrape together the rest . . .

His shoulders slump, and he leans against the pole where the now-silent yellow phone hangs. "It'll take me to my dyin' day to save enough money. I'll be so old I won't be able to finish the thing."

Hal sets down his paper, folds it, and leans over both his folded arms. Being one of the men who buys lobsters from him, he knows more about Bob's income than most anyone in this town. He tips his head toward the counter between them. "You could put a can out." He rummages below the counter and pulls out a rusty Folger's can, slaps a paper over it with some electrical tape, and scrawls *Light the Lighthouse* in thick black ink.

It's generous of him. And Bob, much as he hates to, lets him. But even so he knows that without some miracle, they'll never make it.

It keeps him up nights, thinking of the rocks sewn together with mortar over on the island, of the boxes gathering dust in the boathouse while he figures this tangle out. The hope—false hope now?—given to the people who'd packed those stones with care and sent them off to a stranger in an obscure corner of Maine.

In the dark of night, he wrestles down the only possible solution. So in the morning, sun bright and air clear, Bob skips a good day of lobstering to head over to Bangor. When he returns, an envelope of official papers stuffed in the pocket of his father's old suit, he feels not a lifted burden but the weight of a traitor's brand. He's done it. Sold off his family's land in the mountains. He can almost feel the trees groaning their protest, right in his very bones. He'd hounded the manager of the mill about their policies, their plan to keep the land sustained, not strip it all at once. He'd gotten it in writing, even. And he'd left the mill with enough money to burn a hole in his soul . . . and to buy that Fresnel lens.

He stops at Joe's Landing to call Titan Trish up on that yellow phone again. The only good thing about this day is the way that pinched voice falls silent when he says to order him up a lens.

"I'm sorry?" she says, as if she hasn't understood right.

"No need to apologize, ma'am," Bob says, relishing this. "Just send it right over when it's ready. You'll find I've wired the money already. Have a nice night, then."

"But, sir! There's paperwork to do, and an order like this takes time to build, and—"

"Very good," Bob says. "Send along whatever's needed. Bye-bye, then."

The receiver protests in her tin-can voice as he hangs it with a satisfying final click.

"Things go good?" Hal mutters, buried in his newspaper.

"Ayuh," Bob says. "Real good."

He leaves with the faintest flicker of hope. Just a spark, some-where in the abyss of churning guilt over what he's done to fund this lens. But it's enough to carry him over the weeks and months as he waits, as he draws diagrams of how this "wonder lens" works. The way it takes a solitary light, and simply by the angles and positions of the bulls'-eye-like glass, magnifies it, breaks it up into countless projections of itself, which reunite into one solid, giant beam of light that blazes through dark, reaching out to guide boats to safety.

It's a mechanism that echoes something eternal, something deep inside Bob. Broken things made whole. Light cracking through dark. A cracking that echoes a cleaving of granite buried inside him.

Summer ends, and one cool autumn day Bob walks into the post office to find Jim repeating a scene from the past, leading him out back for an arrival too big for the tiny post office.

Together, he and Ed—a broken soul his Words have recently, mi-raculously, drawn to Ansel—load the crates onto his boat. They're surprisingly light, for the size of what's inside. *"Delicate,"* Titan Trish had told him last week over the phone. *"Don't let its strength fool you. It's intricate. Be careful."* Her voice had morphed from pitying to matronly since his order, and his conversations with her now felt more like checking in with a protective miser. She wasn't dull of intelligence. She knew, no doubt, that something big had been sacrificed to make this happen. *"There's no insurance on this,"* she'd said. *"Go easy."*

The finality of it makes his bones suddenly feel like they're made of glass, too. He and Ed place the crates in the *Savvy Mae* with such tenderness, they may as well have been newborn babes. It puts to mind that far-off echo of a memory, holding little William the night he brought news of his father's death. The same gravity settles in him now.

Across the bay the blessedly still waters take them. *Thank you, Lord,* he prays. Mentally he shuffles through logistics—how they'd get it off the boat, around back to the boathouse. Where they'd store the crates until it was time to mount the lens. The boathouse's back corner, probably. No one ever went back there. Not since Roy had gone away. It seems fitting, somehow, that the crowning glory for his brother's lighthouse would rest there while it awaits its final home.

But all those thoughts fly out of his mind the second they step off the boat. Light is beginning to fade, but there's enough to see clearly that a man sits on the front steps. Head down, something defeated and hard about his posture.

There's something familiar about him. An inkling inches its way up his spine that he should know this man. And yet everything that feels familiar is just the slightest bit foreign, too.

The man looks up—and Bob nearly drops the crate he and Ed are carrying, right there on the path.

"Whoa." Ed steadies him with a hand to the shoulder. "You okay?"

No. No, he isn't.

The man . . . is Roy. The spitting image of his brother the last time Robert saw him alive. Like time had frozen back in 1945 and delivered him nearly two decades later to this moment, to knock the wind clean out of Robert.

His eyes slam shut. He shakes his head to clear this ghost away. But when he opens them again, there he is. Alive as the day, walking toward him with some great burden weighing him down.

Bob swallows. Tries to find words. To move toward the young man. But can't.

There's still a good space between them when the man stops and looks at Bob as if he's sizing up an enemy.

"Robert Bliss?"

Bob swallows back a wave of tremorous unknown. Nods.

"I'm William."

twenty-eight

The kid looks like a thousand-mile road trip rolled up into one person. All dust and weary and lost. Dark circles under his eyes, brown hair falling into his face—a face that looks as if it decided long ago this world wasn't a kind place, and maybe had good reason for that verdict.

He is settling in up in the room Robert and Roy had once shared. Well, *settling in* is probably an overstatement—all he had on him was a worn duffel bag that hung limp and nearly empty.

"What now?" Bob blows his cheeks out, asking the question somewhat to himself, but more so to God. His thoughts are becoming more like an ongoing conversation with heaven, these days—usually more questions than anything else. And this was a big one. *What now?*

What would Eva do? She's away for the night caring for Mrs. Bascomb, who's been ailing. If she were here, she'd shatter this tension with her warmth, work her magic, and get that kid to drop the brick wall around him. What would Ed do? He'd taken off as soon as he figured out who William was, telling Bob he'd be around tomorrow. Sensing, maybe, that there was a lot that needed to happen between uncle and nephew.

So . . . *what now?*

Food. The answer comes quick and hard. A guy needs food, and that kid more than most. He's gaunt, though maybe that's his normal appearance. Bob had no way of knowing. The last picture he has is of a four-year-old on a bike somewhere in Minnesota, beaming up at the camera and, most likely, his mom, behind the lens. After that, Jenny had wed—a Theodore Sawyer—and her letters trickled to a stop, ending with a request that Bob not write anymore. Kindly said, but it had burned. Reading between the lines, Bob assumed Mr. Sawyer wasn't too keen on his wife writing to another man. Bob understood, once he got past his initial anger. And though something had felt off about the request—something unspoken and subdued in Jenny's tone—he'd had no choice but to respect it.

But here, now, was William. Looking for all the world like the second coming of Roy, with a dusting of Jenny's freckles and her blue eyes, too. Surreal.

Bob reaches into the cabinet for a box of cornmeal, pulls a pail of buttermilk from the pistachio-green refrigerator, and some cod fresh caught this morning. The boy needs something hearty. Bob's no chef, but he can fry up a fillet to golden-crisp, and Ed had taught him about a little something called the po' boy. Music to a man's soul—that's what the southern dish is. Bob has no shrimp or oysters, and Ed had declared that using cod instead was like "drinkin' air when what you want's a swig of ice-cold water," but it fills a man up. And that kid needs filling.

Footsteps sound on the stairs, and Bob piles the sandwiches up with tomato, lettuce, hot sauce, and Ed's famous spread. Peppery and savory with all kinds of tang to it.

William hovers in the kitchen doorway. In the light, his clothes show the extent of their wear and want for washing. Button-down shirt that was once sky-blue, now more like mottled clay. A khaki blazer with elbow patches, ripped right up the seam of the right arm. He grips the cuff with that hand, holding the frayed edges together, and Bob realizes his scrutiny is making the boy uncomfortable.

And that's what he is, Bob realizes. Half man, half boy, standing there with his face freshly scrubbed in those soiled clothes, cheeks ruddy, eyes ice. This one's been through the wringer.

Bob slides a plate onto the table, nods toward it. Plants a glass of water there, too, and joins William.

Bob folds his callused hands and bows his head, realizing he'll have to offer his prayer aloud. He eyes the boy, who's frozen with the sandwich halfway to his mouth. He quickly bows his head, as much to pray as to hide the flush of red across his face. He never releases his grip on that po' boy.

"Lord, we thank you for this food. For the day's fullness. And . . ." He opens one eye and sees William with head bent forward, hair falling unruly. "For family. Amen."

William mutters an *amen* and they fall silent, consuming. Not knowing where to start, what to say. The food is the glue holding this hopeless fracture together, and Bob thinks for the hundredth time how God sure knew what He was doing when he made food and gave men stomachs. They need it, and not just bodily.

"You're up from Boston?" Bob says at last. That's where Jenny and Mr. Sawyer had settled, last he knew. There are a thousand questions pounding, but they feel too personal to ask someone who's a near stranger. He has to earn the right, somehow. And he doesn't know how.

William's chewing slows, and he swallows. "A while ago."

"I went there once. With your parents, matter of fact." At the mention of those two people, William fixes his concentration hard on the table in front of him.

He's a paradox. These fine clothes, tailored by the look of them, but bearing grime and wear. His hair, longer than what's polished but not long enough for what's rebellious. His face holds the spark of Jenny's youth and the fervor of Roy's spirit . . . but it is dull, lifeless, haunted. He looks like someone who's been cut loose to drift and hasn't found shore. Not for a long time.

William sets his half-eaten sandwich down, gulps down half the glass of water, and for the first time looks Bob in the eye.

"I . . . need a place to stay for a while," he says at last.

Bob nods, considers. What would a parent do? He hasn't the slightest idea but knows at least that he has to consult Jenny. No matter how long it's been.

"We'd have to phone your mother to see, but we could do that from town tomorrow—"

"No."

The single word is full of defeat and grief.

Bob lowers his sandwich, studies him. There's an iron-strong conviction inside. *You know this sorrow. You have been here.*

Bob grabs a heaped dish towel from the table, wipes his hands on it. Clears his throat. "She's . . . gone," he offers. The last thing William needs is to be made to say it, if this is what's happened.

A nod confirms it, and a pit opens in Bob. But he cinches it tight. Time for that later.

"A year ago," William says, and there's a softening of his voice. "She got sick. It was fast."

A year. Where had the boy been since then? By the looks of things, he's seen plenty in the time that's passed.

"I'm sorry," Bob says. Platitudes run through his head. *She was a good woman. This is a great loss.* And each one is sincere, but none is enough. "She was . . ." An image of Jenny flashes. Girl with wings for feet, weaving through shafts of sun, light on her freckles and dark hair flying. "That girl was life, all wrapped up in a person," he says at last.

William raises his down-turned face, a deepening in his eyes. Unspoken thanks.

There's much to know, still. Where he's been. Where he's headed. But by the look of things, these questions would be burdens to a kid who hardly knows where he is right now. Bob benches the questions, tunes his ear heavenward. *What's he need?*

252

Two words slam him from opposite sides and collide into one single idea. *Home. Hope.* Maybe they're the same thing, when it comes down to it. He also knows that a soul set adrift wants a task, a purpose. No matter how small. As it happens, he's got three crates he can't lift by himself for fear of shattering what's inside. And he can't help thinking there is a reason these two deliveries ended up on his front porch the same night. They're tied to each other, the light and this boy.

"Well, you've got a place here, long as you want," Bob says at last.

In a movement so miniscule Bob almost misses it, William shifts in his seat, shoulders dropping, like a burden's been lifted. He has space—even just a little—to breathe. And Bob knows too well, when you've been without air so long you can't remember another way of life, even a single breath of fresh air is a lifeline.

———

The next morning, Bob creeps downstairs before the sun, scribbles a note for William, rummages for what food he can—an apple, two biscuits, some cheese—and sets it out for him. Out in the frosty morning, he's halfway down the dock when sudden movement sets his pulse racing. A lanky shadow springs from the dock post where he'd been leaning.

Muscles tense, Bob narrows his eyes, barely making out the man's features. "William?"

He stuffs his hands in his jacket pockets, shoulders up. Sheepish. "I . . . thought I'd help."

Bob tosses his sack on board the *Savvy Mae*. "Help?"

"Mom said you fished. For a living."

"That's right," Bob says. "Lobster. You ever been?"

"No . . ." He shuffles his feet. Uncomfortable in his own skin. Seems there's something more he wants to say but can't.

Bob waits.

"I've never been on a boat before," he admits at last.

Bob chuckles. "Well, that's quick enough cured." He slaps his nephew on the back and holds his hand out over the boat, gesturing him on board.

What follows is something akin to watching a newly foaled colt wobble toward its first steps. Bob clenches his jaw to keep back laughter, giving the kid space to find his sea legs. It is a rite of passage, one not to be scoffed at. He fires up the engine and takes the long way out of the harbor. Up into the Weg, out past Grindstone Neck. Slow and easy, until William's grip on the railing becomes less white-knuckled.

He eases the throttle up once they're out in the open, lifting his hand to Gus Packer as they pass him already working at his traps. Bob goes easy once he reaches his first trap. He chooses one closer in, hoping it'll be a good ease-in for William. He slows alongside his buoy, which is tethered to the wooden trap on the ocean floor.

"How do you know which are yours?" William surveys the seascape, probably noticing other buoys bobbing in the not-too-far distance.

"Stripes," Bob says, idling the boat and gripping the buoy. It drips as he pulls it on board showing the Bliss pattern—one thick blue stripe topped by two thin red stripes. "That's our marker. Some will be other colors, other stripes. These ones are ours."

"What happens if someone gets into your trap before you do?"

Bob laughs. "A man who'd do that had better hit the hills running, or the whole of Washington County will be after him. There's honor in this job. Respect as deep as the sea for other men's traps."

As he explains, a hunger lights in William's eyes. He is eager for this honor, for something good and true. Bob wonders what the boy has sacrificed in his time surviving on his own, and what price he is paying for it now. A steep one, by the slump of his shoulders.

Setting the buoy on deck, Bob pulls the rope, hand over fist, forgoing the pulley in these shallower waters. He stops to fling off clumps of seaweed as he goes. The rope pools on the deck until finally the trap shows itself. Long wooden slats domed over a rectangular base, and he can see already the dark sheen of at least two lobsters. The netted opening sports a hole big enough for the creatures to crawl through.

William points to the hole. "What keeps them trapped?"

"Themselves," Bob says. "They could get out any time if they just turn around and go back."

William lets out a rueful laugh, like maybe he understands that more than he wants to say.

Bob pulls the first lobster out, and it waves its claws in protest. He flips it over to check for eggs. There they are, the future, nestled right beneath her. With a toss, he releases her back into the sea.

"What'd you do that for?" William bends over the edge, watching the ripples flow outward from where she's disappeared.

"She's got another job just now," Bob says. "Eggs to hatch. Life to give."

"And the other one?" William points at the trap.

"See for yourself."

William, haltingly, reaches into the trap. Pulls out a starfish.

"Funny-looking lobster," he says, face deadpan.

Bob narrows his eyes, trying to get a read. Is he joking?

The smallest upturn of one corner of the boy's mouth gives an answer. And more than that—the first hint that there might be a door somewhere in the fortress William has around himself. Bob chuckles and tips his head toward the water, where William deposits the starfish.

Reaching in again, he pulls out the remaining lobster, holding him by the back as Bob had done. He flips the lobster over. No eggs.

"He's a keeper," Bob declares, grabbing a large tin bucket from the deck. He plugs the claws with wooden pegs, and William places the lobster inside.

Quickly Bob shows him how to rebait the trap and toss it back in once the boat's on the move again. "Stay clear of the rope, whatever you do."

The next trap, William takes the lead. It's like the boy's all thumbs. His fingers are long and strong, built for work like this, but unpracticed and blind.

A time or two, the frustration in William nearly bubbles to the surface. The boy has a long fuse, but Bob knows too well that the longer the fuse, the bigger the explosion. He's the master of the big explosion himself. And for the first time, he wonders if there's a bit of himself in William, too.

"You're doing fine, son," Bob says, not thinking. The stiffness in William says he should've chosen a different word. He's not Bob's son. "Just takes time."

"That's another way of saying I'm no good at this," William says.

"Nope," Bob says. "It just takes time."

William pulls a lopsided grin, and Bob hopes it's a sign the day will start looking up for him. They drop anchor for lunch, Bob splitting his egg sandwich with William. They'd best make this a short day. A half sandwich won't sustain the kid long, not the way he's working, making his hands raw. And though the bright sun is warming the day, the air is still mighty cold for a boy who has never worked on the water.

Bob ducks into the cabin and readies the boat. "Come on in, William." His name feels strange to say. Flashes of the babe in arms come to mind at its utterance. "How about you steer." He offers him the seat. It will keep his hands out of the wind and work for a while. "So what you do is, to steer it that way"—he points right—"you turn the wheel starboard. Nice and slow, and keep the engine down, too."

William's jaw is set, eyes fixed in concentration on the sea ahead. They're retracing their path from this morning, Grindstone Neck coming up on their right. He'll have to turn the boat to curve around the point and get them into the Weg. Bob stands back, watching the wheels turn in William, the way a vein carves his hand. But as they pass the point, his quick instincts kick in. Seeing they're turning into the cliff, he turns the wheel port side, fast. Too fast. He tries to correct, lurching the wheel back center.

In his panic he's left the motor fast, and the bow is lifting, stern fishtailing.

They're headed toward Everlea Island—and rocks submerged just far enough to be invisible and deadly to a boat. Sensing William's stress spiraling, Bob takes the wheel, lowering the throttle, calming the engine, easing the boat's direction back on course toward the Weg.

He eyes William, offering him the wheel again, but William gulps, shakes his head no. The kid's shoulders are heaving as he tries to catch his breath.

"Happens to all of us at the start," Bob says. "Your dad nearly busted this boat at least twice." He chuckles as William leans forward. "I'm sure your mom told you enough of those stories, though."

"Not really." He shrugs. "Theodore, my stepfather, said it wasn't good to live in the past." The words fall flat and speak volumes.

Bob tilts his head side to side, weighing. "That might be," he says. "Might not. Sometimes the past has a whole lot of treasure to mine. Might be he's missing out, if you ask me."

"Maybe."

He knows he shouldn't, but Bob asks it anyway. "Where is Theodore now?"

"Took a job in San Francisco," he says. "After Mom."

"And he didn't take you with him?"

William shrugs again. "The firm had a penthouse for him. He said"—he presses his eyelids closed, pulling the words letter for letter from where they're branded inside—"it would be no place for a 'young man on the brink of manhood, ready for a life of his own.'"

Bob did the math. William would have barely been sixteen. Reeling in the wake of his own mother's death.

"Like I said"—William's words edge sharp—"he doesn't like to live in the past. I guess I don't blame him." The flatness in his tone says otherwise. "I wasn't really his kid."

Mr. Penthouse is lucky he's not standing in front of Bob. Molten iron springs deep within him, spreads through his veins until he's the one white-knuckling the wheel. Thinking of Roy. Jenny. William. The nerve of the coward whom Jenny gave her life to.

"And like *I* said . . ." Bob schools the ire, looks William straight in the eye. "He's missing out."

twenty-nine

Days pass, the two men finding a rhythm, heading out before the sun, William dressed in a ragged work jacket and either the same threadbare shirt he'd showed up in or the spare he'd borrowed from Bob. They eat lunch out on the waves. Stories and bits of histories come in pieces. Choppy at first, like the waves beneath them. Each one a stitch binding the chasm of time between them, each one pulling that rift together—tighter, closer.

William is not eager to talk about himself, but Bob gathers up slivers of information as they come, pieces them together enough to know the kid has spent a year wherever he could. Sometimes in parks, sometimes in shelters, most recently spending cold nights tucked next to an old chimney in the New Hampshire woods, remnants of an old work camp from the thirties. The kid had gotten the old hearth going again, which turned out to be his salvation and his undoing. It saved him from freezing, but it also brought the authorities out to investigate. They insisted he was a minor still, needed a roof over his head and someone to take responsibility for him. They asked him where he'd gotten the can of beans cooking over the fire—an answer he was ashamed of.

Not waiting around to see what sort of home they had in mind for him, he'd hopped a train to Maine the next day.

Which brought them to now, their jolty routine taking on

rhythm enough to keep this fledgling kinship going. Evenings mean a meal—meat and potatoes of some kind, usually over the campfire out back, the woods walling them in and the night sky their roof. Eva brings out warm apple cider. That cider, and the hands that made it, stitch them all together with their warmth. Bob doesn't want to imagine what this reunion would be like without Eva, and he thanks God once again for creating her and bringing her to him. At night they retire and all is quiet until dawn comes and they repeat it all again.

Until one night, Bob lays in his bed, sleep evading his chase. The old black alarm clock on his bedstand ticks on past midnight. And just as he's about to sleep, lids heavy at last, something awakes him. A *thud*, then a shuffle.

William. But the sound isn't coming from William's room. It's coming from above him. Up in the attic, where Bob hasn't ventured for months. Maybe years. He gets up and steals across the hall, a low light coming from Roy's old kerosene lamp on the bedstand. William's bed is empty, sheets shoved back.

Footsteps cross the floor above him once, twice. He's up there, no doubt about it. Bob returns to his own room, shutting the door. Should he go up? Stay down? Pound on the ceiling with a broomstick like Dad used to when he and Roy were making a ruckus up there? The memory brings a silent chuckle. They'd gotten up to all manner of shenanigans in that attic. Turning crates into cars, inventing a radio that would never work, taking apart the only radio in the house that did work.

Later it had become their finding ground, where Roy first tried his hand at sketching a boat design and brought it to Dad, seeing if it might work. That was when he'd moved his exploits out to the boathouse, and the brothers began to grow on their own paths.

Let the kid smash around the attic. Nothing up there could hurt him. Eventually the stairs creak, careful footsteps bringing William back to his own room, and all falls silent.

In the morning, William is out back chopping firewood—

another skill new to the city boy. And while part of Bob wants to respect his nephew's space, something stronger pulls him upstairs.

Everything is in order in the attic. The old mirror standing sheet-draped, ghost-like in the corner. The two boxcars the twins had labored over, sanded and painted, perched like two rusty relics reminiscing over their glory days. A coatrack, a few boxes . . . and in the center of all, the black trunk, brass-studded and all scratched up.

It's like someone's punched him in the gut. The last person to touch that chest had been their mother, the day she'd gathered all of Roy's things—pulled shirts and pants from his boyhood dresser, books and mementos, treasures of rocks and clamshells. Bob had poked his head up into the attic and spotted her as she sat on the attic floor, a shaft from the window bathing her in warmth as her hands trembled, folding each garment with care. As if each finger knew this was the last time she'd ever fold her boy's clothes, touch the clothes that touched him. He'd lingered briefly, watching her slender shoulders shake when the tears came, the way she wept silently into an old flannel shirt. The way her lips moved in prayer, with words he could not hear and a breaking heart he could feel across the room. She had tucked each item in as if laying it to rest, or storing it up for some miraculous someday.

And now here they are. Clothing pulled out and stacked neatly— but not in his mother's fashion of folding. Jeans and button-down shirts, saltwater boots, and the brown corduroy jacket Roy had worn nearly to threads. His draft letter, crisp as the day it arrived, lying open.

There's something else, too. Bob draws near to the shadowed pile beside the clothes. Two books are stacked squarely. He fingers their worn pages—*Rob Roy* and, on top, the Bible. He lets the edges of the pages flip against his thumb. Stuck between them is the picture from Roy's sick bay wall, the thing he must've fixed his eyes on as his life drained away. His anchor. Beaming Jenny cradling smallest William.

It's been years since Bob delivered this clutch of belongings home to Jenny—the night he'd held William and wished for all the world it could've been Roy's arms, and not his own, wrapping around that baby.

Closing his eyes, his mind plays out what must have happened. Jenny, guarding these things for William, his birthright. Roy's legacy.

William, penniless and with nothing but the clothes on his back, guarding them when life blew him cold and hard out on his own. Bringing them here, carrying them up the creaky old stairs, placing them among his father's things. A homecoming . . . and something more.

A search. Right here in the attic. A kid on the brink of manhood, trying to find the dad he never knew up here in the dust. These are vestiges of a story Bob has lived and relived. He hadn't considered it was also a story William was hungry for.

He gathers it all up, piling it until he can barely see over it, and heads downstairs. Some miraculous someday has come.

When William hits the bottom stair the next morning and rounds into the kitchen, where Eva is mashing blueberries and sugar and Bob is flipping buckwheat flapjacks on the griddle, he is wide-eyed and never looked more like a lost boy.

But it is the look of a lost boy who's just found treasure. In his hands, carried open-palmed like a gift on Christmas, is a shirt of Roy's. "I . . . found this. In my room," William says tentatively.

He's telling the truth. Bob had cranked those clothes through the wash bin yesterday and slung them over a railing behind the boathouse to dry. Eva had caught him and tried to do it for him, but this was something he had to do. When the wind and sun had dried them, he'd smuggled them into William's room along with the rest of Roy's attic belongings.

"You keep 'em," Bob says.

"But . . ." William rubs a thumb over the flannel in his hands.

"Aren't they . . . weren't they . . ." It's clear he's stumbling over what to call Roy.

"Your dad's," Bob finishes. "Yes, and now they're yours." He points the spatula in his hand at the shirt. "As it should be."

Something changes in that moment. Some of the hardness around William drops away. "You sure?"

Bob takes a swig of water from the glass on the counter, nodding, punctuating the nod by planting the glass firmly back in its place. "Never more sure of anything. You ready?" He piles a stack of steaming flapjacks on a plate and passes them to Eva. She ladles on the fresh blueberry syrup and slides the plate in front of William.

He pulls out a chair, slips Roy's shirt over his T-shirt, and sits down in the very chair Roy always used.

Eva steals a glimpse at Bob, and the pooling of water in her eyes matches the surge in his chest.

After that, the change goes deeper. The days get colder, but William, still as green as they come on the boat, keeps showing up. Keeps trying. Keeps almost-steering them into the rocks. If the streets did one thing for him when he was wandering for that year, it was to teach him to keep on keeping on. Until one day . . . he soars. It finds him. The magic of the sea, its rhythm, the dance of it.

Now, dressing mostly in his father's clothes, he's moving in perfect sync with the sea, as if he were born with whitecaps under his feet. And maybe he was. As winter passes, he wants to go out in the boat every chance he can. Even takes it solo some evenings, just to get out. He's on the water more than he's on land, and Bob can't shake the feeling that he's running. Leaving land—and all that he's seen there—behind.

Until one day, in the midst of spring's renewal, the land reaches out a hand as if in truce, offers him a place there once more. They're headed to the Gables, a summer lodge straight across the bay from Sailor's Rest, and one that's seen better days. It'd been in the Flint family for three generations but during the war had fallen dormant, only to reopen around 1950. Abner Flint, who'd returned from the front in France with a prosthetic leg and a heap of tenacity, girded himself with a pile of plans to bring the old place "up to speed." He'd been swinging a hammer and opening one room at a time ever since. The place had an old-world enchantment about it, dark wood and two wings of gabled rooms, tennis lawn and croquet, even a bowling green. In its heyday, it had played host to traveling troupes of performers, plays, orchestras—Ansel's own little corner of big-city sophistication, right there backed by the pines. They'd even hosted a fancy ball every summer, once upon a time. Few of the locals attended. It had been more for the Summer People up from Massachusetts, New Jersey, Connecticut, and New York, along with all their finery.

Abner had caught Bob in town yesterday, asked him to bring by the day's catch if he could, as he had a family coming in for a pre-season visit, as well as a pair of honeymooners from New York City. He said the city's name with button-busting pride, knowing the once-cobwebbed Gables had made a name for itself once again.

Bob and William had pulled plenty of lobsters from the traps, and they dock off starboard in the Gables' private harbor. Rowboats are lined up like school kids bobbing their friendly hello, and William, at the helm, is careful not to knock up against any of them.

"Good on you," Bob says. "You realize that passage you just brought us through is the same one you almost ran aground on the first day out?"

William's sheepish grin says he remembers all too well.

"You're an old hand at it now," Bob says.

William thanks him, and Bob lugs the catch up the sloping knoll toward the kitchen of the Gables. He and Abner make the sale and then stand in the wind, Bob with his arms folded and Abner catching him up on projects around the place. Digging a new well, outfitting the place with clamming gear for a crowd, spiffing up the boats.

"What's wrong with the boats?" Bob casts a glance at the rowboats, eyes drawn to where William's bent over one pulled ashore, running his hands along it. He's been reading through Roy's old boat-working manuals at night, and the sparks going off in his head just now are nearly visible.

"Aw, you know how they get. Ocean beating up on them every which way, all day and all night."

"You pulled 'em in for the winter, right?"

"I might've . . . not."

"Ab."

"I know. Wish I could get a hand around this place and catch up. I've got most of 'em back up and floating, but they all need fixin' of some sort." He swings his arms widely. "The whole place needs fixin'."

He narrows his eyes at William, who's on all fours now, tightening a bolt with bare hands. "That Roy's boy, is it?" When Abner talks, he stretches questions as far as they can get.

"Ayuh."

"Heard about that. He won't be wantin' a job, will he?"

"Can't say one way or another. You can ask, though."

And fifteen minutes later, William is learning that working for Abner might work out just fine. The man likes to talk, barely takes a breath, and William has no problem not talking. He'll get to work on boats, help around the place, and stay mostly unseen when the guests arrive. Being around the people but not of them. On the land, but still stitched to the sea through his work. It's perfect.

Abner's talking about a family coming in a couple of weeks from New Hampshire, how they'll be wanting the boats, and maybe a tennis lesson too, if William knows anything about the sport.

William grows a little green around the gills at this, but he's beaming as they ride home. The days that follow, Bob drops him at the Gables before sunup, and stops in after the day's work to bring him home. And every afternoon, the person who boards his boat is less boy, more man. He walks a little taller. There's color on his face, tan from mending boats and teaching lessons. Not tennis, as it turns out. He couldn't—or won't—hit a ball if his life depended on it. But he's found that some of the kids among the visitors find boat fixing to be fascinating.

He started explaining what he was doing, sometimes letting them try their hand at it, and when Abner witnesses it, he declares, "You've been holding out on me, have you? This is where all the kids are instead of the bowling green, is it?" And he headlines *Boatmaster Classes for the Young* as one of the lodge's new activities.

"Boatmaster classes." William laughs, steering them home and relaying the tale to Bob. "Fancy way of saying 'fixing broken things.'" They have a good laugh, and William slows the engine.

There's a gravity about him. Bob leans forward in his seat, listening. His silence, he hopes, inviting.

"Uncle Bob, uh . . ." He scratches his head.

"Yeah?"

"I wonder if I could . . . I mean . . . could I borrow the boat tonight? Just for an hour, maybe two."

The kid is trying not to show it, but he's a tower of nerves. Won't look at Bob, eyes fixed on the very calm water with a concentration deserved more by a fierce storm. Bob is tossed back to an image of himself just a few years younger than William, all tongue-tied and clumsy in his own skin around a certain girl. He knows what this is about.

"You got it," he says, and William relaxes. When he leaves that night, he ducks his tall form quickly out the door, but not before Bob sees the hair combed and shiny with hair tonic, no doubt from the bottle of Vitalis that has shown up in the medicine cabinet.

This continues for several nights. On the fourth night Bob waits up for him in the library. The night's gone dark around him and he's watching the sky out the window. Stars blinking and moving, great infernos set far enough away to fill mankind with wonder, make him feel small. *"When I consider your heavens . . ."*

He's lost in these musings, the world having grown dark without him noticing and without him flipping on any lights. He's dangerously close to ripping out another paper from the old family

266

tablet and penning more words when the door opens and William enters, a spring in his step.

"So, what's her name?" Bob's voice is gravelly from silence, coming out eerie and threatening from this dark abyss of a room.

William jumps as if he's been ambushed by a panther, and Bob barely keeps himself from laughing. He pulls the chain on the desk lamp beside him, clears his throat so he sounds human again. "I'm not gonna throttle you, son."

And William relaxes. Night and day different from the first time that word—*son*—slipped out. Bob nudges the chair opposite him with his foot, invitation for the boy to come on in.

"You scared me," William admits. "I thought you'd be in bed."

"Not me. There's a story I've got to hear." William sits, his lanky form dwarfing the cane-back chair as he slaps his hands onto his knees.

"So," Bob repeats, "what's her name?"

William looks longingly toward the door. Escape. Then he looks back at Bob and pulls in a breath. "Anneliese."

Bob nods, approving. And waits.

"I . . . met her at the Gables. She's there with her family—they have some connection with Ansel."

"Oh?"

"Yeah, but I don't know how."

Bob shrugs a shoulder. "A lot of people have ties to this place. You'd be surprised. The Gables has been around long enough to pull people in from all over creation, and people like to come see where their grandparents vacationed or where their great-grandparents summered, that sort of thing. It gets inside people, this place does."

William looks around the room as if it's the place Bob's referring to. "Yeah," he says.

"So, Anneliese," Bob says. "When are you bringing her around?"

William goes ten shades of red, and Bob relishes it. He hasn't razzed someone like this since Roy was around.

"I . . . well, see, they're leaving soon, and—"

Bob's laugh comes out easy, and he waves away William's protests. "You bring her if you want. And if not, maybe next summer, eh?"

William's face goes somber, his eyes direct on Bob. "Next summer?"

"If she's back. If you want to."

But William has moved on. It's not Anneliese he's latching onto in this moment, but this "next summer" notion. "You mean if I come back next summer?"

Good gravy, did the kid not yet realize that this place felt more like a home with him in it than it had since Roy had been gone? Sailor's Rest was as good as his. His birthright, even.

Bob leans forward, elbows to knees, locking eyes with his nephew. "I mean if you *stay*. This place is as much yours as it is Eva's and mine," he says. "Maybe not on the deed, but by rights." He shakes his head. "Stay as long as you want. I hope you never leave. You're family."

William stutters his thanks, taking himself off to bed before the moment has a chance to turn to mush. And Bob follows suit a few minutes later, climbing the stairs with a fullness swelling inside.

He's sure that come morning, William will see that this is right, and good, and that he's not staying with Bob and Eva just because he needs protection. He's here because he belongs.

thirty

Sitting in the pew, William is agitated. He hasn't been like this for ages. Bob's watched him since their first Sunday here in the creekside church between Sailor's Rest and town. Over the months he's gone from staring at his shoes the entire duration of the first service to, little by little, coming alive. Sitting a little taller, inclining an ear or, later, his whole self, as the pastor speaks on.

But today? He's like a caged beast. Still on the outside, but a battle waging within. Jaw clenched, hands curled tightly around the edge of the pew. He doesn't open his mouth during the closing hymn and strides out as soon as the *Amen* is spoken.

Bob follows, slowing only to thank the pastor. Turning a full circle, he doesn't spot the boy anywhere. He follows the trail around back—the stream snakes one way around the church, the trail the other, making a sort of island out of the white-steepled building. Behind it, the mountain rises quick and steep, barnacled with mossy boulders and speared with pine-tree growth, making it the favorite haunt of kids during church picnics—the perfect place for hide-and-seek.

Or for a man afire within.

He finally spots William muttering to himself where the stream bends sharp. Bob knows what it is to have it out with the Maker. Is this what's happening? A Jacob-wrestling-with-God moment? He'd best leave them be, then. A man and his God have got to

269

wrestle out the big things. Better than shoving them underground, never addressed.

But William spots him. He hurls a single word at him, voice cracking right down the middle. "Why?"

Bob tries to close the distance, but William's hand is up, gesturing a stop.

"That's a big question, son." Smallest word, biggest question. An age-old paradox.

William shakes his head, eyes wider. A silent reiteration. "You loved your brother," he says, and waits. It's a question, but he isn't sure what the boy is asking.

"Never stopped."

"And then he dies and that's . . . that's just it? You stick his clothes in the attic and just forget? Write off his wife and son? You're just . . . done with them?"

Ice pick to heart—that's what his words are. They pummel him, sending him reeling back to those raw days of bare survival. The battle to let them go, find a life again. The pain of seeing Jenny unable to look at him for the pain it brings her. She'd been a walking skeleton, desperate for change, for breath.

"I was never done with you, William."

He scoffs, breath visible in the cold. "Yeah. I guess that's why you were at my mom's funeral. That's why you knew exactly where I was, what I was going through, after she died, and who I was when I showed up."

Unseeing is he. Blind to all but the only truth he knows—the very real truth of being alone. Forgotten. Abandoned. Passed off. His words rile up anger in Bob—flesh-level anger that hears only his assumptions. But deeper than that, his words are pieces of shrapnel. Splayed across a wasteland, barren and alone—and aching to be gathered up. Why had William waited so long to bring up the question at the root of his struggles? Maybe it's because he is only now ready to hear the truth.

Pain this deep . . . it needs more than words.

"You'd best come with me," Bob says. "There's something you ought to see."

thirty-one

An hour later there's a canyon of silence between them, and a tower of stacked and mortared rocks before them. Bob tries to see it through William's eyes, watching on as the young man circles it, stopping to examine a few of the rocks along the way. The deep rust-colored one, sent from Sedona. A chunk of white marble pulled from a mine in Georgia. Gray in every intensity, from coast to coast and beyond. Bob traces them with his eyes, remembering faces. Stories.

His gaze falls on a bouquet of wilted lilies of the valley beside Luka's blue-streaked stone, and he smiles. Liesl has been here. She comes every few years without notice. She leaves a bunch of flowers on the ground, directly below the stone with a promise etched for the ages. She eventually finds him and Eva before she leaves the area. And this time, he'll be able to introduce her to William. He prays it will be healing for them both.

Near the top, the stone Ed hand-carried all the way from Mississippi is nestled, placed by the hands that cradled transformation. The same rock he took from Michael's grave site with the intent to shatter had ended up here, states away, fused with strength instead.

To William, the tower no doubt looks like a ruin. Unfinished, with heaps of rocks strewn on the ground. They are cataloged there with care—by size, shape, fit, to place pieces as in a puzzle—but to the unknowing eye, it is chaos.

William, though, seems to sense something. He draws back and crosses his arms over his chest. Not challenging. He just waits. Something's shifted in his demeanor. His jaw is still clenched tight, but Bob senses he is ready to listen.

How does one explain something so . . . so unexplainable? Something he still can't account for, the way it all happened? So he goes to the thing he knows best: Roy. Tells William about their escapades, the bonfires, the rock-throwing, the dares. Tells him of conquering this island together, the three of them. Tells of the war and—with care but also truth—tells of his father's death. It seems he knows much of this—Jenny at least told him that.

But that doesn't explain the hollow pillar in front of them, rising out of nowhere.

"There's a grief so deep it leaves a body desperate," Bob says, and looks into knowing eyes. He nods, acknowledging that William perhaps knows even more of this than Bob. "I got there. Clean shattered. Right here on this spot." He scuffs a boot, recalls spilling those tears, mingled with his mother's. "Enough to drive a man mad."

William nods.

"I was on the brink. The grief was so thick around me, I was drowning in it. And then words just punched right through it, imprinted inside like someone had taken a typewriter to my soul and spelled it out, telling me what I was to do. It's the only way I can explain it."

"Explain what?"

"This." He points at the lighthouse. "It was like God just settled right down there in the dust with me and gathered up what was left of me and said, *Now. To build.*"

He would never forget the impression of that voice on his heart. It was the voice of the man who, king of the universe, stooped to wash His own disciples' earth-crusted feet. Who rubbed spit into dirt and used the mud to make a blind man see. Whose royal day of birth was enrobed in dust, right there with the animals in a barn.

That man was accustomed to doing great things in humble places, and it usually involved dirt. Or rocks, as it were. The same God who told a solitary man to build a boat to prepare for a flood when no one had so much as seen a drop of water fall from the sky in all their lives.

Whenever Bob felt the press of attempting something insane for a reason only he could hear, he thanked God for the example of men and women who went before him.

William, hands stuffed in pockets, leans forward and concentrates. Finally, he asks, "But . . . what is it?"

Bob goes to the alcove in the wall of boulders behind them, pulls out the wooden box where lies a now-yellowed news clipping of the words. The poem. The only copy he's ever kept—clipped right from their own *Pier Review*. People had sent more over the years, from the *Boston Globe*, *New York Times*, *San Francisco Chronicle*, places he would never set foot in his life. He kept only the local copy.

He hands it to William who reads it once. Looks at the tower, still not seeing. Reads it again, and Bob can almost see the way the Words enter him this time. Threading through him, from him, round the tower and back.

"I wrote that the night God told me to build, the night your mother told me she was moving away. My last moments with your father were still so fresh, the words came easily." He can hear the crack of the gun salute, see his brother slipping beneath the waves at sundown.

"I'm no writer," he says. "No stonemason, either." He laughs, gesturing at the tower. "But a body does what it's got to. What its soul finds it must do." He moves to the tower, running his hands over the multi-colored stones.

He explains about the rocks, how they came—still come— from all over the country. And how each one, as he mixes mortar, seals rocks together, builds this tower higher, has carved William himself deeper into Bob.

"I stopped writing the two of you after Jenny . . . after your mother married." He falters, unsure how much to say. He didn't want to taint anything to do with Jenny for William. "She explained your stepfather—"

William scoffs, kicking the dirt. "Don't call him that."

Bob nods slowly, pondering.

William speaks. "He never really . . . took to me. When the neighbor kid and I learned to ride our bikes, his dad would run beside his bike saying 'I've got you, son. I've got you.'" William shakes his head. "Theodore just left me to figure it out. Pointed at the bike and went back inside to read his paper."

The story smolders inside Bob, his hands fisting. What he wouldn't give to have shown up on that street, to have run alongside that bike. To have said *I've got you, William,* a thousand times over.

He puts a hand on William's shoulder. William shrugs it back off.

A deep breath in, and Bob tries to explain. "Her new husband . . . didn't like the idea of her writing back and forth with another man. And I can't say I blame him." Let alone one who was identical to her late husband. Bob left that part unsaid.

"Maybe he would have been okay with me writing to you when you got older, but I didn't know where to begin. I was a stranger to you. I convinced myself you had a father and didn't need me muddling things."

William shakes his head. "You didn't have to know where to begin. You just . . . start. Say something." His voice tremors. "Anything."

He's scratching the surface, but something's running deeper than the resentment coating his words.

"I needed you," he says at last.

The air shivers around them, turning chill as the sun disappears behind thick clouds. Pines bend in a gust of wind, haunting whispers through their boughs.

Bob is stiff, words eluding him. How can a body undo a hurt so deep? William, too, stands statue-like, fingers furling and unfurling into fists. This is one of those moments that life hinges on, marking the course of whatever comes next, years and years of it. Will they stuff it down and seal this chasm with mortar, hiding the broken . . . or will they let the hammer above them come down in its full force, split it wide open?

Bob takes a step. Another. And more. Until his feet plant him in front of his nephew, his arms coming around him strong. He waits. The boy remains stiff for a breath, circled there—and then, in the fleeting drop of his shoulders, the unleashing begins. Sobs. Wracking his young body, releasing pain held in for who knows how long. It's a rending and a cleansing. It's a thousand apologies, a thousand forgivings.

When William pulls away at last, eyes red and swollen, he's different. Not healed . . . but held. Like the pieces of him have been gathered right up, and that is enough for now. The rest will follow.

Some of William's youth has dropped away. And in him, Bob sees Roy, rasping his last words with every ounce of strength he could summon. It is time—no, it is long past time—to deliver them.

"Your dad told me to tell you four things." He'd fallen asleep reciting them so many times they were emblazoned on the back of his eyelids.

William's presence is urgent for the words.

"He said he loves you, that it'll be all right, that life is big . . . and God is bigger."

William is still as he lets the message burrow deep. Bob prays the truth of it does its work.

The kid pulls something from his pocket and runs his hand over it. "I found this in Mom's things," he said, looking as if he doesn't want to hand it over. Bob takes in the jagged scrap of paper, handled so much it's worn soft.

He knows it. It's the message Roy passed to him with his last ounce of strength, the one he'd tucked in William's blanket so that Jenny would find it.

"Seventy-seven fathoms," William says. "Once I found her sitting on the end of her bed with it, just holding it."

There's more to the story, Bob can sense, but it's making William uncomfortable.

At length, he spits the words out. "She just sat there and cried, running her finger over the writing. I know it's my dad's handwriting. It matches what I've found in the attic." He pulls in a shuddering breath. "What's it mean?"

This, at least, is a story Bob can be proud of. He tells of Roy and Jenny, their mounting fathoms of love. Something so good . . . it should never have ended. "It's the number of a complete but always-growing love," he finishes. "One that'd give anything to give life."

William's jaw is locked, and all he can do is nod as he stares hard at that paper.

Sensing it is time to move from the past, for now, Bob claps William on the shoulder. "Come, see inside." He leads him to the far side of the lighthouse, where an arched doorway stands, and explains how someday, he'll build a heavy door, paint it red, make it seaworthy. For now, they duck inside the open archway and the walls rise round about them.

At one point, Bob had begun to worry he'd never be able to use all the rocks coming. But when he turned his sights to the inside, he realized the outside of this tower was just the tip of the iceberg. There was the stairway yet to build.

Stone upon stone, spiraling the inner walls of the tower, steps climbed one upon another. They were what allowed him to keep building the tower at its height. Climbing up, scaling the wide ledge at the top as he added new layers.

"We're close," he says, hearing the desperate hope in his own voice.

"We?" William's brows furrow. "Is someone helping?"

Yes, he says, there's Eva, and Ed. But the truth is, he can never be on this island without thinking of the souls of the soldiers—and of the others, like Liesl and Luka—what they gave. It's what keeps him going, though he is weary as the wailing wind. The longer he's worked, the more his eyes burn and his skin chafes and his joints lock . . . the more his heart yearns to light this flame at last and bring others home.

"I'll help," William says, standing just where his father had that last night on the island, the same look of unwavering determination on his face.

A wide smile overtakes Bob. "We're close," he says again. "Now that summer's here the building can start back up. Those crates that came, the same night you did? They'll make up the lens." He shakes his head in disbelief. "Still can't believe we got 'em. It's a miracle, really. And even more of a family legacy." He tells of the tract of woods up the mountain—how it brought his own parents together and now has funded the future of—he hopes—countless more.

He points to the rough but sturdy wooden hut built atop the tower. Only temporary, he explains—wooden beams pulled from the old railway shed behind Birchdown Mountain, walled in with planks and holding up a peaked roof to keep the rain off their heads as they build. It'll all be stone and steel one day.

He breathes in the spiced air of soil and history, thinks of the sale of the family woods that made it possible. "Lifetimes in the making, this is."

It's a feeling that lingers in the coming days, as William joins him more and more on the island. He steals away for work at the Gables each morning, and each evening to see his Anneliese, but tucks in every ounce of building that he can in between times.

On an ordinary Thursday, when the harbor's fogged in and Bob can't go out fishing, the two of them heave and pull and stack and slick mortar like a symphony. Eva sits on a boulder, clipboard balanced on her knees as she sketches diagrams for the top of the lighthouse. Anneliese has a family commitment that evening, which leaves William to work long with Bob. The three are settled into an easy camaraderie with only the crack of a campfire adding to their rhythm as Eva hums, when the sound of footsteps slips in.

"William?" The voice is sweet and light, like the alyssum Eva grows along the front walk.

William stands and swipes work away from his face with his sleeve, trowel in hand. "H-Hi," he says, with a glance at Bob and then back at the young woman. She looks familiar, with dark hair and a presence that suits the mist gentling around her.

William's crossing the clearing to her, and their conversation is quiet, tones bright. This can only be one person. William takes her by the hand, leading her over to Bob, who is joined by Eva.

"Uncle Bob, Aunt Eva . . . this is Anneliese."

The girl offers a hand, and though it's delicate, it is strong, too. Not a stranger to work, despite its porcelain appearance.

"Well," Bob says, enveloping her hand in his and slipping his other arm around Eva. "We're honored to meet you, Anneliese. Seems you've made quite an impression on our William."

William ducks his head and scuffs the ground, but he can't keep from grinning. He turns to Anneliese. "I thought you'd be off with your family."

Her forehead creases. "I am," she says. "That's why I was surprised to find you here. My parents brought us here to meet someone."

"'Us'?" Bob looks around, and two silhouettes approach through the misty veil.

Anneliese nods. "Yes, sir. My older brother and sister." The two young adults approach, their gazes captured upward by the tower. They're dressed in their Sunday best. Simple clothing, but too nice for a hike up the island trail.

"I'm wondering if you have the wrong island," Bob says. "Everlea Island, maybe. There's a fine house there, and the Phelps family moved in there not too long ago. If they're expecting you, we can point you in the right direction. It's easy to get turned around in this fog mull."

He's turning to point beyond the lighthouse, in the direction of Everlea Island, when his name is spoken.

"Mister Robert Bliss."

Bob turns, to find a man he's never seen before. Light hair tumbling out of lines it had been neatly combed into. Black-rimmed glasses and behind them, a haunted but overflowing look he has only seen on one other face before.

Soon, that other face emerges from the mist, lit with unbridled joy.

Connections are firing in his mind faster than he can keep up. The lilies of the valley by Luka's stone. Anneliese's family having some connection to Ansel . . . "Liesl?"

Eva's joy bursts to life beside him as she clasps her hands together before her heart. "But that means . . . Is this . . . ?" She looks to the man, and on to Anneliese. Bob has never seen Eva at a loss for words before. She takes Liesl's hand, rubbing it gently, as if to fill in the words that are too wonderful to be spoken.

"Yes." Liesl's voice is lined in a laugh of her own. "You told me once God does not keep count of miracles. He has surely been too good to us, but . . ." She pulls her hand away, loops it through the arm of her love. "It is true. This is my Luka."

The man steps forward, stretching his hand toward Bob. He grips it in a steady shake. Much is said in his silent stare, as Liesl and Eva erupt into stories. He clasps his hands behind his back in a humble stance, listening to the tale being told. An account of his broken mind and body healing after years, then years of searching for Liesl, his children, a letter to his sister, lost long in the post-war mail . . . until he'd found them, at last.

He wanders over to the tower, fingering rocks one by one as his wife speaks on about his passage to America. Before leaving Europe, he'd learned of the daring rescue of his family by a seaman he owed everything to. And every evening at sundown as he crossed the Atlantic, Luka had paid tribute to the American sailor by saluting toward where he imagined the destroyer had been, and falling to his knees in prayer afterward, to give thanks to his God for the coming reunion.

He'd gathered his wife in his arms there in an October cornfield, hugged his children—including the one he'd never met, Anneliese. He'd taken Anneliese's hand in his, covering her fingers in tender kisses.

And now those fingers are intertwined with William's. These two lives—standing here on this rock, both of them well and breathing because of Roy. Bob can't help wondering—does Roy know? He prays so. Prays there is much rejoicing over this redemption moment that wraps around the eight souls on the island.

Bob joins Luka at the rock, pointing out the stone his bride pulled from the earth for him. And as the man stoops to trace the words *Eines Tages*, Bob longs for the day this tower will do more such home-bringing.

A few months, he guesses. A few months is all it'll take to get there, to light this thing up at last and finally, finally let this memorial live.

thirty-two

Winter is upon them, a magic in the air. Lobster boats sport scarlet bows or wreaths of fresh-cut evergreen. Off-season lobster traps are stacked with care in skyward-stretching pyramids like so many Christmas trees, strung with lights in yards around the harbor for decoration. Smoke perpetually curls from chimneys.

At Sailor's Rest, evenings are spent stoking the fire, drawing up plans for how they'll transport and install the Fresnel lens once spring, and warmer weather, comes. William has given the project a new fire, lending his passion and logistical mind to it with abandon. William's mind lights with an understanding Bob does not have, whenever they speak of the lens, its parts, how so many individual pieces work to make the light stronger than one unified piece.

Over the months, layers had peeled away from the boy, revealing emerging gifts. Leadership—the way he organized the motley crew of them. He'd plant his hands at his sides, narrow his eyes in the way that told the rest of them sparks were going off like fireworks in his head, then being lassoed into order and sense. He'd set out a plan for the day in his quiet and humble way—not demanding power or stepping on what Bob already had in place, but instead coming in and completing it. Learning fast from Bob how to try the stones, lay them out on the ground like puzzle pieces with

281

their handpicked mates, ready to be set in their homes when the time came.

It never ceased to amaze Bob how a rock from one corner of the world, broken and cleaved by time or trauma, held just the right angles, curves, ridges to fit side by side with a stone from the opposite side of the world. William marveled at this, too, and made Bob's science of it into an art form. Checking colors, patterns, light-catching properties for the strongest, most breathtaking effect possible. Watching him was like witnessing a rebirth. His fervor was contagious.

He'd taken to spending nights in the boathouse. There was an old potbelly stove there that had warmed the place when it was Roy's workshop, so while the winter air crept in to frost the beams each night, William slept on a cot by the stove, content to be where his dad had spent his own time creating, measuring, planning. The light would stay on out there till all hours, just as it had with Roy, and the far wall became a working schematic board of sketches and outlines, pinned to the old wood. And more than that, a tribute to the lives. He'd begun to organize and catalogue the letters, photographs, and stories that had accompanied the rocks. Bob had looked in a few times but couldn't follow the intricacies of William's sorting. He's a genius at work, bringing order to chaos. Eva keeps him in steaming hot chocolate, made with milk from the neighbor's cow and her secret ingredient, freshly grated nutmeg.

Six days before Christmas, the three of them are walking along the harbor in town, bundles in hand and Eva's cheeks aglow, eyes framed in laugh lines. She is more beautiful every day, increasing years only adding to her grace and spark. Broader of shoulder than when he'd first come, William takes his lanky form off to the post office and deposits a red envelope into the slot on the door.

Eva elbows him when he returns. "For Anneliese?" His quick grin answers. Letters fly between the two every week, and Bob had stumbled on calendar markings, tallying days until the coming July, when the girl would return to the Gables. If William has anything to do with it, she'll return and never leave. There'll be a ring in the offing, Bob wagers.

Back home, supplies stored up in the cupboards and tree hauled into the sitting room, they spend an evening draping its boughs in strings of cranberry. Frost-sweetened and harvested last month from the bogs a few towns over, only the smallest of the ruby-red fruits have been spared the kitchen to adorn the tree.

Like most of Ansel, they still hold to the old tradition of candles on the tree, lit only for a few carols, a person on standby with a pitcher of water. No one had ever had fire to answer to as a result, but they all took care. There was no end to what fire could do in these parts, as they knew so well from 1947. "The Year Maine Burned," they all called it, and it sent shivers down spines.

All is calm this night—supper, singing with Eva's stumbling piano playing, and bellies full of Mom's hazelnut pie, a recipe Eva had resurrected with much more grace than her attempts at the piano. William stokes embers in the hearth to that perfect warmth where the coals sing like chimes.

"Stay," Eva says, as William jackets himself to head into the night. It's snowing, and potbelly stove or not, it'll be cold in the boathouse. "That bedroom's just going to waste up there."

William could never say no to Eva. The bond they've formed since his arrival had done things to Bob's soul. A son he'd never been able to give her. An unexpected mother after losing one so dear.

"I'll be back," he says, doffing his cap like an old gentleman. He'd scrounged up Bob's old newsie cap and had taken to wearing it on shore, when he didn't need so heavy a covering. "I'll just go out for a few hours."

"You're as stubborn as your uncle," she says, with a wink. The way she says it sings highest praise, and the way she slips into Bob's arms after William has left, pulling him into a dance just like that night on the Charles River in Boston, has Bob's chest full to bursting at the very thought of this woman—in all the wide world—choosing him.

They know "a few hours," in William's universe, might mean well into the wee hours, and so with the peace of a full home brimming with unseen blessings, they retire.

Something wakes Bob. At first all is quiet, but something underlying the dark unsettles him, launches him from his bed. *William.*

He's not in his bed. Nor downstairs. Out in the night the air is tinged with smoke from the harbor homes' fires. He looks toward the dock, where the *Savvy Mae* bobs in a quickening wind as if frantic herself. He turns, everything seeming to slow. Behind the house, an orange glow fills the dark. Sparks shoot in bursts.

That single thought pounds in his chest again—*William.*

He flies, blind to time, space. All he knows is he's in the boathouse now, coughing in a black soup of darkness and angry light. Half the building is afire. Someone's been fighting it—walls are charred, some aglow, some groaning beneath a quaking beam above them.

"William!"

No answer.

Where is he? A prayer pounding with his very pulse. His eyes dart. He's vaguely aware of sweat trickling, eyes burning, lungs wheezing. The structure is alive, walls compressing, expanding, fighting for breath just like him. *Where. Is. He?*

There is movement. From the harbor-side of the boathouse, the end William had set up his world in. A shadow emerges from gray smoke, doubled over and jolting in a fit of coughs.

"William!"

The young man's face jerks up, soot-covered. Devastated. Lugging two buckets, he runs past Bob and straight out to the creek out back, the same one he'd confronted Bob near, upstream at the church.

Bob grabs the bucket Roy always had upside down for a stool and follows. Their legs run in tandem, then in utter chaos. To the fire and back, Bob can't count how many times. It might have been hopeless, the two of them against a ravenous fire in an old place like that but for the snow that night and the week before, and William's dousing everything so quickly.

Somewhere in the haze, Eva joins them. Time warps into a nothingness that feels like an eternity. Until finally they collapse, the three of them watching the place smoke. Flames gone—and part of the boathouse, too. Not all, but a chunk from the harbor end, and they'll keep watch the night to make sure it goes no farther.

Wrapped in a blanket from William's cot, Eva drifts off, head against Bob's shoulder. The hem of her white nightgown is singed, uneven where the fire bit into it. Bob fingers it, throat throbbing as he thinks what could have happened, how close it got to her. This woman who should be clad in silk and diamonds, wearing cotton and ashes as her crowning glory.

He looks up, sensing William's gaze. And what he sees written there closes his throat even more.

"William." He rasps the name out, willing it to chase off the despair on the boy's face.

The boy looks from Eva's hem to the ground between them. He sniffs, swallows hard. It's cold, white moonlight that lights him now, not the eerie red of the fire. It traces his features, highlighting two things: Torment. Guilt.

Lower this time, he repeats the name. "William?"

"I should never have had a lantern in there," he mutters as if in a dream. A nightmare. He shakes his head, eyes growing wild as they shift side to side.

Bob waits.

"I just thought . . . five more minutes. Five more minutes would get the job done. I was working on the pile from the prisoners of war." Face pinched, he winces. "One thousand two hundred and"—he swallows again, throat surely raw—"seventeen. That's how many you have from prisoners of war."

He's talking about rocks now. Almost in a trance. The kid needs sleep. It won't look so bad in the morning. The three of them are alive. The boathouse still stands—most of it.

"They should be in order. What they went through . . . the least they deserve." He pulls dry blades of wild grass from the ground around them, snapping them off. He looks at Bob directly now. "So someone can find them, if they want. What if . . . what if someone comes looking someday? What if someone wants to know?"

He looks fevered. He needs to get inside. But this mad rambling, it wants out.

"What if . . . what if a daughter wants to know? Or a son? They should be able to come here." He climbs to his feet, more old man than young in his stiff movements. Has he been burned? "They should be able to find out about what happened, and how it matters, and how it's going to save more lives, and . . . and that it wasn't for nothing, and—"

He wobbles. Grips a nearby tree trunk, leans his forehead on it. His own story pulsing in his ramblings.

Bob is beside him, guiding him inside. He'll return for Eva and keep watch himself for the rest of the night. But for now, what this boy needs is rest. To close his eyes to the horror he was nearly consumed by. *Is* being consumed by.

"Shh," Bob says. "They will. We'll see to it. You did a good work in there, William." And he had. Even in the dark, Bob could see the boy had guarded those papers with his life. Whisked some of them out of the way, doused the ones he couldn't. Water would dry. Flames would never relinquish. "You did good."

Bob guides him toward the house, but William halts. "Fathoms . . . will burn," he mutters and turns back toward the boathouse in a daze.

Bob's hands are on the boy's shoulders, turning him back toward the house. His chest aches at the delusional mutterings.

"I've got you, son."

Words the boy longed to hear for so long. William's breathing becomes thicker, and he locks Bob's eyes with his own in a silent *thank you*, and a silent plea.

A quick glance back shows Eva's eyelids fluttering sleepily open. He holds up a finger to indicate he'll be back in a minute for her—but she's looking at the boathouse, stricken.

Bob reaches the front door at the same time as Leonard Fink from down the road, who says he smelled the smoke. One look at the black-streaked face of a nearly unconscious William, and he's off down the road to fetch the doctor.

William's almost asleep by the time Bob gets him to the sofa in the sitting room, helps him lay his head down, pulls the deep red afghan up around him. He looks so young. Innocent. Beneath all that black soot, he sees a glimmer of the babe he held so long ago.

And just as he reaches the door to head out in the snow once more, he hears a barely audible murmur. "Fathoms . . . fire . . ."

With a wordless prayer Bob leaves him. But when he gets to where he'd left his bride cocooned against a tree in her nightgown and a blanket, she's gone.

Delicate footprints in the shallow snow and dirt lead into the boathouse. Instantly, his stomach is heavy, hot tar. In a blur of motion he's inside the boathouse, in the smoldering mouth of a dragon who has consumed too much already.

And he sees it in a split-second, happening before he can stop it and yet with the stillness of time slowed. Eva, stooping in her white nightgown, golden hair about her shoulders as she reaches for a scrap of paper on the ground.

The beam above her, shifting at a sickening angle. Unloosed by carbon and soot, its strength burned right out of its sinews.

It falls, and all goes mute as he launches himself toward her.

But by the time he's there, this girl—the one with the crowbar beneath a Boston moon who righted his world in that scarlet dress—is fallen. Pinned, unconscious. Dressed in a growing pool of scarlet. Some madness overtakes him from a place unseen, and he lifts that impossible beam from atop his beloved.

thirty-three

Teetering, skittering right along with his pulse, Bob watches the doctor examine Eva on the sofa William has cleared for her.

There are the surface injuries—the gash along her jawline. The broken fingers where her hand had locked tight around what she'd gone in after.

And then there is the doctor's look, the stroking of his moustache, down and down, with a troubled sigh. This comes when he examines her legs. They do not respond. They may not respond, not ever. He kindly says there are cases where movement is regained after a blow to the spinal cord, but there is gravity in his gaze, too, that says he believes otherwise for Eva Bliss.

But, oh, she breathes. *Thank you, God.* Every muscle in him wants to gather her right up, the way she'd done with the pieces of his soul, mortaring them together as they worked side by side to stack rocks.

The way they might never work side by side again.

No matter. They did not need to work side by side for him to never leave her side. This will be his life now. Caring for her. Whatever it takes.

A breeze from the front door as the doctor departs rocks a crumpled paper on the floor beside Eva. In all the urgency, it had slipped from her hand when the doctor examined her and bound her shattered fingers.

He smooths it . . . and falls numb as he reads Roy's writing. Two words destined to keep coming back and back to him. Bent, it seems, on crushing him. *77 Fathoms.*

This, his brother's proclamation of ever-growing love—is this what it's bound for? Destruction? Hanging his head, he tightly crumples the paper in his hand.

Eva stirs, and there's a gentle touch upon his knee. She's been in and out of sleep since they'd moved her in, and he doesn't know how much she's heard.

Her sleepy eyes flutter open, pale lips spreading into a thin smile. "Unnecessary contrivances," she says.

Her words snatch him back to the night they met. For her sake, he summons a wan smile, remembering their old joke. "Names?"

"No," she says, closing her eyes and rolling her head back on the pillow. "Legs."

So says the woman who scales an island mountain path every day with him. Who counted her war coveralls and the work she did while wearing them as her greatest honor. Who could live ten lives and still never run out of footsteps to take her the places her heart afire dreamed of.

Her courage smites him.

"You know what is necessary?" Her eyes remain closed as she speaks.

A moment passes, and he wonders if she's gone back to sleep. But she reaches out, covering his hand in hers and sliding her soot-streaked fingers down until she opens his hand and touches the paper. "This."

The fathoms. She's not just talking about letters on paper. Eva knows what they mean. To Roy, to Jenny . . . to William, whom she loves unending fathoms of her own—enough to give everything to put this paper back in his hands. She'd known what William's fevered ramblings had meant after the fire—Bob had not.

A mistake he would live to regret every moment. If he had gone in for the paper instead of Eva . . .

Soon her breathing steadies into a deep rest, and he lays her bandaged hand over her heart. Gripping the paper, he heads to the boathouse, bracing himself to face that place.

Wild desperation claws at him, trying to get past the numb wall drawing up around him. Inside, he takes in the north end of the boathouse, with its charred walls and roofless corners. Everything here tells the story of a man—William—who had to make an impossible choice.

Papers preserved.

A pile of rocks, where William is sitting with a soiled rag, scrubbing at the rocks to scour away blackened ash with his own fingers.

His frenetic motion stills, hunched shoulders falling more as he senses Bob's presence.

"You should be sleeping," Bob says. His voice comes out flat, and it sounds faraway.

William turns slowly. "Can't." He stands. "I . . . heard the doctor talking."

Bob's jaw sets. He can't return to those words. "Time will tell," he says. He feels something pulling him up out of these shadows, to be the light-giver William needs right now. But the dull shock weighs him down until his eyes swim.

Time will tell what? Whether his love would walk again? Nothing would stop her from living a full life, he knew. But there had been other things the doctor mentioned. Possible complications of such an injury, to do with her heart. The sort that could end her. He winces, as if that can hold back the encroaching darkness.

"Do you think she'll be okay?" William's look is so fragile, so full of fledgling hope.

Bob will not lie. But how can he tell him the truth? That his fear for Eva is so dark he can hardly swallow around it? He exhales slowly, willing stiff legs to carry him to the potbelly stove. He picks up the metal coffeepot Eva keeps there, swirls it around as if to mix the hot chocolate that's so painfully absent inside. Sets it down and walks mechanically on. His boot crunches over something unnatural on what should be a hard-packed dirt floor. He freezes.

The ground shimmers in a way that is almost beautiful, but it sinks a fist into his gut. A quick scan shows wooden boxes splintered, gruesome in their sharp angles, cradling more shards within. His fingers buzz with numbness coming alive.

This is—*was*—the Fresnel lens. His life's savings, the fruit of his family land. The last hope of the lighthouse . . . shattered to pieces.

This should not wreck him. It's just wretched glass. Eva is alive. William is alive. And yet this last blow somehow piles all the others together and buckles his knees, fells him to the earth like a dead old tree.

Palms breaking his fall, smarting with pain from the glass dust, he looks around and sees only shattered lives. *Forget the lens. Forget the land. Forget it all!* But every shard is a reminder that all he's done is bring grief and hurt upon everyone he loves. All for a stupid tower.

Far off he hears William's voice calling to him. A hand touching his shoulder tentatively. A wavering voice uttering two words—*I'm sorry*—over, and over, and over again.

There's a man more courageous than this Bob buried somewhere in him, trying to break out of this covering of ice to grasp that hand, comfort that voice.

But this Bob—numb, broken, sapped of hope—cannot rise.

And in the morning, William has gone.

thirty-four

Emptiness burrows deep into Annie this night, replaying the story she has pieced together from her own experience and Bess's tale of her father's time in Ansel and the years afterward. The fire. The chasm that years pushed wider, the longer that silence dwelled between Bob and Dad. Months and years given to Eva as she learned to live life from a wheelchair. Bob spent every moment he could at her side, caring for her, carrying her, turning her wheelchair in a slow dance upon their dock every evening until God took her home fifteen years later.

Bob had written letters to William that he'd had no way to send, not without an address. Those years her father had been outrunning his past, fighting in the jungles of Vietnam. And when he'd returned, time had stretched the chasm between the men so wide, neither knew how to bridge it.

Annie's mother had eventually gotten in touch with Bob, sending a birth announcement Bob's way when Annie was born. And he'd done the same, sending Eva's obituary to Anneliese with four words scratched upon the news clipping: *She loved you fierce.* This, then, was how they communicated—through newsprint.

Annie had asked her mother about it once. They'd been in the old green station wagon, packed with suitcases as Anneliese drove

Annie up the coast to stay the summer with this man she'd never met. Why didn't they write more, or speak? "It's between your father and Bob," Anneliese had said, sorrow in her voice. She'd looked as if she wanted to say so much more, but left it at a simple "I only send what—I hope—will mend."

Annie had thought she'd meant the newsprint and had modeled her own communication with Bob after that. It never occurred to her that what Anneliese was sending . . . was Annie. Right into a void Eva had left. Yet somehow that void had turned into a soft place for her to land when she needed it most.

Annie wishes she'd known more, found a better way to bridge the gap. Thinking of each of them shouldering loss upon loss, it shamed her. If Bob would but wake, she might be able to make up for that lost time, somehow. The doctors were beginning a protocol to bring him out of his induced coma, and the next few days would tell much.

Jeremiah had happened upon Bess and Annie halfway through the tale—right when Bob had shown William the tower. He'd sat as rapt as she, listening to Bess's account. The way he had watched her—as if catching every word right along with her and wrapping it into safety in that rugged endless place inside him—left her with a comfort beyond description.

So here in the dark she sits, peering out of the bay window of Sailor's Rest, up into starlight so vibrant it feels like heaven is reaching right down to her.

But what does heaven want with her, after all her years of distance?

The thoughts turn her toward the anchor she feels inside. There is no change in Bob's condition. Margie Lillian has decided there isn't enough time to implement the ferry to the lighthouse for this week's festival. Perhaps she's caught wind of Annie's failed small-town-saving schemes. Perhaps Alpenzell had warned her. It's probably for the best. Chicago is emailing with projects to keep her busy while here, but with every calculation and report she generates, something dries up inside her.

Where do you want me? Her eyes shut around the prayer. *Where do I belong?*

A knock sounds at the front door, and she jolts, looking to the clock in the corner. Eleven fifteen. A quick look out the window shows Jeremiah, unruly hair sticking out from underneath his baseball cap. He looks disheveled, as if he's been up for two nights straight.

Pulse quickening, she opens the door.

"Hey," he says, the word easy but his voice roughened. "Can you . . ." He looks over his shoulder to where Annie realizes there's a second boat bobbing at the end of the dock, small next to the *Glad Tidings.*

"Jeremiah." A smile spreads across her face, her voice. "You finished Roy's boat?"

His lopsided grin answers her question. "Get your shawl thing." His eyes widen, as if realizing his abrupt tone. "If you want to come, I mean."

"Come where?"

"You'll see."

There's no way she's saying no to his veiled excitement. There's a boyish charm there, an invitation to something sacred.

She grabs the knit blanket from its place on the couch, slips on her saltwater boots, and dashes back across the sitting room. Sliding to a stop in front of the small porthole mirror on the wall, she gives her ponytail a tug in a hopeless attempt to add some sort of polish to her near-midnight appearance in jeans and a rustic flannel shirt, procured from Joe's Landing.

Not that Jeremiah will care what she looks like. And not that she should, either.

He's waiting for her out at the dock and offers his hand to help her aboard the *Glad Tidings.*

She wants to ask, to say something about how she thought they were taking the canoe. But something stops her, and as they leave the dock, she sees he's towing the canoe behind.

They pass the harbor, where the school's field lights blaze as vendors work late into the night raising their white peaked tents for tomorrow's festival amid bunting and hanging flower baskets, air laced with cinnamon from someone's test run of funnel cakes. On the green, a bright light shines on Spencer T. Ripley pacing the gazebo, seemingly practicing a speech for the twenty white empty chairs before him.

They pass Everlea Estate and Sully's wind chimes, with their soft lullaby. She feels as if Jeremiah has stretched his hand out to her and they've stepped right out onto the waves on some secret dance floor, while the rest of the world slumbers and toils. It occurs to her that, for the first time, she did not tremble when boarding his boat from the dock.

He takes her north, following the Bold Coast and its rugged cliffs at a safe distance. At length, he cuts the engine, dropping anchor. The moon is high and new, and its pale sliver of light slips into the vertical crevices of the cliffs like liquid silver.

Out here they could shout and not a soul would hear them. A hush has settled about them. Wordlessly, Jeremiah clambers down into the canoe, gesturing for Annie to follow and holding up his hand to help her in, eyes shining.

Once seated, he grabs two paddles. He hands one to her, a question in his eyes. They trade a conspiratorial glance, and although she has no idea where they're going, she feels a part of something grand.

The sound of water rippling around their oars settles into a rhythm, their bodies leaning forward and back in tandem, guiding the vessel.

They slip around a ledge of cliff, into a haven Annie hadn't noticed before. It lay in such a way that at nearly every angle, the cliff appears solid, when in reality one arm of the cliff slips directly behind the other, overlapping to create a corridor of sorts. And that corridor opens into a perfect alcove. A hidden, tiny harbor, like a room in the sea that only they hold the key to. Shallow waters, embraced by sun-heated granite all the day long so that even in the middle of the night, the effect is that of a pool with little water escaping or entering. Stillness and warmth, right there where a cold sea churns just on the other side of these walls.

"Oh," Annie breathes, and cannot find more words.

As she turns to face him, Jeremiah's grin is unbridled. She's never seen it so wide, and it thrills her heart.

"Just wait," he whispers, as they place their paddles across their laps.

There's a sacred hush, and then, boat drifting ever so slowly toward the walls of this fortress, Jeremiah leans forward. "Dip your hand in."

Annie eyes the dark water. "What, so the piranhas can bite my fingers off? You'd like that, wouldn't you? I couldn't pester you with all my note-taking and question-asking, then."

Jeremiah's laugh rolls low and smooth, wrapping itself around her. "Yeah, those tropical Maine piranhas." He holds her gaze and tips his head toward the water. "Trust me." He holds his hand out and waits.

At those words, and at the sight of the hand that dumped sand on the deck of his boat for her, and battled storms just to bring letters that might brighten a soul's day . . . she knows, without a doubt, that she can trust this man. Would trust him a thousand times over.

Eyes fixed on his, she gives him her hand. He hesitates only a moment. Something plays across his face. Regret? Fear? Whatever it is, the look is gone in an instant, determination in its place as he sets his jaw.

He crosses his thumb over her palm, cradling the back of her hand. He stretches his arm out over the water, guiding hers. And then, in a sudden arc of motion, runs their hands, fingers entwined, through the water.

It's like chilled velvet, fierce and soft all at once. Instantly, the liquid darkness ignites. From pitch-black, the water beams a pure Tahitian blue.

Annie gasps and pulls her hand back, holding it to her heart. The night air is cool against widened eyes. She points at the ripples, the bright flicker dying down into a sparse web, like spiderweb lightning.

"What just happened?"

Jeremiah's eyes are laughing. "Do it again."

Annie shakes her head. "Not until you explain that . . . that"—she swirls her finger emphatically—"water electricity."

"Some things are better lived than explained," he says, taking up his paddle. He dips it in, and the outline of the boat and paddle in the water lights in the same way. He paddles closer to the cliffs rising ahead of them, and the small waves that form as a result break against those cliffs. They lighten as they crash, then fade into darkness. He paddles faster, turning their boat in a small circuit until those waves are hitting all the cliff walls circled around them, scattered lights like bright blue fireflies.

He stills his paddling again and lets his fingers comb through the waters, stirring up the light threading through his hands.

It is magic. Pure magic, the kind she hadn't felt since the fairy tales of her youth, or the first time she'd caught her breath and her heart skipped a beat at the sight of a shooting star. Magic, and wonder, and fairy tales, and—

"Microbes," Jeremiah says.

Annie feels cosmic confusion freeze upon her face.

"Microorganisms," he says again, and his voice bears a boyish delight that does not match this laboratory-worthy word. Not out here in the night, where the sea has found a way to hold the stars.

She tilts her head, clears her throat. "Do tell."

"They're like these tiny torchbearers, billions of them. And when something disturbs the water"—he gestures at the illuminated boat outline—"this happens."

Annie releases a breath, her wonder audible. "It's incredible, Jeremiah."

He's grinning from ear to ear.

He scoots forward on his seat and leans in. "Go ahead," he says.

Tentatively at first, she traces the water with her fingertips. A pinprick of light shows, and then a dusting of others. She clenches her fingers into a submerged fist, then releases her fingers suddenly. A cloud of light shines, plays about in ribbons around and through her fingers, summoning laughter from somewhere deep inside.

Soon, she's on her knees in the hull of the canoe, dangling both arms over, tracing shapes and swirls, watching the light trail and surround her. Jeremiah slips to his knees beside her, leans one arm on the boat's edge and dangles the other into the ripples with hers.

She faces him, studies this foreign spark of life on his usually somber face. For reasons she cannot fathom, he's inviting her into something special to him—it's written in the gentle lines around his smile.

"Thank you for showing me this."

He nods . . . and he's pulling words back. Some kind of tug-of-war, until he speaks, finally.

"You're different here," he says.

She pulls one arm out of the water, drapes it over the edge of the boat to better face him.

"Different?"

"Yeah. Just . . ." He gives a small laugh. "Well, look at you. I couldn't have paid you to touch this ocean a week ago."

Annie looks around. "This doesn't feel like the same ocean," she says. Not the same waves that nearly took her mother, carried her father away, buried her grandfather. She shivers and starts to pull her hand out of the water.

But Jeremiah moves his hand beneath hers, light following it as he laces his fingers between hers. His touch anchors her.

He swallows, serious. "Do you know how it works? The light, I mean."

She purses her lips, feigning deep thought. "You came here earlier and emptied a bunch of glow sticks out?" She knows as well as he that this is not the answer, that it's something from that stack of books of his, and he's about to explain how microbes work.

"Close." Jeremiah's got a good poker face. "The microbes," he says, "only have a single cell. And they use it to capture sunlight all day—their sole purpose. At night, when danger comes"—he swishes their hands quickly to light them up—"they don't run. They don't shrivel up or hide. They release that sunlight they've been storing up, right into the darkness. They fight it back by lighting it up."

A shiver runs through Annie as Jeremiah brings their hands up out of the water. He lets his gentle grip linger, studying their hands with brows creased . . . and then he lets her go.

But just as she thinks he'll reach for the paddle, take them away from this place—and an ache springs in her chest at the thought—he swings both his legs over the edge of the canoe, gives her a wink, and tipping the canoe precariously, plunges in.

"Jeremiah!"

Her heart's slamming against her rib cage, sickness and panic bringing back the terror of when her eight-year-old self could not save her mother.

The glow churns with bubbles and movement for too long—and then the sound of breaking water shatters her terror. He's there, head bobbing and mouth grinning, a look of complete bliss on his face. Water dripping off his eyelashes, he swims over and crosses his arms casually over the edge of the canoe. "Well?"

She's furious, and she knows it's unreasonable. Just her adrenaline, looking for a way out, aiming itself at him. "Well, if you think I'm helping you get out of there after a stunt like that, I—"

"Well . . ." He slows the word, scoops it out like he's building her a ramp down to the water with it. "You coming?"

She scoots back, away from him, away from the edge.

Ripples of water ring them, floating there beneath the dark, lit from down under. Everything about this moment is upside-down and inside out. Especially her.

"Annie." His voice is tender, serious. "You're . . . a different kind of phenomenon. You know that?"

Just what every girl wants to hear. But her heart's beating harder against her chest, and she bites her tongue, listening.

"I've never met anyone who loves people as much as you, who's made it her job to study life."

Her shoulders ease, just a bit.

"But for all that love of life . . . are you actually living it?"

Her defenses try to rise, but the truth is pinning them down.

"You float over it on the surface." He palms the boat twice, letting it make his point for him. "Doing these incredible things. But something's keeping you from plunging into it."

He lowers himself into the water, opens his arms wide, the light trailing him.

"You don't want to miss this, Annie."

She leans forward, looking at the water, heat pricking her eyes as the scene swims before her. She grips the canoe edge and leans out, just a little.

And his hands are on her forearms, bracing them gently. Thumbs skimming over her skin, wrapping her in assurance and invitation.

"*I*"—he holds her gaze—"don't want to miss this." He exhales. "With you."

She falters, looking for an excuse and half-hoping it will fail. "My clothes," she says. "I'm not dressed for a swim."

"I don't think you actually care about that."

Touché.

"Plus, I hear phytoplankton don't have a white-collar dress code," he says.

He's treading water in shorts and a T-shirt. If he can do it . . .

Gulping, she dips a hand back in the water. He releases her arm, makes room for her to jump in. And she knows, if she goes in, she's saying yes to so much more than just a midnight swim. It's a leaving behind of her safe distance to life. A dare to live it.

Pressing her eyes shut, she reaches for a prayer, wraps her heart around it, and jumps.

She's engulfed. Skin tickled by the bubbles, senses jolted by the chill. It may be the warmest spot around, but it's still northern Maine in the middle of the night. Not for the faint of heart.

Do not be faint of heart.

Water spins, tornado-like, around her. Twisting her hair into free-floating tendrils, lifting her back up until she emerges into clear dark air, its edges chiseled in contrast to the gentle muted world below.

A rich sound rolls in and beckons her. Jeremiah Fletcher, laughter unleashed in a sea of its own.

She's gasping for air, breathless from the thrill of it. "I'm in the ocean. I'm . . ." She spins, feels something bubbling up from a deep well within her. Her own laughter, sprung from disbelief and delight all wrapped together. "I'm in the waves."

"And?" Jeremiah draws near. "How are you finding those waves?"

A gentle breeze blows, rippling the water around her and lifting her, dropping her, again and again.

"I think they're finding me," she murmurs.

The world goes darker, a mass of clouds covering the moon. There's a fresh life in the air, an imminent something . . . and then it comes. The sky, letting loose, drop by drop. And with each drop, a pinprick of light shines from below. And another, and another—until the whole cove is a shimmering blanket, a dance of water and light.

The wind is picking up, too, the sound of waves crashing harder against the outer walls. They're protected in this cove, buffered by the strong arms of those walls, but the effect is exhilarating and terrifying all at the same time. The power of the growing sea, just a stone's throw away, yet they are out of its reach. Safe.

Blinking against the raindrops, she looks to the sky, then to Jeremiah. He is watching her. No . . . more than that. Reading her, knowing her.

The rain falls heavier now, so intense the whole surface of the water glows, and they clamber into the canoe. He gives her a leg up, she helps pull him in, and they paddle to an overhang on the cliff wall. They are protected there, only a light mist drifting in as the rain collides onto the stone roof above them.

He reaches back, unfolds a damp blanket, and offers it to her.

"Thank you." She wraps it around her shoulders, and a silence settles around them, the water lapping around their boat.

"This sea, Annie . . ." His voice is rough, and he looks off in the distance, as if he can see straight through cliff walls, straight across the country, maybe all the way back to Seattle. "It is wild, and it is fierce."

He stops, but he's not finished. She can almost hear his unspoken words, running up against a stone wall inside.

"But . . ." Annie tries to release a rock from that wall, invite his words through.

Jeremiah shakes his head as if it's a truth he knows despite his long unknowing of it. "There's more, too," he says. "There's light. Right there in the dark. Because of the dark." He gestures at the single-celled wonders lighting up the frigid lagoon with blue pinpricks. "There's courage. There's . . ."

"Magic," Annie says, voice soft.

"You would say that," Jeremiah says, but his voice is infused with something that cuts past the sarcasm and warms Annie. "This sea of yours," he says, serious again, "I hope it has some of that, too."

She swallows around an ache in her throat. What is his darkness? His sea? She wants to gather those waters up, hold them against her very heart.

"Can I ask you something, Jeremiah?"

Elbows on his knees, hands clasped, he looks up at her, and what she sees takes her breath away. A pleading for her to understand. But does he want her to ask? Or to not ask?

She musters her courage, gentles her words. "Your letter," she says, and he drops his gaze again, as if he's going to find an answer between his feet. "Do you . . ." How can she burst into this last holdout in his heart, when he has not invited her? She switches directions. "Is it . . . magic and courage and light, like you said? Or is it the other kind of sea?" Her kind of sea. The ruthless sort.

So much time passes that she wishes she'd never asked, begins to think he won't answer. Maybe it's better that way.

"That," he says at last, "is also something that has to be experienced." He drops his gaze, doing battle over something. And then, a man resolute, he says, "You'd better come with me."

thirty-five

Annie is up and at the dock at four forty-five. It's her first day here all over again, only instead of flying out the front door wrapped in a blanket and hollering her head off to try and catch him . . . it's different.

She is to accompany him on his trek through the dark. The one he takes every day, never speaking of.

Her stomach is doing flips, and it has nothing to do with the fact that Lobsterfest starts today. Nor Bob's state—that impenetrable peace about his fate wraps her still, and ties her heart even more to Jeremiah's.

Jeremiah. That name, that man. A tumble inside has her pressing her hands to her stomach, watching for his light to come on inside the boat.

She couldn't sleep when they returned after the rain let up. She'd lain awake thinking of the man in the boat at the end of the dock, feeling that she was on a precipice—and falling could be glorious . . . or disastrous.

This morning she'd showered the saltwater and plankton away, dressed simply in her jeans and boots, with her hunter green sweater long and warm around her. She'd considered putting on a dress. But this felt more her. And more him. Just . . . right. Natural.

She had, however, spent more time than she cared to admit taming her hair with various heating tools. She didn't know what was ahead, but she felt he was about to open that last, locked chamber of himself. And she wants to cherish it.

Movement outside catches her eye. Illuminated by light shining from above the doorway, Jeremiah emerges from his boat, looking as if he hasn't slept a wink, either, dark circles under his eyes. But those eyes are lit with a fire she cannot name. He's wearing a black fleece pullover with jeans and hiking boots, and she wonders what sort of terrain they are headed for.

Taking her hand in his, he leads her aboard. A somber tone saturates every molecule around them, and it's through this, and ribboning sea smoke beginning to rise in the pale dark of predawn, that they embark.

North they go. Past the Weg, past the cove from last night. Up and up, north and east, the coast always in sight. They pass a few early fishermen out on their boats and he gives them a quick wave, the sort that shows these passings are a familiar thing.

Until forty-five minutes later, he cuts the engine.

She looks around. Ocean, ocean, and more ocean. On land, the unmistakable candy-cane striped West Quoddy Head Lighthouse stands sentinel, its beacon flashing. Out to sea, a paling sky whispers of the coming sunrise.

"This . . . is where you come every morning?"

He nods.

There's a deep gravity in the gesture, and she yearns to understand it.

"What is it about this spot?" She asks it with care, hoping her words carry a tone that shows she will treasure his answer, whatever it might be.

"See that?" He points over the starboard side, a yard out.

She nods, though all that's there is the black-blue of the sea.

"Canada," he says.

She nods again, trying to follow.

"This spot right here," he says, "is the farthest east you can get in the United States." He looks off to where the sky is parting around a radiating point of light, making way for the sun.

"Stand here"—he puts his hands on her shoulders, places her at the bow—"and you'll be the first person in our entire country to be touched by that light when it comes up."

"Really?" She looks out over this ordinary, unassuming spot in a sea of waves, and suddenly, it's extraordinary.

Jeremiah doesn't answer. He's got his feet planted, staring down at something in his hand. The letter.

His grip is firm, thumb pressing it down against his fingers as if he'll never release it. He doesn't look up.

"You know about Melissa," he says at last, and finally meets her gaze.

His wife. Feeling as if she's been caught trespassing, she nods, heat pressing her cheeks. "A little. Bess mentioned her, once."

Jeremiah looks from the letter, to the spot where the sun is going to crest any minute . . . and then to her. He pulls out the pages from the envelope, opens them. He's about to hand them both to her, but at the last moment, keeps the second page in his own callused hands as he passes the first off to her.

Tentatively, studying him to make sure this is what he intends, she smooths the paper in her hands, knowing that somehow, what she's about to read will change everything.

Hey, Fletch.

It feels as if she's reading a note from a friend, this time.

> *I know you're not going to want to read this for a while . . . and that's okay. I love you, is what I mostly want to say. So set this aside, stick it in your pocket, maybe, and these words will wait until the day you just want to hang out a little.*
>
> *Oh, hey. Back so soon? You always were bad at waiting. Like that night of our first date, when you showed up at my apartment door again twenty minutes after you dropped me*

off. You looked so sheepish, standing there with your hands stuffed in your pockets. Your hair was sticking out from under that beanie of yours like it was trying to break free from a prison, and your words were just as unruly. "Breakfast tomorrow."

You said it like a freight train pushed those words straight out of your mouth. Fletch, if you could have seen your face. You looked so horrified that you'd actually said it out loud. "I mean . . . would you maybe meet me for breakfast tomorrow?"

Fletch, I would meet you for breakfast every day for the rest of all time, if I could. I'd do the impossible: wake you before the sun, even get you on your feet and somewhat conscious, drag you out to watch the sunrise, and we'd be the first people in the whole city to see the new day. The first people in our little universe, which may as well be the whole world, if you ask me.

Because I would begin this life again with you a thousand-thousand times, if I could. Sit by the brand-new light of each day to dream with you, be with you.

But, well . . . I won't say it again, since you've already had to hear it from the doctors. I always said I never wanted to go anywhere without you again. And now . . . the biggest journey of all. Yet it's as close as a heartbeat. And even though it's so hard I can't breathe sometimes, there's this peace in it, too. Hard, so hard . . . but good. Because I know Whose you are, and I know you'll be okay.

Leaving you is the hardest thing of all. It's funny, the little things that make my heart hurt. Random things. Thinking of that unruly hair of yours, not getting to run my fingers through it. Thinking of the way you would wrap your arms around me and say something ridiculous and we'd laugh right into each other. I don't like the thought of that laughter stopping.

So I want you to promise me something, Fletch. Don't

let the laughter go silent too long. Don't miss the sunrise too much. I mean, I know you love your sleep, but just once in a while, would you meet the new day for me? Meet it. Be the first one to see it, if you're feeling really crazy. And remember that it's not over yet. This beautiful, messy, hard, glorious life is not over for you, and I'm so thankful. The world needs you, Fletch.

I'll be waiting for you, sitting in the light of a different Son. And He'll meet you at sunrise, even when I can't.

Breakfast tomorrow?

Yours, always.
Mel

Annie reads it twice, and the ache in her chest deepens to a burn, a widening chasm. She can see it, almost. Jeremiah—this man who is, as Bess so rightly said, *all in*—having to let go.

A warm tear rolls down her cheek, and before she can stop it, it drops onto the paper before her. Paper softened by a thousand readings.

She goes to wipe it with her finger, horrified. To mar something so sacred to him—she blows on the wet spot left behind, apologizing in between breaths.

"Oh, Jeremiah. I'm so sorry." For what the letter held. For going and clumsily dropping her own tears on something so precious. For all of it, and so much more.

Her hands fly to her temples as she bows her head, mortified. Heartbroken. For him losing such a woman. For Melissa not getting more time with him. For what she sees can never be, after a love like that.

"This is why you come out here every day."

He nods. "To keep a promise."

Of course. The sunrise. Her heart soars and shatters at the same time—for him to move clear to the far corner of the country, just to be closer to the sunrise. To be the man who first greets it each day, all for a love like this . . .

That is a devotion for the ages. One that should not be infringed upon.

And then he has her. His hands around hers. Taking the letter. Folding it up, pressing it against his chest to flatten it. Another tear comes and this time, a different hand rises to catch it. His. He cups her face in the warmth of his palm, slides his thumb over her cheek, taking the tear with it.

Slowly, silently, he hands her the second page. It's as if it contains his very lifeblood, so careful is he with it.

She reads.

> *P.S.—Fletch. I mean it about the laughter. When you find someone who can laugh right into you and who sees every layer of you and loves you, you'd better promise to not let her go. It's going to happen. It's easier than you think to fall in love with Jeremiah Fletcher.*
>
> *I should know.*
>
> *So don't let her go, okay? Promise me that, too. Go get her.*

Annie's breath catches. She can't bring herself to look at him. She traces her thumb under Melissa's words—*It's easier than you think to fall in love with Jeremiah Fletcher.*

Oh, that truth.

Eyes swimming, she finally lifts them to his.

"Postscript," he says.

She waits. He'll explain, she has come to understand. Blurt first, explain later.

"The p.s.—it comes after you thought the whole story was over."

Her heart feels as if it's going to burst from its cage, the way his voice rakes over his scars and tumbles into a tone of hope.

"Sometimes . . . it's a story all its own."

Jeremiah Fletcher takes a step closer. She can feel the warmth of him, the strength.

"And sometimes . . ." He tucks a tendril of her hair behind her ear, runs his fingers down it. "You start to hope it will never"—his hand comes up behind her neck, thumb under her jaw—"ever"—his free hand meets hers, entwines with her fingers—"end."

Blinding gold light pours over them, the sun climbing from its blue depths. He lowers his lips to hers, hesitates, and then, as if someone has pulled the foundation stone from the wall around his heart and every last stone falls away, his lips meet hers.

The man who when he gives himself gives all that he is, encircles her now with his arms. He is strength and goodness, fire and safety. Maddening stubbornness and unsettling sight, seeing her soul, drawing her close, asking her deep, deep into the water, into this life. Every second that kiss lingers is an offering of his very heart, an asking of hers.

Static breaks from the VHF radio, and a voice breaks through. Jeremiah cups the back of Annie's head, leaning his forehead on hers as he listens.

"*Glad Tidings, Glad Tidings*. This is Bess. Suggest channel sixty-eight. Over."

Annie stiffens. "Bess?"

Something's wrong, for Bess to call from shore. Jeremiah wastes no time in getting to the radio and finding a free channel.

"Bess. Everything okay?" The concern etched on his face says he knows it's not.

A beat of silence, and Annie is beside him.

Bess's voice breaks in, two words. "It's Bob."

thirty-six

Annie paces the waiting room, itching for something to do. She's been here all day, all night, since Bess's call on the radio—that Bob was showing marked improvement . . . and might even be waking up.

Something in her leapt to life at those words. She and Jeremiah had rushed to the hospital, only to be told that this would likely be a long process. The nurses let her and Jeremiah stay in the room long after visiting hours ended. Talking to him, playing a tune, watching with bated breath every time his eyes slowly opened, praying this would be the time they would focus.

And at last, he began to track, to fix in on Annie. Flickers of life, a squeeze of the hand.

It was good. Very good, the doctor said. His motor and eye responses were promising, though his verbal response had a long way to go. The only thing he'd uttered was what sounded like *worm*. Three times he'd said it through the night, the nurse explaining it was probably a vivid dream, that coma patients had to fight through all sorts of imaginings on their way back.

The door opens behind her, and Jeremiah enters, handing her a lidded cup of coffee. He leans against the window, the early morning sun casting shadows over his face. He hadn't left, not for a moment. Had it been only yesterday—a mere twenty-four hours

310

ago—that he wrapped his arms around her? And here they are, a world away. She longs for the safety of that embrace, the hope of that moment. And so much more.

Comfort and peace—*life*—for Bob. Healing for him, and for Dad.

She checks her phone again, willing there to be something from her parents. They were supposed to be home by now. She'd called and called, but their phone just beeped and beeped, a maddening busy tone.

The click of the door sounds as a nurse in scrubs enters.

"He's doing well," she says. Her name tag says *Gina,* and her black ponytail is perky. There must have been a shift change, or it would be Shirley giving the update. "Rest is so important for him right now."

Annie nods. "Of course. What can I do to help?"

Gina looks compassionately at the two of them. "Rest is important for you, too. After all the progress last night, he'll be asleep most of the day. Please, get some rest. We'll be sure to update you the moment anything changes."

Rest. Her body aches for it, but her heart and mind will have none of it. Gina disappears between the double doors, and a hand comes around Annie's side—Jeremiah, smelling of pine and warmth.

Leaning her head on his shoulder, she hears the memory of Bob's rasping voice during the night. *"Worm."* Stretching it, trying to shape it into something more. *Wo-orm.*

William.

"I'll take you home," Jeremiah says.

And in that instant, she knows exactly what she must do. Yes, she must go home. But not to the one Jeremiah's thinking of.

thirty-seven

Storm's comin'.

There's a steady beeping sound coming from nearby. Light out there beyond the red of Bob's eyelids. Something is weighing them down so he can't open them. He'd opened them before . . . hadn't he? His throat burns, parched.

Storm's comin'. The thought comes again, like a persistent nudge to wake him up. Just like it has ever since that storm when he and Roy were ten, the old elbow aches to the marrow when the ocean and air are about to tangle and let loose a blow to ground them all.

He opens his mouth—or tries to. It's like trying to summon life from parched desert land.

"S-s . . ." His tongue sticks to his teeth, and he can't even get the word out. If there's a storm coming, he's got to make sure William is safe. That's all he's ever wanted. *William. Storm.*

"Mister Robert?" There's bustling, a flurry of activity, and a familiar voice. Another voice enters, deeper. Papers rustle, some infernal beeping sounds, and he tries to pull in air. He needs sea air. Not this stuffy old terrarium air.

Everything grows louder, clearer, twisting together into a rope, pulling him out of these dark waters.

He tries again, and a hoarse old whisper comes out. "Storm."

Someone whispers something about a verbal response. "Make the call," they say.

———

Annie grips the pipe handrail, climbing the steps that skirt the cliff. The wind is picking up, but they'd checked all the forecasts and watched the radars as they'd traveled south, almost to Portland, back home to Casco Bay. There was nothing on the radar, nothing over the VHF radio. The wind was par for the coastal course, and with the whole afternoon ahead, they'd have plenty of time to get back to the hospital before sundown . . . with one very important addition on board. She hopes.

She knows these steps like a favorite song, so often she'd skipped up and down them as a child. Never a trace of fear that she might fall off, that the sea below might swallow her right up. The first voice of welcome when her parents first brought her as a squinty-eyed baby home from the hospital, the sea had been a part of her.

Until it wasn't. Until it became the thing that took her parents away for months at a time, that nearly took Mom's life.

A glance down reveals an azure blue, alive with its shifting tones and waves disappearing one into another. And there upon them, the *Glad Tidings*, and its faithful captain—the man who brought back that connection.

Jeremiah is looking up at her. Hand to forehead shielding his eyes from the high sun, but it gives the impression of a salute. He stands stock-still, gripping the rail of the boat. When she'd left him there, there was an energy buzzing from his very frame, a passion that had driven them here and wanted, she knew, to climb the cliff with her. But he understood that this was something she needed to do on her own. He'd given her a hand-squeeze that infused her with the courage to make this climb, to bridge this gap.

He waves, and a peace bolsters her, sends her climbing the rest of the steps, running her hands through the waving lupines at cliff's edge, crossing the groomed lawn.

This place is built from stone, and she loves the story of it. How her father built it from the ground up for his bride, not a penny to their name after they'd purchased the land. How it looks like an extension of the cliff itself, rising like a peaked crown, humble and glorious. It had no name, not like most homes around these parts. They just called it *the cottage*, but it felt like a crowning title.

Even so, she hasn't been back since the Christmas before last. And when she has come, it's never been the same as before Alpenzell. It felt too good and pure for her. Square peg, round hole—that's what it was.

"Annie?" The voice washes over her, the disbelief in it kind. Mom, beaming. She's beautiful. Like always. Paintbrush in hand, she's standing in the doorway of the shed-turned-studio to the right of the lawn. It's nearly overgrown with walls of blooming hollyhocks and clumps of lupine. A streak of violet paint marks Mom's cheek. She rushes forward and wraps Annie in an embrace, smelling of oil paint and cinnamon.

She grips Annie's hand, smearing it with paint and too joyful to care. She laughs, pulling Annie into the studio and over to the old farm sink. "Leave it to me to stain you with paint. Some homecoming, eh?"

Annie laughs, washing her hands and taking in the treasures Mom has on the windowsill. A starfish. A crayon drawing of a boat, colored by Annie when she was six. And something that sends shivers of nostalgia and wonder through her—the old picture of her grandparents. Colors faded on the print from the sixties, smiles vibrant nonetheless. Grandpa Luka and Grandma Liesl. She'd loved their against-all-odds story of reunion after so many years of brutal separation. One for the ages.

Once their three children were well grown, the couple had gathered up their rugged courage and moved back to Germany. *"To redeem the yesterday with the someday,"* Grandpa Luka had said.

Their story reminds her the impossible does happen, that there's hope for Bob and her father.

Her mother hands her a towel to dry her hands, her face falling somber. "How is he?" She's talking of Bob, and they both know it.

314

Annie fills her in.

Her mother's eyes are wide. "I wish you'd phoned that he is waking," she says breathlessly. "We'd have come . . ." She sounds more hopeful than convinced.

"I did phone," Annie says. "No one answered."

Her mother's hand flies to her own forehead. "That phone. Never sits in the cradle right. You remember."

Annie does remember. Her social life in high school had suffered from their defective phone.

Her eyes drift through the studio window, toward the house, where Dad would be.

"Is Dad here? I just thought maybe if I could talk with him"— she admits her pie-in-the-sky dream—"maybe he would come."

Mom is serious as she leads her onto the lawn, and Annie knows she, too, wants this reconciliation. "You can try." She blows a strand of dark hair streaked with vibrant silver from her face. "Those two. They're each more stubborn than the other, and that's a riddle I fear they'll never solve."

A sudden wind chases them inside the house, and Annie gives a glance to the sea, hoping Jeremiah will be all right down there. A new chill sends a shiver down her spine as she steps inside the cottage built by her father's own two hands.

He's seated by the picture window, bent over a workbench—a new addition since the last time she was here. Last time a comfortable couch had hugged the wall below the window, a basket of books to wile away the hours.

Apparently the hours hadn't wiled quickly enough for his ever-sparking mind, for he has turned the whole room into some sort of workshop. Bright gold-toned metal pieces, precision-cut into lengths of curves and odd sawtooth-segments, are laid out on the floor.

A computer screen in the corner shows some sort of engineering program—AutoCAD, maybe?—displaying a three-dimensional diagram of something that looks like an archaic diver's helmet straight out of a Jules Verne novel. All bulbous and ridged.

On his worktable, where his concentration remains unbroken, are several segments of glass-like material. Each curved slightly, with a central disc laid with care in the middle.

"We have a visitor, William," her mother says, voice radiant.

He turns, piercing blue eyes going straight to her. His chair scrapes the floor as he stands, crosses the room. He raises his hands to cradle her face and looks at her as if he's just found long-lost treasure. Those justice-defending arms—perhaps not quite so thick or chiseled as they once were—wrap her up and draw her close.

Annie pauses, surprised at the change in him. He's no spring chicken, as he likes to remind her every month during their phone calls, but she hadn't anticipated the salt-and-pepper of his hair—decidedly more salt than pepper—or the way his shoulders bend, as if the weight upon them is increasing every day. Is this the broad, strong, unbeatable father of her youth? The one who charged into international conflict to defend justice and came home to embrace his daughter?

Stories swirl in Annie's memory. Of her father, young and broken, before he met her mother. Abandoned. Gathered up. Bearing the weight of a guilt he was never meant to carry. Standing here wrapped in arms that doused a burning barn to save a corner of life . . . she feels how this guilt has shaped him. Softened him. Maybe hardened him, too, driven him far away from Bob for too long.

His embrace tightens until all she can do is melt into it, lay her head on his shoulder, let herself be wrapped in this all-encompassing sense of belonging. Until recently—she thinks again of Jeremiah waiting on Glad Tidings—she'd only known such love here with her parents and one other place in her life.

And that was with Bob.

No one has spoken, and yet they all feel this electrifying current zipping around them.

"Dad," Annie says at last, "will you go to him?"

He knows exactly who she means, and his pursed lips declare what his answer will be.

"I can't," he says. "Not yet."

The question she must ask might sound impertinent, so she takes care to curve it into compassion, a need to understand. "Why?"

"I will come," he says, stroking her hair. He glances around. "But I've got to finish something first, and then—"

The pieces shift into place in the scene before her. The animation on the computer screen turning, glass pieces assembled around a cavern made for . . . a light.

"You're building a lens," she breathes.

She has been on the phone with the Lighthouse Society in recent days, asking how she might order a lens apparatus—heart aching a little when she learns the classic lenses are a thing of the past, that what's used now is the same technology as that of siren lights and air traffic control lights. All the mystique and wonder of Bob's original lens . . . gone. Destroyed by fire it was meant to contain.

But here, in her father's living room, is the real thing. If the pieces aren't evidence enough, there's a coffee-stained printout fluttering in the breeze from an open window, held down by a tattered copy of *Rob Roy*. The paper is marked *U.S. Coast Guard. Private Aids to Navigation Application.*

"You did this?"

He nods. "I've had some time on my hands."

"All those trips to Florida." She laughs. "They weren't for consulting, I take it."

She loves him for the telltale red of his face. "Well, you could say I had to consult an expert, about this new technology they're using to re-create Fresnel lenses." He gestures toward the bench. "I had some learning to do for the Paton."

She gives him a quizzical look.

"Private Aid to Navigation."

"This . . . is for Bob's lighthouse?"

His eyes fly to hers. Searching. "You know?"

She nods.

"Ansel never could keep a secret." He stuffs his hands in his jean pockets. "Well, I guess you might know, then, why I have to finish this first."

She surveys the parts of the lens, imagines how grand a scale this is. "This is amazing, Dad." She steps closer, scanning the room, this man, with respect. "But . . ."

His eyes snap back to hers again, concerned. "But . . . ?"

She shakes her head, desperate for him to understand. "He doesn't want recompense."

Dad's jaw works, and she sees in him the shadowed youth who Bob once took in.

She rushes to correct the sting of her words. "He'll be amazed by what you've accomplished, but what he really wants"—he drops his gaze, possibly knowing what she's about to say—"is you." The hardest thing of all for him to bring.

Rain starts to fall against the windows, and her father turns to shut them. He gathers up the application, stares hard at it as if it will give him the answers to all his unspoken questions. Finally, he voices one.

"He's doing all right? Your mom said he was stable, that things are looking up . . ."

Annie opens her mouth to answer, but a muted knock sounds at the door. Her mother opens it, and there stands Jeremiah, face awash with urgency. His shoulders rise and fall fast from what must have been an all-out sprint up those rock stairs.

And then he speaks.

"He's awake. Really awake."

thirty-eight

This place. They're all dead set on keeping Bob here, needles poking him like he's the bull's-eye at target practice.

Well, it's not going to work.

"Where's Annie?" He knows she was here. He couldn't have dreamed her laugh, that voice sweet as spring blueberries, the mandolin. He looks to his visitors.

Bess looks at Ed, who rocks forward in his chair in the hospital room. "She's . . . gone out."

Bob gives him a look, as if the man can see. And knowing Ed, he'll know exactly what's going on.

"All right, all right." The man straightens, holding his hands out in defense. "She's off to Casco Bay."

"Casco Bay." Bob doesn't believe it. She hasn't been there in over a year—not since her ad in Rusty Joe's proclaimed a white Christmas there and he'd written back, saying to get herself up the coast or he'd rope her in like a lobster trap. She'd thought he was kidding.

"Casco Bay." Ed repeats, a note of admission in his voice. "With Jeremiah."

"With . . ." He pictures the lanky lost fellow and his way of carrying his torment with him and his unbending determination. Then he pictures Annie and her ways of music and light, always a little rootless, searching. "Well, at least that part makes sense. But what in tarnation are they doing out there in this?" He flings an arm toward the window, where the sky is blue and the treetops bend gently.

Great. They're all going to think he's lost his marbles. But he knows it in the ache of these bones—those clouds will soon be staging something fierce. One of the needles in his arm comes loose, and something starts beeping.

"They went to get him," Bess says, looking Bob directly in the eye with her chin up, a challenge.

"Went to get who?"

"You know very well who."

William. Something bright and terrifying surges through Bob. Hope.

Followed immediately by something fierce. "They didn't go in the boat," he says, willing it to be true, and knowing the second he says it that that's exactly what they did.

Bess focuses on a loose thread on her sweater, pulling at it. "Anyone tell you yet about Lobsterfest? Rich got us a searchlight that twirls all over the night and makes it seem like real doings. He keeps forgetting to shut it off, though. And speaking of festivals, don't think we all don't know that you up and injured your way into this place"—she twirls a finger around the room—"to escape Bobsterfest."

She's avoiding his question. "Bess Stevens. Did they or did they not take the boat?"

Bess's look confirms it.

"Don't you worry 'bout them." Ed waves it off. But even through his southern-sculpted voice, there's a shadow of worry.

If they are out on the seas, surely they'll take cover on land. And soon.

And if this hospital thinks he'll stay in their web of tubes and needles, they have another thing coming.

320

The radio hums low, the National Weather Service issuing word for word its near-daily statement: "Humid with a chance of rain, accompanied by moderate wind." They might as well be proclaiming that the sky was up and the earth was down. A scant shower from a blue sky was hardly a storm warning. Still, there's an urgency lining the room as her father inclines his ear to the radio.

A look toward the bay tells Annie the seamen are still going about their business, no mass return to shore. They have the best heads on their shoulders when it comes to reading sky and sea— and hopefully, this means they'll have time to get back up the coast. Knowing Bob is awake so far away, and that the ocean could turn on them quicker than fast, she's aching to get on their way.

Jeremiah stands at the door like a runner awaiting the sound of a starting pistol. Annie had made quick introductions once Jeremiah told them of Bess's call. The cell-phone connection had been bad, he said, but it was clear that Bob was awake. What she'd said next was either good news, or bad. A few missed words and then "not long." Not long, what? Until he'd be fully awake? That he'd be alive? In the hospital?

"We need to go," Annie says.

"It will be better if we drive," Jeremiah suggests. He's right, and she looks to her parents, who exchange a grave look.

"Our car is out of commission," her mother says. "Over at the garage in Portland." A look to her husband, and something passes between them. An unspoken pleading. Her father swallows hard, looks to the clock, the sea, the scattered parts of the lantern.

"Here," he says, stooping to roll the metal parts in the drop cloth they're laid upon. He hands a bundle to Annie, one to Jeremiah. Does the same with the glass-like pieces, tucking them carefully but swiftly into a wooden box built to house them.

The phone, back in its cradle, jingles on the wall. It's an older model with a long spiraling cord stretched out from one too many trips to the lawn with it. Mom answers, and they're all still as they try to discern what news there is.

"Yes? Yes. Oh, no. Can they stop him? I see. Thank you very much, Shirley. Yes, do call if you hear more." She hangs up and tells them, "It's good and bad. He's doing well . . . but maybe too well for his own good."

"What does that mean?" Dad asks.

"It means he's left."

"Left?" Annie's heart lodges in her throat.

"Checked himself out against medical advice. He declared he had a literary festival to avoid and walked right out of there. She said he's stronger than most of his age who wake up, but he still needs to be under care, with extensive rehabilitation."

Jeremiah's shaking his head, and she knows if it weren't so serious, he'd be laughing. Maybe even cheering him on. "Stubborn," he mutters.

"Shirley's planning to go over to his house as soon as her shift is done. He needs close monitoring, and support, and physical therapy, and—"

Dad sets his jaw. "Let's go."

There is a weather advisory. Not a storm warning, not even a storm watch. There's a difference, and it should be enough to help Annie breathe easier.

The knot in her gut is tied solely to Bob, she tells herself. But the waves tell a different story. Mom is staying behind to man the phone in case more calls come in. Her connection is better than Jeremiah's. His already spotty cell reception, and even radio communication from the boat, cannot be depended on if the weather turns.

They're going to beat this storm to get back to a force even stronger: Bob. It's rough going in the wind, but it's nothing the three of them haven't seen—especially her father, in all his time at sea. They make good time to Isle au Haut but are forced to slow down as they pass Mount Desert Island, where the waves are get-

322

ting restless. Once they pass Roque Bluffs and are on the home stretch she'll breathe easier.

Jeremiah is at the helm, her father's brow furrowing as he watches the radar, arms crossed. He doesn't like something he sees. He steps out on deck, and Annie follows, searching the sky. White clouds shield them from the harsh sun, a welcome cover.

"Not too bad," she says, waiting for her father's *"Not too bad at that, Annie-girl,"* just as they'd said a thousand times when she was growing up.

But he only stares at the sky, raising a hand to his hair and combing fingers through.

"Anvil," he says at last, and points to two flat-topped clouds in the distance that are trailing points behind them like the shape he's named.

She searches her memory for what that means. "Thunder?"

He turns in answer, heading straight back for the radar screen, checking between it and the charts on the stool beside him.

The clouds morph from white to gray before them, as if someone has drawn a shade over the sun beyond. They gather, growing.

Annie glances in the direction of shore. But as the gunmetal gray rolls in, she can hardly see her own hand in front of her face, let alone any sign of land.

The darkness is so unnatural. They are hours from evening, but night will come. Dark upon dark. And then the trouble will multiply.

Her father throws them each a life jacket, his face grave. They follow his lead in donning them, and time is swallowed up in the white-capped churning as the boat lifts, drops, over and over again. The air temperature plummeting suddenly, Annie's skin pricks in goose bumps.

And then the sky lets loose. Sheets of torrential rain coming at them, the wind driving it like nails. As if the water from above and ahead isn't enough, that wind plows into the waves, pushing them toward the *Glad Tidings,* insatiable.

Jeremiah steps from the wheel momentarily to pull her inside the cabin, his movement swift and protective.

"Squall," he says, his voice low and slow—the imposed calm of someone practiced in the art of staying level-headed in crisis.

Annie's stomach presses against her lungs as the water lifts the boat up and up, then drops them—jarring them to what she's sure must be the bottom of the ocean.

It is not.

It is only the valley between waves. And it's gone the moment the next wave picks up where the other left off. Tossing the boat like a plaything as a wall of black water slams over the rails, wraps itself around Annie's ankles and threatens to take her down.

"Turn into the waves," her father is saying to Jeremiah. "That's it. Now more. Forty-five degrees. Slow it down or we'll—" the boat slams bow first into the next wave—"broach."

Jeremiah cringes, taking the throttle down to near-idle. Just enough force to keep up with the waves and keep some sliver of control. William stands back, his steady presence constantly assessing the storm and the boat, but letting the younger man stand in his newfound footing.

They hit a choppy rhythm, and Annie begins to relax. She joins her father in examining the charts, comparing them to the GPS and radar. They'll need the charts for dead reckoning, she knows, if their equipment should fail. If the squall brings lightning.

Please, God, don't let that happen. . . .

Her dad says something, his voice that of a naval officer, but eyes those of a father.

"Signal-Ann," he repeats.

And just like that she's eight again, the thrill of being her father's signalman, taking over to man the devices. She presses her eyes shut, remembers those blue-sky days of perfection. Before the sea was this raging leviathan.

"Give me the rundown?" He pulls out the old question.

Eyes open, task before her, she fastens her heart to the job and finds courage in it. "Aye aye, sir."

A nod, and instead of standing with hands behind his back, elbows protruding in triangles at his sides as he used to, he's bent over something on the deck, hands working a rope, securing something as he gives the next order.

"Direction."

She looks to the compass, tries to average its bobbing antics.

"Northeast." Which is all wrong, for where they need to be. They'll need to correct west—and hope they see land somehow before it slams into them first.

"Location."

A glance at the GPS. "Forty-four north, sixty-seven west." Getting closer to Machias, Cutler . . . and Ansel. Yet too far out. So many things could keep them from shore. They need to stay glued to the radar so they don't get pummeled by rocks, an island, a log, another boat—anything that the waves could toss at them.

Jeremiah marks it on the chart.

Her dad continues. "Speed."

"Near idle."

"Good. Wind?"

As if to answer for her, a gust blows from the west, a wall of water coming over and at them with relentless force.

"Dad!" Water slaps down over him, right into the house window, and she flails to cover her face with her arm as the window blows straight out from the force.

The boat lists hard, righting itself afterward and reeling over another swell. She's on the deck, scrambling to help her dad up. He yanks hard on the rope and stumbles back to the wheelhouse with her. His strength is worn but fierce.

Jeremiah is steadfast at the wheel, throwing a concerned look toward William, then Annie.

She can almost hear the mental checklist in his EMT brain, looking over the two of them for signs of trauma.

"You okay?" Jeremiah takes one look at William and scrapes out a plastic bin from the corner, tossing him something from within. A heavy jacket. A hat. He's worried about the wet and cold.

"Thanks." Dad dons them both, and Annie sees the way his chin trembles before he stops it. "I'm fine."

Jeremiah's gaze fixes on Annie, intense.

"Me too," she says. Jeremiah's gaze is unmoving, as if he doesn't believe her. He sees too much.

Heaving for breath, her father surveys the damage of the lost window.

He repeats his earlier question, "Wind?" And Annie laughs, humor somehow wending its way into the situation.

"Bad," she says, pointing to the window. She checks the wind speed indicator. "We're at sixty knots." That just pushed them on up the storm scale, blowing straight past Gale, Strong Gale, and Storm.

It was officially a Violent Storm. The category just before Hurricane.

"Waves?"

There's no device for measuring wave height. Her practiced child's eye would have placed her guess based on how high the peaks and swells seemed compared to her six-foot father. And she'd never given an answer over five feet. She pulls the Beaufort Scale printout from where it's tacked up in the house. Sixty knot winds . . . *thirty-seven to fifty-two foot waves.*

"Forty feet," she says, knowing she's being optimistic with that guess.

Her father's face is grave. "Listen," he says, shouting to be heard, "we're in pretty deep. Do you have survival suits?"

Jeremiah points to a hatch out on deck, near the bow. "Two," he says. "In there."

"And you have an EPIRB?"

Jeremiah's face goes white. If her father, the seasoned sailor, is asking about inflatable survival suits, which are basically a wearable lifeboat, and the device that's a last resort call for help . . .

Annie's insides turn to cold, hard metal.

Jeremiah slides his hand beneath the bridge and slaps the wall, where the neon-yellow device is strapped on.

"There?" William affirms, making sure Annie sees it, too. "If things turn bad, whoever can activate that first, does." He hangs his head, then looks them each in the eye. First Jeremiah, then Annie. "I've seen worse. And we can weather this together." His forehead creases deep. "This would normally be the time for us to anchor and ride it out if we had a choice. But . . ."

He leaves the rest unsaid, waiting for them to give their assent. The unspoken concern: Bob.

This moment has been decades in the making. With his health still teetering, and him up and checking himself out of the hospital . . .

She looks to her father and sees unspoken yearning flashing over his otherwise still-as-stone face.

"Let's get back to him," she says.

Jeremiah nods, wincing against the strain the steering and wave-navigating is putting on him. He looks at them for a fleeting second before fixing his eyes back out through the water-pummeled windshield. "I'm in."

It is this that drives them on, the three of them a tangle of activity as Jeremiah and William take shifts steering and securing things outside with Annie amid walls of water sloshing over deck. Exhaustion burns in every muscle of Annie's. Was it only the night before that she'd swum in this very ocean? She shivers at the thought.

Somewhere between the dark of storm and the dark of coming night, the rain pulls back on its horizontal attack, falling vertical.

The moaning wind quiets its lament. A fragile stillness seems on the brink of arrival—and the three of them look at one another. Hoping. Praying.

It's an eerie quiet. The haze about them heavy. They're cloaked in an other-world, out here alone. Waves still rolling larger than life but have rounded into a sleepier dance.

It lasts long enough that Annie begins to breathe again, feels her heart steady.

Please, God. She prays beyond words, not knowing how to

ask for home in this darkness. It seems too much. So much more than just a safe harbor. The bridging of three generations. The healing of unthinkable loss. She doesn't have words for that. Only . . . *please.*

Then rolls the thunder.

And near on top of it . . . lightning.

thirty-nine

Wind beats against the old house, creaking its bones with no regard for its age. Or Bob's. Or his family's.

Every muscle protesting, he rises from Annie's window seat, bent over his walker. He turns it to face the storm outside and can hardly see. With gray sea spraying and the sloshing of ocean over land, like it's Genesis in reverse, water comes to reclaim its territory and swallow the land right up.

All he can think is *They're out there.* Or worse. Bess had come running earlier, hollering about calling Annie, not being able to reach her, then calling her folks' house, and her mother saying they were on their way.

A sea like this knows no friends.

"No." He speaks it into this empty house, defying the shaking in a voice aged a thousand years these past days. He raises his voice. "No! They *are* out there." They have to be. Everything in him—his breath, his gut, his very soul—coils around a prayer all too familiar.

"Bring him home, Lord." Only this time, it is not Roy he's praying for. Roy is safe. He knows that. But William . . . oh, the boy is not ready for that. There is much hurt to be undone. "Bring her home, too. And the other him." Annie. Jeremiah. The two of them together, if they know what's good for them.

329

His gaze falls through the far window. Out to the boathouse, where a blue tarp flaps in the dark like a banshee. Jeremiah's been patching the roof—continuing the job Bob botched. He thinks of that crumbled, burnt-out corner of the boathouse. He'd never had the heart to fix it. Doing so felt like betraying William, confirming the boy's worst fears—that it was all a horrible mistake. But Bob's time left in this life is short now. He knows it. And some desperate part of him thought maybe if he patched up that corner of impossible . . . it might show William that all was covered over, long forgiven.

But he had failed even in that—fallen off a gull-blasted ladder and landed in a dark abyss.

Muscles beginning to shake from the monumental effort it takes just to stand, to pray, he sinks back down, drapes arms over the walker, and hangs his head. He's back in the night with William, flames around them. The boy's face streaked with soot and torment.

"Bring him home," he prays again, but can only see flames, the inferno that drove William away.

The fire that will bring him home.

Roy's voice is in his head, echoes from so long ago, but that seem closer than ever now. *"Tell him I love him."*

How, in this?

Echoes of Roy on his deathbed. *"Don't get stuck in the dark. . . ."*

And for the first time since Bob stood on that island, broken and lost and crazy enough to build, he feels that same unmistakable chiseling of his heart. Again a single word—but this time it burns.

Light.

It is time for that old tower to shine.

He goes to the phone on the table and wishes, for the first time, that he hadn't cut the cord. Pulling out the drawer below the phone, he grips the old Maglite, cold metal handle greeting him like an old friend, its black paint over the etched handle rubbed away long ago.

330

He flicks it on and steps outside.

Somewhere in the dark, howling wind gives way to the thrum of an engine. Things are getting foggy . . . and not just outside. Bob is sweating, shivering, fire and ice. He braces himself inside the alcove of the entryway.

Two figures stagger up the path, heads bowed against the wind and rain.

The yelling is garbled in the weather. But Arthur's voice keeps on, until the words pierce through. "Get inside, you old fool! You got a death wish?" He holds up a white pharmacy bag. "All this medication'll do you no good if you get carried off in this storm." Ed's just behind him, cane helping him navigate the wet paths.

Bob has something a whole lot more pressing than a wish, and it's got nothing to do with death. Pulling an old yellow slicker tightly around himself, he pushes through the haze gathering around his brain and plants his walker down in front of the steps, blocking their path.

"We gotta get to the island," he says. The wind stills, as if to say "Oh?"

There's fury on Arthur's face and pity on Ed's.

Ed responds first. "Now, there's no call for that. You know they can get here on their own. All those fancy gadgets they've got on the boats these days. You going out there won't do anything but put another person at risk."

Arthur's response is not so gentle. "You have any idea what you put this town through, up and nearly crossing over the way you did? If you think we're taking you out in this . . ." He's speaking angry words, but there's a fear in his voice, and it's not about the storm.

Bob puts out his hand to stop them, to remind them who's out there. Spills his plan, every crazy detail of it.

"It's for Roy," he says at last.

Arthur clamps his mouth shut. He's not happy, but Bob feels his memory flip out there to sea, watching the waves take Roy.

The wind is gone. Maybe not for long, and maybe not far out to sea, but he prays it's enough to get them over to the lighthouse.

"I'm goin'," Bob says. "Come or stay as you like. I can't ask you to go out there in this."

Ed speaks slowly, as if he's been gathering up wisdom. "You have got to stay put," he argues. "The chances are . . . well, you know I don't ascribe to the word *impossible*, but this is as close as it gets. And you goin' out there just ain't right."

Bob nods. "Impossible's where the miracles happen, Ed. If I stay put . . . I might have more chance at life, but what sort of livin' is that, when I was *made* to do this?"

Arthur's jaw works. He blows past Bob and into the house. Stairs creak, and something's tumbling around up there. His descent sounds like he's battling a metal giant to get back down.

Out of breath, he steps back out on the porch. In his hands . . . is Eva's wheelchair.

It's just metal and fabric and screws. It shouldn't have the power to undo Bob like it does. But as Arthur opens it up and plants it in front of him, something inside Bob breaks. It is empty. She should be here.

And something inside him soars. This is what she, too, would want.

"You want on that island"—Arthur huffs—"this is the only way you're getting there."

Through a sheen of tears, Bob sits in the chair he pushed down to the dock so many times . . . but instead of spinning his beloved in a slow dance there, the dance takes on new clumsy life as the three men get their blind, near-crippled, stubborn selves onto the boat.

Arthur lets out a dry laugh. "Look at us," he says, his voice graveled with age. "The storm picked the wrong old codgers to tangle with."

He radios the harbormaster, who is waiting on any word from Jeremiah. "We're going to the lighthouse," he says.

"What lighthouse?" Margie Lillian's no-nonsense voice comes through. "Don't you boys dare go out in this—"

Arthur turns his back to Bob, as if that'll keep him from hearing.

"Ya know." Silence. "*The* lighthouse." Still nothing. "The growin's."

"Don't go near that island in this!" Margie barks. "If you think—" Bob reaches over and shuts off the handheld.

And prays the calm holds.

———

"Get down!" Jeremiah shouts. Another blinding flash splits the sky, thunder shaking Annie's very bones. Jeremiah lifts his hands from the metal wheel and grabs a wooden dowel to steer with, crouching. Making himself low to avoid a strike as the highest point. This boat, out here alone, is one giant bull's-eye for the lightning.

"Get below deck!" Jeremiah waves Annie and William toward the stairs, to the place Jeremiah never lets anyone go. His sanctuary.

William is pulling fallen books and debris out of the way, hauling open the door. He goes down, continuing to clear the path, and Annie knows she should follow. But something keeps her. She cannot move, cannot take herself farther away from the man at the helm.

She goes to Jeremiah. He's pleading with her, wordless.

Annie scoops up the hand at his side, threads her fingers between his. These hands, the ones that have saved so many lives . . . how she aches to hold his heart. To belong there. To be with him, come what may.

His hand tightens around hers, his forehead meeting hers in bowed silence. Hair wet, entwining with her own.

She breathes his name. "Jeremiah . . ." Loving the valleys and strength of it, the whole story of him.

"Go," he says. "Please. Get down there."

She shakes her head. "I can't leave you."

"I can't—" The timbre of his voice tremors. Another clap of thunder, another flash. Closer. "I. Can't. Lose you."

And with that, his free hand moves to her face, stroking the curve of her jaw with his hand, running his thumb across her cheek. Pulling her toward him, he lowers his face toward hers, meeting her lips with his.

The wind is regaining its force, awakening again. And with it, the waves. Rising, rising, rising.

Slowly, Jeremiah pulls away.

The air buzzes with electricity, raising the hair on Jeremiah's forearm. She runs her hands down his skin, wishing she could chase away anything that might hurt this man.

"Go," he says.

A pounding on the stairs tells her William's about to come above board to retrieve her. She's endangering them all, staying here.

She feels her heart cracking as she pulls away. She turns, meeting Jeremiah's gaze with a look she hopes tells him she's leaving her heart here with his. And then she grips the wooden banister, stepping down one step, two steps, three—and freezing at a sound so deafening it's surely splintered the entire world.

Electricity, spear-thrown by the sky itself. The force of an entire storm behind it. Colliding with the *Glad Tidings* in an explosion so bright she sees only swimming bits of the boat before her, hazy and haloed.

And all is dark.

forty

Ed taps his shoe against the *Savvy Mae*'s deck, raising his wrist as if he's checking a watch he cannot see. Laughing at his own silent joke. "Think he'll be much longer?"

Bob squints into the dark. They've docked near the school in the harbor, and Arthur had vowed he'd only be a few minutes. Before long, a squeaking sounds, wheels in protest—and the dark shadow of Arthur clatters over the dock with a rusted-out red children's wagon. In it, perched on its edges and spilling over its sides, is the Skyblaster 3000. Rich's searchlight.

It's no Fresnel lens, but it's something. It'll reach a few miles out to sea, anyway.

They can't cross the bay fast enough. But as they round its southern inner curve, Bob takes in a sight that makes him sit forward on his seat.

Small lights, like a string of fireflies, bouncing in a line around the harbor.

The power is out all over town. This can only be one thing.

People. Flashlights. Some old Coleman lanterns. A headlamp or two. Bobbing at a clipped pace, headed toward Sailor's Rest.

Arthur gets the boat close enough to holler. "Hey!" Bob can't see who it is he's shouting to. "What's the story?"

Margie Lillian shouts back. "You're all off your rockers," she says.

"Yeah, so?" Arthur used to have social niceties. They vanished about twenty years back.

"So . . . we're here to help." Margie's voice is iron.

"What?"

"I said we're here to help!"

Arthur cuts the engine.

"There's something you need to know." Margie's tone softens. "The coast guard lost them on VMS."

The sound of hope shutting down rides on the wind.

If the vessel monitoring system dropped them . . . no one wants to put words to what that might mean. It could mean the signal is down, or their electronics—but they all know, it could be that they've gone under.

Bob leans in from his seat on deck. He'd give anything to stand but knows he has to save what little strength is left. "You all go home," he says. "If they're out in this, we'll give them a way home. You go"—he tries to catch his breath—"be safe."

Bess's voice pipes up from the line of lights. "You can't leave us out of this!"

A hearty cheer traveling down the line of faceless townspeople resounds, and before Bob knows it, they're running a makeshift ferry between dock and island. Thankfully the waters have calmed enough here, but off at sea they can see the storm's still thick.

Rich arrives on the last shift, climbing out of the boat and pulling off a sling backpack with metal bars protruding and netted pockets stuffed with survival gear.

"Planning to stay awhile?" Bob leans forward in the wheelchair long enough to shake the man's hand.

"As long as it takes," he says. "Heard you all went and looted my searchlight," he says. There's pride in his voice.

"We did at that. Gonna bring them home," Bob says.

Rich claps him, albeit gently, on the shoulder. "Yes, we are," he says, and starts to climb the path, pulling a CamelBak straw from his backpack and taking a swig. "Stay hydrated!" he shouts back over his shoulder, joining some of the younger men, who are easing the light up the trail. It's in the wagon, but that's not doing much good on the slick runneled mud. Up top, Bess and the others are clearing the way of branches and other debris, making a path to the tower.

Ed, Arthur, and Bess have threatened mutiny if Bob dares set foot on that path. He's been relegated to beach watch, with the promise that Bess will keep him posted by walkie-talkie, and he's not to leave the chair. The lightning offshore has ceased, and if it weren't for this confounded dizziness that keeps lassoing him, he would never have agreed to stay put.

Alone on this island, as he has been countless times before . . . but never feeling more so.

Bess gives the blow-by-blow from the top as the men hoist the spotlight on the count of three. In the background, Bob hears the echoes of their struggles as they leverage it step by step up the wet spiraling staircase.

He holds his breath as they arrive at last on the platform, the one that's waited a lifetime for its light.

He does not like this. There shouldn't be so many men up there. Not with the weather what it is. The wood of the tower is no doubt weak.

He's about to holler across the air waves for them to hurry down. Not another life should be lost to make this light tower possible. But as he opens his mouth and musters all the breath and volume he can, Bess's shout sounds first. Not over the walkie, but down the trail itself. Bob winces against the rain to see up the path—to no avail.

He depresses the button on the walkie. "What happened?"
Silence.

"Bess, is everyone all right." It comes out a desperate statement rather than a question.

"Rich," she says, voice breaking up against storm-induced white fuzz, "on . . . edge . . . cord . . . ankle—"

She cuts out completely.

"Get him a knife!" Bob hollers, digging into his pocket for his own. It's not there.

Bess is holding down the transmitter button because he can hear it all now.

"Who's got a knife?"

Four different voices shout "Here!" and he can just picture them all thrusting their wielded Leatherman knives at the entangled Rich.

He hears Sully's voice. "Cut it loose." Good. They've got a mountaineer up there. "Get him back!"

A second of silence. Another. And then—a fracturing crash once—twice. Silence over the radio.

"Rich," Bob says into the unit. "Is Rich okay?"

Someone hollers that they've got him. Rich is safe. The light is not. Bob makes his way out around shore to the bottom of the cliff, to where the cauldron roils yards away. And in the grip of its white foam, churning shards of the searchlight.

The lights of a small vessel approach the beach, and a stiff, soggy figure steps out. Bob squints. He must be worse off than he thought, hallucinating.

Spencer T. Ripley would not be out in this. He'd be buried in a library somewhere, eating words like dessert.

"Mr. Bliss," the polished voice says.

"So, it is you," Bob says. "I thought maybe I escaped you."

Spencer doesn't laugh. He pulls off his glasses and tries to wipe them dry, finding his soaked sport coat to be of little help. "We heard you were ill," he says. "The festival honored you in your absence, and I came to give you the certificate of recognition for—"

Oh boy. Bob does like a jest with this guy, but he's not about to keep an innocent man out in this. "That's kind of you, son. But as you can see, this is not the best place or time for you to be out. Go on back, dry off."

Spencer looks over his shoulder at the little boat, then back at Bob.

"I'll take you back," he says, eyeing Bob's shaking body with growing concern. "You should be home."

The words float like black splotches across his consciousness. He's fading, he can feel it.

"You ever get that next poem I left for you?"

"Yes, sir. A life well lived is a life well given."

"Gived."

Spencer drops his stare to the beach. "Yes, *gived*."

Bob tries not to relish the boy speaking nonsense words so much. But he can't help a chuckle.

The waves fill a space of silence.

"That's what I'm here for tonight," Bob says.

Spencer folds up the paper Bob has yet to take and tucks it back inside his jacket.

"I'll stay, too," he says, "if it's all the same to you."

Bob looks him up and down. He's a soggy noodle, but there's no denying the courage seeping through. "Attaboy."

Bob asks for Spencer's help fetching something from the *Savvy Mae*. He wants to do it himself but knows he's got to preserve what strength is left for what's ahead. Spencer brings him the requested tackle box.

Bob thrusts a hand inside, his stiff joints feeling like jelly and making practiced fingers clumsy around his tools. But buried beneath a hammer, a spool of fishing twine, and an orphaned work glove, he finds what he needs.

He wraps his fingers around the cool stainless steel, stuffs it in his pocket, and moves his hands to turn the wheels of his chair. But face-to-face with his own weakness, he is forced to ask . . .

"I have a request, Mr. Spencer T. Ripley."

"Anything."

Grudgingly and gratefully, he spits out his request. "Help a guy up a mountain? I'm afraid this old body won't climb it just now. But this soul . . . it has to."

Spencer looks at the steep incline and back at the wheelchair. Without missing a beat, he plants his Oxfords in the slick mud and begins to push.

For once, the young man blessedly restrains his overstuffed

339

noggin. No spouting of rhymes, no quoting "the inestimable Wordsworth." Until now, Bob had cursed the day the kid had showed up on his doorstep. But now . . . even Bob knew he was a godsend.

The ascent invigorates Bob. Saps him, yes, but strengthens him somehow, too. Was this not what he'd climbed this very mountain for, all those years ago? To tell his brother he meant to go to battle for him?

That battle has come.

Spencer wheels Eva's mud-caked chair into the clearing to find the group huddled under the stone overhang, fussing over Rich, whose shoulders are draped in an old tarp.

Rich sees him first. Stands and approaches him slowly, his lanky form limping.

He clears his throat. "I'm awful sorry, Mr. Bliss."

The rain falls steady. But the torment on Rich's face speaks of an entirely different storm, one deep-running.

"It's not your fault. I owe you my thanks," he says.

A quick glance around shows a sea of somber faces. He knows that look. Defeat. It has no place here. This island has housed it too long already.

"Hey," he says to the huddled group. It's a simple idea and needs a simple introduction. "Know what lit lighthouses before they had lenses or generators or even windows? Before all the fancy fixings?"

Sorrowful faces stare blankly at him.

He leans in and utters that single, magical, terrifying word.

"Fire."

Silence meets him. Followed by a low, resonant laugh. Ed, with that rolling pitch of understanding, laughing with his arms crossed over his chest, seeing what no one else does.

"Crazy, Robert Bliss. That's what you are." His laughter tapers off, and he shakes his head and stoops, feeling for sticks on the ground. This man whose own country refused him wood for a house . . . gathering wood up into his arms. "Point me where to go," he says. "I'll build your fire."

And in that single act—the stooping down to the ground and holding wood up, the darkness cracks open. Hope seeps back in.

"Thank you." Bob pulls in all the breath he can. "If we assemble a line from out here, on up the stairs, we can pass whatever we find up there until we have enough."

Arthur saunters over. "You don't mean . . ."

"We're going medieval, Arthur. Going to torch this thing until they see it and come on home."

"We can't do that," Arthur says. "It's not what this place was built for."

Bob crosses the small clearing, runs his fingers across the tower's wet stones. Thinks of the lives they represent. The families who dragged rocks, mailed rocks, scraped together pennies to ship a piece of earth for this moment.

"It's exactly what it was built for," he mutters. "Fire won't harm these stones. We'll pile on as much as we can on the platform, and—"

"It won't burn long enough," Arthur says. "If we wait for the coast guard when the storm's passed, there's a better chance—"

"This is just kindling," Bob says. He looks up, and in the tiniest sliver of moon emerging from the dark clouds, sees the makeshift roof, the beams.

It might only burn a short time, but God is not bound by time. He could make as much of a second as He could an eternity.

Bob leans forward and grabs a fallen branch, passes it to Rich, who passes it on up the line that's already forming. And when the platform is piled to the roof with storm debris, leaves, whatever they could find that would flame, and everyone is clear to safety again, Bob sets his hands on the wheels Eva had gripped year upon year and pushes himself to where he can grip the stones, steady himself along.

Ignoring the protests of his friends, he shoves a foot on those steps for the first time since William left. With every ounce of strength he can muster—and some he cannot account for—he grasps the stone handholds along the way. Each one a life. Each one cherished. Rocks crying out, ushering him on to trust the One who brought him here . . . for such a time as this.

And at the top, head reaching into the now-packed alcove of the platform, he pulls out his scavenged artifact from the boat.

Brushed steel. State of the art. Exclusive to the Sharper Image, as Rich liked to remind him. And destined never to touch a crème brûlée in its life. He releases the torch's safety latch and presses down the ignition. Bright blue flame hisses. He ratchets the gas lever all the way to its highest setting, aiming it at the grasses and papers, leaves, and other tinder piled before him.

"Come on," he says. They're damp, not catching. "Come on . . ." His fist trembles, the continued pressure asking much of his atrophied muscles. "Light," he says, a prayer to the Maker of fire. "Please . . ."

He braces his shaking hand with his other, and waits.

A spark.

A smolder.

Another spark. The sweet scent of spent leaves burning. They flicker into light, embers dancing over their veins until they ignite, taking on the work of the torch and passing fire to the next thing, and the next.

Urgent shouts rise from below. "Get down!" Bob shakes himself into the present and does just that.

But on the painstaking journey down the stairs, joints creaking and heart pumping hard, he pauses, his weathered, wrinkled fingers bracing against the wall beside him.

He is caught here. Some strong force stills him, harkening him to listen, to take note of the snapping fire above him . . . and the scaffolding of stone around him.

He slides his palm over the gentle strength of those rocks and remembers the faces from the photos tucked into boxes with those rocks, the stories penned with care on tear-splotched pages, arriving from around the country. He sees Liesl, the horror and hope of what she'd been through etched in her face as she unwrapped that stone from her threadbare handkerchief.

He sees Omaha Beach. U-boats. Paris celebrating, bathed in light. He sees the frozen passes of Russia, winding river currents in Burma, jungles in the Philippines.

The stones begin to warm beneath his touch, jolting him back as someone reaches for his hand from below to help him down those last steps. The pillar dances with shadows and echoes, the fire above crackling to greater life.

Out in the night, the others are gathered a safe distance away. He pauses before joining them, watching as he sits against a boulder away on his own, off where he and Roy had their last bonfire.

It's as if time and space scooped up that fire and transported it to here and now, where this vaulted bonfire takes shape. Flames growing in strength until they engulf the roof, escape the bounds of the open beams, and lap rain from the sky.

It rages. Brave into the storm. Bold into the night.

Spencer T. Ripley sidles up near him.

"Everything all right, Mr. Bliss?"

Arthur comes up on the other side, listening.

Bob has only one thought, watching the flames. "Now that," he says, pulling in a shuddering breath, "is poetry."

forty-one

A daze. Dark daze. The first thing Annie registers, there at the top of the boat stairs, is the soles of black Grundéns boots.

Jeremiah.

She moves toward him and feels the muted beat of steps behind her. Her father. His mouth is moving, but all she hears is a foggy, shapeless voice.

He stoops, brushes her tangled hair out of her face. *Are you okay?* She sees his words more than she hears them.

She nods. She's okay . . . she thinks. But Jeremiah is not moving. She points, says as much, and as they both run to him, the air breaks through the fog and sounds become clearer. Thunder is receding. But there's a noise somewhere that's new, unsettling. She can't quite place it.

Jeremiah's face is to the side, head bleeding, unconscious.

"Did he get hit?" she asks, the question making her voice waver. She remembers the blinding flash of lightning.

"It could be, but I don't see any burns, and"—he listens for breathing, checks his pulse—"he's alive. I think he fell with the force of the hit to the boat and struck his head."

"We should wrap it," Annie says. The rushing she hears grows louder as she unfastens her life vest, pulls off her outer jacket, and with her father, lifts Jeremiah's head gently into its fold. Her hand lingers. The burning in her ribs swelling, recalling Melissa's letter to him. She runs her fingers through Jeremiah's dark, unruly hair, for Melissa . . . and for him. And—there is no ignoring it—for hope.

They wrap the wound the best they can, and William looks toward the direction of the sound, down in the hull.

"We're taking on water." He moves quickly to the bridge. Setting Jeremiah's head down gently, Annie tears herself from him and switches on the GPS to see how far they are from land.

Nothing happens.

She does it again and then tries the plotter.

Black screens.

The VHF radio is silent—every channel, dead. There will be no Mayday call from them. No one to hear what their broken boat cannot send.

William tries the engine, and Annie hears the faintest noise in response. "At least that's not completely fried," he says.

"But even if we can move, where will we go?" She looks to the chart, where Jeremiah noted down their last coordinates. But the water has swept away his pencil marks, chewing up the paper in its wake.

They're back in 1890, with nothing but the invisible stars to guide them, and the hope of a lighthouse to reach them.

"I can get the engine up," William says. "But it'll do no good if we don't stop that water." He squints, looking out on deck. "There." He points to a hatch whose trapdoor is flapping in the slowing wind. Water sloshes down in sheets. "Can you fasten that?" He thrusts a hand flare her way. "Use that to see. I'll check if there's a manual pump for the bilge. We've got to get some balance back."

She nods, swallowing. On the floor, Jeremiah begins to stir but does not wake. "What about—"

"I don't know." Her father's voice is sad. "He might be fine in a few minutes. Or he might need a hospital, fast. Depends on if there's brain bleeding. I think he'll be okay, but—"

Annie swipes away the hot tears. Her father squeezes her shoulder. "The best thing we can do for him right now is get this boat going."

Her marching orders.

She nods and steps into the night. It's cruel, almost, how quickly the storm has calmed, moving right along as if it hadn't just chewed them up and spit them out. A mist lingers, but the rain is light, the waves seeming like dwarves at three feet, compared to the monstrosities of a few minutes ago.

But the clouds still cover the night. They could be miles off course. Blown clear to Nova Scotia, for all they know. She lights the flare, lets its red glow bring enough light to guide her to the hatch.

Hinges creak a warning. *Too close*, they seem to say as she creeps closer to the bow, to where the waves still splash over the railing, sending pools of cold.

Kneeling, she tucks a rogue length of rope back into the compartment. She grabs an empty tin pail from within and bails out the small hold, then seals the lid down tight.

Her work is done. But something keeps her here, beckons her farther, closer to the bow. She stands, gripping the rails where they meet at the front of the boat, and waits, wind lifting storm-matted locks from her neck.

Her flare sputters into darkness. It's just her, the night . . . and the waves, spraying a fine mist over her.

This baptism of water sends a chill through her. Making her wish for her mat of sand from Bob. Something solid to stand on out here in the unknown. Afar off, the wind wails a hollow sound, tugging her to her knees, palms down.

Somewhere between the wind's lament and the steadying lap of the dark waves, so close she can taste them . . . she feels it. The whisper of a truth she can hear the tune of.

"On Christ the solid rock I stand . . ."

She spreads her fingers, aching for the comfort of solid ground.

"All other ground is sinking sand . . ."

She holds her breath, goose bumps rising to a keen awareness that something is about to happen.

Here, in the middle of the dark abyss with no land in sight, the
Rock of Ages offers himself to her.

"What is it?" she whispers.

Ahead, the waves gentle into a rolling sheet, reflecting the smallest sliver of moon.

"Please," she prays, her voice small in the great canopy of the
night. "Guide us home."

All is still. She waits on the precipice of the dark, face-to-face
with these waves, crying out to their Maker.

And then, from the quiet, comes the sound of hope. A rumble—
but not thunder, and not from above. Her palms against the
wooden deck tremble with it.

The engine.

Thank you. She cannot force the words past the ache in her
throat.

She knows they are not home free, but somehow, she looks at
these unpredictable waves and is not overcome by the old fear.
She sees the waves that built a tower, that carried her grandfather home to heaven, released her mother back to life, before
she was born. The waves that rocked Annie to sleep as a baby,
that carried her parents far from her, yes, but nudged her back
to them, too. Waves that tore her heart in two, and waves that
caught that heart when it landed in Ansel in pieces, just weeks
ago. She sees dark water that sparks with blue light as Jeremiah
takes her hand and stirs the lightkeepers to life. A grit and a
beauty, a grace.

These are the waves that have brought her home. To these
people, this place . . . and to life.

Her own salt tears drop into them, head bowed.

And then comes a voice. Strong and sure, right around her
heart.

Lift your head, Annie Bliss.

She remembers Josef Krause, the very words he heard right out
here on this sea. A God so personal He sounded like a fairy tale
to Annie, sometimes.

And yet . . . as she opens her eyes, lifts them, and peers through the veil of night . . . she sees it.

Impossible fire. Blazing like the sun, atop a tower. They are close—a few miles, maybe.

Home.

———

There are flames, and there are shadows. Spinning. Bob staggers toward the cliff, bracing himself against a tree safe enough back. Watching.

He's submerged, heart, mind, and soul, sounds muted like he's underwater. His own pulse marking time.

"Please." He can't hear his own voice, but parched lips form the word.

"Please." Dredging the prayer up through rubble.

No sign of anything on the horizon. Clouds breaking open, rain letting up, fire dimming from the tower as it consumes the last of its fuel.

His muscles, too, are dimming fire. He drops to his knees. Grips earth, grips jagged hope.

"Please." The strength of the storm does not change whose waves these are. There is One mightier still.

And then it comes. Carved like the day heaven told him to build. Words, right upon his heart. *Lift your head, Robert Bliss.*

He does.

It is dark. Waves, black; moonlight, white. All of it empty. He tells himself to breathe, makes his tired lungs reach for more air. The scene before him blurring until . . . there. Breaking into view between the islands yonder, the dark figure of a boat.

The waves below are loud and strong and morph around him until it's fog. He fights to hear what the others are saying, to not lose these dark blips of time as burning exhaustion claims him. He thinks somewhere in the clearing he sees Annie—drenched and wild-eyed, searching. Breathtakingly whole. A tall figure beside her, bandaged about the head and holding her hand, the two of them rushing toward him. He tries to keep watching. But in this swirl of night and smoke, light and stone, here on this soil charred with the bonfire of two brothers long ago . . . he cannot fight for consciousness. He has given all the fight he has to another battle.

And just before this heavy weariness claims any vestige of lucid thought, he feels his weak limbs—limbs that once lifted stone—gathered up into strong arms. Lifting his eyelids with every bit of strength he can pull from the dregs inside . . . he sees blue eyes.

William.

The arms of the baby who stirred the air from a kitchen basket, now a grown man. Pulling Bob close to his chest, where a strong heart thuds hard. He speaks.

"I've got you, Bob."

And although his voice has thickened and deepened, it still holds traces of the boy who showed up on Bob's doorstep all those years ago. The voice that trembled as he told the tale of learning to ride a bike, needing those words, needing Bob.

"I've got you."

epilogue

"Every wave in that big old blue sea is a story."

Bob told me this a long time ago, his voice brined with wind and water.

I remember my little-girl laugh, trying to count them before they disappeared. I thought it impossible then. I think it impossibly beautiful now.

It's spring in Ansel, which means two things: Bess is firing up her griddle for the season . . . and the town is trying to figure out what to do with the stream of people who keep coming and coming.

It started last summer, after the storm. The *Pier Review* ran a piece about the lighthouse and our miraculous rescue. The weather experts confirmed that it was just that: miraculous.

Jonesport picked up the story, then Bangor and Portland—and then the *New York Times*. Someone had caught a video clip of us from shore before we disappeared too far off—waves looking for all the world like they'd swallow us whole. The clip went viral. And then someone from *TIME* magazine came out to do a piece on it all.

Bob—with a little help from Rich—slipped the memory card

351

from their "newfangled digital camera." Never did a face hold more glee.

They managed to put a picture in, anyhow, from their own archives—the one of Bob, all those years ago. And next to it, a full-page picture taken from out on the water, showing the light-house. Completed. Radiant.

After that, they started to come. Not the rocks—the people. Widows. Widowers. Sons. Daughters. Grandchildren. Great-grandchildren. Come to see the testament to legacy and courage of their soldiers, stones mortared together to light the way home.

They crowded into the boathouse on their pilgrimage to see the letters and pictures so carefully kept. Some of the documents water-rippled from being doused by a brave soul in a fire long ago. All of them cataloged with care by those same hands, hands that have mounted a true lens upon the light tower, and hands that have helped Bob into the boathouse every day since the doctor grudgingly gave his leave. Dad and Bob have swung hammers side by side as they've turned the old boathouse into the best museum I've ever seen. A rustic, living, light-shaft-woven hall of history.

Only the fierce Maine winter stopped the influx of people, and now with mud season coming to a close and summer around the bend, the tide of visitors is rising again.

Halfway through those snowy months, a package came for me—from all the way across an ocean. A picture: the familiar faces of Alpenzell, holding up that *TIME* article and grinning bright as the day. The mayor wrote in his formal English: *We are proud to be a part of your story, and for you to be a part of ours.* Though the program we'd begun together had a rough beginning, with a few prudent adjustments requiring time commitments and scheduled payouts of stipends, it was flourishing, as was the village.

Bob framed that letter and likes to make me blush about it. But I know the truth as deeply as he. A thing redeemed from a place of brokenness is a humbling honor. And priceless.

Arthur comes to help whenever he's not out fishing. Ed comes, too, always with a big smile—one probably having a lot to do with a certain mountain woman whose Victorian silverware brings music to his world. Sully's with him more often than not, looping her arm through his and letting her long white braid brush against his hand.

And just yesterday, two visitors tagged along, up all the way from Mississippi. Hosea Jones and his grandson Jimmy, come to see a certain stone, beaming ear to ear. Jimmy in particular lights up at this place, and he can't stop poring over his application for one of the new grant-funded positions to obtain oral histories from relatives of the tower soldiers. It took all my courage to write that grant proposal, and I'm undone with gratitude at seeing this program come to life in Jimmy's soul.

And then there's Jeremiah, who stayed away those first few nights after the storm. By the time we reached shore, he'd regained consciousness and insisted he didn't need medical assistance. And that night he moved his boat. Once Bob was stable and settled at home, with Shirley bustling around like an efficient whirlwind to keep him in his place, it took me two days to find Jeremiah anchored over by Ed's old driftwood shanty.

When I finally came upon him, I worried his injury had taken on infection. He was in that old shanty, pacing the floor in what looked like a fevered fog, like he was bent on wearing a ditch into the ground.

He took one look at me there in the doorway and froze. All covered in scruff, hair damp from washing himself in the sea, he had on that same old T-shirt from the first day I saw him. *Go Away*, it said. The *Please* he'd written in was fading.

His face reflected the same message. Grim, eyes fierce, almost desperate. Longing for something—or someone—he could not have.

The letter was out, planted on the mantel with a stone.

So I turned to go, to hide the tears that came despite me gritting my teeth and wishing them away. What had I thought? That just because we'd survived a storm together—just because he'd shown me a sunrise—and sure, just because he'd gone and hooked his prickly, stubborn, maddeningly *knowing* heart right into mine, that he could somehow find it in his heart to love me?

He deserved his space, and clearly wanted it. I could at least give him that.

I returned to Sailor's Rest and started packing. Bob and Dad needed time together. Jeremiah needed space. And I . . . I didn't know what I needed. I needed to go back to Chicago and put in my notice—that was certain. Going back to spreadsheets and analytics after living—truly living—within the heartbeat of a town like this . . . it wasn't possible.

This was where I belonged.

Maybe if I avoided Jeremiah for long enough, I could convince myself that friendship with him was enough. *More* than enough. To have his kindness, his blustery dry humor, his presence even as a friend . . . Surely it was worth it to put to rest this living devotion growing inside of me.

And then the knock came.

Everyone was away for a dinner in town. It was just me and that old creaky house. And when I opened the door, Jeremiah.

It wasn't so much the look on his face as his presence, the way his hands were stuffed in jeans pockets, looking like captive things. His whole self held back by some barely harnessed force.

He did not say a word. The air was charged, and I wondered if the lightning had somehow gotten trapped inside this man when it struck the boat.

Slowly, he dropped his gaze to the ground and let it linger there. Like he was trying, in his silence, to tell me something.

"Jeremiah?" I said at last.

He lifted an eyebrow and looked at me—a spark there: part hope, part mischief—then dashed his gaze back down just as quickly.

Only he wasn't looking at the ground. He was looking at his T-shirt. He held out the hem of it, as if trying to read it, scratching his head. I couldn't help feeling I was part of some skit, not picking up on my cues like I should.

Go Away. Same old T-shirt. With that faded-out word on top: *Please.* But there, in the glow of the porch light, I saw he'd added something more. An arrow, pointing up from between the words to where he'd scrawled one word: *Don't.*

Please Don't Go Away.

I swallowed. Heart skittered, daring hope.

He took my hand in his, covered it with his other. So warm . . . so secure.

He leaned in, lowered his voice to just above a whisper, and said, "Ever."

We locked eyes. He must have seen the question pounding. Did he mean it? Was this just fevered ramblings? Did he truly want this? Or did he need medical care quite urgently?

He sank to a knee and took my other hand, too. "Please don't go away ever, Annie Bliss."

I sank down in front of him, running my hand over that face and wondering how, *how* in all the world, such a man could offer himself to me.

The Great Wall of Jeremiah was lying on the ground. Nothing between us but air and two pounding hearts. I searched his eyes and saw forever there.

"I'm all in, Jeremiah Fletcher."

He pulled me to himself in an embrace that was the beginning of a lifetime of together, hearts beating right into each other. He slipped something on my finger. Smooth and warm and feeling of the ages.

"When I asked Bob and your father," he explained, "first they told me I'd be off my rocker not to hitch myself to you. And then"—he traced the wooden ring on my finger, his touch tender—"they gave me this."

It was Grandma Jenny's ring. Dad had shown it to me a couple of times over the years. I hurt for her, for this woman I'd never met, and yet I lingered on the deep devotion she and my grandfather had shared, even in so short a time.

Such a mighty thing to begin a life with this heritage.

I looked at my EMT-postman and wrapped his hand in mine, locking them together right then and there.

His name is my name now. Jeremiah and Annie Fletcher, who are building a house on a certain island. We are to be the caretakers of a lighthouse, you see. And every story that it guards. We will open that boathouse to the wayfarers who have traveled far to see their family's stories. We will ferry those pilgrims across the bay, carve out a place for them here on the island as they linger until dark and watch as the light shines in a dance, a light pattern all its own: long, long, short-short-short. Twice in a row, and then a beat of darkness.

Morse code, for those who know it. The number seventy-seven, casting forth the story of a life, a love—of hard-won hope etched on a scrap of paper pulled off a destroyer—in a few small blips:

77 fathoms.

author's note

I like to think about that little post office in Ansel, its mail slot in the door. The sea breeze pulling it open and shut, creaking in fledgling attempts at a song.

If I were there, I'd pull open that tarnished brass slot and slip a note inside addressed to you. It would say:

Dear Friend,

With this book, I offer you my heart. It isn't much, perhaps, but these words were sown with tears—both those of grief and those of joy—and deep, deep hope, which I pray might be even a small gift to you.

You see, when I look back at where this tale came from, so much is a blur. But one single thing is clear. It came from a place of being held. A place where God gathered up all of me in my brokenness in a time of deepest grief and just closed His grip around me tight, holding me close to His heart. There in the dark was a pair of nail-scarred, love-etched hands that stooped to gather up and tend each broken piece, His heart aching right with mine. Hands and heart whose way is to cherish, to take that brokenness and somehow, with tenderness and strength, summon forth light. Hope.

This is my prayer. That in the midst of any caverns of grief, chasms of tribulation, anything that has marked or cracked your life, the God who plunges right into your turmoil with you—*unter wasser,* as Liesl would say—will wrap those shards up and do His work.

In his Narnian world, C. S. Lewis called it "The Deeper Magic from Before the Dawn of Time"—that one innocent would offer His own scars into a broken place, to bring life. Tolkien called it the "Eucatastrophe"—the good catastrophe. Jesus called it His very purpose: "I came that they may have life, and have it abundantly" (John 10:10).

Lift your head, brave one. This life is a storm, no doubt about it. But oh, the One who holds those waves, who holds our hearts. What it is, to think of facing this storm in His hands, wrapped in a love that is fathoms—infinite fathoms—deep.

He loves you fiercely. And as Roy would say, there's a whole lotta light.

May it shine right into you.

—Amanda

acknowledgments

I so hope you enjoyed your time in Ansel, dear reader. This town is a medley of countless generous people who took the time to help create such a place. I owe them all a thousand thank-yous.

To our online community, who never fails to chime in with brilliant names and ideas when I post questions on Facebook or in my newsletter. It delights me to no end that many of this town's details come from you! It's always hard to choose from the wonderful suggestions, but I have Sondra Kraak to thank for naming the *Glad Tidings*. Lori Benton, who dubbed the small-town paper *The Pier Review*. Rachel McMillan and Lesley Gore, who when asked about favorite classic black-and-white movies, chimed in with *It Happened One Night*. Ansel thanks you for giving texture to the town!

To Martha Artyomenko, Gail Hollingsworth, and Emily Bergstrom, who each offered pieces of their own courageous relatives' World War II experiences, which inspired some of the stories held by the stones in this book. You may recognize glimpses of Martha's grandfather, Hans Vogel, who immigrated to the U.S. from Germany as a boy, then bravely took up his linguistic roots as a young man to serve the U.S. in Germany, saving lives. There's a reference to Gail's father-in-law, Berle Dean Hollingsworth, and his bravery transporting soldiers in a U-boat to Omaha Beach on D-Day—a day so much of the war hinged on. And Emily's great-grandfather, Arthur Busboom, who wrote in a letter to his bride, telling of V-E Day in Paris: *"It seemed good to see all the street lights on again, and I think they had every light they could find in Paris lit last night."*

To these men, and to all the Greatest Generation, we owe so much. We may never understand the breadth and depth of what was given. But as we try, and learn, and grow . . . we are thankful. Beyond words.

And to our nation's brave soldiers, past and present. Thank you, to you and to your families. A novel—or a thousand of them—is insufficient thanks. With all my heart, thank you for what you do.

To the experts who patiently coached me in aspects outside my realm of knowledge. While I've done my best to reflect authenticity in each of these departments, any accidental oversights are on me and not these brilliant minds. I owe my thanks to Jordyn Redwood and her knowledgeable medical input. Jeff Gales and the United States Lighthouse Society, for walking me through both technical and historical aspects of our nation's beloved beacons.

Sharon Mack and the Machias Bay Area Chamber of Commerce, who went above and beyond and hunted down personal, local accounts not recorded in history books and inspired me to no end. Historian Valdine Atwood, who provided such details to Sharon. Dawn Lamoureaux-Crocker and Craig and Annette Parsons, who took time to patiently relay their own harrowing experiences in sudden storms at sea, and to answer this landlubber's questions.

Tina Ingemi, who didn't blink twice when I wrote again and again and again, asking more Maine questions and savoring her boundless, beautiful answers. You helped me fall even more in love with Maine, Tina. Thank you!

Aura Moore, who provided me with local history and connections, and whose kindness and patience emerged even more as one of the first readers of this story, to keep a "weather eye" on my Maine facts. While many elements of this story are purely fictional—the town of Ansel, the island, Bob's hospital—my hope is that the magic of Maine still shines through.

To friends whose very heartbeats are woven into each line of this book and my life. How I cherish you. Joanne Bischof, faithful kindred spirit and bringer of hope and a dash of beloved spunk, whose beautiful heart inspires me at every turn. Lesley Gore, who never ceases to bring a smile through her wit, a tear through her understanding, or to astound me with insight and wisdom. Wendy Lawton, agent and friend, whose bookshelves are lined with timeless treasures, just as is her heart. Kelli Standish and her ceaseless encouragement and stalwart friendship over the years.

To selfless authors who have offered encouragement along the way on this writing road. Laura Frantz, Dani Pettrey, Sarah Sundin, Cynthia Ruchti, Jocelyn Green, Rachel McMillan, Elizabeth Byler Younts—your words and kindness have meant the world!

To Bethany House Publishers, and beyond-intrepid editors Raela, Karen, and Elizabeth for taking this windblown tale under your wing. I still get this little-kid smile in my heart when I think of my childhood self, curled up with the Mandie mysteries, dreaming of one day writing a book for this publishing house that exists to bring hope, light, and encouragement. Thank you, with all my heart. It is an honor to walk this road with you.

To my family. Each and every one of you. How I love you. How my heart beats with the story of you and gives thanks for the miracle of you. What an Author we have, who would be so gracious to let me know and love you!

To my beloved Ben. This love for you is an ever-rising tide. Every hint of romance written, comfort given, laughter shared in these words—it comes back to you.

And finally . . . the Rock of Ages. When writing one of the hardest scenes of this book, finding myself tangled in the storm right along with Annie, I stumbled upon a quote from C. H. Spurgeon: "I have learned to kiss the wave that throws me against the Rock of Ages."

Thank you. For being the gentlest and safest of landing places. For the gathering. The holding. The piecing together, the building. For your strength, your tenderness. Your grace.

Thank you for being our Light in every storm.

Amanda Dykes is a drinker of tea, dweller of redemption, and spinner of hope-filled tales who spends most days chasing wonder and words with her family. Give her a rainy day, a candle to read by, an obscure corner of history to dig in, and she'll be happy for hours. She's a former English teacher, and her novella, *Bespoke: A Tiny Christmas Tale*, was met with critical acclaim from *Publishers Weekly*, *Readers' Favorite*, and more. She is also the author of a novella in *The Message in a Bottle Romance Collection*. *Whose Waves These Are* is her debut novel. Readers can connect with her online at www.amandadykes.com.

Sign Up for Amanda's Newsletter!

Keep up to date with Amanda's news on book releases and events by signing up for her email list at amandadykes.com.

You May Also Like . . .

Annalise knows painful memories hover beneath the pleasant façade of Gossamer Grove. But she is shocked when she inherits documents that reveal mysterious murders from a century ago. In this dual-time romantic suspense novel, two women, separated by a hundred years, must uncover the secrets within the borders of their town before it's too late.

The Reckoning at Gossamer Pond by Jaime Jo Wright
jaimewrightbooks.com